I0685087

Maidens of Epodlo

Book 1

Antwanesta Agape and the Mystery of the Red-dot Moon

by

Thomas David Valentine

Thomas David Valentine

Maidens of Epodlo Book 1 Antwanesta Agape and the Mystery of the Red-dot Moon

First Edition

Copyright © 2016 Thomas David Valentine

Valentine U.S.A.

First Publication 2016

ISBN-13: 978-0692723418 (Valentine)

ISBN-10: 0692723412

Maidens of Epodlo, Book 1 — Antwanesta Agape and the Mystery of the Red-dot Moon

Acknowledgements

Thank you to:

my niece, Shelly for her kind assistance with the cover art;

my brother, Bob for help on the math;

my sons, Victor and Gregory who listened to my ideas;

my friends, Azra and Bruce for photography of the author;

my many, friends and relatives for moral support;

and most of all my wife, Angela, the SSPW* in my life, for her love, tolerance, and patience.

*strong, smart, passionate woman

Thomas David Valentine

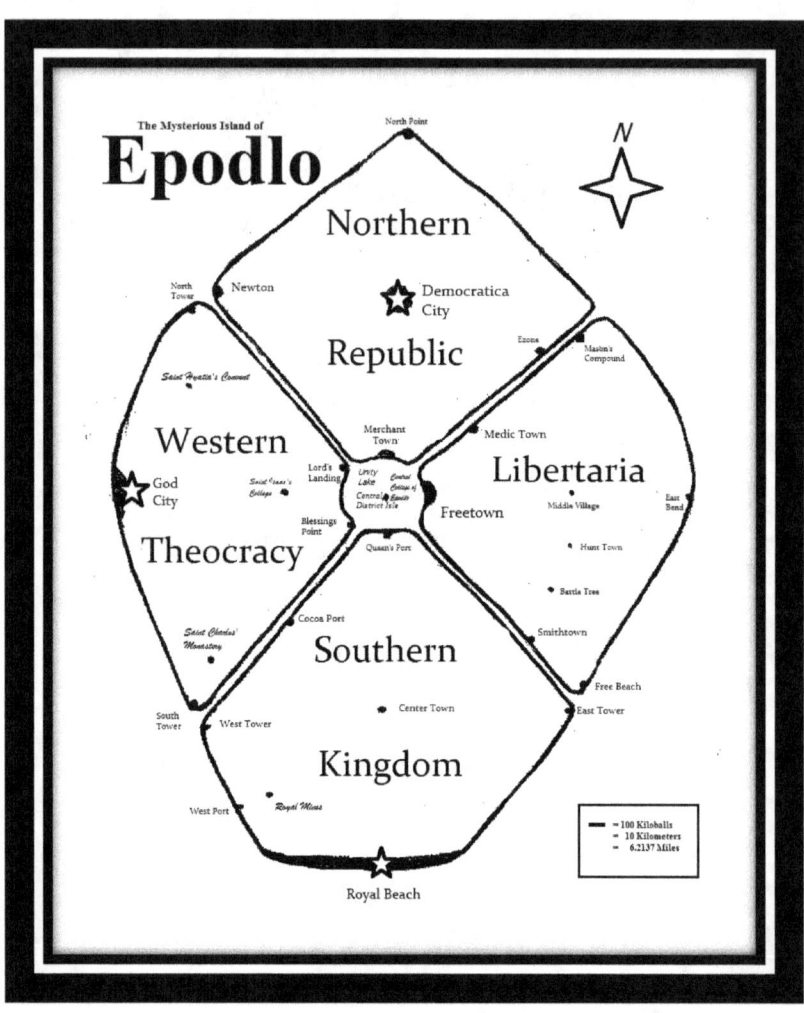

The Mysterious Island of

Epodlo

Northern

North Point

N

Newton

North Tower

Democratica City

Ezona

Mason's Compound

Republic

Saint Hyatia's Convent

Merchant Town

Medic Town

Western

Lord's Landing

Saint Isaac's College

Unity Lake

Central District Isle

Central South College

Libertaria

East Bend

God City

Middle Village

Blessings Point

Freetown

Theocracy

Quaan's Port

Hunt Town

Battle Tree

Saint Charles' Monastery

Cocoa Port

Smithtown

Southern

Free Beach

South Tower

West Tower

Center Town

East Tower

Kingdom

West Port

Royal Mines

= 100 Kiloballs
= 10 Kilometers
= 6.2137 Miles

Royal Beach

Central District Isle

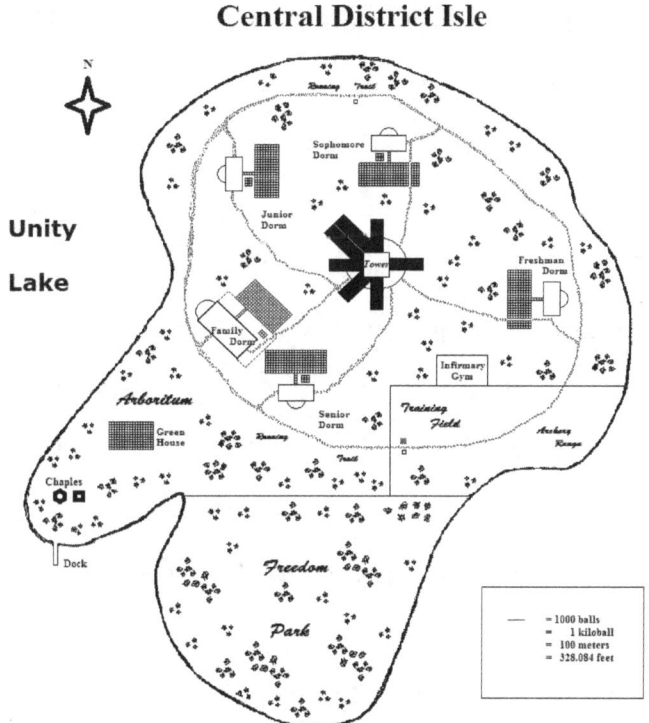

Central College of Epodlo Campus

Contents

Thomas David Valentine

Character List

Alphabetical by Category and First Name

The Maidens:

> **Antwanesta Agape** (Ant), Freshman (Theist, Theite)
>
> **Feli (Felisianna) Smith** (Bunny-brain), Freshman (Humanist, Republican)
>
> **Gretchin Quadrapopis** (Retch) (Sweetheart), Freshman (Libertarian)
>
> **Xiny (Xinonina) Stewart, Handmaiden to the Queen** (Sinny), Freshman (Royal)

Classmates:

> **Ballsar Gardener**, Freshman (Royal)
>
> **Barthon Stewart**, **Baron,** Sophomore, Xiny's brother (Royal)
>
> **Celina Pentapopis**, Freshman (Libertarian)
>
> **Darwood Tripopis**, Freshman (Libertarian)
>
> **Efunius Cutter**, Freshman (Humanist, Republican)
>
> **Eltwando Agape**, Freshman (Theist, Theite)
>
> **Fargitch Plumber**, Freshman (Royal)
>
> **Gregor (Prince Gregorious) Regalis**, Sophomore, Lissy's cousin (Royal)
>
> **Hardy (Hardington) Weaver**, Freshman (Humanist, Republican)

Maidens of Epodlo, Book 1 — Antwanesta Agape and the Mystery of the Red-dot Moon

Harolod Agape, Junior (Theist, Theite)

Histina Bowright, Freshman (Humanist, Republican)

Jillissa Agape, Junior (Theist, Theite)

Levisina Fletcher, Freshman (Royal)

Lissy (Queen Yvalissa) Regalis (Hinny), Freshman (Royal)

Mulucia Butler, Freshman (Royal)

Oluga Keep, Freshman (Royal)

Petina Tripopis, Freshman (Libertarian)

Quistina Unipopis, Freshman (Libertarian)

Relisha Metropopis, Freshman (Libertarian)

Rollo Mason, Freshman (Libertarian)

Roost Hunter, Freshman (Royal)

Sal (Salbird) Keysmith, Sophomore (Humanist, Republican)

Tear (Tearesia) Tripopis, Sophomore (Libertarian)

Wondina Metropopis, Freshman (Libertarian)

Xeris Plumber, Freshman (Royal)

Yarvan Quadrapopis, Freshman (Libertarian)

Zell Fisher, Sophomore (Humanist, Republican)

Professors:

Elonora Agape ("the Black"), math professor (Theist, Theite)

Thomas David Valentine

Gerluke Boatman, archeology professor (Humanist, Republican)

Illi (Dean/Governor/Judge Illisima) Smith, (Humanist, Citizen of Central District Isle)

Irigon Agape ("the Red"), religion professor (Theist, Theite)

Kaye Solider, history professor (Royal)

Largot Cook, weapons professor (Royal)

Morgont Medic, science (Nature) professor (Humanist, Republican)

Risky (Dr. Betriski) Sexapopis (Risky Sex), physician, physical training professor (Libertarian)

Clergy:

Father Alfonzo Agape, priest in Lord's Landing (Theist, Theite)

Mother Bethunia Agape, priestess in Freetown (Theist, Theite)

Bishop Korack Agape, Bishop of the Southern Kingdom (Theist, Theite)

Bishop Salestina Agape, Bishop of God City (Theist, Theite)

His Holiness Pontiff Thomas the Sixth (Theist, Theite)

Mother Vissina Agape, visiting priestess at Central District Isle (Theist, Theite)

Parents:

Chief Councilor Alfide Stewart, father of Xiny and Barthon (Royal)

Maidens of Epodlo, Book 1 — Antwanesta Agape and the
Mystery of the Red-dot Moon

Azunia Smith, Attorney at Law, mother of Feli
(Humanist, Republican)

Comaz Fisher, Father of Zell (Humanist,
Republican)

Daro Pentapopis, Pop Three of Gretchin, Pop Five
of Risky (Libertarian)

Dothina Agape, mother of Antwanesta (Theist,
Theite)

Frontaris Mason, father of Rollo (Humanist,
naturalized Libertarian)

Ottarian Dipopis, Pop One of Gretchin, Pop Two of
Tear (Libertarian)

Pargog Metropopis, Pop Four of Gretchin, Pop Two
of Risky (Libertarian)

Picius Smith, father of Feli, ichthyologist (Humanist,
Republican)

Quinis Metropopis, Pop Two of Gretchin,
(Libertarian)

Uvinia Mason, mother of Rollo (Libertarian)

Others:

Captain Carlon Knight, military officer (Royal)

Dr. Colorianna Grocer, physician (Royal)

Duggy (Naragadug) Baker, cousin of Zell
(Humanist, Republican)

Dussy Dipopis, stable carl (Libertarian)

Evy Pentapopis, stable carl (Libertarian)

Ifarbis Agape, man on lake shore (Theist, Theite)

Jandarian Solider, Chief Royal Plumber for Central College of Epodlo (Royal)

Jarn Smith, Illi's Father (Humanist, Republican)

Karis Pentapopis, brother of Gretchin (Libertarian)

Lander Quadrapopis, brother of Gretchin (Libertarian)

Mars Sexapopis, brother of Gretchin (Libertarian)

Tolmov Unipopis, man in forest (Libertarian)

Umbar Tripopis (Bari), man in forest, notorious vandal (Libertarian)

Lieutenant Victorani Keep, military officer (Royal)

Wago Tailor, cousin of Zell (Humanist, Republican)

Zellick Dipopis, baby (Libertarian)

Zillestra Agape, swimmer (status in transition)

Chapter 1

The Enrollment

After a long interstellar voyage, the mothership was stalled for
repairs and the final preparation for the invasion of the target
planet, a planet with a breathable atmosphere and an
abundance of liquid water.

"Antwanesta, please bring me a glass of water."

"Yes, Mother."

A teenage girl, with red hair past her shoulders, filled
a glass by pulling a lever made of an incorruptible alloy. Saint
Isaac's blessing flowed clear and pure. She gulped the water
down, unseen by her mother. The girl refilled the glass and
brought it as requested. Antwanesta then set about clearing the
dishes form the evening meal. The dishes too would be
washed with water delivered by technology which applied the
laws of Saint Isaac to deliver God's blessing. Of course
natural laws did not *belong* to Saint Isaac. He just discovered
some, long ago. All laws were God's laws, excluding what
people in the North regarded as *law*. All had to obey God's
laws even the atheistic Humanists, whether they believed in
Him or not.

All seemed very normal; that was how Antwanesta
wanted it to appear.

"Thank you, Dear," her mother said in a soft neutral
tone.

After a pause, "Are you excited about school, Dear?
Its just a week away."

1

"Yes, Mother," the girl replied in a casual tone which revealed no hint of excitement.

Antwanesta was in fact excited and anxious, but she thought a passive tone was best. She had been reminded just weeks ago that it was best to keep her feelings and thoughts to herself.

"Are you going to the church again tonight, Dear?"

"Yes, Mother."

"Father, was so very right about the power of prayer. You have really turned around since you started praying in earnest each night. With all your talk about that vile place on the lake, I thought the golden demons would never let you go," her mother said with sincere relief.

The father of which her mother spoke was not Antwanesta's real father. Her real father was always with her, but only in spirit. That was what she was told, and that was what she believed. Father Alfonzo, was flesh and blood. He had been a key figure in Antwanesta's life for eighteen years. He had been there for her thirty-sixth day blessing, and advised her throughout childhood and adolescence. She had gone to Father Alfonzo with all her fears and regrets. When she had considered going to the Central College of Epodlo, rather than Saint Isaac's College, she went to Father Alfonzo first. He advised her to consider each of the six virtues, to pray, and to have faith in God. He also had reminded her that the Pontiff had severed relations with Central College for good reasons. People her age had died in recent years. They died taking the very sinful path she had been contemplating.

Antwanesta wasn't contemplating going to the college on the lake any more. Her thinking had evolved from that point. She had gone from contemplation to planning and from planning to preparation. At this point there was nothing

left to contemplate. All that was left was the execution of the
plan, and that was to occur tonight.

Antwanesta took leave of her mother as she had for
the past few weeks. Before exiting the small pink-stoned
house she used the toilet one last time, not knowing when she
would have access to another stone-rimed hole with its round
blue button to operate the bidet appliance and its round red
button to blow dry her intimate parts after washing. *God bless
the Royal Plumbers*, Antwanesta thought. This sentiment was
sometimes said, and much more often thought, by Theites
when a toilet was available at a time of urgent need.
Antwanesta did not have such urgency now, but she knew the
voyage ahead would take several hours, and the Royal
Plumbers would well-deserve their blessing upon her arrival.

Out the door Antwanesta went into a clear windless
night. This night the buildings of Lord's Landing looked more
red than pink. There was a full moon. She had planned for the
weather. That was easy to do. August 31st always had a calm
clear night. It was last year, the year before, and so far as she
knew, there was a calm clear night every August 31st from the
beginning of time. The moon was another matter. It had its
own cycle, 28 days. Antwanesta knew the cycle well. The
moon was like the older sister she never had. She knew
tonight's moon would be full, but she judged that, on balance
its brightness would help, as much as hinder her. The
disadvantage of the full moon was that she could be more
easily seen, both on the lakeshore, and in the water by the men
patrolling in boats. The advantage was that she could use the
moonlight to navigate. She would be able to see the shore of
the homeland she was leaving (the Western Theocracy), and
later the tower on Central District Isle, which was the college
campus.

Antwanesta wore the traditional thick black robe that
was customary for women and girls of the Theocracy. She
had worn such a robe, in varying sizes, since her first birthday.

3

It extended from the base of her neck to her ankles. This attire had been designed to facilitate the cultivation of both the virtues, modesty and chastity. The robe could be uncomfortably hot this time of year. Antwanesta was blessed that Lord's Landing was in the relatively cool northern part of the Theocracy. She was also blessed that no virtue required clothing beneath her robe. Beneath she wore only her bronze Holy Hexagon pendant. Air could flow freely and cool her, to some degree, even in the Summer.

The church was in the center of Lord's Landing, just ten kiloballs down the hill, about a seven-minute walk. Her formerly-white cotton shoes moved at a brisk walking pace along the path of stone pavers. What might have been called *roads* in millennia past were merely *paths* or *trails*, not just here in the Theocracy, but in the other nations as well. There were no vehicles, no wagons, or carts larger than a man could push or pull, and no beasts of burden.

To eat or harm an animal would be a clear sin against peace. Likewise, to use products which were the result of killing would be sinful, but what of harnessing an animal for service? Would that be a sin? Perhaps the question had never been asked, since such creatures only existed in parables, legends, and in history long before God's guidance had been delivered by the sea. Antwanesta had no time for philosophy at the moment. She was going to church. As was her usual habit on such occasions, she was in a state of contemplative prayer as she walked. Her contemplation was intermittently interrupted by her silent recitation of memorized trigonometric tables. Antwanesta was passionate about both God and mathematics. She saw no conflict in this, because surely math is the purest of God's energies.

She reached the church which was on her left as she entered the central square. At the square's perimeter were commercial structures. All were closed both because it was night and because, on Sunday, the stores and service establishments were closed all day. Though quite unnecessary, the door of each had a red circle hung upon its face.

She had approached the six-sided house of worship from the rear, since she was coming from the west. Like all larger buildings the base of the church was made from cubic pink granite native stones. They were stacked three tall. The stones at the end of each wall had been cut at the angle needed to permit the corners to fit tightly together. Antwanesta proceeded to the east face of the church, where there were two tall black doors, each with the shape of a hexagon on it. These doors had no red circle, not even a hook for a red circle to be hung upon. The doors were not locked. They were never locked. The church was never closed. Why would anyone be denied access to God's house? God never stopped blessing his people. No enemy would be so possessed by evil as to desecrate the holy place. The soldiers from the South were reputed for their polite behavior, and their kingdom maintained quite friendly relations with the Theocracy. Even the shamelessly godless people of the North were hostile only in words, not action. The savages to the east came only to deliver fertilizer, stone, and more recently manufactured goods. They never came past the docks. God had indeed blessed the island of Epodlo with peace. Antwanesta made the sign of the hexagon from her forehead to her navel and back again. Then she entered the church.

In the church there was a hexagonal sanctuary with thirty-six rows of long simple wooden benches. At the far wall, which was oriented toward the Holy Hexagon in the sky, there was the familiar symbol of the Holy Hexagon visible through an opening at the center of a wooden wall (iconostasis) adorned with eight painted icons. On the left of the center opening, from left to right there were Saint Nicolas, Saint Charles, an image of Saint Hypatia's naked and bloody body being attacked by a mob wielding the shells of extinct mollusks, and Saint Hypatia again, holding a large book of mathematics in her arms. To the right of the opening, the first

5

icon was of empty golden space representing the ineffability of God. To the right of that, were Saint Thomas, Saint Isaac, and Saint Albert. The Holy Hexagon was a representation of the six virtues which guided Theists in daily life.

The church was unoccupied except for the devout Antwanesta. She walked toward the hexagon, knelt before it and prayed. She prayed aloud, but in a soft respectful tone, "Merciful God, grant me your energies, that I may cultivate love, modesty, chastity, peace, forgiveness, and faith." She repeated this thirty-six times, and made the sign of the hexagon six times.

If there were ever a time to be quick and perfunctory in her ritual, it was now. Antwanesta needed to move quickly. She needed to get as far as possible before day break to avoid detection. However, she tarried. She was drawn as usual by the Holy Hexagon. It spoke to her, or it sung. Often a corner would sing in a clear pure tone. Sometimes two or more corners would sing in harmony. Now, as had so often been the case in recent months, she heard dissonance. This moral noise in her mind did not offend or repulse her. It drew Antwanesta. It called her. It called her, but not to stay. The compelling dissonance called her to *go*!

She stood, and departed from the church the way she had come. She continued east down to the lakeshore. She reached the shore about one kiloball north of the docks where products were imported from, and exported to, neighboring lands. To her right was a stand of dense low bushes which had been allowed to remain in place to protect the point which marked the transition from Unity Lake to the Northwest River. The roots of the bushes held the soil, mitigating erosion during the three major storms each year. It was in these bushes that Antwanesta had hidden the components, and now the finished product, of her labors. She had worked in secret while she was believed to be praying in church these past few weeks. She had gathered light logs and thin rope from the shore of the lake and the bank of the river. The ropes she had found had been carelessly discarded during inspection of manufactured goods imported from the Northern Republic and the wild land to the east. From the logs and ropes she had made a raft. The raft was slightly wider than Antwanesta's shoulders, and its length measured from her neck to the middle of her thighs.

The moon was bright in the nearly cloudless sky. The moon had a great red circle centered on its now fully illuminated face. This perfect red circle was commonly known as the *red dot*. The dot was uniform in color, covering two-thirds of the moon's face, and totally featureless. It glowed red even when it was not on the half of the moon illuminated by the sun. The dot had been there all of Antwanesta's eighteen years. It had been there through the lifetimes of all now living and their ancestors for many generations. It had in fact been there for 984 years. The very calendar system now used originated with its appearance. This year was 984 A.Q. The "A.Q." stands for "after quake." The dot appeared in the year zero A.Q., and no one seemed to be able to satisfactorily explain why.

This moon casted a red glow upon the lakeshore, and Antwanesta feared it made her far too visible. There could be no other night. Classes would start in two days, and the weather tomorrow night would be much less favorable. She had no choice but to act despite the red moonlight, and act *now*.

This black-robed, red-haired girl, who really did not comprehend her own emotions, much less God's will, removed her shoes and placed them on top of the raft. She clutched the raft to her chest holding her shoes between her breasts, pressing her Holy Hexagon pendent against the skin under her robe. With her right hand she dragged a long straight stick she had also scavenged. The stick was like a narrow pole, twice as long as she was tall. She waded into the

7

water trying to minimize splashing. She was waste deep when she heard the first yell.

A man's voice shouted, "You there! Sister! No! Don't do it!" The man ran toward her.

Antwanesta pushed against the lake bottom with her stick. She tried to get too deep for the man to reach. She did not recognize the voice at first. The man was Brother Ifarbis Agape. All Theites had the same surname, except the rare few who had immigrated from other lands or had descended from naturally conceived people who failed to maintain chastity. This man was God-kissed so he had to be an Agape. "God-kissed" was a designation given to the minority of Agapes who had genetically dark skin, flat noses, and tightly curled black hair.

Brother Ifarbis boldly ran into the water. He grabbed at Antwanesta's ankle. She instinctively kicked, and pushed out farther with the stick. He gripped her right foot.

"No Sister, don't," the man pleaded. Theites referred to each other as "Brother" or "Sister" because they were all children of God.

She pushed back with her stick. The stick hit the man's left cheek. Her foot slipped free. She was now too deep for the man to safely reach. Blood dripped from her brother's cheek as he stepped back for a safer footing. He made the sign of the Holy Hexagon and hastened back to shore. He then ran for help. Brother Ifarbis ran to find Father Alfonzo.

Shortly Antwanesta was too deep for her stick to push against the bottom. She was horrified, not by the depth, but by what she had done. She had drawn blood. This was a sin against peace, an assault against her own brother, and against God. To make it worse the man she had assaulted had been trying to help her, trying to save her life. She committed

this terrible sin for reasons she could not even explain to
herself.

Antwanesta could not allow herself to continue her
introspection. Like her brother at the shore she could not
swim. The risk of drowning was real, and the probability did
not leave margin for distraction. She would have rather
entered the water further south, but this would have increased
the risk of capture. She had measured the speed of the current
toward the river and had calculated that if she took a vector to
the southeast the suction of the river could be overcome.

However, she knew she had another problem. She
had been discovered. The men from the Theocracy would
soon come for her in boats. With no wind, only rowboats
could be used. She might yet evade her pursuers.

She was paddling with her arms now. After half an
hour her arms hurt. She paused for a moment. A shoe was
pressing into her sternum. She shifted the cotton shoes so the
soles were against her rather than the rougher uppers. She also
pushed them down to her belly to mitigate the chaffing which
had been occurring near the inner portion of the base of her
right breast. The shoes had pushed the fabric of her now
saturated robe against her skin, and what had been discomfort,
which she could ignore, was now pain. She wished she could
peel off her robe. It did not help her here. Were it not for her
log raft the wet robe would drag her under the water. Even if
God miraculously granted her the ability to swim, modesty
demanded that she wear this robe. Whether she made it to
Central Collage or, as was more likely, was pushed back to the
Western Theocracy, she could not arrive naked. No Theite
would be so bold, so brazenly sinful. It was better to die in
virtue than to live in sin. This was a basic axiom demonstrated
by many saints. No, she would hold to her robe, as she held to
her now wavering faith.

Antwanesta was wrong. She was wrong that there
was not a Theite so bold. She did not know that some nine

kiloballs away, no farther than a yell could carry, in the same lake, and with the same mission; there was another eighteen-year-old. This young woman was bold. She had left her robe and her Holy Hexagon pendent on the shore, for while Antwanesta was building a raft, Zillestra Agape had been clandestinely teaching herself to swim.

Antwanesta and Zillestra had gone to the same schools as children. They were classmates but not really friends. It was not that they were adversaries or that they disliked each other. They just never became close. They had never had more than a superficial conversation. It was not that they had nothing common. They lived in the same town, had the same culture, and even shared the same heavenly Father. They did not talk of fears, doubts, or plans for the future. The future was set for them. They would go to St. Isaac's College for four years and then to St. Hypatia's Convent to submit themselves for annunciation. Their mothers had both been through the process. Both of their mothers spoke of the ecstasy of God's presence. The two young women were very much the same, even in their unspoken ambivalence about life and their vague sense of confusion and frustration.

Zillestra had begun the journey a full hour before her former classmate. She also entered the water from a more favorable embarkation point than Antwanesta, who needed cover for her raft. Zillestra had also traveled faster, but now she was traveling in the wrong direction. She was moving back toward the Theocracy, not due to discouragement or disorientation, but due to exhaustion. She had started strong. When she tired she could roll over and float on her back to rest before pushing further east. However, as the night progressed, the resting floats grew longer, and her progress toward the school stalled and then reversed. The perpetual westward current prevailed.

Antwanesta's progress had stalled too. The rope lashing the logs did not fray or loosen as she had feared, but the logs, so buoyant at the start of her voyage, were now becoming saturated with water.

How long had it been, three hours, more? She had deliberately hydrated herself earlier, to avoid risks which might be associated with drinking the seemingly clean lake water. She had also just as deliberately evacuated her bladder just before exiting the house. Her bladder was now full again. She had a fleeting thought about the immodesty of releasing its contents. Her subconscious responded to the absurdity of her reluctance faster than her rationalization could be formed. She released the flow and felt the warmth on her thighs, and spreading to her knees. Her tension was briefly relieved.

Her mind was now free to reflect on her situation. She could not even see her destination. She knew the odds were very much against her success. She oriented herself to a new mission, *survival*. She silently recited the prayer of the Holy Hexagon thirty-six times.

Zillestra had reached a similar realization. She was floating on her back, white torso breaking the surface of the still smooth water seen only by God's red eye. There was no one who actually believed that the red dot moon was literally God's eye. It was a comforting metaphor. The perfection of the round red dot in the center of the moon's Earthward face was now illuminated by the sun. It seemed to be a reminder of God's presence, but Zillestra took no comfort in it. Zillestra had found she could conserve energy by swimming backward on her back. She would try one last time to swim to the center of the lake. Swimming backward her face was to the west. She would be able to see if she were making progress against the current. She did not pray.

Antwanesta could only face in the direction she was trying to travel. She could not roll on to her back. If she did, she would likely fall off, and be dragged down to depths by her saturated robe. She was uncomfortable, tired, and sore. She had to go back. She was beginning her turn to face back

11

toward the Theocracy when she saw something in the water. It was not Zillestra, though she was almost close enough to see. Antwanesta saw a rowboat. She thought it likely to be a boat from the Theocracy with men from church looking to take her back to the land from which she had fled. It could be a boat from the Republic, but why would it be out here? Back before she was born people fished at night. Now however the only fish in the lake were tiny minnows half the size of her smallest finger. To live, that was what mattered now. She was on a sinking raft without the ability to swim. Whoever, was in that rowboat was an angel from God. Father Alfonzo often said God puts angels just where they are needed. When Father Alfonzo said "angels," he did not mean supernatural creatures with six wings and many eyes. He meant human beings, the imperfect tools which God uses to actualize His energies.

"Help. Over here!" Antwanesta yelled.

The bow of the boat turned in her direction, and she saw the oars move.

Zillestra, could also see the boat, and could hear the yell of a girl in the water, she paused and watched. She would judge her next move based on her observation of the fate, of the girl she assumed to be similarly situated to herself. *We learn from experience. It is often less costly or painful to learn from the experiences of others,* Zillestra thought.

As the boat drew near, Antwanesta could see, in the red moonlight, the head and back of a man who was facing the stern of the boat as he rowed. As the bow neared her she said weakly, "I am right here."

"You'll be ok. I'll get you," said a man's voice, as he shifted his body to face her.

The boat was large for a one-man rowboat, almost eighty balls long. It was made of wood, and had metal oar locks. It smelled of alcohol and chicken manure. The man quickly pulled the oars in, so they would not slip form the locks while he brought the young woman aboard. With the bow of the boat close to her head, Antwanesta's view of her rescuer was obstructed. The man reached over the starboard gunwale. His left hand reached Antwanesta's upper right arm. Between him pulling and her pushing with her feet against the waterlogged raft, she boarded the vessel. Her cotton shoes slipped off the raft and into the depths.

Antwanesta lifted her head, and got her first clear look at her savior. Before her on the deck of the small craft was a bearded man with no clothing except a belt which served no purpose, but to hold the sheath of a knife more than half the length of the mans naked thigh.

A savage, Antwanesta thought.

The man without clothes smiled at the shivering Antwanesta, and said, "You're a free woman now. I'll give you a ride."

Antwanesta was shocked and scared. She did not have to go through any moral calculus with the Holy Hexagon to know what virtue was at risk here. She backed toward the bow shuffling her bare feet. As she did she saw a crossbow on the deck at the barbarian's feet. *What kind of angel had God sent?*

Before she could further process what she was seeing, she heard a voice from behind her. "Are you ok over there?" It was a man's voice, but not deep enough to be a mature man. She did not look back, because she was transfixed with fear by the beast of a man not ten balls in front of her.

The naked man-beast yelled back spewing the odor of liquor from his mouth, "This is a free woman, Repub! She doesn't need to be chained up by your laws! She just won her freedom from the Theos!"

13

Thomas David Valentine

Antwanesta opened her mouth to speak, but no words came out.

The voice of the boy-of-a-man behind her spoke, in a firm but civil tone. "I agree sir, she is free, and I respect her autonomy. She may of course stay with you if she pleases, but I am bound for Central College, and I think that is where she wants to go."

The drunken man picked up his crossbow and said, "She's free, and I will protect her freedom! You Humis talk the good talk, but democracy has made you all slaves of the majority. Listen girl; if you want freedom, come with me. I'll show you freedom. I'll show you a place where you don't have to hide behind wet cotton in the heat of the Summer."

Antwanesta jumped off the port side of the bow. The equilibrium of the boat was upset, and the bearded, naked man tumbled to the deck. Antwanesta would have sunk quickly to her death, but the young man was ready. He had a wad of rope in his hand, and he threw it square into Antwanesta's head as she hit the water. The panicked Antwanesta thrashed and grabbed. Her fingers caught the rope. She was underwater holding her breath, but she held the lifeline. The young man pulled the rope taut, and shifted his weight to the side of his light rowboat opposite from where Antwanesta was submerged.

The young man yelled, "Climb!"

She did climb, despite not having heard the young man's entreat. Antwanesta climbed the rope, one hand over the other, until her head breached the surface. She gasped, and grabbed the starboard gunwale of the aluminum boat with her right hand. The left hand followed, and she pulled herself over the gunwale as the young man leaned over the port side too keep the boat from capsizing.

14

The older bearded man in the first boat, was bleeding, having hit his head as he had fallen to the deck of his boat. He was dazed, drunk, confused, and angry. He grabbed his crossbow, already loaded with a bolt, and leaped unsteadily to his feet. His head rose faster than did the blood his brain needed to function. He collapsed forward again onto the deck. As he fell the crossbow discharged. The bolt struck the younger man in the left deltoid. The tip of the bolt did not penetrate, but the razor sharp edge of the bolt's head gashed the young man's shoulder. The sleeve of Zell Fisher's white cotton shirt would soon be the same color as the red dot on the moon, now sinking low in the western sky.

In spite of his injury Zell shifted the bow of his small boat away from the larger one that Antwanesta had vacated, and he rowed. He was in the middle of the boat. The wet mop of a girl was sitting at the stern with her bare feet submerged in a puddle of water accumulated on the aft deck. The puddle sloshed to the stern with each stroke of the oars.

"There's a blanket there," Zell said as he nodded to a dry portion of the deck. She picked up the neatly folded blanket and wrapped it tightly around her shoulders, with her long wet robe beneath it.

"I'm Zell, Zell Fisher. What's your name?"

"Antwanesta Agape. Your bleeding. Are you ok?"

"Nothing Risky Sex can't fix, replied Zell"

"What!?!"

"Risky Sex is the school physician. Her real name is Betriski Sexapopis. She is our physical trainer too. The students call her Risky Sex, not to her face of course, or in front of other professors. She's great."

Zell was a fit brawny nineteen-year-old with light brown to blondish hair. He was wearing a white cotton shirt

15

with long sleeves, one of which was now quite bloody. His pants, also of cotton, were beige and held up by a deer leather belt. He also wore deer leather boots. From his clothing it was clear this was a Republican.

The term *Republican* was used to refer to a resident of the Northern Republic, just as *Theite* was the name politely used for residents of the Western Theocracy, and *Royal* referred to people of the Southern Kingdom. However, to be a Royal one had to be *of the blood*, that is a member of one of the few intermarried families of the Kingdom, not just a resident. Most people in the wild lands to the east called themselves *Libertarians*, though only the most informed and courteous of outsiders would refer to them as such. In the Republic the term, *Northerner* had also come into common use, just over the last century, as cynicism over democracy had grown. Most citizens of the Northern Republic would regard *Republican* or *Northerner* as equally polite and having the same meaning.

Most Republicans, Zell included, were Humanists. Humanism was generally classified as a religion, though most Humanists would object such a classification. The Humanists rejected all things supernatural, and saw human need as the objective measure from which moral decisions could be empirically justified. Humanists were contrasted with the Theists, who devotedly believed in God, but who seemed quite content to leave the concept of God left undefined. Both Theism and Humanism had traditions, rituals, axioms, and norms; and though they had many core values in common, their practitioners generally shared a mutual distrust.

There was a third boat in the water, even larger than the first. Two pairs of oars propelled the craft toward Zell's boat. The larger boat swiftly overtook the smaller one. It came along side. Antwanesta recognized the man in the middle of the boat. He was Father Alfonzo, a tall man in a long black robe, with a brown goatee. There was a silver hexagon shaped amulet hanging from his neck suspended from a silver chain.

"Antwanesta, please my dear, think about this. Your mother must be terribly worried. Please come with me," said the priest; in a firm, clear, but gentle voice.

"Father," said Antwanesta.

"Come with me my dear. God loves you. He wants what's best for you," said the priest in a sincere voice.

"I don't want to come," Antwanesta replied.

Father Alfonzo gently asked, "Why Antwanesta? Why leave the people who love you, and want to protect you?"

"Because I, I, I want to learn. I want to understand. You and Mother have told me the same things for eighteen years, and I have no idea if you are telling me the truth. I want to know who I am. I, I, I don't know! I need to know! Is that so wrong? I want to escape from my ignorance. I want to learn from people who are not just like me, people who really know things."

The cleric added, "You are a beloved servant of God, Sister Antwanesta. God has a wonderful plan for you. Don't turn your back on Him."

Antwanesta retorted, "I want my own plan!" at first not realizing the selfishness and arrogance implicit in her words. "I want to *make* my own plan. I don't want to be told what to do. I don't want to be intimidated into accepting someone else's ideas. I want to figure the world out for myself." Shocked at herself, she started to weep.

Then there was a yell from the south of both boats, "Help!" It sounded like a girl in trouble. "Help!"

"Row!" shouted the father. As the larger boat pulled away, Father Alfonzo looked at the weeping Antwanesta and said, "Have faith in God, Sister. He will always be with you." He made the sign of the hexagon giving God's blessing to the confused young woman he had blessed the first time as a tiny red-haired baby such a very short time ago. A tear came to his eye as he turned to scan the water for his other lost lamb.

Zell, rowed in silence, as Antwanesta wept.

Several minutes later Antwanesta asked, "Will they let me in, in the school? Can I be admitted?"

"Sure," said Zell. "They will be thrilled to see you. Theites are rare now, since your god-man cut relations with the school."

"The Pontiff is no '*god-man*.' He is God's representative on Earth." replied Antwanesta, a bit put off by Zell's crude choice of words, especially given her fragile emotional state.

"Sorry, I respect your right to believe as you wish," said Zell. He wanted to add, "Even if it is irrational," but he thought better of it when he considered that this girl had already jumped out of one boat because she did not like what she heard.

Antwanesta said, "It still looks so far. Can you row so long?"

"Notwithstanding the old adage about Republicans and rowboats, I will get you there."

As time passed, the predawn sky was starting to lighten. Antwanesta could see the silhouette of the school tower on the eastern horizon.

Antwanesta asked, "Is that it?"

"Yes," said Zell. "You will have to get used to a few things, but if you have enough compassion, reason, and creativity, I am very sure you will adapt, and love it."

"Thank you, Zell. I needed to hear that," she said. Then she added, "Why were you out there?"

"To find someone like you." Zell replied.

Antwanesta, blushed.

"I want to save people like you from ruthless totalitarianism cloaked in religion," Zell continued. "I want to rescue women form the illusion of God."

Antwanesta did not know what to think of Zell, but she was getting eager to leave the boat. She silently prayed until they reached the shore.

They hit the shore of the Central District, the campus of the Central College of Epodlo at twenty-seven minutes past dawn, September 1, 984 A.Q.

"You caught one Mr. Fisher. Good work." A man in a robe similar that of a priest, but shorter, greeted the boat. The man was beardless, in his early 50's, and he had thinning red hair. Antwanesta knew he had to be from the Theocracy. "Welcome Sister, I am Professor Irigon Agape. Are you ok?"

"Yes," Antwanesta said, her eyes darting between the man and the tall, pink, stone and glass tower behind him.

"What is your name?" The man inquired.

"Antwanesta," she replied knowing that to him the last name was obvious.

"I'm glad to see you, even if it does mean I lost my bet with the dean. She said we would have a couple of students from the Theocracy this year. I should know better

19

than to question her predictions. She seems to know everything."

The red-haired professor then noticed Zell's arm. "You're hurt Mr. Fisher. You better see Dr. Sexapopis about that." He then noticed a woman approach, and said, "God puts angels just where they are needed."

A very fit, lean, muscular, yet distinctly feminine woman, with suntanned skin and blond-streaked shoulder length brown hair, ran up, and began to examine Zell's arm. Antwanesta looked at her with shock in her face, her eyes wide and mouth agape. The women tending to Zell's arm was totally and absolutely *naked*.

Chapter 2

Roommates

"My cousins will retrieve the boat in the afternoon," Zell told Professor Agape. Dr. Sexapopis escorted Zell away. Antwanesta could not even thank the heroic boy, shocked as she was by the doctor's nudity. The bare physician, with her arm supporting Zell, walked east toward the infirmary, which was in a two-story rectangular building with the gym at its ground floor. Antwanesta's eyes followed the firm bronze buttocks of Dr. Scxapopis, until Antwanesta caught herself, and looked at the exterior metal bracing of the school tower instead.

Professor Agape, who seemed to take no notice of the doctor's nakedness, directed Antwanesta to a door at the end of the southwest wing of the sprawling six-winged ground floor of thirteen-story glass and steel tower. She entered the indicated door, now not even conscious of her bare feet. She followed a sign to a desk manned by, whom she correctly presumed to be a senior student assigned as a clerk to receive new freshmen. The clerk asked her name, country of origin, and birthdate. Antwanesta provided the three required pieces of information which the clerk recorded. The clerk then showed her the location of the freshman dorm on a map. Next he gave her a student robe and a room key. He told her the student robe was required to be worn on campus at all times, except in designated areas including the dorms, baths, training field, gym, running trail, and Freedom Park. The clerk also identified her room number as 327, and told her she could change into her robe in the toilet area down the hall and to the left.

Antwanesta walked to the toilet area and remembered that she had lost her shoes. That was a problem she would need to resolve later. The toilet area had six stalls behind a wall with a rectangular wash basin two balls across and the length of all the stalls together. *Six toilets*, she thought, *one for each virtue*. She smiled at the absurdity of finding divine purpose in plumbing. However, at the moment the plumbing was a welcome blessing. Alone in the area she quickly shed her wet Theite robe, and slipped into her new student attire (a black robe thinner and shorter than the one she had just removed). Then she entered the third toilet stall to accept her blessing. The walls of the stall were floor-to-ceiling polished granite of the type familiar throughout Epodlo. The top-stone and blue and red buttons were identical to those in her home in the Western Theocracy. She felt quite comfortable except that the stalls had no doors. She thought this a bit immodest, but as she was alone, the point was moot at the moment.

Antwanesta washed her hands at the basin. There was no mirror. A deerskin rucksack rested on the floor next to her right foot. From a stall, behind and to her right, she heard a young woman's voice.

"Hi, I'm Gretchin."

Antwanesta knew it would place the toilet sitter in an immodest situation, if she turned to face her, so she did not turn around. She stared at the wall and said, "Hi, I'm Antwanesta."

Gretchin removed the awkwardness of the situation by finishing with her blow dry, and coming to the basin. "I'm pleased to meet you, Ant. I guess you are a freshman too."

"Yes" she replied, not knowing how to react to being called "Ant." That word had no meaning on the insect-free island of Epodlo.

"Let's walk over to the dorm together," Gretchen Quadrapopis said in a sincerely friendly tone.

Maidens of Epodlo, Book 1 — Antwanesta Agape and the Mystery of the Red-dot Moon

Gretchin was two balls taller than Antwanesta. Her skin was suntanned. Her hair was dark brown as were her eyes. Even in her robes she looked thin, and clearly had no bust. Her face was naturally very pretty, but she was unaware of that fact. Her extroversion and bravado were mostly subconscious artifices erected to conceal a deep insecurity. She doubted her value as a person and most especially as a woman, though Antwanesta could not detect Gretchin's weaknesses.

They walked out on toward the freshman dorm.

"I guess when you're washed up, the men are really excited by your red hair," Gretchin said casually.

Antwanesta's face turned red with both embarrassment and a touch of anger. The statement shocked Antwanesta on a number of levels. For one, she certainly did not aspire to "excite" men. Chastity was one of the six virtues of the Holy Hexagon. For another, this was no way for a young lady to think, much less talk. The idea of exciting men was highly offensive. For a third, how could a Royal, which she presumed Gretchin must be given her tanned face and arms, be so blunt and vulgar, and yet maintain such a high reputation for tact and curtesy? There was also a forth. She thought, *I must be hideous as a drowned rabbit after the ordeal in the lake.* The wet cat analogy did not come to mind, because the only cats of which Antwanesta had any awareness, were the lions in religious parables. Antwanesta, replied with, "I'm not interested in men."

Gretchin then said, "Whatever, I'm happy to hear it. The more lesbians in the world, the more men there are for me. Not that I have anything against women. It's just that men have an obvious anatomical advantage I appreciate."

Antwanesta's face was now the same shade as the dot on the moon. Gretchin was *not* Royal. S*he must be a libertine from the wild lands to the east.* Antwanesta was now silent.

She would be glad to reach the dorm, and rid herself of this barbarian girl.

The two walked around the south of the tower complex, and east along a path.

"What floor are you on?" asked Gretchin cheerfully, concealing her wish that the stiff Theo prude would be housed far from her.

Antwanesta, coldly asked, "Are the three-hundreds on the third floor?"

"Yes," said Gretchin, her forced cheerfulness starting to falter.

They crossed a foot bridge over an array of glass panels and entered the dorm from the south end. As they climbed the stairs they passed two freshman boys wearing black student robes identical too their own.

"This is a girl's dorm isn't it?" Antwanesta, asked Gretchin.

Gretchin replied, "The Humanists disposed of 'separate but equal' ages ago. Freedom prevails here. As freshman there will be just girls in our rooms. Also freshman and sophomore baths are still segregated as a concession to the Theocracy."

Antwanesta wanted a change, but this was coming at her all too fast.

The two reached the landing of the third floor. Their eyes were immediately drawn to the men wearing golden armor standing near the left wall close to the far end of the hall. The young women walked toward the men. They both saw the number on the door between the men, 327.

Gretchen smiled and said, "Men are waiting at my door already. I knew I'd love this place."

The realization hit Antwanesta that she and the lusty savage were roommates.

Gretchin then asked, "Why to do Royal soldiers use short swords rather than long ones?"

The sergeant on the right replied, "Short swords are much faster than long swords, Miss."

"That's what I thought," Gretchin said in a tone of exaggerated resignation.

Both of the armed men enveloped their own lips to avoid cracking a smile.

Gretchin then said curtly, "Open up. This room is mine."

The sergeant then said in a calm businesslike voice of a government official performing his duty, "Disrobe please."

Antwanesta froze in terror.

Gretchin, smiled, dropped her rucksack, promptly removed her robe, folded it once, and draped it over her right arm. Like Antwanesta, she had no clothing under her robe. The lean bronzed Gretchin stood there proudly displaying her nude body for the soldiers to inspect.

The sergeant with the dispassionate composure of an experienced medical professional said, "May I inspect your bag?"

"No," replied Gretchin.

"We can walk you to the dean, and have her persuade you to let us inspect it. That seems like a major waste of time," said the sergeant in a calm gentle tone.

"OK," said Gretchin, handing her rucksack to the sergeant. She agreed that talking to the dean would be a waste of time.

After inspecting the bag and finding only deerskin and rabbit pelt clothing, the sergeant said, "You're clear."

The corporal to the left of the door, spoke to Antwanesta, "You too please, Miss."

Antwanesta, could not react. Her mind was an emotional battle field, a cratered waste land. So much had happened to her, so fast, she could not process it.

Gretchin came to the rescue. "Good luck getting under that robe. She's a Theo, fresh off the boat."

"My apologies Miss," said the corporal, "I assumed you were from the Republic. The Kingdom has nothing to fear from the Theocracy."

The sergeant knocked on the door.

The firm clear voice of a young women responded from within, "Enter."

The golden clad guards snapped to attention and opened the door to the dorm room. Gretchin, still unclothed, and Antwanesta still in a daze, walked in.

The room was small. The door was near one corner, and opened across from one of two open windows on the opposite wall. Between the windows there was a bunk bed made with a plain pine frame. Directly across from one bunkbed, and near the door, was an another identical bunkbed. At the far end of each bed was an armoire with four drawers and a cabinet. One small wooden table and chair was at the far end of the room lit by one of the windows. A single closet filled the wall at the end left of the doorway.

Before them stood two other young women, each wearing identical bright white tunics. Each tunic had a V-neck which extended to the base of the sternum. The skirt portion of the tunics extended half-way down the deeply tanned thighs. Slits at the center of the thighs allowed ventilation and freedom of movement. The slits were invisible because they were covered with rectangular sections of cloth, also bright white, which hung from the waist and were coterminous with the rest of the skirt portion of the tunic. The rectangular pieces were narrower than the thighs beneath. The tunics would be regarded as extremely immodest in the Theocracy, but with naked Gretchin standing next to her, Antwanesta felt they were much less so. Both young women had blond hair. The taller and fuller of the two had mostly straight hair which curled in uniformly at the neck, and stopped short of her shoulders. The shorter one was of the same height and bodily proportions as Antwanesta, but more lean and firm in muscle tone. Her hair was also just short of her shoulders, but with a mousey wind-swept look. The taller one was between Antwanesta and Gretchin in height and a bit heavier especially in the chest and in general musculature. She was no Risky Sex, but her love of swimming conditioned her well. At 6.1 <u>balls</u> in weight she was still trim and fit, despite her ample bosom.

The larger of the two said, "I am Lissy, and this is Xiny. You are our roommates I presume?"

"It appears so. I'm Gretchin, this is Ant."

"Antwanesta," interrupted the tired, dirty, frazzled girl, now returning to her wits. "What's with the guards?" While saying this she hung her still damp Theite robe on a hook on the foot of the bunk nearest the door.

"I do apologize for that, Antwanesta," Lissy replied.

Xiny, continued as if she and Lissy were somehow just one person, "Lissy is her Royal Highness, Queen Yvalissa Regalis, Monarch of the Southern Kingdom. The guards are for her protection."

Lissy, just as smoothly proceeded with, "Here I am just Lissy. For four precious years I can be just another girl. Xinonina Stewart is my loyal handmaiden, forth from the

27

throne, and the daughter of my trusted and able chief councilor. Here she is my dearest friend, Xiny."

"Fine with me Your Hinny. You and Sinny *are* just girls to us free people anyway," Gretchin jabbed.

Lissy registered no offence on her face, but there was a hint of some weakness in Xiny's golden armor of curtesy. It was just a flutter in her facial expression, but Antwanesta could tell that the handmaiden was hurt by the disrespect shown to her Queen.

The relationship between Lissy and Xiny was far more complex than the brief description the two personable young women had so summarily provided. A handmaiden in the Southern Kingdom is no mere serving girl. Personal service to a queen or princess is part of the role, but she was also, a counselor, confidant, and an extension of the Queen herself. Xiny was Handmaiden because she was the oldest unmarried female in the second ranking family.

Xiny was also forth in the line of secession to the throne, not because she was Handmaiden, or even because she was daughter of the appointed Chief Councilor to the Queen. Her proximity to the throne was defined by birth and blood. The reigning family held the honorary sir name, "Regalis," and now consisted of but two remaining members. Each family which came to the throne exchanged its common sir name for the name, "Regalis" in accordance with long-held tradition. Lissy and her cousin Gregorious were the last of their bloodline. Gregorious was nineteen, one year older than Lissy. However, Lissy was the daughter of the prior King, so the role of Queen, much to Gregor's relief, fell to her.

Another matter necessary to understand the traditional system of interrelationships in the Kingdom, is the method by which marriages are arranged. Each Royal, every citizen of the Kingdom, is designated to marry the person of the opposite sex whose birth was nearest in time to their own, among the pool of eligible unmarried citizens. Royals become eligible for marriage when the woman graduates from college and man both graduates from college and completes four years of military service. Since graduation typically occurs at age twenty-two, marriages generally are arranged when a woman is twenty-two and a man is twenty-six. When a man is discharged from compulsory military service, he marries the graduated woman closest to his age. Marriage partners are predictable years in advance if no surprises occur. Complexity ensues when an untimely death reshuffles the effectively betrothed pairs. Due to this risk, relations, both sexual and emotional, among the those who expect to marry, are strongly discouraged, and in the case of sex, regarded as a gross breach of social norms although not of actual law.

Similarly, sex that might result in progeny would constitute a serious threat to the bloodline. Therefore, Royals, male and female, were expected to be chaste until marriage. Given their deep devotion to custom, duty, honor, and consideration of others, this mandate was seldom breached, at least not in a way which might produce unsanctioned children. Also, given Royals' extraordinary capacity for discretion, such rare breaches were never subjected to gossip, and thus knowledge rests only with participants and witnesses.

Lissy and Xiny did not want to overload Antwanesta and her uncultured companion with these details. It was not the sort of thing Royals would discuss in casual conversation with outsiders in any case.

After the brief introduction provided, Lissy said, "Xiny and I want to get a bath before the orientation lunch. Come with us. You definitely need a shower Antwanesta." The Queen picked a piece of algae from Antwanesta's flattened mop of red hair.

Antwanesta needed and wanted a shower very much. She smelled like the lake, and felt worse than she looked. However, for Theites, bathing is an activity which people do alone. To bathe in the sight of others would be the height of immodesty.

"The baths here are spectacular. My great-great-grandfather designed them. The freshman bath is just down stairs. You will love it," Lissy added, while removing her tunic simultaneously with Xiny. Antwanesta now had three naked roommates.

"I can't," she said, "The guards will see me."

Xiny scurried to the door. She spoke to the guards as if she were fully clothed. She instructed them to close their eyes when Antwanesta passed them.

The guards replied in unison, "Yes, Handmaiden," as if Xiny were their superior officer. She was in fact the voice of the Queen, and they would never hesitate to obey her as such.

As Xiny re-entered the room, she undid the clasp on Antwanesta's robe, and pulled her robe down to the floor. Antwanesta now, without her consent, had been brought into conformity with these strange girls who she had only just met. After folding Antwanesta's robe and placing it on the lower bunk behind the place where Antwanesta had hung her wet Theite robe, Xiny took Antwanesta's hand, and all four exited into the hallway. Antwanesta was too tired to put up any real resistance, and too filthy to say no to a bath.

At the end of the hall Lissy and Xiny both ducked into a toilet area leaving Gretchin and Antwanesta briefly at the top of the stairs. Gretchin looked into Antwanesta's eyes and saw the anxiety. Then with a tenderness Antwanesta would not have thought possible from the savage girl, Gretchin said, "Don't worry. Hinny and Sinny are Royals. They would jump off the school tower before they would fail in their duty to be nice to you."

Xiny and Lissy emerged, and they all proceeded down the very steps where, just several minutes before,

Antwanesta and Gretchin had passed the robed boys. Down to the basement they went. First left then another left down a sloped passageway. The passageway opened into a room with wooden benches and empty hooks on the wall. The room had two small skylights, but most of the light in the room came from a wide opening across from the door through which they had entered. There was a closed door on the right end of the room. The four young women proceeded directly across from where they entered. There was a wider opening into a longer sloped passageway brightly lit by sunlight through skylights which together spanned most of the ceiling. The passage way was divided down the middle with a low granite partition about as high as Gretchen's upper thigh. The four proceeded down the right side of the passage, with Gretchin a few steps ahead of the others. Antwanesta was very uncomfortable walking nude down this unknown passage with these strange girls of very recent acquaintance. Her discomfort would soon turn into acute humiliation.

Three boys, also unclothed, were walking up the left side of the passage. At the sight of them, Antwanesta covered he left breast with her right hand and her right breast with her right forearm. Her left hand shot to cover her pubic area. She blushed in red splotches. She positioned herself such that, as much as possible, Lissy and Xiny would be between her and the three nude young men.

Lissy and Xiny were immediately recognized by the boys. "Hi Cousin!" shouted the shorter of the two blondest ones.

"Gregor, Barthon!" Lissy replied with a welcoming smile.

The third boy would have been recognized by Antwanesta if her eyes had still been open. It was Zell Fisher. Lissy and Xiny extended their hands to be kissed by the Royal boys in accordance with their custom. Gretchin who had pulled her shoulders back so far her ribcage protruded with

31

unnatural prominence, eagerly extended her hand to Zell, who smiled and kissed it with a mixture of politeness and amusement.

Lissy and Xiny understood Antwanesta's situation, and tried to assist in her in the futile effort to achieve invisibility. Lissy introduced Gretchin, who's eye's scanned Zell up and down, before locking her view on his eyes. She broke her gaze briefly to acknowledge Gregor and Barthon, but Zell clearly had the focus of her attention.

"This is Zell Fisher, our roommate," said Gregor. He then told Zell, "This is my cousin, Lissy and Barthon's sister, Xiny."

"I have heard nothing but high praise for you both," shared Zell.

"Of course" added, Gregor, "without Lissy a vast mountain of responsibility would fall on my head. She wears the crown well. Long live the Queen."

"I'm just Lissy here, Zell," Lissy said.

Xiny added, "Why are you, sophomore boys in the freshman bath?"

Barthon replied to his sister, "Our bath is closed for repairs. Some glass in the roof was broken. Plumbers need to drain the main pool and remove the glass. It will take weeks to pass the Chief Plumber's inspection. Mr. Solider is very cautious."

Gregor and Barthon both noticed the contorted white and red speckled wreck of a girl crouched behind Xiny desperate to be unseen. As Royals they felt almost instinctively that they must aid her, so Gregor said, "You girls need to get wet. We'll see you later."

Zell nodded his head to Lissy as his way of saying,
"Although I find the concept of monarchy a fundamental
affront to human dignity, I respect you as a person."

Lissy being amazingly perceptive in the art of
reading body language, got the gist of his meaning and smiled
politely.

The boys walked past, and Zell said without turning
his head to actually look back, "Good to see you again,
Antwanesta."

Antwanesta's red splotches grew redder. Her eyes
closed tighter and she began to whimper.

Lissy said, "They're gone now," in a soft comforting
voice.

Antwanesta opened her eyes only to see Xiny's
tanned buttocks right in front of her. As Xiny turned
Antwanesta fell with a loud splat on to the rough granite floor.
A tear ran down her left cheek.

Lissy and Xiny in unison each took one of
Antwanesta's arms and lifted her. Lissy spoke softly into her
right ear, "You are ok, Antwanesta. See that curve to the right
ahead. After that turn there will be no boys, only girls."

Lissy and Xiny walked Antwanesta with *their* power
not hers. Gretchin was several steps ahead daydreaming,
oblivious to the plight of the frightened Theite girl.

The four rounded the corner, and saw the freshman
women's bath for the first time. It was a magnificent sight. To
the far right was an enormous rectangular swimming pool, 500
balls across and 1000 balls long. Along the end and side
nearest to the entry were round pools of water thirty balls in
diameter. Most were hot and churning. The large and small
pools had rounded edges tiled with tiny pink opaque glass
squares. To the left of the round pools at the end of the large
rectangular pool, there were showers. The four rows of eight

33

showerheads were suspended, from the trusses of the high glass-paneled ceiling, by long pipes. The Royal plumbing was indeed divine. Only five of the thirty-six showerheads were occupied. Each showerhead had a fob suspended from its middle point. Among the showers were short stone pedestals. Each with four stone cups. To the left of the showers was a stone panel with access behind from either end. The left wall beyond the stone paneled area was stone up to twenty-five balls then was a metal grid to the ceiling. This allowed more sunlight in. Several clean white towels hung on golden bars left of the opening where the four had entered. The ceiling was supported by four massive granite columns, one at each corner of the large pool. Wide steel trusses coated in gold also supported the glass-paned ceiling at ten-ball intervals. Aside from the vulnerable glass above the room, bracing seemed over-engineered, as if to withstand a massive earthquake. The right wall was stone up to the end-truss of the glass paneled ceiling.

Lissy and Xiny lead Antwanesta to the showers proceeded by Gretchin. The four young women took white liquid soap from the stone cups and lathered themselves. Antwanesta, who was coaxed by Xiny, slowly began to surrender her tension, and enjoy the warm water of the shower.

Lissy said to Xiny, more by way of explanation to Antwanesta than as instruction to Xiny, "Gretchin and I will go swim while you help Antwanesta get ready for training tomorrow."

Xiny took Antwanesta by the hand and lead her behind the stone panel, where there was a cosmetic room. Here there were tables, mirrors, and cabinets filled with all sorts of cosmetics and toiletries, free for common use. In the middle of the room were four clean shinny massage tables covered in a soft, smooth, black material. Xiny gestured for Antwanesta to sit on the third table. She did. Xiny explained that all the women at the school shaved their legs and under their arms, and that if Antwanesta did not, she would stand out in a "most unpleasantly immodest way." Xiny told her not to worry, that she had shaved Lissy many times.

Antwanesta said nervously, "Just the legs and under the arms?" looking down at Xiny's tidily trimmed blond pubic plumage.

With a smile Xiny said, "Yes, I will leave the rest of your hair as natural as Gretchin's."

In just a few minutes they were back at the showers rinsing off the shaving soap residue.

Xiny then took Antwanesta to the churning hot pool second from the door. They slipped below the water and into paradise. Antwanesta's soar tired muscles finally felt relief. After a few minutes of silent bliss, they were joined in the pool by Gretchin and Lissy.

They conversed briefly about nothing, and were then joined by a black-haired beauty who sat on the rim of the tub across from Antwanesta. Antwanesta realized she could reliably identify the nationality of the twenty-or-so women in the bath by a combination of skin tone and hairstyle. The young woman before her, with the light skin an intermediate degree of pubic hair trimming, was from the Republic. This was later confirmed by her use of Humanist idioms like, "Life is not a dress rehearsal," and "Reason rules."

After testing the water and the company, the black haired young woman slipped the rest of the way into the water. Her name was Felisianna Smith. She went by "Feli." She said she had no known relationship to Dean Smith. *Smith* was a common name, not as common as Agape, or Metropopis, but common both in the Republic and in the Kingdom. Feli was amiable and outgoing, much more pleasant than Antwanesta expected a Humanist girl would be. It was Feli who first asked Antwanesta how she came to be at the school.

Antwanesta told the tale of her voyage. Feli, Xiny, and Lissy listened with interest. Gretchin who had been lost in reverie was shaken to attention only when Antwanesta got to the part about Zell Fisher. Gretchin then peppered her with questions about what Zell said and did. It soon came to light that Gretchin had not even noticed that Zell had had a bandage on his shoulder when they met in the passageway. The others laughed at this realization, even the ever-polite Royals.

To Gretchin's further intrigue, Feli said she grew up with Zell in the Republic town of Newton. She said he was very nice albeit sarcastic. "He and I have a similar sense of humor," Feli added. "We get our jokes when no one else does."

Gretchin asked if she and Zell were a couple. Feli said that as young teens she and Zell had practiced kissing and caressing together, but that she had known him so long he was like a brother to her. She added that there was no romantic chemistry, but that he was still a close and dear friend.

After a few more pleasant moments, Feli excused herself to go find her roommates, one of whom Gretchin knew from Freetown, to prepare for the lunch orientation. Before parting, Feli spoke to Antwanesta, Xiny, Lissy, and Gretchin each in turn. She called each by name, and gave each a sincere smile, warm eye contact, and individualized parting words. To Antwanesta she said that she liked her, and looked forward to becoming very close friends. To Xiny she said to forgive her for being so forward, but that she felt that Xiny was already her close friend. To Lissy she also apologized, saying she was sorry for treating her as an equal, but that the egalitarian ethic of her Humanism left her no option. To Gretchin, she said, "Gretchin, Sweetheart, I really do think Zell might go for your type. If I were him, I *definitely* would." As Feli withdrew from the pool she said, "I look forward to hearing Dean Smith speak at lunch. I really admire her. I don't understand why she is called the *Demonic Dean*."

Chapter 3

Orientation

Upon returning to the dorm room the four roommates dressed. Lissy and Xiny dawned their white tunics and school robes. Xiny let Antwanesta borrow a tunic and white cotton shoes. The immodesty of the short and low-cut tunic was covered by her school robe. For Gretchin the school robe and a pair of dear skin sandals was the totality of her outfit. Who would wear animal hide clothing on the first of September?

The four walked over the foot bridge which spanned the bath roof, and across the campus to the main tower building. The main, body of the campus, that portion to the northeast with the tower at its center, had several groupings of trees arranged in odd numbers three to seven. Each grouping was of but one variety of but a handful of species of oak, pine or maple, pollinated by only the wind. Several random clumps red and silver maples also grew along the lakeshore in places having self-seeded there. The lawn was dark green, soft and free of weeds.

The freshman dining hall was on the first floor of the tower complex, in a different wing from the administration area where Antwanesta had met Gretchin. The four young women arrived in the dining hall seven minutes before the appointed time of noon. There was no problem finding a place where all four could sit together. The room was no more than half full.

Most of the dining hall was occupied by several rectangular wooden tables and benches. These were set in parallel ranks perpendicular to the main entry door and to a dais at the opposite end. On the tables were clean empty plates and eating utensils. On the dais was one table and one bench, no different from the others in the room, and one simple wooden podium.

Before noon the last of the freshman students arrived. No student wanted to displease Dean Smith with tardiness the day before the start of class. She was reputed to have expelled students from the school during past orientations. However, that was not for tardiness. It was for sitting on the railing of the tower breezeway.

With all the students in matching robes, it was hard to tell the nationality of the students. Surely all the girls from the bath were here, but Antwanesta could not recognize any of them, except Feli who was two tables forward. There was one student of who's nationality Antwanesta could immediately identify on sight.

Eltwando was a God-kissed boy. He was tall with naturally dark skin, short curly black hair, a flat nose and full lips. This young man was obviously from the Western Theocracy, and he had his own story.

Eltwando had lived in Saint Charles' Monastery, for six years. Theite boys go to the monastery at age twelve. There they are educated and protected from the distracting temptation of women and girls. Life in the monastery was in no way brutal or unpleasant. It was a contemplative life of prayer and service. The large granite monastic compound was near the southern end of the Eastern Theocracy. The location was hot in Summer but presently mild in Winter. The senior monks at the monastery were kind, gentle, and understanding; but Eltwando had missed his mother, and his mother missed him.

Eltwando's trek had not been as arduous or perilous as Antwanesta's. His escape was, what one might call, an inside job. He had crossed the Southwest River to the Southern Kingdom in row boat which had secretly been

prepositioned for him. He arrived at a point on the bank
northeast of West Tower. In the Kingdom he was escorted, as
planned by his mother, by very polite soldiers to Queen's Port.
From there he sailed with several Royal students to Central
District Isle, where he was greeted at the arboretum dock by
his loving Mother who took him directly to the small Theist
Chapel on campus. There he and his mother both thanked God
for the reunion and wept with joy.

Promptly at noon the main door opened, and in strode
five people in black robes. The robes were much like student
robes but with color along the front edges. The color varied to
identify the specialty of each professor.

At the head of the procession was a thin, attractively-
shaped woman of no more than average height. Her hair was
dark brown shoulder length with several strands of grey mixed
in. She looked younger than her fifty-six years. Her expression
was stoic. She marched directly to the dais and podium, while
the four professors took places on the bench behind the table
on the dais.

Without any pause, the dean began to speak.
"Welcome to Central District Isle, and Central College of
Epodlo. "I am Illisima Smith. I play many roles in this place.
Most significantly to you, I am your dean. I serve as head of
this school at the pleasure of the Board of Regents. I am also
Governor of Central District Isle the totality of which is
occupied by this campus. It's a beautiful place wouldn't you
say?"

There was polite applause from the faculty behind
her and enthusiastic applause from the students. This brought
a small tight smile to the dean's face.

She continued, "Please, refer to me as "Dean or Dean
Smith" and extend an analogous curtsey to your professors. As
Dean and Governor, I am an absolute dictator with unbridled
discretion. Any laws and rules which exist in the Republic or

39

elsewhere do not apply here. Any rights, privileges, and liberties you enjoy in your homelands apply to you here, only to the extent that *I* permit them to do so. This may seem to you harsh or unfair. However, if you don't find my governance to your liking, you have absolute freedom to board a boat to your homeland, and never return. However, if you speak to some upperclassmen, you will find that on the whole students love it here. This is a multicultural institution and getting used to people who differ from you, may require some adjustment on your part. If you give it an honest try, you can adapt, make friends, and love this place just like your more senior peers."

Then the Dean half turned and extend her right arm to the table behind. "Here with me are your professors," she said with a tone of pride and some approximation of kindness. The professors were introduced left to right, Professor Kaye Solider, Professor Elonora Agape, Professor Morgont Medic, and Doctor Betriski Sexapopis. These professors will teach History, Math, Nature, and Physical Training respectively. She added, "Each of you will be assigned an advising professor to counsel you and help you adjust to any cultural or emotional challenges you may face." Notices about your first counselling session will arrive in your dorm room via mail slot."

The red-haired Professor Irigon Agape was not among those at the table because he did not teach freshmen. He taught Religion to the sophomores. Students referred to the Religion professor as, "Professor Agape the Red," and the Math professor as Professor Agape the Black." The name referred to hair color not race. Race was an alien concept, lost to history in the distant past. The only use of the word "race" was for running competitions. The red-headed people and the God-kissed were not races, just people with rare characteristics which had only distinctly appeared in the last century, and only within the Theocracy.

"Lastly, I want to speak of rules. I grew up in North Point the deepest and coldest depth of the Northern Republic.

As the Republicans among you know, the Republic is full of rules. There are rules on how to behave, how to conduct business, how to regulate personal life. Even intimate relationships are formalized and regulated by the legal institution of marriage. I grew to hate rules, and when I first went to Libertaria I learned I was not the only one. I have a strong affinity for Libertarians. However, I understand, that for people who do not have a strong sense of personal responsibility, rules are an unfortunately necessary expedient. The ancient philosopher, Plato, who is venerated in the Western Theocracy, once said, "He who does no wrong needs no law." Our friends in the Southern Kingdom exhibit this truth well, with their habit of curtsey and their commitment to duty. However, for those of you who have come here with a less-than-fully-formed moral sense, we have rules. There are five:

1. Show respect for your instructors, staff, and fellow students;
2. Comply with the dress code;
3. Comply with direction from your instructors and posted signs;
4. Don't disappoint *me*, and added just this year;
5. No weapons on campus except in Weapons Training class or as used by the Kingdom soldiers, or Professor Cook."

There were groans and boos from several of the Libertarian students and a few Republican students as well.

Dean Smith added, "Rule Five is an accommodation to the Southern Kingdom to meet special security needs during the next four years, much as Freedom Park is an accommodation to Libertaria and the wearing of black robes in most areas of campus is an accommodation to the Western Theocracy. The Board of Regents must strike a reasonable balance among the varied cultures represented here, and I personally believe the board is doing a very good job." The dean did not mention that the board always accepts her recommendations.

"I have one last point before I leave you today. The person, who tossed the rock on the sophomore bath roof yesterday, can expect to receive swift justice consistent with the precedent set down in response to the most recent prior incident of vandalism."

Several of the students knew to what prior incident she referred, but Antwanesta did not. Umbar Tripopis was a freshman student at the Central College of Epodlo five years before. He painted graffiti on a wall of the tower's first floor. He was caught. Dean Smith in her role as Central District Isle Judge, sentenced Mr. Tripopis to probation on the condition that he personally remove the graffiti with only his own toothbrush. For nine hours he worked with no break, allowed only to drink water. He was about to collapse with exhaustion when Dean Smith pronounced his efforts inadequate. She then expelled him, and exiled him from Central District Isle with the recommendation that he be drawn and quartered by deer. Her recommendation was widely accepted as just in Libertaria. The recommendation may have been effectuated were it not for the fact that Libertaria does not have a government, and thus could not impose or apply the sentence. Upon his return to Free Town, Umbar found he was barred from the three largest brothels. The smaller brothels soon joined in the ban at the insistence of both customers and employees. Umbar's name has thereafter been associated with gross dereliction of personal responsibility and the consequences thereof.

The Dean finished with, "My schedule is tight. I will now turn you over to Dr. Sexapopis, for some important remarks about nutrition before you have your first meal here at the school."

"Thank you Dean Smith," began Dr. Sexapopis, as the dean exited the room. "Before you have your first meal at

Maidens of Epodlo, Book 1 – Antwanesta Agape and the Mystery of the Red-dot Moon

Central College, I want to make you aware of the results of a study of nutritional habits and death from cancer. Epodlo has four distinct cultures with varying dietary habits. The Western Theocracy were a strict vegetarian diet is the norm has the lowest death rate from cancer, and an average longevity of 69, with some people living past 80. My homeland of Libertaria, where meat consumption is highest, has the highest death rate from the same disease, and an average life expectancy of 56." Many, who misunderstand Libertarian culture, assume the short longevity is the result of violent trauma. The reality is that death from violent trauma is very rare in Libertaria. In the Kingdom and in the Republic death from cancer is at an intermediate rate, as is the consumption of meat. The overall death rate in the Kingdom is higher, but much of that differential is attributable to genetic disorders. Many of you will want to remind me that correlation does not prove causation, but this is a very robust relationship. The dietary difference is the most plausible explanation proposed for the variation in cancer deaths. In Central College we provide dietary choices which conform to the customs of each of the four cultures. If you choose rabbit, chicken and venison you will have it. However, each of you is free to choose what you eat regardless of the culture in which you were raised. I have given you this information. It is up to each of you to make your choices. The food will now be served."

Applause followed, more for the food than for the professor or her information.

Servers dressed in grey shirts and pants brought trays filled with a wide selection of food, and set them at intervals along the axis of each table.

Antwanesta said a short prayer, made the sign of the hexagon, and took a selection of vegetables including some especially good-tasting lentils. Lissy, Xiny, and even Gretchin took only vegetables as well, but only Antwanesta was nauseated by the mere sight of cooked animal flesh.

Antwanesta observed the selections made by her roommates. She was especially surprised at Gretchin eating no meat, but she did not remark upon it.

The kitchen staff served each student a glass of wine, and a plate of fruit for desert. Fruit was relatively expensive, due to the labor required for hand pollination. However, with efficient production of fruit in the Theocracy, and the Kingdom, supply was generally adequate, but with seasonal variations.

Gretchin, Lissy, and Xiny said they would explore the campus after lunch. Antwanesta was exhausted, and said she just wanted to sleep.

After lunch Antwanesta returned to the dorm. She brought back Gretchin's sandals and student robe. Gretchin had given them to Antwanesta to take to the room when they stepped onto the spur of the running trail. Gretchin wanted to run and to visit Freedom Park. They had left Xiny and Lissy in the school tower building to locate classrooms, and shop for supplies in the market in the central atrium at the tower's base.

Antwanesta spoke briefly to the guards and then entered the dorm room where she found an envelope on the floor near the door under the mail slot. There was no addressee on the envelope, just instructions about recycling printed in ink, and a series of letters and numbers written with a carbon pencil, all stricken through, except the last which read, "FRD327." Antwanesta opened the envelope to find a listing of counseling appointments for her and her roommates. Gretchin was to meet with Dr. Sexapopis tomorrow, after her last class which conveniently was Physical Training. Lissy was to meet with Professor Solider the following day. The day after was Xiny, also with Professor Solider, and Antwanesta with Professor Irigon Agape.

After disrobing and folding her robe and the borrowed tunic, Antwanesta climbed into the lower bunk nearest the door. She recited the prayer of the Holy Hexagon thirty-six times, and went very soundly to sleep.

Gretchin went for her run. The trail spur, which extended from the freshman dorm to the running trail circle, was considered part of the running trail, and therefore outside the area designated by the dress code for mandatory robe use. Gretchin was in full compliance with the dress code when disrobing there. The trail spurs allowed students to go directly from dorm to running trail without the burden of clothing. Thus a student could leave clothing in the dorm room, pass nude through the hall, down the stairs, and to the running trail. The trail intersected with the north side of the rectangular training field, south of the building which housed the gymnasium on the first floor and the infirmary on the second. The southeast corner of the training field rectangle was cut off by the lakeshore. Within the training area, and between the running trail and lakeshore, was the archery range. Rather than running south toward the training field Gretchin ran north, counterclockwise. The trail curved left to the west, behind the sophomore dorm and near the first maples beginning the seasonal transition from dark Summer green to the warm hues of Autumn. The clean, well-tended path was paved with sand, and was wide enough for five runners to run abreast, but runners ran in both directions keeping to the left, in conformity with an uncodified norm which had historically allow right-handed swordsmen to pass blade to blade. Therefore, runners generally ran just two abreast. Gretchin passed other runners as the trail curved south behind the junior dorm. Encircled by the trail and the dorms was the sun-flashing, thirteen-floor tower of glass, stone, and steel, the top of which was visible from every point on campus, not directly behind a building or tree. Gretchin passed the point where the trail passed just 1200 balls from the western shore where Antwanesta first set foot on the Central District Isle just about nine hours before. Our slender, tall, bronzed runner then gracefully glided southeast, on lean, muscular, tanned legs, passing between the five-story family dorm on her left and the arboretum with its greenhouse, chapels, and dock on her right.

About three quarters of a lap around, as she approached the western entry to the Training field and near the outdoor showers, she found the young woman she had hoped to encounter. Gretchin's sister Tearesia Tripopis was up ahead. She was 2.3 balls shorter than Gretchin, attractively fuller in the hips and far from her sister's flatness. Tearesia, had a head of thick short straight brown hair and the same Summer-tanned complexion as Gretchin.

Gretchin ran up beside her and said, "Hey, Tear."

Tear screeched, "Retch!"

The young women kissed each other quickly on the lips in accordance with the custom of their homeland for greeting sisters.

Tear asked, "How do you like it?"

The two young women began to run side-by-side, as Gretchin replied. "I like it so far."

"Did you draw good roommates?" Tear asked further.

"I'm in with a queen, her handmaiden, and the only Theo girl in the class."

"Royals are great," Tear said, "I've never been with a Theo. I have two Royals this year too." Tear further explained that all three of her roommates were new to her this year, and "*all boys.*"

Upon hearing this, Gretchen felt both admiration and jealousy. She asked, "How did you manage to do that?"

"Their roommate from last year wanted to be with someone else. Barthon, Gregor, and Zell had a space. I volunteered to fill it," Tear responded.

"You're with them?" Gretchin said with shock at her sister's good fortune.

"Yes," She said with a smile.

"Can I have Zell?" Gretchin asked with a bluntness that made them both laugh.

"That's up to him not me," replied Tear.

The two spoke about family issues a little. Gretchin checked to see if Tear knew about the secret she was keeping at her mom's directive. Tear confirmed, "I know the deal, and I will be totally *Royal*." The term, *Royal* had come to mean, *being discreet* or *maintaining a secret*, because Royals were known for their power cultural tendency to avoid gossip and maintain confidences.

They conversed the remainder of Gretchin's second lap. Then Gretchin said she wanted to visit Freedom Park. Tear said she didn't have time to go with her today because she needed to buy school supplies, and meet with one of "her boys." They both showered off the sweat at the outdoor facility in the training field. Then with a parting peck on the lips went their separate ways.

While Gretchin was running with Tear, Lissy and Xiny were in the tower locating their classrooms. All freshmen had the same classes in the same rooms. Lissy and Xiny only had three rooms to locate, because their other class, Physical Training would be held in the training field adjacent to the gym and infirmary building. History, Nature, and Math would be in the tower. The rooms were quickly found, and the two Royals went down to the atrium to shop. The interior of the tower was amazing. It was hollow inside up thirteen floors to a glass roof which allowed in the sunlight. There were breezeways surrounding the open core and a winding staircase on the west side of the building. The breezeways with their golden metal railings were on floors three through thirteen. Floor two had only a small balcony facing the open core from the north and a small breezeway near the stairs to the west. The thirteenth floor had meeting rooms and even a courtroom. Floors eleven and twelve were offices and apartments for faculty members. Floor ten was the library. Floors three through nine were classrooms. Floor two housed the dean's office and large private apartment.

At the base of the core was the atrium, with tables chairs and decorative planters. From the Atrium sprawled six wings including the four eating halls, an auditorium and the administration wing.

Shopping was quite sparse by Royal standards. Several tiny shops around the perimeter of the atrium sold clothing, and school supplies. Lissy bought cotton shoes, and two Royal-style white tunics for Antwanesta, so she would not need to borrow form Xiny. She also bought Antwanesta a beige cotton rucksack. At the school-supply vendor she bought four boxes of carbon pencils and four notebooks. Notebooks are very expensive because the supply of paper-pulp pine trees is limited on Epodlo, and no paper is imported from other lands.

The cost was not a problem for the Queen. Most students are dependent on debt to finance school supplies and higher education in general. The only lender on Epodlo is Royal Bank, owned by the Southern Kingdom itself. Debts are repaid through labor after graduation.

Gretchin passed from the exercise field to Freedom Park. The adjacency of the two was convenient because the school robe requirement did not apply to either place. The park had stands of large trees in groupings of odd numbers up to thirteen. There were oaks with broad canopies, tall erect pines with branches only near the top, and majestic magnolias with long branches brushing the ground. There were many low flowering shrubs, but they only bloomed in the Spring. Flowers were prized due to their rarity. All flowering plants that required insect pollination were long extinct. These shrubs had been propagated through cuttings. The magnolias had been perpetuated through the ages by Theist monks who had pollinated their mother plants in the southern part of the Western Theocracy, ostensibly because the white flowers symbolized God's sinless purity and the red seeds the blood of His love for all humankind. The air was fresh and woody. Gretchin closed her eyes for a moment to take in the fragrance of the trees and soft sound of the breeze rustling the branches above her.

On a warm September afternoon most of the people in the park were unclothed like Gretchin. The park's tall trees reminded Gretchin of her home in Libertaria. Gretchin, however was not homesick. She was on the prowl, a lean cat hunting her prey. Gretchin would not understand the cat metaphor since no cats existed on Epodlo, or anywhere so far as she knew. A cat would need to be described as a short-eared carnivorous rabbit to give her an idea what one might be like.

The tanned slender Gretchin, fresh and clean from her shower, approached two young men playing chess on a small stone table. Gretchin stood right beside the table for a minute seemingly unnoticed by the chess players who were deeply focused on their game. A white pawn took a black bishop immediately diagonal to the black king. The bishop had been removed from a square at the edge of the board a half a thumb's length from Gretchin's warm anticipation. One player said. "mate." The players, still seemingly oblivious to Gretchin, began to set up the board for another game. Gretchin walked away in disgust. She thought that, if that was a chess player's idea of *mating,* she wanted nothing to do with them. Ballsar Gardener and Roost Hunter played on.

49

Thomas David Valentine

She then walked over to a group of Republican boys talking about politics, or was it religion? One young man said that democracy should be deleted form some manifesto. Another said that the failure of democracy in the Republic was not an invalidation of the principle, just an aborted execution. A third was optimistic about the prospect for successful democracy for no stated reason. He also added that the first fellow would surely get an A in Dean Smith's special studies class. *Whatever these small shriveled boys were talking about, it was boring*, Gretchin thought. She walked away.

In a few minutes Gretchin was heartened. See saw a man looking in her direction with a smile and eyes of desire. This young man looked handsome and *functional.* He was craning his neck just to look at her. This was what Gretchin wanted. *No. No not that.* The man was not craning his neck to look at her, but to look *around* her. Gretchin turned to see. It was Professor Solider lounging on a rock reading a book. The young man was looking at the history teacher, a woman twice Gretchin's age.

"Hi Gretchin, you look hot," came a young man's voice from behind.

"Yarvan, you look like a man in need of a stable."

Gretchin knew Yarvan from Freetown in Libertaria. She also knew he wanted a Northern girl. "You trolling for snow does?"

"Yep," Yarvan said. "Nothing against you Gretchin. If I could have 100%, you would be hard to resist, but I know you. You won't give it all."

"I sure wont. It is egocentric, arrogant, and unrealistic for a man to think he has the power to please a woman *by himself* for a lifetime."

"Northern girls don't see it that way."

"I know the most Northern of Northern girls, and she
knows how to manage a stable better than anyone. Watch
yourself Yarvan. Even snow does have to face reality."

Gretchin had enough. All she liked in Freedom Park
was the trees, tall erect pine trees. She left and returned to the
dorm.

When Gretchin arrived Antwanesta was sound
asleep. Gretchin climbed into the bunk above her. Gretchin
was left with only her own thoughts. She was tired and
frustrated. All she could do was lie down and relax herself.

Lissy and Xiny went to the arboretum with their shopping
spoils neatly packed in Antwanesta's new rucksack. Two
soldiers followed at a discreet distance. As the girls entered
the arboretum, they met Feli and Zell on their way out. Feli
greeted them warmly, and Zell politely. Feli volunteered that
they were returning from a meeting of the Humanistic Charity
Organization, HCO. Lissy suggested she might make a
contribution.

Feli said her contribution would be very welcome.
"They are collecting donations of sperm, and recruiting
surrogate mothers to help reproductively disadvantaged
people. A Royal womb would be greatly valued, she added."
Feli said she had declined to serve, upon learning the proposed
stipend was too low to aid in her financial plans.

Xiny said she and Lissy would decline too.

Feli then said that Zell was a "generous donor."

Zell smiled and then said, "If you are looking for
Barthon, he is down past the greenhouse talking with the head
solider guy."

Lissy said, "We weren't looking for him, but we will
greet if he is here." No doubt Xiny's father, the Chief
Councilor was using his son, Barthon to communicate

51

delegated duties the captain. Chief Councilor Alfide Stewart had always instilled in his children, and in the young queen, the importance of delegation. He said far more times than Xiny and Lissy could count, "*A leader must delegate not do.*" This was what he called the "Second Principle of Ruling." The First Principle was, as the Royal women also well knew, "*Substance over form.*" He said a leader must focus on the larger picture and not attend to petty or cosmetic details.

Feli and Zell took their leave, and proceeded north toward the sophomore dorm. Lissy and Xiny walked toward the very large greenhouse. In the distance to the left of the greenhouse, past some wide pine trunks, they could see Dr. Sexapopis in her faculty robe walking briskly in the direction of the gym and infirmary building. The two Royals then proceeded west of the greenhouse. Past its corner they could see Barthon and Captain Carlon Knight.

The captain saw them and told Barthon. Barthon jogged over to meet his Queen and his sister. Captain Knight followed with shinny golden armor clanking. Fortunately for Captain Knight, Royal armor is not heavy. The captain's armor was the same as his soldiers except his shoulder plates were painted red instead of the bare gold-gilded aluminum of the common inductees, or the blue of Lieutenant Keep, who was his second in command. The armor consisted of a chest plate and attached shoulder plates plus two rectangular plates the same dimensions as the thigh vent covers to which they were attached on the soldiers' otherwise standard Royal white tunics. The armor provided almost no protection from bolts, arrows, or sword thrusts. The armor appeared largely decorative, a clear violation of Xiny's father's First Principle. In fact, the light armor made since in the hot climate of the Kingdom. Soldiers would quickly tire and die of heatstroke in more robust armor. The Kingdom population, policed by the soldiers, was well-behaved, and there had been no war since the great disastrous conflict over 200 years ago. This bright shinny armor identified authority and function. That was all that was needed.

As Barthon and the captain reached the Queen and handmaiden, Captain Knight clicked to attention and smiled brightly.

Lissy said, "Greetings. At ease, Captain Knight. Have you anything to report?"

"Yes, my Queen. A serious weakness in our security deployment has been identified. I have given orders to rectify the situation," replied the officer.

Lissy inquired, "What weakness?"

"In the cosmetic preparation area of the bath, there are razors which could be used to assault you with speed and lethality."

Lissy asked, "You're not going to remove the women's razors are you?"

"No, my Queen. We were told that would be disruptive. We are posting guards in the bath. They will insure that the razors do not leave the cosmetic area."

"That does sound like the least disruptive approach. Which of your men identified the risk? I want to thank and commend him."

"The matter was communicated to me by one of your door guards, but the risk was identified by your roommate, Miss Agape."

After a brief discussion with Barthon, the Royal women returned to their dorm room to find two sleeping beauties sprawled on their respective bunks. Lissy kissed Antwanesta's forehead, in a silent thank you. She then woke her and Gretchin to go to dinner.

The fare was quinoa, beans, brown rice, fruit salad and a broader selection of wines than at lunch. There were meat choices as well, but again Antwanesta's three roommates joined in her vegetarianism. Antwanesta's curiosity got the best of her, and she asked why they did not eat meat.

Lissy said that her Chief Councilor advised her that her health was the health of the Kingdom, and she should always follow the best nutritional advice except when courtesy required otherwise.

Xiny said she followed Lissy's example and her father's advice.

Gretchin said that Risky was well respected in Libertaria and she followed her advice "to be more like…, to be healthy."

At dinner they planned the school day. Xiny reminded Gretchin of her counseling appointment. Lissy told Antwanesta that the two of them would be together in the first class, Physical Training, and that they needed to have breakfast before Gretchin and Xiny in order to have time to return to the dorm to remove their cloths. "All physical training classes are in the nude of course."

Chapter 4

First Day of Classes

Before going to sleep Antwanesta did as she had always done
every night since as long as she could remember. She prayed
aloud the prayer of the Holy Hexagon. On her fifth recitation
Gretchin interrupted from the bunk above her, "Is your god
deaf or dim-witted? Why does he need to hear the same words
over and over?"

Antwanesta was shocked, hurt, and offended by the
remark, but she only said, "This will just take a few minutes."
She then resumed her recitations and continued to the thirty-
sixth one. Then she said to her crude new friend in the bunk
above, "Prayer is not about what *God* needs to hear. It's about
what *I* need to say."

Gretchen said nothing.

Antwanesta was no longer worried about her
modesty. After her horrifying and then very pleasant
experience in the bath, Antwanesta had performed her moral
calculus. In places such as the bath or even physical training
where the prevailing norm is nudity, it would be more
immodest to wear clothing, and thus draw attention or imply
some special status above others. Nudity in such situations
was in fact modesty. At least that was the rationalization she
had created. Now instead she was concerned about a different
virtue of the Holy Hexagon. She was concerned about her
chastity. She was not worried that she would be violated, or
that she would lose control and give herself to some young
man. The sin she feared was subtler. She had long been told
that sins of the heart were as bad as sins of action. *Pluck out
your eye if it leads you to sin*, went an often quoted passage of

55

scripture. Antwanesta feared that the sight of naked young men would evoke lust within her heart. She feared the sight would arouse her and lead her to have forbidden desires.

The next morning there was a slight chill in the air as Lissy and Antwanesta walked together along the feeder spur to the main loop of the running trail which would take them to the training field, where they had been told to meet their class and Dr. Sexapopis. A gentle breeze off the lake kissed parts of Antwanesta's body which had never before even been seen by the sun.

Lissy said, "I am so glad you are with me, Antwanesta. I would feel nervous about going to my first class without Xiny, if I didn't have you the give me courage." She said this mostly to show Antwanesta that they were together, that she understood Antwanesta was uncomfortable, and could sympathize with her. Lissy's words, which seemed belied by her confident demeanor, were however, largely true. She was not worried about being naked outdoors and in public. Everyone was in that state south of Beach Trail back home at Royal Beach. Lissy was in fact a little anxious about being without her devoted handmaiden and best friend Xiny.

Royal Beach was the city name of the Southern Kingdom's capitol. The city stretched along the south coast of Epodlo. In general, people in the capitol and throughout the Kingdom wore white tunics identical to what Xiny and Lissy wore the previous day when they met Gretchin and Antwanesta. However, in the Kingdom's capitol, just north of the actual *beach,* was a long walking path called Beach Trail. There was a custom, so firm and consistent it may have just as well have been codified into law, that people must be clothed north of Beach Trail and nude south of it. The trail itself was a transition zone where clothing and nudity were both acceptable. There were exceptions for sun hats and for Bishop Korack, who was a special case in a number of ways. Because of this custom the young Queen had spent hours most every day of her life nude among her subjects. To Lissy nudity was nothing, so long as it was applied in accordance with the prevailing custom.

In Libertaria nudity was even more ubiquitous. People there were nude outdoors all summer and indoors all year, except while cooking of otherwise doing something which required clothing for practical reasons. Thanks to the engineering skill of the Royal Plumbers who serviced all of Epodlo, not just the Kingdom; all homes and other buildings had a very good heating system based on geothermally heated water from deep below the soil. Indoor settings were warm even in Winter, and even in the Republican North. Therefore, indoor nudity was not deterred by cold.

In the Northern Republic, where the climate was cold, people were clothed most of the time. However, there were indoor heated public swimming pools, and clothing would serve no purpose while swimming. Feli's mom used to take Feli and the neighbor boy, Zell to the pool quite often. Nudity was just normal.

Only in the Theocracy had anyone ever made an issue about covering the body with cloths apart from style, protection, or warmth. There people wore their black robes or long-sleeve shirts and pants outdoors and in. Theites did disrobe to bathe, but this was only done in a closed room very much alone. Antwanesta had been to the Theocracy's beach on the west coast just a couple of times. On those occasions she just waded in up to mid-ankle. At age four she had hiked her robe above the knee and was scolded. Of course she never swam.

By contrast, now she was walking in the light of the morning sun. Her white buttocks, her breasts with pointy pink nipples, and her vulva topped with bright red hair were all *out there* for the world to see. Beside her was Lissy, her large breasts with wide areolas bouncing as the two young women

57

walked. Lissy seemed even more naked than Antwanesta with the Royal trim of her blond pubic hair.

They arrived at the designated area of the training field, where the running trail intersected with the exercise yard. On the other side of the running trail she could see Professor Cook's Weapon's class practicing archery equally nude. It seemed strange that even a weapons training class would require a state of undress. Archery maybe, but how would they practice with swords?

Antwanesta instantly discovered that her fears about having unchaste thoughts were unfounded. The sight of naked young men did not arouse her in the least. She did not feel lust. She felt only pity. These boyish men, with their diminutive flaccidity exposed to the chill of the morning air, were in fact far less interesting than her fellow female students with the variations in the shape and color of their feminine features. Antwanesta did not find her fellow women arousing either, but at least she could appreciate them on an aesthetic level. Even the handsome Royal men like Ballsar Gardener and Xeris Plumber were not impressive without clothing. Antwanesta observed that the pubic hair grooming convention she had seen among Royal women did not apply to men. She thought this for the best.

Feli was there. She smiled, winked, and waved at Antwanesta and Lissy, but stayed among the young men with whom she was talking. Two of Feli's roommates were also there. Antwanesta did not know their names. From the hair styles and complexions Antwanesta could tell one was from the Republic, the other from Libertaria. The Libertarian seemed nervous. Antwanesta thought this odd, since obviously Gretchin was very comfortable nude, and assumed that was just how people were in the East.

Many of her classmates did not seem to share Antwanesta's indifference. Many of them, both male and female were looking in her direction. At first she thought it was Lissy's large breasts which attracted the attention, but she soon realized it was *her*. Her skin was white but not so much whiter than many of the girls from the Republic. Even her pink nipples were not unique in this group. It was her *red hair*. Red hair was the only thing which set her apart. The red plumage atop her vulva, made Antwanesta feel increasingly immodest. Her blush of red splotches was returning, mostly across her chest, centered around her hexagon pendent.

She was saved from this attention and the unease she felt about her increasingly interested peers, by the approach of their instructor. Dr. Sexapopis was striding toward them across the field from the direction of the gymnasium, in all her athletic perfection. The professor wore nothing, and carried a small purple notebook in her left hand. Only the outermost third of her breasts bounced as she walked. The remaining portion was heavy pectoral muscle. Despite her lean muscularity she did not look masculine except maybe in size. Betriski Sexapopis was every inch a woman. Her brown hair was streaked with blond on her head and similarly speckled below.

All eyes were on this goddess of a professor as she spoke her first words. "Today we run," she began. "First I will lead you through warm-ups. Make three rows across." While leading the students through stretches and bends, she explained that grades in the class were based on athletic performance. Running, weight lifting, and swimming would each be tested. The grades on the three tests would be averaged to produce the final grade. As she finished the warm-up, she added, "You will have to just do the best you can today, but women whose bounce leaves their breasts sore may see me at the end of the lesson, and I will take measurements for cotton halters to use next time." She jogged onto the running trail, saying, "I will set a pace that will win you an A on the test in three weeks. We are doing two laps. If you get sick, do not vomit on *my* trail. Let's go."

Thomas David Valentine

The runners spread out behind Dr. Sexapopis. A
clump of boys followed her closely at first. Later most would
fall behind. Antwanesta and Lissy stayed side-by-side. They
fell to the end of the line due both to Lissy's encumbrance,
and Antwanesta's lack of endurance. Even at eighteen her past
lack of running came at a cost.

They ran counterclockwise. They passed behind the
westward-facing freshman dorm on their left, with lakeshore
about three kiloballs to the right. The running trail followed
the shore at about this distance passing behind the sophomore
dorm which faced south also in the direction of the tower. The
runners passed the junior dorm with Lissy and Antwanesta
bringing up the rear. Lissy was supporting her breasts with her
arm. Antwanesta's bounce was small enough to be tolerated,
but she thought she would need a halter too. They passed the
arboretum and family dorm. Antwanesta was winded passing
the senior dorm though Lissy did not seem to tire. They
reentered the training field from the west. As they neared the
end of training field, they saw the sophomores of the weapons
class shooting their bows. Most of the archers were Royals.
There were a few Antwanesta thought were Libertarians, and
one Republican, Zell. All of the archers hit at or near the
center of the target, except Zell, whose arrow slid through the
grass well to the left. Antwanesta smiled at him. Zell smiled
back.

The faster runners were about to pass Antwanesta
and Lissy on their second lap. First one then another passed.
Next Dr. Sexapopis passed. As she did, she said, "The halter
will help you next time Miss Regalis." A few more runners
passed as they reached the junior dorm again. One boy seemed
to be using Lissy and Antwanesta to set his pace. He followed
three strides behind much of the rest of the lap. Antwanesta
saw the archers had now switched from using bows to using
crossbows. This yielded similar results for Zell. Antwanesta
laughed. Zell again smiled.

60

When they finished they joined the group of girls
who were having measurements taken by Dr. Sexapopis. Lissy
and Feli had their measurements taken, but Antwanesta did
not. She found her breasts to be quite firm.

After an outdoor shower and then a return to the
dorm to dress, Antwanesta and Feli, now in black student
robes, were off to Nature class. Lissy went to History.

In Nature, Xiny and Antwanesta sat beside each other
on the second row. Feli sat in front of Antwanesta. Eltwando
sat in the third row near the door. Before the professor came
in Eltwando said, "Greetings Sister." Antwanesta smiled and
replied, "Greetings Brother." Two boys Antwanesta
recognized from the third floor were there too. There was also
a girl with a purple ribbon in her hair Antwanesta thought may
be one of Feli's roommates, but the professor came in before
Antwanesta had time to ask Feli about her.

Professor Medic entered. He had light brown hair and
was a thin man, eighteen balls tall. It was clear he was a
scientist and a Humanist. His first words to the class were,
"We call this class "Nature" to appease the Theists, but I teach
Science."

The word *science* had fallen into disrepute among
Theists because of the way it was sometimes used by
Humanists. Humanists saw the fulfillment of human need as
the goal of every moral choice. Once human need was
accepted as the great good, from which all virtue could be
derived; morality, in their view, became an empirical process
much like science. The merit of any moral choice was derived
by this method. Good was that which could be, as a matter of
objective fact, demonstrated to be in the best interest of
humanity. Theists objected to this approach. For Theists the
goal of morality was to serve God. God was of course
benevolent. The fragments of scripture which had survived the
ages were clear on that point. God loved humankind, and
though loving and even serving fellow humans was a central

61

way to achieve God's will, it was God's will that truly mattered not the petty needs or desires of sinful humans.

This rift between Theism and Humanism generated friction between the Theite West and the Republican North. Tension was felt even in the great pluralistic hub of Epodlo, that was the Central College. The college was governed by a board of four regents, one from each of the nations it served. The Pontiff, who ruled the Theocracy, had long threatened to withdraw the Theocracy's regent from the board because of concern that science was being taught in biased ways which were counterproductive to actual education. Stated more bluntly, the Pontiff thought young Theites were being corrupted and brainwashed by the secular Humanists, who by their own admission believed that God either did not exist or was not relevant to humanity.

The Pontiff made good on his threat four years ago by withdrawing the Theite regent. The last straw which lead to the Theite regent's withdrawal, was the discovery that, through complex obfuscation with various business entities, the dean of Central College owned business interests which involved very disreputable practices. The dean did not resign, did not divest her interests, did not apologize, did not even acknowledge the existence of her business interests which were plainly evidenced by a careful examination of public records. Her response was to appoint a proxy regent to act on behalf of the Theocracy. Her selection was Irigon Agape, the Religion Professor.

Irigon was no stranger to conflict with the Pontiff. Professor Irigon Agape had long championed a philosophical position which was widely rejected by Theists and Humanists alike. It was a position for which the professor's published works had earned him the label, "heritic." Irigon Agape was a determinist. He believed that free-will was a fiction that did not exist in reality. In his case at least he was right. He was very much under an irresistibly compelling influence in his

own life, Illisima Smith, the very dean who appointed him.
Irigon categorically supported Illi, which was presumably the
reason for his appointment.

The first Nature class was about measurement and
the related geology. It was just a review of what everyone
knew. To conduct measurement, you needed balls. Balls were
used to measure length, volume, and mass. How is it possible
to use the same unit to measure for length, volume, and mass?
The answer is that there were in reality three distinct units
given the same name.

The three balls were all based on an object which
occurred in nature, called a "native ball." Metals were found
deep below the rich black soil of Epodlo in the form of
spheres. These native balls, if uncorrupted by oxidation or
erosion, all had the same mass, but varied in volume
depending upon the element of composition. For example, a
native ball of aluminum was much larger in volume than a
native platinum ball, but weighed the same. The gold native
ball was the standard used for measurement because of its
invulnerability to oxidation. Iron for instance could never be a
dependable standard because it was inevitably found badly
rusted. The official standard ball of gold was maintained in a
glass display case at the Newton Museum in the town of
Newton at the western tip of the Republic.

The standard gold ball had a diameter of one linear
ball. Its volume was one (ball) of space, and it weighed
exactly one <u>ball</u>. An odd fact, lost to history, was that in a time
thousands of years ago the diameter of a gold ball would have
been measured as exactly ten centimeters. Thus if a person
from ancient time appeared in Epodlo she could easily make
conversions of linear measure. Ten balls equaled one meter.
That assumes a temperature of twenty-five degrees Celsius.
The variability of a metal's density with temperature was a
source of error in measurement, but for practical purposes it
did not matter much.

Antwanesta asked Professor Medic why native balls existed; what natural process had generated them.

The professor praised her question and admitted he had no satisfactory theory to explain how the balls had formed. He added that the Theist explanation that they existed to demonstrate God's perfection and love was not the least bit satisfactory, because the principle of parsimony disfavors the introduction of complex concepts from outside the scope of empirical evidence.

Antwanesta took no offense at this answer. She had long thought the same, but when she had voiced such an opinion at school in the Theocracy, her teachers were less than sympathetic.

Antwanesta's next class was History. She sat with Gretchin near the middle of the room.

Professor Solider was a Royal, and she taught history from a distinctly Royal perspective. The first week of classes was to be about the War of 783 between the Southern Kingdom and Libertarian "Terrorists." Professor Solider said the war was "horrendous," and "devastating."

Gretchin, smirking, asked what the casualty count was.

Professor Solider said, "eight, including five Royal soldiers and three Libertarian guerilla fighters." The war was devastating to the Kingdom because the loss of five unmarried men changed the coupling expectations of almost every unmarried Royal citizen.

The professor then proceeded to explain the marital conventions of the Kingdom. As she did, Antwanesta began the understand the situation in which her Royal roommates, Lissy and Xiny, found themselves. When they graduated they would be paired with husbands, not of their choosing. Their husbands would not even be chosen by well-meaning parents

or a wise match-maker. The marriage would not be
determined on some formula with an algorithm based on
scientifically supported criteria of compatibility. No, it was
just a matter of who of the men, newly discharged from the
army was the oldest. The oldest man in the marriage pool
would marry the oldest woman. Then the next oldest man and
woman would be paired, and so on, younger and younger until
only men or only women remained. The leftovers would
remain single until next year when they would be the oldest,
and thus first to be paired. Love, convenience, attraction,
personality, and everything else did not matter. For Royals
marriage was just an accident of birth.

No wonder Lissy so valued these four years of being
"just another girl." It was not just that the full yoke of her
duties as Queen would rest upon her shoulders. After
graduation she would not even be free to be with one she
loved. Xiny would face the same fate, duty-bound to marry the
next man up.

After History, Gretchin joined Xiny at the afternoon
session of Physical Training, and Antwanesta went to Math
with Feli. In Math, Feli introduced Antwanesta to two of her
roommates Celina Pentapopis and Histina Bowright. They
were the ones Antwanesta had seen in Physical Training.
Celina had brown eyes, long straight black hair and was petite
in stature. She had a tendency toward anxiety, not about
nudity, but about almost everything else. It was her fear of
failure which lead her to study hard and become the best
Libertarian math student in the class. Histina was medium
height with long wavy blondish hair tied in back with a thin
purple ribbon. She had bright blue eyes, and a small mouth.
She was from the Republic and was a devote Humanist. She
had a sarcastic streak like Feli, but her sarcasm was wielded
with a more reckless disregard for the feelings of others. Feli,
in contrast, was just playful. Antwanesta recognized Histina
from Nature class as well as Physical Training.

Thomas David Valentine

"Pleased to meet you, Antwanesta," said Histina, "I saw you in Nature this morning. cherry girls do stick out. You didn't disrupt science class with creationist comments; I guess that means you are in recovery. Keep a positive outlook and you will be God-free in no time."

Before Antwanesta could react or even count how many ways she had just been insulted, the professor came in. Professor Elonora Agape immediately gave the students a diagnostic quiz which contained fifty progressively harder problems. Professor Agape said she would review the quiz answers and adjust the content of the class to match the needs of the students. She walked among them as they worked. The professor smiled as she passed Antwanesta. This was a rare student from her own culture, a sister, (a daughter of the same Father). Professor Elonora Agape had an even larger smile in the class before when she had passed Eltwando. He too was her countryman, and her brother, but Eltwando was something more. Just over eighteen years ago he had been in her very womb. Eltwando was her son.

Antwanesta did all the problems and checked her work three times. The last forty questions were too hard for most of the students. Feli got to Problem 43 before she was stumped. She even solved the hardest of the trigonometry problems. Neither Celina nor Histina could get passed Problem 35.

Gretchin missed out on the archers. Weapons class was only in the morning. Otherwise the class was much the same as with Antwanesta and Lissy.

Eltwando was there. He drew the curious eyes of his fellow students, just as Antwanesta had. However, Eltwando was neither self-conscious, nor concerned about modesty. His mother had briefed him on what was coming, and explained that it was God's will for him to be here. He also knew how to control unchaste thoughts. The senior monks at the monastery had taught him a special technique to expel his lust. He could

resist even the beautiful young women he saw so vividly
displayed before him, for the moment at least.

The short back curly hair of Eltwando was in stark
contrast to the long blond hair of the tall fit Royal, Roost
Hunter, but to Gretchin they were exactly the same. They were
both handsome, well-mannered men who would *never*
consider being in her stable.

At Physical Training, Gretchin did not stay side-by-
side with Xiny. "Excuse me Sinny," she said as she ran ahead.
She ran stride-for-stride with the Dr. Sexapopis for the first
lap. Then she increased speed on the second, and sprinted past
the fastest young men to finish well ahead of them. Gretchin's
lean smooth form was well-suited for both speed and
endurance. Xiny finished near the middle of the pack.
Gretchin had a long soothing shower in the open air. Then she
walked over to the crowd of women waiting to be measured
for halters. Gretchin was not waiting to be measured. A person
who has no feet needs no socks. Gretchin was waiting for her
counseling session. Gretchin and Dr. Sexapopis walked up the
exterior staircase to the professor's office in the infirmary
above the gym. The esteemed nude doctor opened the door
and then closed it behind Gretchin.

Risky and Gretchin then kissed on the lips.

Chapter 5

Counseling

The kiss was just a quick peck, like the one Gretchin shared with her sister Tear the day before.

"It's good to see you here, Retch." said Risky.

"It's good to be here, Risky."

"Have I been *Royal* enough for you?'

"*Royal* as the Queen. I should know she's my roommate."

"I understand the Queen is very sweet."

"She is. Was she your idea?"

"What, her Grand Imperial Deanship listens to me? You know she has her own mind, and there is no convincing her of anything."

"The putting me with the only Theo girl in the class was *her* idea not *yours*?"

"It was hers, but I heartily approve of it."

"Why?"

"Theites have it hard here, especially now with the Pontiff going bunny-brains about the school. Miss Agape needs friends. You are rough on the outside and fuzzy on the inside. That is just what she needs to adapt."

"Ant is ok. I like her. Her ideas are deer dung, but she has a good heart."

"You like your roommates. That is one thing I'm supposed to ask you about in this counseling session. I'm also supposed to ask about your family. Shall I just say you love and admire your dearest sister, and live to one day be just like her."

"You are as sarcastic as a snow doe."

"Sorry, Retch. We are both Mom's daughters."

Risky and Gretchin did have the same mother, and two of the same fathers. As a Sexapopis, Risky had six fathers. Gretchin, a Quadrapopis, had four. They had two fathers in common. With Tear, Gretchin shared only one father and no mother. Risky and Tear were not sisters because they had no common parents.

In Libertaria surnames are assigned by the mother, the only person who really knows who the potential biological fathers are. Generally, a mother designates fathers who may in fact be the biological father, but sometimes a dear male friend is designated with his consent. The naming scheme includes the names Unipopis, Dipopis, Tripopis, Quadrapopis, Pentapopis, Sexapopis, and Metropopis. The last name being for children with more than six designated fathers, or none.

"Pop misses you Retch, why don't you reconcile with him?" asked Risky in a gentle and slightly pleading tone.

"Drop it Risky."

"If I can forgive him you can."

"This counseling session ends now if you keep going with this," said a visibly frustrated Gretchin.

Risky paused. Then she said, "How do you like it here?"

"It's great. I made friends fast. The professors are nice,"

"What about your favorite subject?"

"I don't know. Tear has a cute roommate, but she has the inside track on him. The boys from home still want older women or snow does. The Republicans are so *respectful* they don't know I'm a woman. Professor Soldier explained today why Royal men won't give it inside. I don't even see the rare Theo guys as men. Celibacy is not as amenable to my taste as it is yours."

"I thought you didn't want to talk about that, but since you raised the issue; there is more to love than sex. I'm sure you will find men who will love you so much that you will understand that. Just give it time. You *are* just eighteen."

From her counseling session Gretchin went to the dorm in time to join Xiny, Lissy, and Antwanesta for a bath. After they settled in the warm pool Feli again joined them with her characteristic process of sitting on the side to get used to the temperature before going all in.

There was an odd dynamic between Gretchin and Feli. Gretchin was obviously jealous of Feli's close friendship with Zell. There was contempt in Gretchin's tone whenever she spoke to or about Feli. Gretchin often referred to her as "*your* friend, Feli." She didn't even give her a pet name. To Gretchin, Xiny was *Sinny*, Lissy was *Hinny*, and Antwanesta was *Ant*. Equally odd was that Feli who was so extremely kind to everyone else, sarcastically referred to Gretchin as *Sweetheart*. Despite the tension the young friends enjoyed the bath and the opportunity to just soak and talk.

The next day class schedule was the same, but Lissy and Antwanesta adopted the practice of going to breakfast in the space of time after Physical Training and before the second class, rather than before, to avoid running on a full stomach. After the last class it was Lissy's turn for counseling. She met with Professor Solider in her office on the twelfth floor. A guard took a station outside the door.

"Greetings Miss Regalis, said Professor Solider as Lissy entered, wanting so much to say, "my Queen," but duty-bound to follow an order to the contrary. Lissy responded cordially and the counseling session began.

"Please forgive me if I ask intrusive questions. Dean Smith insists I touch upon certain personal areas, which we Royals would normally not discuss. It is to identify problems so that I can help you resolve them."

"I understand," said Lissy warmly.

"How do you like it here so far?"

"I love it. Everything is as good as I imagined it would be."

"Do you feel safe?"

"More than safe. My cousin was here last year with just two guards. I have thirty. I have never met anyone with ill will toward me. I think I am more than secure enough here."

"History is full of war, treachery, and violence. You have lived only in a time of peace. This is not the norm. It is the exception. You are the reigning monarch of the most powerful nation on Epodlo. I respectfully suggest you be more circumspect and cautious."

"Thank you for your prudent guidance."

"How about your roommates? Are they working out ok?

"Oh yes, they couldn't be sweeter."

"Even Miss Quadrapopis?"

"Yes, Gretchin tries to be tough, but on the inside she is a very kind, loving person. I am very pleased to share a room with her."

71

"She has considerable disrepute and infamy in her family line. Be careful not to trust her."

"I will *not* hold Gretchin responsible for the actions of her kinsmen. Anyone who seeks to harm me could get past ten Royal guards with more ease than overcoming Gretchin, I assure you."

"What about Miss Stewart?"

"Xiny is the most devoted friend for which anyone could ask. She would never be disloyal."

"Agreed, Miss Regalis. Every member of the Stewart family would sooner die than fail in a duty to you." I did not mean to suggest otherwise. I mean how is your relationship with Miss Stewart?"

"She is my best friend. I love her more than I love anyone in the world."

"Do you depend on her?"

"Yes, very much, without her I would be totally lost."

"I see. It is a great vulnerability for a monarch to depend too much on any one person. Do you not agree?"

"You are right of course, but that's just how it is. What do you suggest I do?"

"Nothing really radical is necessary. Just try to develop some interests and relationships independent of Miss Stewart. Keep an eye to the future, and understand that, what she is to you now will not be what she is to you in four years."

Professor Solider then moved to another subject area. "I'm supposed to ask about your family. I know that Prince Gregorious is all you have."

"Gregor, keeps me grounded. Whenever I take the burden of monarchy too seriously for my own good, he brings me down to Earth. As both my support and the Kingdom's contingency, he serves better than any other could."

"How about your duty? There are many temptations in a place like this. Do you fear any risk to the blood?"

"None. I know my duty and will follow it to the letter. I have Xiny to protect me, if I were inclined to falter, but I am not."

"Your subjects could ask no more."

Lissy and Professor Solider concluded the session.

The following day Xiny had a similar session with Professor Solider. The professor emphasized the development of Xiny's independence even more. Xiny professed devotion to her Queen, but likewise acknowledged that it would be best for her to become more independent.

When Professor Solider asked Xiny about risks to the blood, Xiny lost her cheerful, gentle demeanor, and said, "I will serve my Queen. The bloodline will flow however *she* commands."

Professor Solider was shaken by this response. She felt that she offended the Queen's handmaiden with her intrusive question, and begged her forgiveness.

"Greetings Sister," said Professor Agape the Red as Antwanesta entered his office.

"Greetings Brother," replied Antwanesta with a smile.

"I think Dean Smith will grant us some latitude in these sessions. Alone in my office, you may call me 'Brother Irigon,' if it makes you feel more comfortable."

"Thank you, Brother Irigon."

"So how goes it, Sister Antwanesta?"

"I love it so far. My new friends are wonderful, and all my professors are excellent."

"You must have adapted to God's will well. Most Theites have a hard time at first. Those who resist God's energies are destined to suffer. Don't you agree?"

"I guess so."

"Careful you will be a heritic like me. You may have heard I am in a state of disfavor in the Theocracy."

"I have."

"Does that trouble you?"

"Not really."

"Why not?"

"I have met several friends here who are different from me. Our differences help us learn from one and other. If you are considered a heritic, it probably means you have much more to teach me."

"With that wisdom I could probably get you an exemption from my Religion class next year."

"Please don't."

The professor smiled. He then asked, "So, all is well with your roommates?"

"They are the best friends I could hope to find."

"No problems with *modesty*?"

"That was hard the first day, but my roommates took care to protect me from humiliation while I sorted things out."

"How did you sort things out?"

"I applied a principle my friend Feli calls relativism.
I interpreted the virtue of modesty in the context of my
circumstance. I bent like a willow and weathered the storm."

"You are a wonder Sister. I do look forward to
having you in my class next year."

"How are things with the family back home?"

Antwanesta's heart sank. After a long painful pause,
"I don't know."

"I assume your mother worries about you. Perhaps
some communication would help."

"Communication? How?"

"A priestess comes over from the Theocracy each
Sunday to perform the liturgy for the Theists here on the isle.
Just write a letter, and go to church. I'm sure the priestess will
be happy to ferry your letter to your mother."

"Oh, Thank you Brother."

"Does anything else trouble you Sister?"

After another pause, "Yes."

What?

"When I was leaving the Theocracy a man tried to
stop me. I hit him with a stick and hurt him. I sinned against
peace."

"Was the man badly hurt?"

"I don't think he was. I cut his cheek. He bled a
little."

"Did you intend to hurt him?"

"No. I just wanted to push him away so I could go."

"I do see the sin here, but it is not against *peace*. It is against *forgiveness*."

"I don't understand."

"Forgive yourself, Sister. I'm sure God and the man have *already* forgiven you."

Antwanesta smiled, and then said, "I have a question, but I think it is too personal to ask you."

Professor Agape responded, "Personal to *you* or personal to *me*?"

"More to you."

"How about we do this? You ask the question, and if I find it too personal, I will refuse to answer, but I promise not to be offended or judgmental. Ok?"

"Ok. Do you still believe in God?"

"Your question is *not* too personal, but it is highly complex. I will answer it in a way that I think you are ready to receive. Yes, I believe in God. However, my conception of both the terms, *believe* and *God*, I would expect, differ from yours. For now, just let me say that the God I believe in, as a fifty-two-year-old man differs greatly from my conception as a child, a teenager, or as a young adult. The nature of the ineffable logos cannot be captured by the human mind. We can only participate in God's energies much as matter responds to gravity, but we can never truly *know* God. We can only *become* Him."

Antwanesta thought Feli was deep. Brother Irigon was somewhere past the far side of the Earth. She wanted to ask for clarification, but decided she was not ready to handle more. "Thank you Brother. I was right. You clearly have a lot to teach me."

While Antwanesta was with Professor Agape. Feli was just down the hall with Professor Medic. Professor Medic began the session with a handshake, and the conventional pleasantries. After Feli said she felt things were going well, the professor asked her about her roommates.

She replied, "They are suitable to their purpose."

"What is their purpose?"

"To occupy my dorm room without annoying me too much."

"Have you made friends with them?"

"It depends how you define the word, 'friends.' As the term is conventionally used, no."

"Do you have friends?"

"Yes."

"Do you feel supported by and connected to them?"

"Yes."

"Can you elaborate?"

"I have met eighty-nine members of the freshman class; and have analyzed their personalities, applying three separate systems of psychological categorization. Based on my analysis, I have selected those persons who have the greatest utility relative to my goals, and made them friends. I have twenty-two people I would label as 'friends' including upperclassmen. Of those, five are either close friends or have been targeted, through rational analysis, to become close."

Have you analyzed the faculty as well?

Of course.

Professor Medic's curiosity was aroused. What can you tell me about me?

"You are very idea-oriented and have a very high capacity for abstract cognition, but average to low emotional intelligence. You value reason, logic, and self-control, not just because of our Humanistic culture, but because you fear emotion, especially emotions relating to sexual and romantic interests. Unlike most people your pupils dilate in the presence of Dean Smith. This suggests…"

"Enough! Never mind. How about your family? Are things ok back home?

"Mom is a lawyer and dad is a scientist, so they don't make much money. Life has always been a struggle, and I have always been a financial burden. My parents love me very much, and I love them. I want to become financially independent, and be responsible for myself."

"That is commendable. I'm sure your parents are very proud of you. Are you having any problems *here*?"

"I am very well adjusted, except for my insistence on paying my own way rather than going into debt with the Royal Bank like my classmates. By the way, I very much enjoy your class; I look forward to it every day; and of all my professors you are the one with whom I feel the greatest sense of identification. I feel we are very much alike; analytical, and logical, yet wary of our emotions and fearful of passion. I am so glad to have such a kindred mind as you for my counselor."

"Thank you, said Professor Medic a bit sheepishly."

"Have a good day Professor. We can talk more about *you* next time if you like."

"Good day Miss Smith, Professor Medic responded weakly with a nervous grin and dilated pupils."

Maidens of Epodlo, Book 1 – Antwanesta Agape and the Mystery of the Red-dot Moon

Feli had amazing seductive power. Despite a deep insecurity about mixing sexual intimacy with psychological attachment, her emotional intelligence was very high. It enabled her to pick up on subtle cues in people's behavior which told her, at a basic level, who the person was and what the person wanted. It was not just her beauty and extroversion that made her so magnetic. She could almost subconsciously change her apparent personality to penetrate the psychic barriers of others. She was a social chameleon who could be whoever she wanted. What Antwanesta was to mathematics, Feli was to social skill. She was not just an organic genius. She was a self-trained expert who earned her skill through study, thought, and practice.

Feli's social skill would be very dangerous in the wrong hands. What would Gretchin do if she could seduce most any man at will? However, Feli was a Humanist in the truest since. She did not use her power selfishly at the expense of others. She knew she owed a moral duty to the fellow members of her species, and she took her duty as seriously as any Royal.

On the way to the bath, Antwanesta shared Professor Agape's religious insight with Feli. Feli was very pleased to hear the enigmatic wisdom, and said she really looked forward to Professor Agape the Red's class next year. This was the real Feli speaking. She really did have an interest in religion. This shared interest was one reason she had chosen to cultivate Antwanesta as a friend. Feli of course did not believe in anything supernatural, but she was very curious about the evolution of religion as a psychopathology. She conjectured that religion was a genetically acquired anomaly of the brain. Feli thought Antwanesta to be an especially interesting case-study in that Antwanesta was both intelligent and curious. Intelligence and curiosity were characteristics generally thought to be lacking among the religious. At least that was the view which prevailed in the North.

Antwanesta asked Feli how it went with Professor Medic.

Feli said, "It went as I expected. I like him and he likes me."

When Antwanesta, Lissy, Xiny, at Gretchin later returned from the bath they found an orange colored envelope on the floor. The note inside said that all four were summoned to the Dean's office, Saturday at 9:00 AM, *tomorrow*.

Chapter 6

The Dean's Office

Antwanesta said her thirty-six prayers, but then could not sleep. *Why did the Dean want to see us? Was it me?* She had broken no rule she could identify. She offended no professor. She was putting in a good effort in Physical Training, both in running and weight lifting. In Nature, Professor Medic praised her for recognizing the recent extinction of the large marine fish was an example of the law of natural selection first proposed by Saint Charles. She was very attentive in History, because Lissy and Xiny had given her a real reason to care about how things worked in the Southern Kingdom. In Math, Professor Agape practically let her teach the class. She respected everyone, and complied with the dress code. She had done nothing wrong.

The Theocracy! Maybe her coming to Central College caused some political controversy. Would the Dean send her back? *No, this isn't about me. If it were me, why summon Lissy, Xiny, and Gretchin. Lissy! That's it. Lissy is the Queen of the Southern Kingdom. This must be about her, about her security, or about special rules for roommates of the Queen. This has to be about Lissy.* With that thought Antwanesta became calm, and went to sleep.

Lissy and Xiny had already fallen asleep. They thought it was about Lissy too. Lissy and the Dean were both heads of state. They knew each other before Lissy became a student. They had negotiated the terms of Lissy's status. Perhaps the Dean/Governor wanted to renegotiate terms. Perhaps Illi thought she could use the roommates for leverage in some way. Lissy and Xiny did not worry. Politics was part of their daily existence. They had both hoped to put politics aside while here at the school, but they knew they could never fully control a diplomatic counterparty. They had worked with Illi in the past. Whatever the problem was, they would address it like rational women.

Gretchin also slept. Like Antwanesta she knew she had done nothing wrong. She had lived under the rule of a strong domineering mother for eighteen years. Dean Smith could be no worse. To Gretchin, this was just more of the same. She would deal with *whatever* in the morning.

After waking, Gretchin insisted Antwanesta join her in a run. It had rained the last two days and Physical Training was just weight lifting. Antwanesta agreed. What is a day without nude exercise? Lissy and Xiny went for a swim and a massage. They would all go to breakfast together, and then up to the Dean's office on the second floor to see what was up.

Antwanesta, Lissy, Xiny, and Gretchin were not the only ones with a Saturday morning appointment. Zell and Feli were off to the infirmary to meet Dr. Sexapopis. Donation collection for the HCO had been moved from the Humanist Chapel to the infirmary, so that Risky could get the seaman samples in the freezer faster. Medical facilities throughout Epodlo had small freezers which operated on *medipower* (electricity). No one understood medipower except senior Royal Plumbers. Even their understanding went little farther than *plug it in.* Medipower worked, and it ran important medical equipment. That was all the doctors cared.

Zell was coming to make a donation. Feli was his mandatory witness. The sponsor organization for the HCO's Reproductive Assistance Program, required samples to be collected under the supervision of a medical professional. This was to protect against contamination of the sample to the detriment of the recipient. A school rule applicable to faculty prohibited physical fraternization with students. To avoid the appearance of impropriety Dr. Sexapopis and Dean Smith agreed that such collections would be witnessed by a third party. Donors were allowed to bring their own witness.

Heterosexual men always wanted female witnesses. For Zell, Feli was the natural choice. She was a close friend and she had seen it all before. Zell was the most generous donor because he had Feli as a witness. Most men who had women in their lives close enough for mutual comfort as a witness, had girlfriends who did not value their boyfriends' charitable inclinations.

Feli and Zell walked to the infirmary on the running trail to avoid having to wear student robes. The air was too cool to be nude on the running trail without actually running, so they were clothed. Zell wore khaki pants and a white tee shirt. Feli wore the best of her three blue cotton dresses.

The standard Republican cotton dress was very popular, even among students from outside the Republic. It was really a marvel of simplicity, comfort, beauty, and functionality. The standard dress was quite casual really. It was little more than a long cotton tee shirt tapered at the waist. Its cotton fabric was thicker than a common tee shirt, but it hugged a woman's body in a close but comfortable way. The neckline was high and round, again like a tee shirt, but with a thick rounded hem. The dress emphasized the contour and texture of breasts while providing gentle support as well. The length of the dress was typically to the middle of the lower portion of the thigh, where it ended in a simple flat hem with no frills or lace. The only flaw the dress seemed to have was that if a woman sat and her legs were not crossed, there was nothing left to the imagination. This was of no concern at the college where nudity was the norm in some places; and where it was not, the drape of the student robe made up the difference. The dress could be bought in black, white, blue, purple, olive, or pink. The dark colors were much more popular than the light.

Feli's thrifty wardrobe consisted of three of the standard dresses, all blue, but with three degrees of fading. The oldest was obviously too small. With Feli's growth and the garment's shrinkage, it now would only reach the level of her pubic bone. The deficiency of the dress was amplified by the contrast between the black of her pubic hair and the lightness of her skin. She only wore this oldest dress in the dorm where most of her peers were nude, or under her student robe where it was unseen. The second dress was longer, to the middle of her thighs. It was only too reveling when her arms were lifted or she was walking up a stairway. She wore this dress mostly to save ware on the newest one. It was the newest dress she now wore walking along the trail with Zell. It was darker than the others, and in nearly new condition. It extended to her lower thigh. She wore this dress when she wanted to make a good impression.

Zell had walked alone from the sophomore dorm to the freshman dorm where Feli lived on the second floor with Histina, Celina, and another Libertarian named Petina Tripopis. Zell picked up Feli and they walked together south along the running trail to the training field and up the stairs to the infirmary.

Dr. Sexapopis, in her white lab coat, met them with a kind smile. She escorted Zell and Feli to a private examination room. Zell disrobed and folded his khakis and tee shirt neatly on a chair. He sat on the patient table for the procedure. The professor, or physician, as her role now was, held a clear sterile glass bowl to receive the specimen. She asked Zell in a warm yet detached way to please begin.

Feli thought of eight different sarcastic remarks, but she withheld them all, she did not snicker or wince. She very professionally conducted her job as witness.

It literally was a job in a way. While donors received only the pleasure of giving. Witnesses were paid a small fee. This fee was negotiated between Dean Smith and the sponsor of the Reproductive Assistance Program. The fee was to create an incentive for witnesses to offer their time. The fee was quite generous, given the small amount of time required and the fact that standing and watching for misconduct, which would never occur, was easy and in no way unpleasant.

Gretchin, Antwanesta, Lissy, and Xiny arrived at the dean's office in their black student robes as required. Gretchin's boldness lead her to enter first, Lissy and Xiny's curtesy lead them to be last. Antwanesta was just there in the middle silently reciting the prayer of the Holy Hexagon in her mind. They entered the outer door from the west second floor breezeway, just right of the building's winding stairwell. To the right was a small desk and chair. The chair was unoccupied. Perhaps it was used by a secretary or an assistant on weekdays. Just forty balls further and straight ahead there was an open door to Dean Smith's inner office. The dean was not in her black faculty robe, but in a standard Republican dress of deep purple. The dress flattered even Dean Smith's fifty-something-year-old figure, or perhaps it was her lean fit figure which flattered the dress.

The Dean asked the four students to take a seat, gesturing to a wooden bench in front of the dean's desk. The desk was nothing extravagant. The whole small room was surprisingly plain for a woman of such status and authority. Covering two thirds of the wall behind the desk was a glass window. The third of the wall to the dean's left was occupied by what appeared to be a closet. It was a small enclosed space with a door near the northwest corner of the room. There was a third door on the north wall with a sign which read, "Private."

The Dean sat in her chair, and the four young women sat on the bench, Xiny, Lissy, Antwanesta, and Gretchin in order from left to right from the prospective of facing toward Dean Smith.

"Thank you for coming so promptly," the dean began in an almost kind, civil tone. She continued. "I have asked you here to share some information, information which I want you to receive accurately, and in the company of your social support system."

This sounded as if it would be bad news if social support were needed. Bad news for whom? The dean's gaze tracked back and forth evenly among all four students.

"Earlier this week, before classes began there was an incident."

Was this about the rock on the roof of the sophomore men's bath? They had nothing to do with that.

"In the lake waters to the west, two people disappeared under circumstances which support the conclusion that they drowned."

Antwanesta went cold.

"A young women named Zillestra Agape and a priest, Father Alfonzo Agape are presumed dead."

Antwanesta was shocked. She had never been close to Zillestra, but her loss reminded her how close she had come to death that night, and how very real her own mortality was. Father Alfonzo had been the only human father Antwanesta had ever known. Her heavenly Father was always with her, and always would be, but to lose a man she loved as a father was indeed a blow to Antwanesta.

Lissy put her arm around Antwanesta and said, "I know it hurts, but you will be ok."

Antwanesta started to cry, and then said, "It is all my fault."

"It is not your fault, Miss Agape," interjected Dean Smith. "The four Theite men who survived the capsizing of the vessel, said Father Alfonzo died trying to save Zillestra, not you. You were on Mr. Fisher's boat at that time. Any belief that you are somehow the cause is irrational."

"Father Alfonzo wanted to save me. If I got on the boat it may not have capsized."

"That is just speculation, Miss Agape. If you were on
that boat you may have drowned too. You do not know. If you
don't know, you cannot be held responsible. You are not to
blame Miss Agape. If there is blame at all it should be
allocated to the Theist culture that prevents people from
learning to swim, or the Theocratic hierarchy which prohibits
the free movement of its citizens. Wherever, culpability may
lie, it is *not* with you. The egocentricity necessary for you to
believe otherwise would be a gross sin against your precious
modesty."

Antwanesta, could not counter Dean Smith's logic,
but she still felt terrible.

Dean Smith said there was one more thing
Antwanesta needed to know. The Theocracy had adopted two
new polices in response to the tragic loss of Father Alfonzo
and Zillestra. A wall was being built in the Theocracy along
the lakeshore, and young people, who were suspected of
inclination toward going to Central College, were being
detained. Dean Smith warned Antwanesta that if she returned
to the Theocracy for Hypatia's Day or Newton Day break, she
might be detained and confined. The Pontiff had determined
that detainment and confinement were not violent, and thus
did not violate the virtue of peace. This was seen as especially
true, if the detainment or confinement was performed for the
protection of the person whose liberty was taken.

Dean Smith finished with "Miss Regalis, Miss
Stewart, I know the two of you are well able to address Miss
Agape's emotional needs. Please do so. Miss Quadrapopis, it
may interest you to know that the four Theite men who
survived owe their lives to being rescued by a certain Pargog
Metropopis."

Gretchin responded, "He probably sank the boat."

Dean Smith shot an angry look at Gretchin and said,
"Respect is a basic rule with which I expect you to comply.

Thomas David Valentine

Regardless of his past wrongs, your father deserves your respect. Is that understood?"

Gretchin did not reply.

"You may go," Dean Smith said to the four.

Antwanesta was too lost in her thoughts and grief to have heard the exchange between Gretchin and Dean Smith.

Lissy and Xiny heard and understood, but Antwanesta would not hear of it from them.

Lissy suggested they take a walk in the arboretum, knowing that the Theist Chapel was there, and that it might be of comfort to Antwanesta to go and pray.

As Zell was getting dressed, Dr. Sexapopis spoke to Feli. She said that she was impressed with Feli's clinical demeanor, and asked if she would be willing to serve as witness for men who did not have their own witness to provide. Feli consented, and said she might even be able to recruit more men to make donations. Thus began Feli's second entrepreneurial enterprise. The first was a clothing innovation which she had licensed to a manufacturing company.

As the four roommates walked from the tower to the arboretum, Lissy told Antwanesta that she was more than welcome to come to Royal Beach for Newton Day break. They could celebrate Saint Isaac's Day together. This thought did cheer Antwanesta slightly.

As the four approached the Theist Chapel Antwanesta made the sign of the Holy Hexagon. The four black robed young women then entered. The interior of the chapel looked very much like the church in Lord's Landing, but in small scale, with just eighteen rows of benches. The iconostasis differed somewhat. The icons of Saint Charles and Saint Hypatia had swapped places. In place of the depiction of the naked Hypatia being brutalized with mollusk shells, there was a second depiction of Saint Charles with his long white

88

beard and bald head sitting astride a giant tortoise. Antwanesta understood that this difference was due to the fact that the church in Lord's landing was dedicated to Saint Hypatia, while the chapel on Central District Isle was dedicated to Saint Charles.

Antwanesta knelt on the floor near the front of the chapel facing the Holy Hexagon. There she recited her prayers. Lissy, Xiny and Gretchin all sat quietly together on a wooden bench. They huddled together a little closer than they otherwise might have, just because this place seemed a little creepy to them.

Antwanesta said her prayers and got up. She turned to her roommates, and said, "Let's go." As she passed through the outer door she made the sign of the Holy Hexagon. As she exited the hexagon-shaped building, she saw the purple doors of a building just one hundred balls in front of the Theist Chapel. The doors had equilateral triangles on them in the same style and proportion as the black hexagons on the doors through which she had just exited.

Antwanesta asked, "What is that?"

"It's the Humanist Chapel," replied Xiny.

They walked on, Antwanesta in the lead.

"Where do you want to go now," asked Lissy.

"The bath. Will you please teach me to swim, Lissy?"

"Of course, Antwanesta."

The bath was more full than usual, but even with thirty-one young women divided among showers, swimming pool and soaking pools, there was plenty of room.

Xiny and Gretchin swam laps together while Lissy gave Antwanesta her first lesson.

"First you must overcome fear of water." Lissy said while they waded in at the shallow end.

Antwanesta did not know if her experience in Unity Lake made her more or less afraid of water, but she trusted Lissy with her life. Lissy supported Antwanesta with her arms as she floated on her back. While floating completely secure in Lissy's support, she looked up at the heavy golden roof trusses and the glass panels they supported. She could see the clouds slowly drifting across the blue sky. She did not think of God looking down upon her nakedness floating in the water. In the Theocracy she had been told that Humanists mischaracterized Theism as a belief in an anthropomorphic supernatural being who lived in the sky. In the week she had been on campus none of the Humanists she met had expressed such a misapprehension. Feli was the only Humanist with whom she had talked about God at any length, and Antwanesta was impressed with how knowledgeable Feli seemed to be about Theist doctrine and traditions. When Antwanesta looked at the sky she did feel God's presence, but He was not *up there* someplace. He was within her and in the love of the dear friend holding her with such kindness.

Once Lissy felt Antwanesta was comfortable on her back she had her to rollover on her belly. Again Lissy held her and asked her to put her face in the water, and hold her breath. Over the course of the next hour and a half Antwanesta learned to float on her own, tread water, and rabbit paddle. Afterward she was tired, and Lissy helped her to the familiar warm pool where Xiny and Gretchin were soaking.

Antwanesta told her friends she wanted to write a letter to her mother. She wanted to tell her that she was sorry for scaring her, that she was ok, and that she had the most wonderful friends taking care of her. She also wanted to explain why she had behaved so impetuously, but she couldn't. She did not know herself. It was like she had been driven by some force which was her, but not her. She didn't understand herself what that meant. This was something

unconscious, something less than, or more than, rational. She
did not know how to explain *why*. She decided that the "I'm
sorry" and "I'm ok" were the most important things to
communicate anyway.

While the four roommates bathed and conversed in the
soothing warm water, Feli was at the table in her dorm room
developing her plans. She laid out her marketing campaign.
She even tested her solicitation on the men next door. Fargitch
Plumber, as expected, politely refused. He would not
surrender his sperm to impregnate a foreign woman. That
would be a gross offense against the bloodline. Darwood
Tripopis and Efunius Cutter were both very enthusiastic about
the charitable cause, and in their consent to have Feli as their
witness. Eltwando was a surprise. Feli had assumed he would
decline on the basis that such behavior would violate the
virtue of chastity under the Holy Hexagon. Feli imagined how
Antwanesta would respond if a similar request were made of
her. Eltwando *consented* to participate. At first Feli thought he
did not understand the request. She explained in detail, Dr.
Sexapopis, the clear bowl... Eltwando understood. He even
thanked Feli for being willing to assist in what he called *the
ritual*.

After the bath and before dinner, Antwanesta had one last
request of her friends. "Let's go shopping," she said. The four
were now dressed in their student robes. Underneath Lissy,
Xiny, and Antwanesta each wore their Royal white tunics,
Gretchin wore just rabbit fur thigh warmers.

Antwanesta browsed each of the small shops
surrounding the atrium.

A clerk in the school supply shop explained to
Antwanesta the system of credit under which goods were sold
on Central District Isle. Under the system, which was
sponsored by Royal Bank, all student purchases were financed
in the same way as room, board, and tuition. *How could I be
so stupid to believe I would have a free ride for four years?*
Antwanesta thought. She now had a taste of Feli's aversion to

91

debt. Antwanesta's mathematical mind quickly jumped to the question of what the interest rate would be. She was told that the rate applied would depend on the prevailing rate of interest at the time payment became due. It was with some relief that Antwanesta learned that interest would not be due, or even begin to accrue until her graduation. This would in effect give her a four-year interest-free float on all purchases made today. The clerk added with a smile, "The sooner you buy the more you save."

Lissy further explained that graduates who could not otherwise pay were given jobs in the Kingdom suited to their aptitudes, so that the loans never went into default.

Antwanesta was too prudent to go on a spending spree. She wanted to have a long discussion with the financially savvy Feli before going too deeply into a hole. However, she did find one thing she just had to have, a standard Republican dress. She chose black, as it would clearly be the most modest.

Lissy and Xiny also got into the spirit. They each bought a standard Republican dress too, in white. Gretchin did not. Her refusal was not due any political objection or even a love of fur. Gretchin had seen and even admired the cut, practicality, and style of the standard Republican dress. However, one or the distinguishing features of such a dress, the one that most made it appealing to men looking at the wearer, was the way it hugged, supported and emphasized breasts. Such an emphasis was not in Gretchin's interest.

The next day was Sunday, Gretchin would go to the gym with her sister, Tear, and then go to Freedom Park to *hunt*. Lissy and Xiny would sleep in, and maybe study a little. Antwanesta would go to the liturgy at the Theist Chapel. That night they all slept well in happy anticipation of the Sunday to come.

The next morning, Antwanesta wore her Theite robe under her student robe. That way she could conform to

whatever norm prevailed during the liturgy. She made the sign
of the hexagon and entered the Theist Chapel.

Midway down on the left, was Professor Agape, "the
Red," Antwanesta's trusted and admired faculty counselor.
On the second bench from the front, on the right, was her
respected math instructor, Professor Agape, "the Black." On
the math instructor's left was a woman with light brown hair
in her late thirties or early forties. To the professor's right was
her son, Eltwando. There were five upper-class students
peppered among the benches. They all wore student robes.
The only person in the room other than the priestess who did
not wear standard school attire was the woman beside
Professor Agape, "the Black." She wore a Theite robe.

The woman turned her head as Antwanesta
approached. Antwanesta knew that face. It was *her mother*.

Chapter 7
Mother

Antwanesta's mother smiled and beckoned her daughter over to sit beside her. Antwanesta came and sat. They could not speak during the liturgy. That would be rude and disrespectful. They sat side-by-side as the priestess, Mother Vissina, conducted the familiar sacrament.

It was not strange to see a priestess conducting the liturgical service. Theism did not limit roles by gender, beyond those necessitated by variations in the human anatomy which God created. There *was* sexual discrimination in the Theocracy however, and it went all the way to the top. With one prominent exception, the Pontiff always selected priestesses for assignments in foreign lands. Being inexperienced with women, the Pontiff held the opinion that women had a lower level of sexual desire than men, and that with age the desire would sink to such a low level that the risk of a priestess succumbing to the temptation to sin against chastity would be much lower than with priests. This, the Pontiff thought, was of particular importance in places where the dominate culture was far less modest than in the Theocracy.

There was also sexual segregation in staffing Saint Charles' Monastery and Saint Hypatia's Convent. This was also to minimize temptation toward sin against chastity and modesty.

In Freedom Park, Gretchin was on the hunt. It was cool this Sunday morning. Only the a few of the sixty-or-so visitors to the park were nude today. Gretchin wore her rabbit fur thigh warmers and a deerskin loin strap with small greyish brown triangles of rabbit fur suspended from it, draping in front and back, and covering almost nothing. She also had a rabbit fur halter. This might seem ironic given that Gretchin had nothing to halt. However, the mere existence of the halter suggested that there may be something of interest concealed beneath. The feminizing effect on Gretchin's appearance was quite dramatic. Several men's eyes drifted in her direction. Perhaps hunting would be good today.

Lissy and Xiny were alone in the dorm room together. The guards were just outside the door, but in Royal terms this was total privacy. For the first time in a week, they could just relax and be themselves, no secrets, no duties, no curtesy, just total freedom to share their love with each other.

During the service at the Theist Chapel, the priestess lead the small congregation in the recitation of the Symbol of Faith, the Theist creed which had been passed down with some translation through millennia. *I believe in the ineffable Creator, Maker of all things material and conceptual, His seed, the Template for human perfection which shares the nature of the Creator and is of one essence with the Creator, and in the Spirit which dwells within each of us, and guides us in the service of God. I look forward to the unity of God's people, my perpetual participation in the Logos, and life in the hearts of those God has loved through me.*

Back in Freedom Park, Gretchin was noticing the masculine attention she was receiving. She recognized one set of eyes. Darwood Tripopis was in her math class. Most Libertarian men preferred older women or Northern women with their perverse customs, but Darwood was looking at her in a way which suggested he liked what he was seeing. She approached him and began a conversation. There seemed to be the beginning of some chemistry between them. However, Darwood said, "Too bad I'm promised to Risky Sex later today…" *How could he do this? The jerk insulted my sister and me in the same sentence.* Gretchin's expression went from warm to a sort of livid nausea. Mostly to protect herself from consequences of the violent outburst which was ready to explode from within her, she said nothing. She turned on her heels and walked rapidly away.

After several minutes of silent rage, Gretchin decided not to let one idiot spoil an otherwise beautiful day in the park. She aimed her sights on another young man. Salbird Keysmith had not been looking at Gretchin, but he was handsome, though somewhat short. Sal was a sophomore who, the previous year, had roomed with Zell, Gregor, and Barthon. This was the roommate Tear had replaced this year. Sal was from the Republic. His Father was, as the surname suggests, a lock and key smith. His mother was a lawyer, like most mothers in the Republic. His father's business was quite successful, having a monopoly in the making of locks and keys. His mother took mostly pro bono cases since the oversupply of lawyers, and burdensome regulation of the profession made paid work generally not worth the trouble. Sal grew up in Merchant Town, the most Southern Republican city, right Unity Lake.

Sal asked questions about Freetown. When a Republican man asks about Freetown, one assumes he just wants to know about the famous brothels. However, Sal seemed more interested in the small shops in the center of town. He also asked about how well immigrants from the Republic were integrating with the local culture. He did not seem curious about Gretchin personally.

Gretchin asked bluntly why he had left Gregor, Barthon, and Zell. Tear had said they were all nice. Sal agreed they were nice, and that they were still good friends, but that he had some other friends he wanted to get closer with.

Gretchin dug for insights on Zell, while Sal just wanted to discuss intercultural tolerance in Libertaria. They were talking past each other to the satisfaction of neither. Then

Sal said that it was good talking with her, but he had to meet a
friend at the bath. This left Gretchen back on the prowl.

Another man caught her eye, Hardington Weaver.
Hardy was another Northerner from Merchant Town. He was
tall and muscular, with black hair and a very masculine
jawline. Gretchin was forward in showing her interest. They
made small talk a few minutes, but he put his foot in his
mouth even faster than Darwood. He said he wanted to get to
know her better, but that Feli, "had him signed up for twice
this week."

Gretchin's eyes widened, and at that moment, over
Hardy's broad left shoulder, she saw the blue standard
Republican dress with *Feli* in it. Feli was speaking with five
men at once. One of the man made a clearly vulgar gesture, to
which Feli nodded and smiled. Without giving Hardy a parting
word Gretchin began marching toward Feli.

As she reached Feli, Gretchin said, "What are you
doing?"

"About the same as you, Sweetheart, hunting men,"
Feli replied with a smirk.

"What's with the notebook, can't keep up with them
all?"

"That's right. I need at least twenty per week."

"I've had it with your sarcasm!" With that Gretchin
stormed away.

Feli continued with her campaign. She signed up
more men for the reproductive assistance program in one day
than had participated in the last three years combined.

At the end of the liturgy Antwanesta hugged her own mother
and was greeted by Mother Vissina. Then she went out the
door with her mother. They made the sign of the Holy

Hexagon, hugged again, and walked over to a granite table behind the chapel. They sat and talked about the past week.

Antwanesta's mother of course was terrified when Antwanesta disappeared, and was even more so when she heard Zillestra and Father Alfonzo had drowned. However, she was heartened by the report form the men who survived the capsizing of the boat, that her daughter was last seen alive in another boat with a college student. She prayed nonstop, and then her prayers were answered. She received a letter from her old college roommate, Elonora. The letter said that Antwanesta was safe and doing very well at the school, and that God had sent three of his best angels to be Antwanesta's roommates. *Thank you, Professor Agape, "the Black,"* Antwanesta thought.

But that was not all. The Bishop of God City, herself came to the house, and told Antwanesta's Mother that it was God's will that Antwanesta attend Central College, and serve God as a witness exemplifying His energies.

"So tell me about your week, Dear," her mother finally asked.

Antwanesta, didn't know what to say. She knew she had to edit her tale for parental consumption.

"My roommates are the best. One is Queen of the Southern Kingdom," Antwanesta began. "Xiny and Gretchin are sweet too." She left out her acculturation to a new variant of modesty. She talked about her classes and the very Godly faculty counselor. Antwanesta would have shown her mother parts of the campus, but everywhere was across the *running trail* from the arboretum.

As Antwanesta was about to run out of safe things to say, her mother broke in with, "Oh, I forgot to tell you. When Bishop Salestina came to see me, she also said I was requested to come to the convent for a visit."

"A visit with God? Your 42, isn't that too old?"

"I asked the bishop the same thing. She said that God was not bound by any rules, and she would not question His will."

"When will you go?"

"Next week. I will stay for one year, longer if God blesses me with annunciation again."

Soon the priestess returned, and spent several minutes getting to know Antwanesta. Antwanesta asked her about the new policies in the Theocracy, the detentions and the wall.

Mother Vissina confirmed that the construction of the wall was rapidly commencing, and it would stretch from Lord's Landing to Blessings Point. It was being erected of native stone cubes so no cutting was required. If Frontaris Mason, the stone magnate in Libertaria, were not already the richest person in Epodlo, this wall would surly make him so. At three blocks high and 347 kiloballs long, the wall would require 104,100 native blocks, all transported by sailboat. Antwanesta did this calculation in her head in less than on second. She did not know Mr. Mason's profit per block, but she could calculate his income tax bill, zero. Frontaris Mason was no fool. He moved from the heavily taxed Northern Republic to the land of true freedom several years before, and never regretted it for a moment.

As for the policy of detaining young people at risk of fleeing into sin, "Yes, regrettably the Pontiff is adamant that drastic action to protect children from exposure to sin is more than justified. He says it is the clear will of God," Mother Vissina told Antwanesta. "If you go back to the Theocracy you will surely be detained." The priestess further confided that several of the bishops had advised the Pontiff against this course, but to no avail.

Antwanesta's Mother then asked with a note of concern, "Where will you go for Saint Isaac's break?"

"Lissy and Xiny have invited me to Royal Beach. I'm sure I will be well cared for with them," Antwanesta responded.

"I'm sure God will always be caring for you," said her mother.

"Indeed it is so," added Mother Vissina.

Mother Vissina, told Sister Dothina (Antwanesta's mother) the boat would soon leave. Antwanesta hugged her mother goodbye, and then both her mother by blood, and her mother through the church, left.

Antwanesta felt so relieved to have gotten to speak with her mother. She had not fully realized the depth of her own stress due to feelings of guilt about the way she had left her mother to suffer in worry. Her Mother was taking Antwanesta's rebellious action better than Antwanesta could have ever imagined. She even had time at the convent to look forward to. The relationship with her mother was intact, and her mother was happy. *Praise God. Thank you for this blessing.*

Mothers in the Theocracy were usually very close with their daughters. The Father was omnipresent, but not exactly there in a physical and personal sense. Mothers gave birth at the convent and stayed for a year thereafter while nursing the baby. Mothers had fond memories of Saint Hypatia's, both because of the joy of the annunciation process, and the pleasure of being with a new baby in a supportive environment. There were no men at the convent, only nuns who lovingly cared for both the mothers and babies. Mothers were not invited to a second annunciation until their first child reached adulthood. This practice of sequential rather than concurrent children had developed because it was discovered

that having two children in house together lead to strain on the
virtue of peace. Siblings fought each other and also strained
mothers' patience to such a degree that they often sinned
against peace in their hearts if not in action.

       The Relationship between Antwanesta and her
mother was pretty typical. Antwanesta was very close with her
single parent throughout childhood. As she entered
adolescence Antwanesta wanted more and more autonomy.
She questioned her mother's authority, opinions, guidance,
and view of the world. Antwanesta resented being told what to
do, by both her mother and her society. As her adulthood
approached she began to see going to Saint Isaac's College as
a destiny imposed upon her by a mother and a paternalistic
society which would not allow her to be herself. Antwanesta
did not even know who she was, but she wanted to be a person
of her own making, and she wanted to understand the world of
which she was a part. Perhaps it was this more than anything
which set her on the path to her break with the known
predictable reality, and jump in the lake on a quest to find
herself.

       In the Republic motherhood was different. Typically,
men and women formed pair bonds. They often married.
Marriage in the Republic was a legal covenant which bound
two or more people in a set of complex legal obligations and
privileges. With rare exception there were only two people in
a marriage. Though polygamy was a legal right, few people
practiced it, and then only for practical reasons like qualifying
for a government subsidy. Marriages were solemnized either
by a notary or a Humanist celebrant. In either case the
complexity of voluminous statutes and centuries of case law
applied to many mundane details of married life. No one
wanted to be subject to the impossible burdens imposed by a
myriad of irrational, vague, and contradictory laws; so every
married person entered into a marital agreement to waive the
plethora of legal privileges which would be their spouse's
burdens. The only benefit of the legal complexity was that it

provided employment for lawyers who otherwise would likely be migrant farm workers in the Theocracy. Many lawyers preferred the farm work because of the higher pay and better working conditions. However, farm work was seasonal, so some negotiated marital agreements only in the Winter.

Feli's parents were in a strong committed monogamous relationship. Azunia and Picius Smith loved each other, and they loved Feli. They were model parents. Both were very rational and loving. They exemplified their Humanistic values. From her mom, Feli learned to rationally analyze the motives and behaviors of other people. From her Father, Feli leaned to love science. Feli got the best of both, and both were loving and generous.

The generosity was mostly limited to time and emotional commitment. Feli may well have been spoiled, if her parents had the money to spoil her. They did not. Like ninety percent of Northerners, they were poor. Every day was a financial struggle. Many of Azunia's clients were in the food industry, and so legal bills were often paid in food. However, bartering did not relive her parents of the oppressive income tax liability. At least they always had food. Poverty was like a third parent to Feli. From poverty, she learned thrift, caution, and fear. From fear came the desire to control both her circumstances and herself.

In Libertaria mothers played the most central role in the lives of very young children, though the burdens of motherhood were often shared among a broad sisterhood and with devoted servants. As children grew older the plentiful nurturing fathers played an ever larger role. Mothers focused on careers usually as medical professionals, women of the brothel, entrepreneurs, or arbitrage investors. Men were generally not very ambitious. In a state of freedom women tended to want to work while men tended to want to play. Men played with children or pursued hobbies while women earned

their means of support. Such is freedom. Generally, the people
of Libertaria were happy with the way freedom worked out.

Gretchin's Mother maintained s mid-sized stable. The
word, *stable* no longer meant, a building in which domestic
horses were housed. Horses were long extinct; and only
existed in stories, legends, and tales of ancient history. The
word, *stable* now had a different meaning, and everyone knew
what the word meant. A *stable* was a woman's collection of
lovers, usually. but not exclusively, men. Women collected
men. Generally, the richer the woman the larger her stable.
Gretchin's mother was rich, but her stable was not
proportionately large. Currently she had six men to service her
needs. She gained or lost and average of one per year. Lately
she neglected to replace the older ones with younger ones,
largely due to the fact that she was just too busy to fully fulfill
her sexual desires. She did keep her youngest man near her,
and he was always eager to be of service.

Gretchin's mother was a successful entrepreneur. Not
only did she have a controlling interest in the three largest and
most famous brothels, she had maintained business interests in
all four nations of Epodlo. With her wealth came political
influence. She was used to getting her way, even with her
headstrong children. Gentleness and nurturing was a job for
men. The mother of Risky and Gretchin was a tough woman
in a challenging and dangerous world. She protected her
daughters from her enemies, her notoriety, and the corruption
of indirect power; by insisting that her children keep their
maternal parentage very confidential.

Gretchin headed back to the dorm to drop off her clothes
before running with Tear. As she walked in she saw Lissy and
Xiny together in Xiny's bed in an state of intamacy. Gretchin
smiled and said, "don't get up, I'm just dropping off my fur to
go run with Tear. Gretchin was back out the door before Lissy
and Xiny could even give her a proper greeting.

Gretchin knocked on Tear's door in the sophomore dorm. Tear's roommate opened the door. "Hi, Gretchin," said Zell.

"Hi, Zell." *Wow, he remembered my name.* Gretchin's heartrate quickened.

"Hey, Retch," said Tear hopping from a top bunk. "Ready to run?"

"Yea. You want to run with us Zell?" Gretchin asked the question with a hopeful tone and wide eyes.

"No thanks, Gretchin. I'm going for a swim. Maybe another time," said Zell in a polite even tone, which did not betray whether or not he was looking forward to that possible future time.

Tear rushed Gretchin out the door. They hit the trail, running counter clockwise as usual.

"Any luck yet?" Gretchin's bluntness would not be considered rude or nosey by Libertarians, especially sisters.

Tear replied, "I'm with two Royals. If I don't keep my mouth shut about them, they won't so much as let me warm their pillows.

"How about Zell?"

"He goes out with Feli, and comes back limp."

"Feli again? She is everywhere. She's sucking all the water out of the lake, and leaving us like stranded minnows drying on the bed."

"She's not so bad. I think she's nice. She seems to really like you."

"Like me? She likes to torture me more like it."

104

"I don't think so" persisted Tear. "When I met her, the first thing she said to me was, 'Your Gretchin's sister. If that Sweetheart is your sister, I love you already.' The way she said it, I can't believe it was a lie."

"Sarcasm. Feli is the world champion at sarcasm. She said that when she is with Zell they are practically speaking in a sarcastic code, only the two of them can decipher. She said they jump between 'first level' and 'second level' sarcasm, as if I'm supposed to know what that deer dung is. I don't trust a word out of her mouth. Antwanesta loves her, says that she is *so* deep. I know what she's deep in."

During the run Gretchin and Tear passed several runners. On the second lap they came up behind two young Royal women.

Upon seeing them Gretchin asked, "What are those?"

Tear Responded, "Cotton thigh warmers."

"That's a good idea, they are much more washable than rabbit," said Gretchin.

"I bought a pair at a tower atrium shop. I will wear them when it gets colder."

"Is white the only color?"

"Mine are grey. I have seen black too. I heard that they are made back home in Freetown by one of Mason's companies."

Gretchin and Tear picked up the pace and ran past the two Royals, who were freshmen, Levisina Fletcher and Mulucia Butler.

As they ran past the arboretum on their third lap they saw Antwanesta speaking with Jillissa Agape, a junior who came to the school two years before, via the Republic, after catching a ride on a merchant boat. Jillissa was explaining the history of the relationship between Central College and the Theocracy. Gretchin and Tear exchanged waves with Antwanesta, and continued along the running trail. They ran past the senior dorm and then into the training field.

As Gretchin and Tear were at the point where the running trail leaves the training field to head north behind the freshman dorm they saw something curious. There was a man standing in the area between the freshman dorm and the glass roof of the freshman bath. That was clearly an area requiring a student robe. However, the man wore nothing at all except a black hood on his head. He was holding what looked to be a telescope. The object was long, dark, and pointed up in the direction of the dorm. No, not a telescope, a crossbow, yes that was it.

Lissy stood up from the lower bunk on which she had been sitting. She took two steps toward the table. A crossbow bolt whizzed through the window.

Chapter 8

The Attempt

Gretchin and Tear saw the shot. The hooded man dropped the
crossbow, and ran south toward Gretchin and Tear, who
sprinted in his direction. He reached the south end of the
freshman dorm. As the man entered the door he removed the
black hood, and the door slammed behind him. Gretchin saw
him only from behind.

Gretchin reached the door first. She ran up the stairs,
taking four steps in a stride. She was on the third floor when
Tear reached the door. Tear went down the stairs to continue
the chase, thinking the shooter may have sought concealment
in the bath.

Gretchen reached the dorm room, after passing one
guard sprinting down the hall to the stairs. He and Gretchin
were both too hurried to exchange words. The dorm room
door was open with the other guard inside sword drawn.

To Gretchin's relief, Lissy and Xiny were both
unhurt. They were now dressed in their white tunics. Both
seemed quite calm given what had just happened.

The bolt had impacted the wall above Gretchin's
bunk. If Gretchin had been there, she could have been hurt or
killed. Gretchin gave no thought to the threat to her own
mortality. She was just pleased to see her dear friends safe.

Tear raced down the slope to the freshman men's
bath. As she entered, she scanned the large room for any sign
of the attacker. Most of the thirty-or-so bathers turned to look
at her. A woman in the men's bath was an unusual, but not
unwelcome, sight.

107

Zell saw his roommate, and climbed out of the large pool where he had been swimming.

Gretchin decided to stay with Lissy and Xiny because they were down to one guard. The other had gone to report to Lieutenant Keep.

Tear told Zell what had happened. He said he had seen no one enter the bath but her. They ran up the sloped passage to the room at the top. The room had a door which opened to a tunnel passage to the gym. The heated passage was used to travel from the dorm to the gym when weather was unpleasant. Just inside the door Zell found the black hood.

Zell still had the hood in his hand when a Royal solider arrived.

"Halt! You are under arrest!" the solider shouted.

"It's not me! The guy you want must have run up there!" replied Zell, with more urgency than fear.

"I just brought Zell from the bath. The shooter must have run to the gym through the tunnel," added Tear.

"We all stay here until I'm relieved," said the solider firmly.

"I saw the shooter," Tear protested. "This is the logical escape route. You need men at the gym!"

Captain Knight and Lieutenant Keep both arrived at the Queen's dorm room. The captain asked for a report. The guard who had been on duty explained the situation.

Just as the guard finished, the solider arrived from below with Zell and Tear. "Captain, I have a suspect and a witness."

"Report," said the Captain curtly to the arriving solider.

"I found this man in the bath cloak room with this black hood in his hands. I arrested him. The Libertarian woman was with him. She says she saw the shooter, and that it was not this man."

The captain turned to Tear. "What did you see?"

Tear quickly said, "I saw a man wearing only a black hood shoot a crossbow from outside toward this room. He ran into this building through the south door. Zell found the hood inside the door to the gym tunnel passage."

"Lieutenant Keep, take some men to the gym and see what you can find." The captain turned back to Tear. "What did the shooter look like?"

"Tall, muscular, with a skin complexion like mine. His hair was blond or light brown." Then turning to Gretchin who was now sitting on her bunk, "Retch did you see more?"

Gretchin added, "I saw him from behind as he entered the building before the door closed, his buttocks were narrower than Zell's."

Turning to Zell, Captain Knight asked, "What is *your* story?"

"I was swimming down in the bath. Tear came in. She's my roommate. I went to her, and she told me a crossbowman shot at Lissy's... I mean the Queen's, room. Tear was chasing him. I went with her. I opened the door to the gym passage, and found the hood. Your solider came and arrested me before we could head to the gym."

Captain Knight then asked, "Why were two Libertarians and a Republican trying to chase down a dangerous would-be assassin?"

"Lissy is our friend," responded Zell, Gretchin, and Tear in unison to the captain's inquiry.

Lissy smiled.

Captain Knight turned to his Queen.

Lissy said, "They are my friends, and I trust them as much as any Royal. Zell, you are no longer under arrest."

Antwanesta was oblivious to the recent events. After conversing with Jillissa, Antwanesta walked contemplatively back toward the dorm. She thought of what Jillissa had told her. Jillissa was a devote Theist, but she had altered her faith to better accommodate her own needs. When Jillissa found chastity was not consistent with the needs of herself and her boyfriend, Harolod; she changed her nightly prayer and her image of the Holy Hexagon. She replaced chastity with courage. Antwanesta did not know how to feel about this. On the one hand she admired Jillissa. On the other she felt Jillissa had cheated in some way. It was immoral to change the tradition of wisdom which had been faithfully passed down by generations of Theists before them. Was it not the height of immodesty for Jillissa to place herself in the position to rewrite ethical principles for her own convenience? Clearly Jillissa was so consumed by her lust that she purged an entire virtue rather than conform to the true good. Antwanesta prayed that God would have mercy on her new friend. Antwanesta worried that she too might be tempted to act as Jillissa had. Was she any less vulnerable to sin? She too felt lust. She never acted upon it, at least not with another person. If a desirable man offered himself to her, could she resist him? What about women? She had grown very fond of her friends. Could her platonic friendships turn into something else? Lissy and Xiny seemed to be more than friends, and Gretchin was almost a caricature of sexual liberality. What if her friends tried to seduce her? As her anxiety rose, and her heart raced, Hardy Weaver ran past on the running trail with a "Hi, Antwanesta." She reflexively turned and saw Hardy's sweaty masculine body. She could see Hardy's muscular legs running away. As Antwanesta inhaled, the chemistry in her inner brain responded to molecules her conscious mind could not perceive. Antwanesta began to tremble. *Why must God tempt*

me so? Antwanesta thought. She prayed for God to lead her
away from temptation.

Antwanesta took a straight line from the arboretum to
the freshman dorm because she was wearing her student robe,
and therefore was not required to be on the running trail with
its tantalizing pheromones. *Thank God*, she thought, then she
quietly recited her memorized trigonometry tables. The direct
route to the freshman dorm took her south of the family dorm
and north of the gym. As she was approaching the freshman
dorm from the southwest she noticed several Royal soldiers.
There were four jogging toward the gym, three others were
looking at the ground between the dorm and the bath roof, and
one was guarding the outer door at the south end of the
building.

"What is going on?" Antwanesta asked the solider at
the south door. Antwanesta was familiar with the solider
because he sometimes guarded the dorm room.

"I am not at liberty to say, Miss Agape, but the
Queen is unharmed." This was the soldier's attempt to balance
the values of discretion and curtesy.

Antwanesta rushed up to the room which now had
four guards rather than two. One of the guards opened the
door for Antwanesta to enter. She went in. The captain turned
and nodded to her. Lissy, who was standing, hugged
Antwanesta, "We're ok. Don't worry," Lissy said with a
reassuring smile.

The captain took his leave from the Queen, assuring
her that the attacker would be caught, and that the enhanced
security measures would be applied with the greatest of
curtesy and respect.

Zell and Tear excused themselves to return to their
own dorm. Gretchin joined them to retrieve the fur garments
she had left in their room. Zell, Tear, and Gretchin walked
along the running trail toward the sophomore dorm. Zell was

in the middle with, Gretchin on his left arm and Tear on this right arm. Zell could not help but feel affection for the two Libertarian women, who were now with him as his stress level was diminishing.

Zell, said, "Thank you, Gretchin for supporting me back there."

Gretchin tried to think of a clever reply, but settled on, "You're welcome."

As they reached the half way point between the freshman and sophomore dorms the three encountered Gregor and Barthon coming the other way. The two Royal men were wearing their white tunics in contrast the to the nudity of Gretchin, Zell, and Tear. Gregor and Barthon had heard about the attempt on Lissy's life from a solider, and were coming to check on her and Xiny. Tear assured them they were ok, but that of course, Xiny and Lissy would want to confirm their well-being to them.

Zell, Tear, and Gretchin reached the room in the sophomore dorm. Gretchin slipped into her rabbit fur loin drape and halter. Tear pecked her sister on the lips to say bye. Zell hugged Gretchin, no longer wet, having had ample time to drip dry after his abrupt extraction from the bath earlier. Still embracing her he drew back his head, and looked into Gretchin's eyes. He said, "Thanks again." Zell released her. Tear smiled at Gretchin. Gretchin left through the door.

Gretchin had so many emotions. She had just been hugged by Zell, and he felt so good. Someone tried to murder Lissy. She was jealous of both Tear and Feli. What emotion was most powerful? She did not know. Yes, she did. Anger at the man who tried to kill one of her best friends had to be at the top of the list. Gretchin headed back to the dorm room. The soldiers were on the trail of Lissy's attacker. Gretchin just wanted to be with Lissy and Xiny. She wanted her friends to feel safe, and she wanted the assurance that any attacker would have to face *her* to get to them.

Lieutenant Keep reached the gym. He questioned all the students present as well as Dr. Sexapopis. None had seen anybody enter through the doorway from the tunnel. However, the door to the tunnel was not visible from most areas of the gym. There had been at least two other students recently exercising, who had left before the arrival of the officer and his men. Those students could not be identified.

When Gretchin arrived back at the room she found only her roommates plus Feli, who had rushed to see Lissy and Xiny as soon as she heard of the attack.

"Hi Sweetheart," beamed Feli at Gretchin." Xiny just told me how brave you were."

Gretchin did not return the greeting. "Let's go get something to eat," she said.

Xiny with a glance to Lissy said, "We need fifteen minutes to get the men in position."

Feli said, "I need to run. She hugged Lissy and Xiny. "If there is anything I can do for you, I'm yours. Ok?

"Thank you Feli," replied Lissy.

Feli left to assist Dr. Sexapopis with the appointments Feli had lined up for the afternoon.

After the soldiers had time to reach their stations, Lissy, Xiny, Antwanesta, and Gretchin went to the freshman dining hall.

In the days and weeks that followed the investigation continued, and security became central to life. Lissy could no longer dismiss the presence of her guards as an overly protective extravagance. Xiny, Gregor, and Barthon were given authorization to carry weapons. Gregor and Barthon each carried a dagger in a scabbard mounted on a belt. Xiny's dagger was strapped to her left thigh with a special scabbard that held the dagger handle down for quick access with the

113

right hand. Gretchin wanted to carry a dagger too, but Dean Smith would not allow it. Lissy had at least four guards everywhere, except inside her dorm room. Even in the dorm there were always four guards outside the dorm room door. There were also at least two more patrolling the ground outside the freshman dorm. Even Gregor was assigned two body guards.

No sooner than the new glass arrived for the sophomore roof, Jandarian Solider was tasked with changing every lock on campus.

Antwanesta refused to carry her own dorm room key. She insisted it be held by a dorm room door guard. Her reasoning was logical. The key would be valued by someone intending harm to Lissy. Anyone seeking to take a key from Xiny or Gretchin would die in the attempt, even if Gretchin had no dagger. Antwanesta, as a pacifist, could not defend the key. She was therefore an easy target, a weakness in Lissy's defense.

The soldiers were very diligent in their commitment to their Queen's protection. Several volunteered to extend their duty hours to provide added security to the freshman women's bath. Sixty more soldiers were brought from the Kingdom and they occupied the vacant rooms in the freshman dorm.

The investigation yielded little. The crossbow and the bolt had been stolen from a cabinet in the gym. There were only four keys to that cabinet, they were held by Professor Cook, Dr. Sexapopis, Dean Smith, and Jandarian Solider. All four of those keys were secure and accounted for. The head on the bolt was not a field tip such as used for training at the school. It was a hunting tip of the sort commonly used in Libertaria for killing deer with minimal suffering. The long sharp bladed edges of the bolt head would insure that wounded prey bled too fast for it to escape unprocessed. In Libertaria, to inflict unnecessary suffering, or to cause the vain death of an animal, was seen as irresponsible. To allow rabbits

114

and deer to become overpopulated to the point of starvation would be all the more so. Libertarians believe strongly in responsibility, because liberty is always in direct proportion to it.

The bathers in the freshman men's bath were interrogated. None could confirm Zell's statement that he had been there at least an hour before Tear's arrival. Even Sal Keysmith did not notice him, even though he knew Zell very well.

The hood was crudely hand-sewn out of student robe material. Anyone could have made it. It was not a useful clue. It did not even indicate that the assailant was a student. Anyone could acquire such material. The attacker could have used it to appear to be a student.

A break in the case occurred three weeks after the attempt. There existed a fifth key, and it was missing. Sal Keysmith had a set of master keys he had made in his father's workshop. The set included a key which would have opened the lock on the archery cabinet in the gym. The set of master keys was missing.

Gregor was aware of Sal's special set of keys. He and Barthon had used one of Sal's keys to open the archery cabinet the past year, to use equipment for weapons practice. Last year Gregor and Barthon were only freshmen, but at the school, weapons training was an elective for sophomores. They did not want their shooting skills to go rusty for want of practice. At that time weapons were allowed on campus, and no one cared that they used equipment from the cabinet. They always returned it after use.

Gregor asked Sal about his keys. Sal checked his drawer, and found they were missing. Gregor and Sal went to Captain Knight to report the discovery.

Captain Knight asked who knew about the keys.

Thomas David Valentine

Sal said, "Barthon, Zell, Gregor and me, no one else."

Zell and Sal were, due to the fact that the sophomore men's bath was closed, in the freshman men's bath at the time the shooter had access to the bath. Sal had a witness who confidently said Sal had been in the bath at the time of the shooting. Rollo Mason, son of Frontaris Mason, said he had been with Sal in a hot pool. He said he had no doubt on that point.

Again evidence seemed to be pointing at Zell, but the Queen was sure he was blameless.

In Theism the thirty-sixth day after a birth was a time of celebration. For Antwanesta her trip to Central College seemed like a birth, complete with breaking water. Today was the thirty-sixth day since she jumped in the lake. It was now clearly Autumn on a breezy cloudy October day. Antwanesta walked to the chapel after Math. She wore both her Theite robe and her student robe. This time the Theite robe was for warmth rather than modesty or compliance with norms. She said her prayers and left. The cold air persuaded her she should give herself some warm cloths as a gift for her thirty-sixth day. She had seen runners in the Smith & Mason cotton thigh warmers, as well as ankle and arm warmers. She went to the tower atrium shop and bought three sets of each. All were black. The thigh warmers had the deficiency of leaving her intimate parts exposed to cold air, but from Antwanesta's perspective, keeping genitalia cold was consistent with virtue.

After four weeks at the school the routine was well established. Classes were now generally easy, except that grading was always on a curve, so the students were always in competition with one and other. This did not matter to Antwanesta. She was at the top of all of her courses except Physical Training. She was only average in running, below average in weight lifting, and was the worst swimmer. However, her skill in swimming had greatly improved due to diligent practice and Lissy's guidance. As the temperature

116

grew colder and daylight shorter more time was spent in the
baths. After dinner each day Antwanesta, Lissy, Xiny, and
Gretchin were in the bath, swimming laps and then soaking in
the warm bubbling pool. Feli was there only about half the
time because, she was always busy, working with Risky or
discussing investment opportunities with business oriented
students, like Rollo Mason, Hardy Weaver, and Sal Keysmith.

Late in the afternoon, when Antwanesta returned to
the dorm, a guard opened the door. Only Xiny was in the room
even though there were still four guards outside.

"Have you seen Lissy?" Xiny asked urgently.

"No," said Antwanesta.

"She was here forty minutes ago. She ordered me to
stay here. She also ordered the guards outside the door not to
follow her. It's not right. Something's wrong. Gretchin went
looking for her," said Xiny anxiously.

"Let's go find her," said Antwanesta as she changed
into her black standard Republican dress, and thigh warmers.

"I can't," said Xiny. "She ordered me to stay."

Xiny tied the lace on Antwanesta's thigh warmers.
Then Antwanesta put her student robe back on.

"I'll go tell Captain Knight, Gregor, and Barthon,"
said Antwanesta. Then she went out the door.

Chapter 9

Long Live the King

Gretchin arrived at the senior dorm which housed the Royal officers. She asked the first solider she saw where she could find Captain Knight. The solider immediately told her only because he recognized Gretchin as the Queen's trusted roommate. Gretchin beat on the captain's door until it was opened. Before Captain Knight could speak, she said the words she had prepared to efficiently convey the nature of the urgent situation. "The Queen told Xiny and the door guards to stay at the dorm room while she left unguarded. We believe she is in danger."

Without a word the captain knocked hard on the nearest door. He shouted through the door, "Up and out! The Queen is in danger!" A sergeant answered the door. The Captain added, "Assemble the men out front, *now*! The Queen is missing." The sergeant ran up the hall beating on doors. Captain Knight then asked Gretchin what else she knew.

Gretchin said, "This is not like Lissy. She never excludes Xiny from anything. She never gives Xiny an order to not follow her. I think she is under some outside influence."

Captain Knight asked, "When was she last seen?"

"She left about an hour ago. I was not there. If I had been I would have followed. *I don't take orders*."

Captain Knight then asked her to please find Gregor and Barthon to apprise them of the situation.

Gretchin replied in the affirmative, and ran in the direction of the sophomore dorm.

Antwanesta ran down to Feli's room and knocked on the door. Celina answered. She said Feli was with Risky at the infirmary. Antwanesta asked Celina to ask Feli to check on Xiny upon her return.

Antwanesta was then off the find Gregor and Barthon.

Gretchin reached the sophomore dorm before Antwanesta. She found only Gregor in the room. With a brief explanation from Gretchin, Gregor said. "I want to talk with Xiny." They ran together along with Gregor's two body guards toward the freshman dorm. It was odd to see runners in student robes especially when accompanied by soldiers in golden armor. They met Antwanesta half way. Gregor asked her to inform Barthon and Tear in the cafeteria. Antwanesta then went west toward the tower.

When Gregor and Gretchin reached the dorm room the four guards were gone. Captain Knight had reassigned them to the search for the Queen. He was able to do this because a standing order had given him authority to redeploy troops. He did not have the power to relieve Xiny of her order. When Gregor and Gretchin arrived the captain was trying to persuade Xiny that she could at least leave the room to use the toilet. She said she would follow her Queen's order to the letter. Gregor told the captain to supervise the troops, and that he would deal with Xiny.

"Does Lissy love you?" Gregor asked to Xiny.

"Yes," said Xiny.

"Do you really think that by telling you to stay here, she meant that you could not step outside the room to use the toilet?"

119

"No."

"Then go use it, and get back in here to help me figure out what could make Lissy leave you and her guards."

Xiny and Gretchin both left and returned.

Gregor then asked, "What would make Lissy risk her life?"

"The Kingdom, the family, or her friends," replied Xiny.

"You know all her friends. Is anyone in trouble?"

"No."

"The Kingdom, do you know of any threats to the Kingdom?"

"There are always threats to the Kingdom, but I don't see why that would make Lissy disappear."

"Family? That's just me."

"No,"

"How about your blood? You Royals are bunny-brains about blood," Gretchin interjected.

"Gretchin!" said Xiny.

"It's ok," said Gregor, "She is helping Lissy. I thought Antwanesta was the smart one."

"No, I am. Ant just plays with numbers," said Gretchin.

"Gretchin is right. If someone could convince Lissy that I was seduced by a woman…," Gregor said.

"No. She would tell you and me," said Xiny.

"Yes, she would. Good try Gretchin," said Gregor.

Antwanesta found Tear in the sophomore cafeteria.
Barthon was not there. Tear said he went to the bath.
Antwanesta brought Tear up to speed. Then they both went to
the infirmary to find Feli.

They found Feli behind a curtain where Hardy was
making a donation. Risky scolded Antwanesta and Tear for
intruding on Hardy's privacy. Hardy, said, "It is ok. The more
the merrier."

Antwanesta apologized to Hardy and Risky, and
explained the urgency of the situation. Risky told Feli, she
could go. The next two donors could either reschedule, or the
witness protocol could be relaxed in an emergency with the
donor's consent. Darwood and Eltwando were both regular
donors who could be trusted not to fabricate allegations of
impropriety.

Antwanesta, Tear, and Feli went to Freedom Park to
search for Lissy. Antwanesta had never been to Freedom Park.
She never had a reason to go, until now. Antwanesta and Tear
took off their bulky student robes for greater freedom of
movement. Antwanesta had her black standard Republican
dress and cotton thigh warmers. Tear was in her fur loin drape,
and halter. Their robes were draped over their arms as they
searched among the trees and bushes. Feli had left her robe at
the infirmary, and was in her second best blue dress.

Antwanesta was propositioned by three separate men
in ten minutes. She began to question the modesty of her black
dress. Antwanesta had a quick solution to the unwelcome
distractions. She put her Holy Hexagon pendent on the outside
of her dress. Antwanesta said the pendant would work as a
plainly visible, "I will not copulate with you," sign. It worked.
Men kept their distance.

Lissy was not to be found in Freedom Park, the arboretum, the tower, or the baths. Even Jandarian Solider, who knew places on the isle known to no one but him, found nothing. She was gone. Antwanesta, Gretchin, Tear, and Feli all went to their beds at 3:00 AM. Tear returned to her room and found Barthon and Zell as worried about her as about Lissy. Gregor was with Captain Knight planning to search beyond Central District Isle.

Some soldiers did find one thing out of place. There was a boat just off the north shore of the isle. It was Zell Fisher's boat. Technically it was his father's boat, but Zell and his cousins, Naragadug (Duggy) Baker and Wago Tailor were the only ones who ever used it.

The following morning, Lieutenant Keep, asked Zell about the presence of his boat offshore, in sight of the sophomore dorm. Zell said he had no idea how it came to be there, or how a shirt, belt, and pair of pants came to be wadded up on the boat's deck.

Antwanesta, Gretchin, and Feli each planned to skip some classes to stay with Xiny so she would not be alone in the dorm room with her worries. Antwanesta skipped Physical Training. Feli would explain Antwanesta's absence to Risky. Feli returned and Antwanesta went to Nature. Professor Medic would be disappointed that his favorite student was absent, but Xiny needed Feli more than he did. Antwanesta would take good notes. She also planned to skip Math. Professor Agape, would just have to teach the class herself.

Antwanesta had been looking forward to Nature class until the horrible distraction of late. The topic was to be the moon. She had always been very curious about the moon. Why does it have a red dot? Why is the dot centered on the Earthward face? Why does the dot appear to cover exactly two-thirds of the moon's face? Why is the distance of the moon relative to its diameter such that it creates an image the same apparent size as the larger and more distant sun? These questions had long troubled Antwanesta. See knew the answers. She had been told in elementary school. She was told again in middle school. She was given a more detailed explanation in high school. *God shows his perfection by inserting improbable regularities in the universe. Reality is the product of God's willful and intelligent design. He shows us His perfection every day and every night. Just as He shows us the six virtues with the black Holy Hexagon in the western sky, and the white Holy Hexagon which washed up on the beach of His chosen people. He made a dot which is 66.66666...% of the face of the moon. God is forever reminding each of us about the path to theosis, the way to Heaven.* This is what Antwanesta had been consistently told. Why was it not enough? It was enough for her mother. It was enough for Father Alfonzo. It was enough for the Pontiff himself. How immodest could she be? Why should *she* deserve something more?

Antwanesta wanted more. She knew full well that Professor Medic was a Humanist and a man of science. She also knew that every Humanist would wipe the mud off shoes, with the supernaturalistic explanations which passed for truth in the Theocracy. Histina Bowright sarcastically theorized that the red dot came from a menstruating goddess. Antwanesta wanted to hear a serious explanation form a thoughtful Humanist. She just wished she were in the mood to hear it.

Antwanesta's worries were not the only things to inhibit her enjoyment of the class. Professor Medic's explanation was disappointing. "The prevailing theory is that the red dot is actually a vast lava field resulting from magma being drawn or expelled from the moon's interior," said Professor Medic. "It is centered of the Earth-facing side because the Earth's gravity creates a tidal pull on the magma which has melted the thin crust of the moon's surface."

"Tidal pull? You call that parsimonious?" Antwanesta interrupted with less tact than her normal manner

would impose. "If such a thing as tidal pull existed, we would experience a proportionately smaller tide on the water here on Earth. We live on an island; I think we would have noticed."

Professor Medic took no offense. He was pleased to see a student with passion for his subject, a critical thinker no less. "We just don't know, Miss Agape. Sometimes we have to bridge the gaps in our knowledge with rational conjecture."

"You mean faith?"

"No, I don't. Faith is belief in something with no empirical basis. In this case we don't know all the details, but we have experience with gravity. We know quite a bit about gravity, thanks to Isaac Newton. It is expected that a body as massive as the Earth would exert a gravitational force on the moon sufficient to pull a fluid through a shallow crust."

"Why does our ocean have no tide?"

"Presumably the mass of the moon is too low to generate enough gravity to create a tide in the ocean."

"What about the fact that the percent of the moon's face occupied by the dot is 66.666 percent like the six virtues of the Holy Hexagon?"

"So what? The bright white part of the moon is 33.333 percent like the three Humanistic virtues. It's *just* a number. The universe has coincidences in it."

"I suppose the fact that the sun and the moon are the same size to our eyes because of their relative distances and diameters is a coincidence?" Antwanesta's voice was clearly skeptical in tone and her brows were raised.

"That is more parsimonious than the idea that the moon is artificial and made by extraterrestrials homesteading planets with liquid water. You can make anything up, tie it to pretty numbers, and make it seem amazing and mysterious.

124

Yes, what you described is probably a coincidence. We don't need to attribute every stray oddity to a divine hand." After a brief pause Professor Medic added, "Thank you. Miss Agape has just demonstrated what I like to see in my class (critical thinking). For next time, I want each of you to bring in a written list of three or more phenomena, other than the moon, which seem too orderly or complex to be the result of natural processes. I want serious thoughtful examples, not jokes, Miss Bowright."

At 11:00 AM a sail boat arrived at the dock at the tip of the arboretum lobe of Central District Isle. A middle-aged man, in a white Royal tunic and a narrow blond goatee, stepped on to the dock followed by two soldiers. He walked to the tower where Captain Knight had set up a situation room from which to direct the search for the Queen. When the man walked in the captain snapped to attention. The man in white had news. When the captain heard it, his head fell in disappointment. Then the man in white, Chief Councilor, Alfide Stewart, said he wanted to be directed to his daughter. He then went straight to Room 327 in the freshman dorm.

Feli was lying on Gretchin's bed. When the knock came, it was Xiny who rushed to answer. She saw her father. She hugged him and began to cry. Feli hopped down, and asked shall I leave you alone. Xiny's father said, "No, please stay." He then introduced himself, as did Feli. Xiny added through sobs, "Feli is one of my best friends."

Chief Councilor Stewart looked Feli in the eye and said, "My darling girl will need her friends now. Will you promise me to care for her after I must go?"

"I will. I love Xiny deeply, and others here do too. We will do absolutely anything for her."

"Thank you, Feli. You lighten my heavy heart."

Xiny then said, "How?"

125

"It was quick. There was no evidence of rape or torture, but she is gone," said Xiny's father.

Xiny then embraced Feli hard as if letting go would send her into a freefall.

Gretchin came to the door in her fur halter and loin drape, her robe hanging on her left arm.

When Xiny, saw her she released Feli and said through tears, "Father, this is my roommate, Gretchin, another very dear friend." Xiny hugged Gretchin.

Gretchin did not know what to say. She just hugged Xiny and wished she could suffer her pain for her.

"I'm very pleased to meet you Gretchin," said Xiny's Father. "Thank you for being Xiny's friend."

Gretchin, responded, looking into Xiny's eyes, not her fathers, "We love your daughter, very much." She then held Xiny's head tightly to her chest.

Feli said to Xiny's father, that she needed to go, but would return in two hours, and that Antwanesta would be with Xiny before Gretchin left. Feli kissed Xiny on the temple, and did the same to Gretchin. Feli then whispered to Chief Councilor Stewart, "At least one of us will be with her at all times."

After Feli left, Xiny composed herself and said, "I must see her."

"No my dear. You will say your goodbye at the funeral with the whole grieving Kingdom."

Barthon and Gregor came to the door next.

As they entered Chief Councilor Stewart knelt on one knee and bowed. He then said, "Long live the King." Barthon,

Xiny, and the guards all followed his lead. They bowed. "Long live the King."

Gretchin, remained standing, and gave Gregor a tentative wave with her fingers.

Xiny and Barthon were told by their father to stay at the school until the funeral which was scheduled for Sunday. Gregor would have to come to the Kingdom, and be seen as a model of strength and courage in this time of crisis. Xiny at first resisted staying, but relented after receiving a stern look from her father, who said he had to be able to focus on his duties. He wanted Xiny with her friends, and away from the stress which the Queen's untimely parting would mean for the Kingdom.

When Antwanesta arrived at the dorm room. Barthon was still there with Xiny and Gretchin. Antwanesta reported that classes were canceled for the rest of the week and all of the following week to allow students to process the tragic event, and that student counseling sessions would be held for any student desiring counseling. Barthon excused himself, and said he would check back with Xiny in the morning.

After Barthon left Gretchin said, "Let's eat."

"I'm not hungry," said Xiny.

Gretchin then added, "Let me rephrase that. We are going to the dining hall. You, Sinny, are going to eat. Your only choice in the matter is whether you feed yourself, or I feed you."

"I thought Libertarians believed freedom," said Xiny.

"I do. I'm free to feed you so that you can be free to not starve."

"I think I like that, said Xiny, I've never had a handmaiden before. Will you give me a massage after dinner?"

"If you swim ten laps in the pool I will, replied Gretchin quickly, knowing that Risky advocated aerobic exercise as the best antidepressant medication in existence."

"Xiny, Gretchin, and Antwanesta, went to the freshman dining hall. Gretchin did feed Xiny, bite-by-bite. Xiny almost smiled."

Antwanesta was pensive. She was trying to figure out what could have lead Lissy to leave Xiny and her guards to meet her death. There had to be an answer, and nothing would keep her from it.

After dinner Xiny, Gretchin, and Antwanesta went to the bath where they were joined by Feli. Xiny put in her ten laps. Then she and Gretchin went to the cosmetic room where Gretchin gave Xiny the massage she had earned.

Antwanesta and Feli were together in the hot pool, thinking and sharing conjectures. They were trying to understand who would and could have killed their dear friend.

After the bath Xiny had a further imposition to request of *her* new *handmaiden*. She asked Gretchin to lie with her on her bunk. Gretchin complied, willing to do whatever it took to relieve Xiny's grief. Gretchin was lying on her back like some great long skinny plush animal. Xiny cuddled up to her from the left side. She put her head next to Gretchin's ribcage. There she fell soundly asleep listening to the slow strong rhythm of Gretchin's very large heart.

Chief Councilor Stewart had relieved Captain Knight of command, and placed Lieutenant Keep in charge of a much reduced Central District Isle guard. Lieutenant Keep was also delegated full authority over the local portion of the murder investigation. The Chief Councilor only wanted "expeditious

justice, no reports, no consultation, and no requests for
direction." Lieutenant Keep was to help his nation get past this
tragedy as quickly as possible. The lieutenant was left with
eight soldiers and expectations that seemed well beyond his
ability, but he had faced worse.

Lieutenant Victorani Keep had reentered to the army
after a tragedy in his personal life. He had completed his
mandatory military service. He was discharged as a senior
sergeant and entered the pool of men eligible for marriage. He
was paired with a smart, kind, cheerful, and beautiful twenty-
two-year-old woman. They married in accordance with
tradition, exchanging vows of commitment and fidelity until
death and beyond. His lovely bride died of heart failure at the
wedding reception without ever even physically
consummating the union. His only living relatives were his
sister and his niece, Oluga who was a now a freshman at the
Central College.

Early death by heart failure due to a congenital heart
valve defect was very rare, except in the Southern Kingdom.
There it was very common. The population was dangerously
inbred. Several recessive genetic disorders flourished. Heart
failure and stroke were common in the Kingdom, and occurred
in a much younger patient population than in the rest of
Epodlo.

Victorani Keep was a widower. There was no
provision within Royal culture for remarriage. Everyone had
one chance at marriage, only one. Victorani's prospects for
love and family life were over. He refocused himself on his
career. Having served honorably and effectively in the service
of his country during his conscription, it was natural to return
to the work he knew well. He had applied for, and received a
commission as an officer in the Royal Army. It was an honor
to be second in command of the Queen's guard. It was a credit
to his competent and devoted service that he was now in
charge of a key part of the investigation into Queen's murder.

He was very capable of carrying out the duties delegated by Chief Councilor Stewart. He was intelligent, resourceful, diligent, and determined to perform his duties well.

No one had the slightest clue that Victorani Keep would be the first to fall in the war which was soon to come.

Chapter 10

The War

As Xiny half woke she felt the warmth of the body next to her. She thought it was Lissy. *I must have had a nightmare. That was it.* As she slid her hand across Gretchin's chest, it became obvious that Xiny was not with Lissy. The grief returned, but Xiny was comforted by Gretchin's presence. She held Gretchin close to her. Xiny then saw the depression in the bunk above. In the past such a compaction of the upper bunk mattress was an indication of Lissy's presence. Now it meant Feli was there. Feli was there for the sole purpose of comforting her. This heartened Xiny more. She then looked over to the red hair and pale skin of the young woman on the bunk across from her. She knew she was surrounded by friends who loved her. The intimacy Xiny shared with Gretchin, Feli, and Antwanesta was different than what she had had with Lissy, but she felt their love and she loved each of them.

In the sophomore dorm Tear woke to the sound of rain. She hopped from the bunk. She kissed Barthon's bare right buttock, and Zell's lips. Both were sleeping in their bunks. "Up boys" she said, "time for yoga." Barthon groaned. Zell was silent in slumber.

Tear sat in cobbler's pose stretching her firm bronzed inner thighs. The water-heated floor felt warm against Tear's bear skin. She knelt, and leaned forward to child's pose. Then arms and legs straight with rump up for downward deer. She went through the warrior poses and then stretched back into a bridge. She held the position for several seconds. Then she released. She worked slowly through her regular routine. With her pelvis over her head she remembered she was late, five days late. That's not much, but for Tear it was strange. She was normally as regular as the weather. She planned to check with Risky, if her period did not come in the next two days.

There was a knock at the door. She opened it without dressing or asking who it was. There were two Royal soldiers. This did not seem strange. Until Gregor's departure for the Southern Kingdom, there had been two Royal guards outside the door since the crossbow attempt on Lissy. "Good morning, Miss Tripopis. Please excuse us. We have orders to search this room."

"Barthon," Tear called calmly, "Some of *your* people are here."

Barthon got up. "What do you need Sergeant?"

"We have orders to search this room, Baron Stewart."

"Why?"

"Mr. Fisher is a suspect in the Queen's murder."

"You have no right to search *my* room," said Tear firmly.

"You are wasting time," said Barthon, to the soldiers.

Zell, woke and yawned. "You got a warrant?"

"We don't need a warrant in the Central District. Your Republican rights don't apply here, said the solider."

"Go ahead. I consent," said Barthon. "Let them follow this rabbit trail to a dead end, so they will redirect their investigation in a productive direction. We all want the Queen's killer brought to justice."

"I don't consent!" said Zell. "Civil liberties are not to be disregarded."

The soldiers began to search.

"Don't worry, Zell. They will find nothing and leave," said Barthon.

"That's not the point," said Zell. "We must stand up for liberty."

Tear smiled at Zell. *I'll make a Libertarian of him yet,* she thought. Tear then turned to one of the soldiers. "Hand me those," she said to the solider rummaging through her drawers. "And those," as the solider handed a fur halter to her. "The thigh warmers too, the fur ones."

"What's this?" The other solider held up a small pointed metal object, knowing full well it was a crossbow bolt field tip. "Who's drawer is this?"

"The drawer is mine," said Zell. "That arrowhead is *not.*"

The solider then held up a set of keys.

"Those keys are not mine either."

"You're under arrest, Mr. Fisher."

Tear kissed, Zell on the lips. "I'll get Xiny. She'll kick solider boy's prostate to the dot on the moon." With that and a scowl at the soldiers, Tear exited the room.

Tear jogged under the grey clouds to the freshman dorm. Mercifully the rain had stopped as it always did on this date every year. Tear reached room 327 and knocked. Antwanesta opened the door just as freely as Tear had opened her door twenty minutes before. Tear explained what the soldiers had found, and that Zell had been arrested.

Feli jumped down from the bunk above Xiny's, and pulled on her blue dress. She would need to go to her own room to get her student robe.

Tear pleaded with Xiny, "Please make them stop."

"I can't. I have no power anymore. I am not the voice of the Queen. Only King Gregorious, or my father can turn them around," said Xiny.

Then Feli jumped in, "I have known Zell all my life. He could not have killed Lissy."

"I believe you, Feli, but it is out of my hands," said Xiny, "Lieutenant Keep won't be persuaded by me saying that Zell couldn't do it just because my friend says so."

Feli replied, "You may be powerless, but I'm not. I'm going to see Dean Smith. You're with me Sweetheart."

"Me? Why me?" said Gretchin.

"Because you're my courage," said Feli looking into Gretchin's eyes with a *you-will-not-question-me-on-this*, air of command.

Gretchin dressed in fur loin drape, halter and robe. She followed Feli, to get Feli's student robe on the second floor. Then they were off toward the tower.

As they approached the tower they saw Dean Smith marching along the walkway toward the senior dorm. Feli and Gretchin ran to catch her.

"Dean Smith!" yelled Feli as they drew near.

"I know, Mr. Stewart told me," said Dean Smith without turning or slowing her pace.

Lieutenant Keep came out the east door of the senior dorm with two of his soldiers. Dean Smith, Feli, and Gretchin, met the three golden-armored men at a point directly east of the senior bath roof and five kiloballs west of the gym.

"Greetings, Dean/Governor. I was just coming to you with a report," said Lieutenant Keep.

"I heard you have arrested one of my students. What do you intend to do with him?"

"He will soon be on a boat to East Tower. We have good evidence against him."

"There is no extradition treaty between the Central District and the Southern Kingdom. You can't just *seize* one of my students."

"Of course not. I was coming to see you, to ask your permission. You will certainly want to cooperate under the circumstances."

"I will not be cooperating, Lieutenant. Permission is denied."

"I had hoped it would not come to this, Dean/Governor. I have armed men. The Kingdom will not be denied justice."

"I don't intend to deny justice to the Kingdom, or to Mr. Fisher. If you have good evidence, the case will be tried *here*."

"The body was found on Royal soil. We have jurisdiction."

"I have the defendant, Lieutenant."

"Actually *I* have the defendant, Dean/Governor."

"Mr. Fisher was arrested on District soil, and he is still on it," said the Dean smugly.

"Not for long, replied the officer."

"You have just threatened to use force under color of national authority to seize a person subject to Central District protection. That is an act of war," said the dean with a provocative, haughty tone of resolve.

"With all due respect Dean/Governor, we are not at war."

"Yes, we are," replied Dean Smith with an arrogant smirk. "Miss Quadrapopis, you have just been conscripted. Remove your robe and hand it to Miss Smith. Then relieve Lieutenant Keep of his sword."

Gretchin removed her robe and handed it to Feli, with a wink. Then, without a word, Gretchin kicked the lieutenant hard in the chest plate with her left foot. He fell back onto the ground. Then, with no hesitation, Gretchin did a hand spring and landed with her right knee bent directly above the officer's trachea and her left foot on his right wrist. Gretchin grabbed his short sword from its sheath with her right hand. Then pivoting on her left arm she swung both legs under the solider to Keep's right, who was frantically grabbing at the handle of his own short sword. He fell hard on to the moist ground. Gretchin rolled on top of him placing the ball of her right foot under his chin and slamming the butt of the lieutenant's sword into the wrist of the soldier's sword arm. Gretchin snapped up the second sword and summersaulted into a standing position facing away from the last solider. She spun herself low while holding the swords perpendicular to each other so as to block anticipated swings from above and from the left.

Neither swing came. The terrified soldier said in a timid voice, I don't want to hurt you, Miss.

Gretchin smiled with a look both taunting and flirtatious. She then dropkicked him in the chest while parrying his tentative sword swing in midflight. The solider fell backwards to the ground, the skirt of his tunic, and the two golden rectangular plates at its front, flopped up unto his abdomen revealing is genitalia. His sword was still in his right hand. Gretchin was standing. She placed a blade to the left of the man's scrotum, and said coldly, "Yield, or I sever your bloodline."

The Royal soldier opened his right hand wide
releasing his sword. Gretchin withdrew her sword and picked
up his with another smile. She handed one sword to Dean
Smith and another to Feli. Gretchin had to close Feli's fingers
around the handle of the sword. Feli was just standing mouth
agape and trembling.

"A glorious victory. The Central District has defeated
the Southern Kingdom," Dean Smith announced. "I shall now
dictate terms of peace. You will release Mr. Fisher on his own
recognizance. He shall remain on Central District Isle until his
trial. You shall provide a sailboat and two soldiers, fresher
than these, to escort these two girls to Newton to arrange for
Mr. Fisher's defense counsel. As an accommodation to the
Kingdom's desire for swift justice, trial will be this-coming
Saturday at 8:00 AM."

"Saturday! I don't even have a prosecutor," protested
Lieutenant Keep.

"Yes, you do," responded Dean Smith in a
sarcastically gentle tone. "You have the very best attorney
licensed in the Central District."

"What? Who?"

"You, Lieutenant."

"I'm not a lawyer, and I am not licensed to practice
law here or anywhere."

"You are now. Welcome to the Central District Bar.
Your identification number is 0001. Now get these girls on a
boat. The expedited trial schedule will no doubt be a challenge
for defense counsel as well."

Lieutenant Keep obtained a boat and two clean
uninjured soldiers to take Feli and Gretchin to Newton.

The two soldiers who Gretchin had fought went to
the infirmary. The first was shaken-up. To hear him tell it, he

had fought a hulking brute of a Central District commando, "as tall as a D-unit," (whatever that is). The other soldier was more lucid. He had a cut on his inner left thigh from when Gretchin withdrew her sword. The soldier was cheerful and unconcerned about the injury. He was clearly pleased to receive his sutures from the trained, experienced doctor.

Both soldiers would be regarded as heroes back in the Kingdom. They lost the war, yes, but they made it through the melee without any disruption to the bloodline. This was better than any costly victory. Ironically, had one, and only one, of the soldiers been killed, much of the bloodline would have restored to its state before the Queen's death. One female was removed from the chain of marital pairings with Lissy's passing. The loss of one male solider would have reset most future pairings to where they were before the loss of Lissy. The soldiers did not think of this, and fortunately few of their countrymen would either. Even those who did would never be so uncourteous, even in thought, to consider an untimely death as something to be desired or preferred. Heroes they indeed were.

Gretchin was irritated that the dean would not even let her shower before boarding the vessel north. After the boat set sail, Feli dipped up a bucket full of lake water. She and Gretchin washed and picked the mud and humus from Gretchin's body and fur garments. At least her student robe was clean. As a *solider on duty*, Gretchin had been exempt from the dress code as she walked to the arboretum dock. After becoming relatively clean she slipped back into the student robe for warmth.

The boat moved at a good pace, even with little wind, because the water current was with them. As they sailed northwest, Feli learned the names of the soldiers and gathered enough information from them to assess their characters. This was Feli's way. Know everyone, but keep emotional distance from all but a safe dependable few, and hold no one person too dear. "Diversification of emotional assets," she called it. Feli

then turned her attention to the friend she had come to love.
Gretchin was one of her "core assets." Feli feared she might
have too much invested in Gretchin, but fear and greed make a
market, and she had no inclination to divest.

She saw in Gretchin's eyes that she too had become
emotionally invested, but not in her. "I'm worried about him
too, Sweetheart," said Feli, reading Gretchin's face.

"Is your mom a good lawyer?"

"The best," replied Feli, not really believing her
words.

"She also loves Zell. When Zell and I were kids she
took us to the public bath four days a week."

"You grew up bathing with Zell?"

"It was more just swimming and playing. Mom was
there, and Zell was like the son she never had. Mom will get
Zell out of this. I know it. *Your* mom will help too if needed."

"What do you know about my mom?"

"Patina told me. Her mom works at one of your
mom's brothels."

"That's supposed to be a secret, Gretchin said
nervously."

"I discerned as much from your tendency to avoid the
subject of your mother. I told Petina to keep the secret. She
agreed in exchange for math tutoring and massages. I was ok
with that, until she tried to extort me for more. I told Petina
that the secret was not yours but your mother's, and that if she
breached secrecy, she would have your mother to answer to.
That worked. I don't even give her massages any more. I do
still tutor her as a compassionate kindness."

"So I owe you some massages?"

139

"No, Sweetheart. You owe me nothing."

"Why do you call me, *Sweetheart*?"

"The same reason you call Antwanesta, *Ant*, and Xiny, *Sinny*.

"That's just a Libertarian custom among sisters and female friends, said Gretchin."

"Yes, but do you know the psychomechanics of the custom?"

"Uh, no. You're the only *psycho mechanic* I've ever met."

Feli explained. "You pick a slightly irritating nickname for a woman you like. This angers her at a subconscious level producing general emotional energy. You then cultivate that energy into affection."

"You are one manipulative rabbit," said Gretchin with both offence and admiration.

"So are you. We all are. I just operate at a conscious level."

"Does it work on men?"

"No, their brains are wired differently."

"Is there a way to manipulate them?"

"Yes."

"How?"

"That knowledge is too dangerous for you to have."

"I knew I hated you," said Gretchin in a tone softer than the words.

"All in accordance with my master plan, Sweetheart."
Feli smiled with convincing, though artificial confidence.

As Feli and Gretchin disembarked from the vessel at
the Newton dock. One of the Royal soldiers informed them
that the orders were to escort the young women *to* Newton,
not *from* it. Before Gretchin could resume military hostilities,
Feli said that her Father had a good boat, and the Royal vessel
was not needed.

"There is the Newton Museum," Feli said, pointing
proudly to a large rectangular white building on a hill. Its
whiteness was especially distinct amid the common pink
granite buildings surrounding it. It was also made of pink
granite, but a white coating had been applied to make it stand
out as the symbol of knowledge and reason it was intended to
be. "I worked at the museum last Summer. I'd love to take you
there, if we had time, but I need to brief Mom about Zell."

"Yes, Zell is our mission," Gretchin agreed. "Get me
out of this cold air. I need more fur."

"The house isn't far," Feli assured her shivering
friend.

Feli and Gretchin entered the house to the surprise of
Feli's parents, each of whom hugged Feli.

"This is my friend, Gretchin."

After a brief exchange of conventional pleasantries,
Feli said, "It's Zell. The Royals have accused him of killing
Lissy."

"You can't be serious? Zell would never do such a
thing," replied her Mom.

"Of course not. Someone is trying to frame him. He
needs you, Mom."

"I'll be on the boat at first light. Have dinner, and tell
me all you know."

141

Feli's father served soup with cabbage, beets, beans, and chicken. Feli ate Gretchin's chicken explaining that Gretchin was a vegetarian.

"But you don't just *take* it from her bowl Dear," scolded her mother.

"It's ok, Mom. Where close," said Feli.

"Oh, yes we share everything," Gretchin added with mock enthusiasm.

Feli gave Gretchin, a stern look and said, "You go take a shower, Sweetheart, and then get some sleep while I explain things to Mom. You still smell like the lake."

Feli's mom and dad exchanged glances. Picius Smith showed Gretchin to the shower and where to find Feli's room. While Feli explained all she knew of the charges and evidence in Zell's case, Gretchin fell asleep in Feli's small bed.

After Antwanesta recited her prayer thirty-six times she asked, "You want me to join you over there?"

"Please," said Xiny, half expecting Antwanesta's sense of chastity would prohibit her from lying next to another person no matter how platonically.

Antwanesta crossed the room in two steps, and slid beneath the blanket with Xiny.

"Thank you," Xiny said, "I know I seem like a child, having to be put to bed. It's just that without you I feel very alone, and it is hard to sleep."

Antwanesta replied, "Even when I'm not here, God is always with you, Xiny,"

"I don't feel any gods. I just feel you."

"I'm just the instrument God uses, Xiny. The love you feel is from Him."

142

"You don't love me?"

"I do love you Xiny, but human love is not pure and perfect like God's. In a classical formulation there are three kinds of love. *Agape*, like my name, is God's love, love in the ideal form, unadulterated by human imperfection. *Philia* is brotherly love. It is the imperfect shadow of God's love. Then there is *eros*, which is sexual love. It is love corrupted by base desire. Feli has a different formulation also in the form of a triad. Feli is a Humanist, so she ignores *agape* altogether. She divides love into three separate, but related neurological processes; attraction, passion, and attach…." Antwanesta realized that Xiny had fallen fast asleep.

The next morning there was a knock on the door to Feli's Newton bedroom. "You need to get up girls. We need to eat breakfast, and hit the water," came to voice of Feli's father.

Gretchin woke. "I see why I didn't freeze to death. You make a nice thick comforter."

"Who are you calling thick? I only have fat in places you wish you had it," replied Feli.

"On you or on me, it kept me warm last night, so thanks. Maybe the boys are right about you snow does."

"Anything for you, Sweetheart," replied Feli with her usual sarcastic tone.

After breakfast Picius piloted the sail boat grant money had bought for his aquatic research. He transported his wife, Azunia, daughter, Feli, and her friend, Gretchin to Central District Isle. Tacking upstream on the Northwest River was not easy. Feli helped her dad with the sails. Gretchin conversed with the skilled attorney who had given birth to the very strange irritant which had entered into her life. It was more of a deposition than a conversation. Feli's mother was curious about how Gretchin and Feli met, and got to know each other. Gretchin entertained herself by evading Ms. Smith's questions. After two hours Azunia was no closer to understanding just what kind of relationship Gretchin and Feli had, but she came to really like Gretchin.

Like most Humanists, Azunia was very accepting of same-sex couples, although her desire for grandchildren made her less than enthusiastic about her daughter being in such a couple. However, after talking with Gretchin she warmed to the idea. Then Gretchin started to comment about how difficult monogamy must be, and how a stable should have at least three men. This left Azunia totally confused. She broke off the conversation with Gretchin and went back to planning a defense strategy for Zell.

It was past sundown when the boat reached Central District Isle dock. Picius would stay with Azunia in an apartment provided in the mostly-vacant family dorm. Feli took her mom to see Zell. Gretchin went to her dorm room anxious to see how Xiny was fairing.

The next morning Azunia made several legal motions. She moved to be authorized to represent Zell without a license to practice in the district. That motion was granted. She moved for a continuance. That motion was denied. A third motion for expedited discovery rules was granted. Her other motions, seven for dismissal on various theories, were all swiftly denied. Azunia next focused on evidence and witnesses.

Xiny, Antwanesta, Gretchin, and Feli each had counseling sessions scheduled. First Gretchin would meet with Risky. Next Feli would meet with Professor Medic. In the afternoon Antwanesta and Xiny would meet simultaneously with Professor Agape the Red, and Professor Solider respectively.

Gretchin arrived at Risky's office above the gym. After the door closed they shared the customary sisterly kiss. Then Risky opened with, "How's Xiny?"

"She's strong, but losing Lissy is almost more than anyone could take. Ant, Feli, and I are all over her. We don't

144

let her out of our sight; we even take turns sleeping with her. Feli was with her last night. Xiny seems calm enough, but I think a little more stress will break her."

"Is she getting exercise?"

"Only because we make her. Running, swimming, pumping iron. We train her like a solider."

"Good, that is just what she needs. How are *you* holding up, Retch?"

"I don't know. I think I'd feel worse if I didn't have to pretend to be strong for Xiny. I'll be ok." After a pause Gretchin continued, "Can we talk about one of those subjects we don't' talk about? I don't mean Pop Four. I mean about what happened with you."

"What about it?"

"You're twenty-nine, Risky, and so far as I know you don't have a stable. I know men want you, lots of them. When will you move on?"

"Would it comfort you to know that I have a lover?"

"Yes. Who?" Gretchin sat up and leaned forward with interest.

"We are not ready to reveal our relationship."

"Your *what*?"

"I'm entitled to some privacy don't you think?"

"*No*, not from me. I'm your sister."

"Sisterhood carries with it some privileges, but I don't have to tell you all my secrets."

"*Secrets?* You're as bad as Mom."

Risky lowered her head, and looked Gretchin in the

145

eyes.

"Ok, not as bad as Mom, but why all the secrecy?" said Gretchin.

"That's my business. You'll know when we are ready to share our relationship."

"Ok, I'm glad you found someone to be happy with."

"What about you, Retch? How is your stable coming?"

"Don't ask? I only wake up with Xiny and Feli"

"You gave up on boys?"

"You know about Xiny. Feli dragged me up to Newton to retrieve her Mom to defend Zell. Newton is apparently short on both beds and heat. At least she was warm."

"Feli's great. You could do worse."

"I want more functionality than she has to offer. I'm sorry Risky, I didn't mean…

"That's ok, Retch. There are more important things than getting you vagina filled. Love is the real prize, not sex, but if you find them both in the same person you are a big winner."

Feli went to the tower for her counseling session with Professor Medic.

"How are you, Miss Smith?"

"I'm well, Professor."

"I understand you were close to the Queen. I'm sorry."

"Lissy was a good friend. I'm glad I have more of them."

"I know you are adept at social networking. It is all very scientific to you, isn't it?"

"Yes, replied Feli, I try to apply reason to manage passion and grief."

"Do you fear passion?"

"Yes, I do. Is something wrong with that?"

"You tell me?"

"Fear is another dangerous emotion, almost as bad as passion. I need to work on fear too."

"Don't discount passion, Miss Smith. Passion will take you where reason will not follow."

Later Antwanesta was with Professor Irigon Agape.

"Are you well, Sister Antwanesta?"

"I have many blessings, Brother Irigon.

"Do you see the loss of the Queen as a blessing?"

"I do not, Brother, I see it as a test."

"How so?"

"*God did not create a universe of perfection. We live in a place of necessary suffering and pain. Were it not so, virtue would have no meaning. If all were perfect, there would be no need for modesty. If there were no lust, there would be no need for chastity. Peace would have no meaning without the possibility of conflict. If there were no wrongs, there would be nothing to forgive. If there were no hatred, love would have no meaning. If certainty were ours to grasp, faith would have no utility,*" recited Antwanesta.

"Where did you come by this wisdom, Sister?"

"I read your book, of course."

"I am truly blessed to have you read my book, and all the more so to hear it quoted so flawlessly from your memory. Thank you, Sister."

"Thank you for writing the book, Brother. You are so wise. Why did you not become a priest?"

"It is not for me to know why God put me where I am. However, I have noted that the Humanist students are more likely to be receptive to God's wisdom when conveyed through a heritic than through a priest."

"I'm sure you are right. Feli is the only Humanist I know who is sincerely curious about our beliefs. May I ask you a question about virtue, Brother?"

"You may, if you promise to think critically about my answer," replied Professor Agape.

"I don't understand why chastity is a virtue. Sex is just a means of reproduction. Why should it be a sin?"

"You look to reason to justify ethical principles. Perhaps education among you and your Humanist friends, flows both ways. I believe the virtue of chastity is misunderstood, even by most Theists. Chastity is not the avoidance of sex *per se*. It is *saving* sex for a mutually committed, loving relationship between people dedicated to reflecting God's energies."

Concurrently Xiny was with Professor Solider.

"My condolences on you great loss, Miss Stewart. How are you?"

"I'm a wreck," responded Xiny. "I would be totally lost without my brother, Barthon and my dear friends. Barthon visits me twice-a-day, and I have friends who would do anything for me."

"Your closest friends are not Royals. Do you think they can understand your grief?"

"I love them, and they love me. There is nothing else they need to understand."

"Humanists and Libertarians are tolerant of our ways, but Theites have a long history of being less so. Do you think you can trust Miss Agape to be so close to you?"

"I trust Antwanesta. I know she loves me unconditionally."

"I am glad you have strong social support. Please remember I am at your service too. Also if you feel depressed, Risky can prescribe drugs, though I know she regards exercise as the best medication."

"You called Dr. Sexapopis, "Risky," in front of me. It is odd to see you breach protocol, Professor Soldier."

Professor Soldier replied, "I know who Risky is to you."

Chapter 11

Trial of Zell

The courtroom on the thirteenth floor of the tower was filled to capacity. It seemed to be filled with judges because most people in the room were wearing black robes. A smaller number were in golden armor, including Victorani Keep seated behind the prosecution table. Azunia Smith was in a professional dark purple suit with a thigh-length skirt.

There was a jury box, but no jury. Over defense objection, this was to be a bench trial. Judge Illisima Smith would preside. In the absence of a jury, the jury box held a collection of witnesses. Gretchin, Tear, Barthon, and Xiny were there, as well as were several Royal soldiers, Professor Cook, Sal Keysmith, Wago Tailor, and a Royal physician.

Azunia Smith sat next to the defendant, Zell at a table. Feli sat behind a wooden railing behind Zell and her mother. Antwanesta sat next to Feli.

Promptly at 8:00 AM, Judge Smith entered the courtroom from a door behind the elevated judge's bench. All present stood. The Judge sat; and then the attorneys, witnesses and audience sat.

"Let's begin with some preliminary matters," said Judge Smith. "Ms. Smith, you and I share a surname, this may create the appearance of bias. Are we related?"

"Yes, your honor I am proud to call you my cousin," said Azunia Smith.

"To be more specific, I am your second cousin twice removed, am I not? asked Judge Smith."

"Yes, I believe that to be correct," replied Azunia Smith.

"Have we met before this case?"

"Only once, when my husband, Picius presented a paper here at the college."

"Lieutenant Keep, do you wish to move for my recusal based on my relationship with defense counsel?"

"I do not, Your Honor. Few in the Kingdom are as distantly related as the two of you," said the prosecutor, Lieutenant Keep.

"Very well. Are there any additional pretrial motions of which to dispose?"

"Your Honor, I wish to renew all of my prior motions for dismissal and in the alternative I again move for a jury trial," said Azunia Smith.

"All are again denied."

"I also wish to move for a continuance to allow a fair amount of time to prepare a defense. I have been on this case only three days. This is not fair to Zell. I can't give him a competent defense without more time to prepare."

"I have every confidence in your competence, Ms. Smith. Motion denied."

"I again move for change in venue to the Republic."

"Denied."

"I move for sequestration of witnesses."

"This is an educational institution, Ms. Smith. I believe the educational value of the witnesses being present exceeds the risk that their testimony will be corrupted by hearing each other. The motion is denied."

"Prosecutor, do you have any preliminary motions?

"I do not, Your Honor."

"Let us proceed to openings then, said the judge.

"Excuse me Your Honor, I do not see a scribe taking down the record of this case," interjected Azunia Smith.

"None is needed. I have a very good memory," responded the Judge.

"What about the record on appeal?"

"I am the Central District appellate court too."

"I wish to record my objection to the same judge serving at both the trial and appellate level."

"Your objection is so registered," Ms. Smith. "Proceed with your opening statement, Prosecutor."

Lieutenant Keep rose and spoke. "May it please the Court, the evidence I will present will demonstrate beyond a reasonable doubt that the accused defendant, Zell Fisher did on September 7, 984 A.Q., shoot a crossbow bolt into the window of room 327 of the freshman dorm here on the campus of the Central College of Epodlo, on Central District Isle, with the intention of assassinating the Monarch of the Southern Kingdom, Her Majesty Queen Yvalissa Regalis. Further the evidence will show that the same Mr. Fisher did on October 5, 984 A.Q. kidnap and brutally murder our beloved Queen by bludgeoning her to death at a location unknown, and depositing her body in the Southern Kingdom just west of

Queen's Port. The defendant's opposition to the monarchy has been stipulated. Keys and a crossbow bolt field tip, found in the possession of the defendant, connect him to the first attempt on the Queen's life. The defendant's boat and his blood-soaked clothing connect the him to the murder." The Prosecutor then sat in his chair.

"Ms. Smith," said the judge."

Azunia Smith stood and spoke, "May it please the Court, all of Epodlo grieves the loss of Queen Yvalissa Regalis. She was loved even by those averse to monarchy as a system of government. The defense will show that there is ample room for reasonable doubt in this case. The testimony, which the prosecution will present to you today, will be shown to be without credibility. Many of the witnesses see themselves as having a duty to do as they are told, regardless of truth, and indifferent to legal consequences associated with willfully concealing that truth. All the physical evidence presented today will be less consistent with Zell committing a crime, than with Zell having been framed by a person or persons unknown. It has been stipulated in this case that Zell was openly opposed to monarchy as a system of government, as are many in this room. It has also been stipulated that there is no evidence of personal animosity between Zell and the Queen. Further, it has been stipulated that Zell has engaged in direct political actions against the policies of a foreign government, namely the Western Theocracy, *not the Southern Kingdom*. However, it has also been stipulated that there is no evidence of Zell using violence in his political activism, even on the occasion when he himself was shot with a crossbow while engaged in protecting the life and liberty of a young women destine to become one of the Queen's best friend's. The evidence will *not* show that Zell killed the Queen. An honest appraisal of the evidence will reveal that the real murderer is at large, a *continuing* threat to the Kingdom, and to all people of Epodlo. I hope we can dispose of this distraction quickly so that resources may be reallocated to

153

finding the actual killer, and bringing the justice we *all* ardently desire." Azunia sat.

"You may call your first witness, Prosecutor," said Judge Smith to Lieutenant Keep.

"Thank you, Your Honor."

"I call Royal Physician, Colorianna Grocer.

Dr. Grocer took the witness stand. Judge Smith asked, "Do you affirm under penalty for perjury that the testimony you give in this matter will be the truth."

"I do."

Lieutenant Keep examined the witness on the state of the victim. Dr. Grocer testified that she had examined the body of the Queen, and that she died from a crushing trauma to the head consistent with a violent blow with a blunt instrument swung downward.

The witness was turned over to Azunia Smith for cross examination.

"Dr. Grocer, you have not brought with you any physical evidence that Yvalissa Regalis is dead, have you?"

"No."

"We have only your word that the alleged victim is even dead."

"I'm sure some soldiers could testify to that as well. I am just the most qualified to speak to the issue of death and its cause."

"You speak of *Royal* soldiers don't you?"

"Yes,"

"You too are a *Royal* are you not?"

154

"Yes."

"You take your duties as a Royal physician very
seriously don't you?

"Yes, I do."

"You take you duties as a Royal citizen very
seriously too don't you?"

"Yes."

"If your Queen told you to lie, you would wouldn't
you?"

"Objection! The question calls for conjecture,
assumes facts not in evidence, and exceeds the scope of the
direct examination," said Lieutenant Keep, now on his feet.

"Overruled. I will allow the question," said Judge
Smith looking at the witness.

"Yes, I would obey any order from my monarch, but
a dead monarch gives no orders."

"I have no further questions of this witness," said
Azunia Smith.

"I next call Tearesia Tripopis," said Lieutenant Keep.

Tear testified about seeing the man shooting the
crossbow at Lissy's window. She conceded that the attacker's
height and muscularity was consistent with that of Zell.
However, she said that she was sure it was not him. "I know
my own roommates. The attacker's hair was too blond and he
was shaped more like Barthon than Zell," Tear said.

"Blond hair? You said the attacker wore a hood,"
asked Lieutenant Keep.

"Not that hair, his pubic hair."

Lieutenant Keep then asked a series of questions which demonstrated that Tear was really too far to make out such fine details reliably.

Gretchin was next on the stand. She had run ahead of Tear, and gotten a closer view of the assailant. She had even seen the back of the attacker's head when he pulled off the hood. She confirmed the blondness. She also expressed confidence that the attacker was not Zell.

On cross-examination Azunia Smith asked how Gretchin could tell the attacker was not Zell. Gretchin began to describe the specifications of Zell's buttocks compared to those of the attacker.

Lieutenant Keep objected that, "Miss Quadrapopis is not qualified to render an opinion on the shape of men's buttocks."

Azunia Smith, responded, "I may well be able to qualify Miss Quadrapopis as an expert."

Lieutenant Keep said, "She's my witness. If Ms. Smith wants her as an expert on men's buttocks she should do it in her defense, not cross-examination."

The judge ruled, "I will take judicial notice of the fact that Miss Quadrapopis *is* an expert on the subject of the shape of men's buttocks, and weigh her opinion for what it is worth. Please move on Ms. Smith."

Gretchin smiled with pride.

Azunia had no more questions for Gretchin in cross.

Sal Keysmith testified about his missing keys, which were introduced into evidence. He also testified that he had not seen Zell in the bath on the day of the first assassination attempt.

Xiny testified about Lissy's order for her to stay in the dorm room.

Zell's seventeen-year-old cousin, Wago Tailor was called to identify the boat and the circumstances of its disappearance from his home in Merchant Town.

A soldier testified about the order he and his comrades had been given by the Queen to not follow her. Soldiers were also used to introduce physical evidence, the hood, the crossbow bolt, the missing field tip found in Zell's armoire with Salbird Keysmith's keys, and the bloodstained clothing in the Fisher family boat.

All the evidence was admitted, despite the defense objection that the keys and bolt head were obtained through a search which was in violation of internationally accepted conventions. "I didn't sign any conventions," said the judge, "and as you well know, the Republican Constitution means nothing here."

After the soldiers testified, Victorani Keep rested his case.

Most of the motions made in the case by Azunia Smith had been denied by Judge Smith. Her next motion was almost perfunctory. She still had her own witnesses to call for the defense, but as she had done in a hundred cases before, she had to make the motion which had always been fruitless. It would be malpractice not to make the motion, despite its futility. She moved that the case be dismissed for facial insufficiency of the evidence.

Judge Smith, responded with, "Motion granted. The defendant is not guilty." She slammed her gavel with finality.

There was shock. Both attorneys (Azunia and Victorani) were too stunned to speak for a second. Then Azunia turned and hugged Zell.

Zell was pleased with the outcome, but it was what he expected. He knew he did not kill Lissy or try to kill her. He also had confidence in Judge Smith and Ms. Smith too. He knew Illisima Smith was more than smart enough to see that he had been framed. Zell's naive confidence in the reason and compassion of his fellow humans did not lead him astray *on this occasion*.

Zell found the hug from his neighbor, Ms. Smith a little uncomfortable. In his childhood she had been his first crush. She had been the object of countless hours of his young fantasy life. Now here she was hugging him like he was something infinitely precious that she almost lost.

Feli leaped over the rail. She looked Zell in the eye, reading his mind. Zell blushed. As Azunia released Zell, Feli hugged him with equal enthusiasm.

Antwanesta did not leap over the railing to congratulate Zell. She did not want to get caught up in the hug-fest. She even stepped back away from Zell. She knew that Zell was a temptation for her, and she did not want her passion aroused.

Judge Smith's gavel came down and brought the courtroom again to silence. The judge then said, "Lieutenant Keep, I suggest that you have your men arrest the true murderer while it so easy to do so."

Lieutenant Keep had only just recovered from the blow of his sudden loss enough to shake the hand of opposing counsel. He looked around the courtroom and said, "Who?"

"What do you mean, Lieutenant, the logically obvious suspect of course."

Victorani was both embarrassed and offended that Judge Smith would humiliate him so. At least the rest of the people in the room seemed equally dumbfounded.

Maidens of Epodlo, Book 1 — Antwanesta Agape and the Mystery of the Red-dot Moon

"Come now," said Judge Smith, "This is a place of higher learning, a place where minds are developed and trained. Surely someone can explain who killed Queen Yvalissa."

As if the courtroom had become a lecture hall, two hands went up. One from Barthon, the other from Antwanesta.

Judge Smith said, "Hold Mr. Stewart. I want to hear what Miss Agape has to say."

Antwanesta stood, and with anxious confidence said, "If we assume the killer was the one who planted the keys and field tip in Zell's armoire drawer, it had to be a person with access to Zell's room after the lock was changed. The keys were held by Gregorious Regalis, Barthon Stewart, Tearesia Tripopis, and Jandarian Solider. Also Gretchin Quadrapopis often visited her sister Tearesia in the room. Gretchin and Tearesia both claim to have seen the shooter who made the attempt on Lissy's life. If that story is a fabrication, they would both have to be in on it. I don't know Tearesia well, but I know Gretchin loved Lissy, and could not kill her. They are both therefore excluded. Gregor has an obvious motive, becoming King, but he is too short to meet the description of the shooter given by both Gretchin and Tearesia. Mr. Solider has the characteristic blond hair of a Royal and the height and muscularity, but I have seen him on the running trail, and I can confirm that his buttocks do not meet the description given in such vivid detail by our resident expert. That leaves only Barthon, who could have induced Lissy to order Xiny and her guards to not follow, by asserting that Gregor impregnated a foreign woman. The mere existence of a Libertarian woman as a roommate makes such an allegation credible. The boat could have been stolen by Royal soldiers who were ordered to maintain secrecy."

The courtroom was silent, as all eyes fell on Barthon Stewart.

"Thank you Miss Agape," said Judge Smith, "What do you have to say for yourself, Mr. Stewart?"

Barthon replied, "Antwanesta is correct. I saw a chance to bring my family closer to the throne and I took…"

Barthon was hit in the nose by Gretchin's right fist. The left fist struck the same target before soldiers grabbed both Gretchin and Barthon. Blood flowed down Barthon's face from both nostrils.

The Judge spoke, "Miss Agape you are clever! I assign you to employ your considerable intellect to the formidable task of keeping this girl under control. Miss Quadrapopis is now your charge. If she commits another act of unsanctioned violence, the *two* of you will be transferring the Saint Isaac's College."

Gretchin shook free of the soldiers, but did not resume her assault on Barthon.

Judge Smith continued, "Remove this man from my island. I surrender him to his countrymen."

Antwanesta went to Gretchen to assume her new duty. Barthon was dragged away.

Xiny, in a state of shock, walked out the door to the railing of the thirteenth floor breezeway.

Without so much as a pause, she threw herself over the railing toward the floor of the tower atrium below.

Chapter 12

Xiny's Leap

Gretchin and Antwanesta had seen Xiny as she passed out the
door. They sprinted to her. As Xiny went over the railing,
Antwanesta and Gretchin each grabbed an ankle. Either of
them alone would have been pulled over, but the power of
both together kept Xiny from falling to the floor twelve stories
below. The drape of Xiny's black student robe inverted and
hung from her chest covering her head and arms. The skirt of
her white tunic splayed open like a flower reveling the golden
scabbard and dagger chained to her thigh.

Gretchin and Antwanesta did not have the strength to
lift Xiny. and they could not hold her for long. However, help
was on the way. Risky and Feli were racing down the stairs to
reach Xiny from the twelfth floor breezeway below. This race
was easily won by Risky, who took each flight of stairs in two
bounds, and then sprinted to Xiny. Risky kicked off her shoes
and leaped barefooted onto the twelfth floor breezeway
railing. She wrapped her arms around Xiny's abdomen. Risky
leaned back away from the perilous drop, and yelled, "I have
her!" Gretchin and Antwanesta released their dear friend to
Risky and the power of Antwanesta's most ardent prayers.
Risky fell back on the floor of the breezeway with Xiny,
bending her head forward to avoid impacting her skull on the
floor. Risky used her own body to cushion Xiny against
injury.

161

Feli ran up and removed Xiny's scabbard and dagger. She tossed them to Gretchin who was now approaching. Gretchen caught them with one hand without breaking stride. Feli then pulled the student robe down from Xiny's face. Feli looked Xiny in the eye, nose-to-nose, and said, "You are going to be ok, Xiny. We love you." Feli and Antwanesta pulled Xiny off Risky, holding her in case she tried another leap. Gretchin gave Risky a hand up.

Risky said, "We are going for a walk, Honey." Xiny began to cry as Risky took one arm and Feli took the other. Antwanesta and Gretchin followed closely behind as they headed down the stairs. Gretchin stopped at her locker on the way down, and deposited Xiny's dagger and scabbard there. Gretchin then ran to catch up to her friends. They walked across campus to the infirmary assuring Xiny that she would be ok.

"Take this. It will help you relax." Risky gave Xiny a pill and some water. "Do you want to stay here or go to your room? I will stay with you either place."

"The room," Xiny replied.

The four walked her to the dorm room before the tranquilizer took effect. Xiny fell asleep in Feli's arms. Feli got up from the bed gingerly.

Risky whispered to Feli, "I'm not going to let Xiny out of my sight tonight. Will you cover the infirmary tonight and tomorrow, so I can stay with her?"

Feli, more readily than Risky anticipated, said, "Yes, I will serve Xiny in any way I can. Just explain to her why I am not with her at the funeral. I don't want her to think I abandoned her."

"Of course," Risky replied. "My apartment is yours while I'm gone." Risky turned to Gretchin and Antwanesta.

162

"You three girls go get lunch, and bring something for Xiny
and me."

Barthon was taken quickly to a waiting sail boat, by
Lieutenant Keep and six soldiers. The boat did not stop at
Queen's Port. It went, with a favorable current and wind,
down to the mouth of the Southeast River, to the port town of
East Tower. King Gregorious had ordered the whole
population of the Kingdom to Queen's Port. East Tower was
deserted. The soldiers left Barthon in a dusty cell with just
food and water. He would have to endure his shame alone,
while Keep and his soldiers tacked back up river to the funeral
as commanded.

Risky lay on Antwanesta's bed across from Xiny, who now
was asleep under the influence of the sedative Risky had given
her. Risky looked over at Xiny. As the school physician, the
psychiatric health of the students was her responsibility. She
had also spoken with Xiny's father, when he was at the school,
and solemnly promised that she would protect his daughter.
However, Risky also had a special relationship with Xiny
which they both maintained in secrecy. Risky had known Xiny
for many years, and entrusted her with her very heart. Xiny
was the very lifeline which connected Risky with romantic
love.

That night Feli was alone in Risky's bed. She wondered how
many men had fantasized about being in her present location.
Of course they did not fantasize about being in Risky's bed
alone, but at least some would not be too disappointed to find
Feli there instead. Feli did not spend much time thinking about
other people's sexual fantasies. Her thoughts quickly shifted
back to Xiny. Xiny had become one of Feli's core friends. Feli
had already lost Lissy. To lose Xiny too would hit Feli hard.
However, it was not her own psychological health Feli was
concerned about now. She wanted Xiny to recovery from her

163

shock and depression, and to learn that there really can be life after the loss of a great love.

The irony struck Feli. Xiny now faced the dreaded circumstance which Feli took such pains to avoid. Xiny's emotions were invested too heavily in one person, the loss of whom was devastating. Feli expected Xiny to recover, and yet her own fear of such prospective grief lead Feli to avoid romantic love. She wanted close friendships. She wanted sex. However, she wanted to draw these two volatile chemicals from separate flasks, and keep them separated at all costs.

Feli was ruled by fears. She didn't fear crowds, heights, social rejection, being alone in this big building at night, or the prospect of dealing with serious injuries and medical conditions without Risky's professional expertise to guide her. She feared being out of control. She wanted to control her financial security, and she wanted to control her emotional destiny. She managed her social life to avoid passion and excessive attachment. She did not want to fall in love or be bound by commitment. Feli wanted to be independent, both financially and emotionally. The biggest impediment that Feli faced trying to meet this goal however, was Feli, herself. She cared too much for Xiny, for Gretchin, and Antwanesta too. Even Zell was a risk for her, albeit a well-managed one.

Feli savored this time of solitude. She loved her friends, but to be alone like this was precious. She breathed. She relaxed. She slept.

Back at the freshman dorm Xiny awoke and asked Antwanesta to lie next to her. Antwanesta complied. Xiny chose Antwanesta, because her affection seemed less secure. Xiny knew Gretchin would do anything for her, without question. She had similar confidence in Risky. Antwanesta was another story. This was a girl who put her devotion to an unseen supernatural being above her flesh-and-blood friends. Xiny knew Antwanesta would not submit to her will like Gretchin,

Risky, or Feli. That is why Xiny wanted to hold *her*. She did
not want Antwanesta to slip away. This sweet red-haired
young woman, naive, yet wise, had stumbled into Xiny's
heart, a very spacious place, having been so recently vacated.

Gretchin felt a little hurt that Xiny chose Antwanesta
to lie with her, but she got over it in three seconds, as she
stretched her body across the full expanse of her bunk. Xiny
took up less space the *bunny-brained quilt* of a girl who piled
on top of her in Newton, but for Gretchin a bed to herself was
second only to a bed with a *man* in it, maybe two, ok three.
That was the theory. Gretchin had never actually had a man.
She had never had sex with anyone, but herself. She wanted
sex of course. Oh, did she want it. However, lusting in one's
heart just isn't the same, regardless of Theist conceptions to
the contrary.

Even sex didn't interest Gretchin now. One dear
friend was dead, and another was crushed by grief. Gretchin's
thoughts turned to tomorrow's funeral. Gretchin did not like
the idea of funerals. In Libertaria people were just buried
summarily, without ceremony. Death was the ultimate loss of
freedom. No one liked death, and yet no one could avoid it.
Why dwell on such a thing? Life is for living, not for dying.
Gretchin and all the King's deer and all the King's men could
not bring Lissy back. It was time to get over it, and move on
with life.

Antwanesta did not mind lying with Xiny. This was
love in action, comforting her friend. If Xiny were a man,
Antwanesta might see the situation differently. If she were
lying naked in a bed this close to a man, her thoughts would
turn in an unchaste direction. With Xiny she was safe. Lying
with Xiny was like lying with herself. Even their bodily
proportions were the same. In the dark, blond hair and red hair
are the same, and tanned or white, the skin of both was in just
shades of grey. Antwanesta would comfort Xiny, and Xiny

would fall asleep. Antwanesta was God's instrument comforting a traumatized girl in a time she needed it most.

Risky slept on Antwanesta's vacated bed, under Gretchin's, instead of the bunk above Xiny's which used to be Lissy's, and was used by Feli in recent sleepovers. Risky chose the lower bunk, just in case Xiny made a break for the door for another suicide attempt.

Risky grew up in Libertaria like her sister, Gretchin. However, she saw the pending funeral from a different perspective. She saw Xiny's presence at the funeral as a step for Xiny to take, in the process of healing her psychic trauma. Xiny must accept that Lissy is gone. Once that was done, Xiny could open her heart again, to accept and give love. Risky knew emotional trauma, not like this, but almost. Her loss was not so great, or was it? Risky would leave that question to philosophers and romantic poets to ponder. She had moved on. What's gone is gone. One must make do.

Risky now wanted to be reunited with her lover. Life could be so hard; so complicated; with so many rules, customs, and beliefs in the way. At least the funeral would be a chance for Risky to be with her lover. They could not be intimate. They could not even let on that they were a couple, but they would be in the same place at the same time. They had to hide their feelings until they could again truly be together.

In the morning Risky and her three girls dressed in Royal white tunics. Risky had her own. Xiny gave Gretchin one of Lissy's tunics. It was short on Gretchin, but just a little, not like Feli in her most shrunken blue dress. Gretchin looked good in Royal garb. Wearing identical clothing, the similarity between Gretchin and Risky was more pronounced. Gretchin was thinner and flatter. Risky had more bleaching of her otherwise dark brown hair. Xiny knew that Gretchin and Risky were sisters, but being a Royal, she did not give away their secret sisterhood. She had not been told to keep the

information quiet, but she could think of several reasons why
Gretchin and Risky might want to keep it so. They also
dawned their black robes for breakfast and the walk to and
through the arboretum. They took two rucksacks for the four
of them the to have a place to put their robes once they
boarded the boat.

Feli said her good-byes to her parents. Azunia and
Picius sailed north, with plans to shop in Merchant Town
before later heading down river, home to Newton. They would
be in the boat, on the lake under the open sky, together, *just
the two of them*. They could anchor between Central District
Isle and Merchant town, and enjoy some romantic moments.
Though long-married, they each had a deep, enduring passion
for the other. Their passion stood in ironic contrast to their
daughter's fear of emotional intimacy. Perhaps it was the
obvious power of the passion shared by her parents which
intimidated Feli into being so canny. To lose one's will to
another person is indeed a frightening prospect.

At breakfast Risky was proud of her little
vegetarians, eating oats with sliced fruit. Feli was still at the
infirmary, but she would leave briefly to see them off at the
dock.

Antwanesta had forgotten something. It was
something important. She forgot that today was Sunday, the
Sabbath day, the day she had always gone to the liturgy at a
church or chapel. Antwanesta was so preoccupied with Xiny,
she had even forgotten God. As she passed through the
arboretum she saw the Theist Chapel. She asked her
companions to take the route in front of the chapel. She could
at least bow and make the sign of the hexagon at the door.

She was about to bow when she saw it, something
strange, something she had not seen before, at least not on the
door of a church or chapel. Such things were for stores. It was
common practice throughout Epodlo for stores or restaurants
to display a red circle on the door, to indicate that the

167

establishment was closed, that business had stopped for the day. It was especially easy to find a red circle on a door in the Theocracy on Sunday. All businesses closed in the Theocracy on the Sabbath, to allow time for concentrated prayer and scriptural study. The church never had a red circle. Churches never closed. Even if services were not being held the church was always open for people to enter for prayer.

There was a note below the red circle. It read:

Today's liturgy will be held in Freedom Park, under the sun to comply with the papal directive for retreat to nature to pray for mercy.

Antwanesta was shocked. She had never heard of such an event.

Unknown to Antwanesta, the red circle was not just here. It was on every church door in the Theocracy. It was even on the missionary churches in Libertaria and the Northern Republic. The door of the missionary church in Royal Beach had no circle, only because the whole city had been emptied by order of King Gregorious. All Royals were assembling at a field near Queen's Port, for the Queen's funeral, except Barthon Stewart of course.

"We have to go Miss Agape. We are on the last boat." It was Risky's voice. Antwanesta hastily made the sign of the hexagon, and followed Risky and her friends to the dock.

As Risky, Xiny, Gretchin, and Antwanesta were about to board, Zell trotted up, as did Feli. Feli said her goodbyes hugging and kissing both Xiny and Zell. Feli did not hug Risky because of the rule against physical fraternization between faculty and staff. She did not hug Antwanesta, because Antwanesta saw hugging and kissing as leading to prurient desires. She did not hug Gretchin because she did not want a punch in the nose.

Antwanesta wanted to make small talk with Zell. She did not know why. It just seemed like the polite thing to do. She asked if he got his boat back. Zell replied in the affirmative, and that his cousin, Wago had rowed it back to Merchant Town.

Then Antwanesta asked, "What was that you said about rowboats and Republicans?"

"When?"

"When we were on your boat coming to the college."

"I don't remember. It must have been the old joke?"

"What old joke?"

Before Zell could answer both were distracted by the arrival of the last passenger on the sailing vessel. Dean Smith had boarded.

The dean removed her robe and handed it to Risky. Risky turned to Gretchin, who turned her back to let Risky put the dean's robe in her rucksack. Gretchin registered no reaction, as if the dean often stored things in her rucksack. Antwanesta noticed this. Perhaps it was just the *whatever* attitude common in Libertarian culture. All the black robes were now in rucksacks. All of the passengers and crew of the boat wore white Royal tunics, except for one. Dean/Governor Smith did not wear one. She wore a smart dark purple suit, very similar to the one worn by Azunia Smith at the Zell's trial just the day before.

The dean approached Xiny. "You have my condolences," Dean Smith said stoically.

"Thank you," replied Xiny is a similarly emotionless tone.

"I have been approached by the Royal Department of Archives to arrange for a student to review and edit Lissy's

169

documentary legacy. I can think of no student better suited to the task than you. You could do it in the slot where you now have History, as a special project. Please tell me you will accept."

"Ok," said Xiny, a little surprised.

"Very good. I will inform Professor Solider. Come to my office instead of her class for the rest of the year."

"Your office?"

"Yes, we need a secure place for you to review the documents. We can't have anything getting lost, and then later being mischaracterized by persons seeking to discredit Lissy."

"That makes since, I guess."

"I'll see you there then," Dean Smith replied with a smile and a wink. Excuse me, I must speak to the captain."

Dean Smith walked to the stern of the boat.

Xiny was pleased to have a new purpose, a new role, a new *duty*.

As the boat approached Queen's Port, a makeshift shrine could be seen on the shore. It was a wooden scaffolding with white cotton and paper ribbons attached to it. There were also a few white stuffed teddy bunnies, the evolutionary descendent of the extinct teddy bear. In prior millennia such a shrine would be covered in flowers. However, every culture in Epodlo would consider the use of the severed sex organs of another species, for such a purpose, as being in very bad taste if not perverse.

Queen's Port was a tiny trading village. Beyond, to the southwest, was a vast crowd of Royals, in their white tunics, assembled in a large grassy field. The tradition of wearing black at funerals was lost to history. Within the sea of white there were sparkles of gold, the soldiers standing with their families. Amid the crowd were small white buildings thirty balls tall and twice as wide. These were portable toilets. God bless the Royal Plumbers. Along the edges of the crowd were black boxes, ten balls tall and five balls wide, tethered together with what appeared to be long black ropes, which ran along the ground between the boxes. Each black box was elevated on a base of crisscrossed metal supports twelve balls high. People who had in the past attended large gatherings would recognize the black boxes as some of the many minor miracles Royal Plumbers could perform. To the east of the crowd stood a temporary stage, curtained in black with its back portion shrouded from view.

Passengers and crew disembarked and walked to the crowd. There were ten rows of folding wooden chairs at the front of the sea of white. Some chairs on the second row had paper signs reading:

Governor, Illisima Smith; Doctor Betriski Sexapopis; Handmaiden, Princess Xinonina Stewart; Handmaiden's Friend 1; Handmaiden's Friend 2; Handmaiden's Friend 3; Handmaiden's Friend 4. Xiny told Zell that "Handmaiden's Friend 4" was for Feli, but that she would be honored to have him sit there as her proxy.

On the stage there was a podium, and a row of chairs. At the center of the front of the stage sat a wooden box, draped with a white Royal flag. The box was unmistakably a casket. The casket was closed concealing the fact that it was empty.

Chapter 13

Earthquake and Tsunami

King Gregorious was sitting in the curtained area behind the stage reviewing the script for his speech.

"Pardon, Your Majesty. Soldiers have arrived with important news from the Central District. For your ears, Sire."

"Send them in."

The aide let the soldiers in, and then left the room.

The soldiers bowed.

"Report."

Your Majesty, please forgive the intrusion. Lieutenant Keep sent us. "Zell Fisher was found not guilty, and Baron Barthon Stewart admitted to the Queen's murder."

Gregor looked as though he had been punched in the gut. "Admitted? Where is he now?"

"Lieutenant Keep took him to East Tower for your disposition."

"Thank you, Sergeant. Join the crowd and pay your respects. Tell no one of this."

"Yes, Sire. Both soldiers bowed, and departed."

To the southeast, in the dungeon at East Tower, there were sounds of footsteps in the darkness.

"How are we on time?" Barthon's voice was oddly calm for a man recently arrested for commission of a heinous crime, and locked alone in a dark cell.

"Just a few minutes behind," said Barthon's coconspirator. "Hold the lamp while I figure out which key works. One of them better work, or *your* funeral will be next."

"Sal won't let me down. His set of keys will open anything."

"You and I both expect a lot from our friends."

Click, went the lock.

"I owe old Salbird a kiss," said Barthon.

"If that was sarcastic, it was unkind of you to say."

"It was not sarcastic. I am truly grateful that Sal has a fetish for keys."

"You would be surprised what the Northerners call sarcastic."

"I had Zell Fisher for a roommate. I know my sarcasm, level one and level two. He gave me lessons. You should hear him and Feli go at it. It's like they have another language."

"I've heard them."

Barthon and his savior went up the steps through some deserted hallways to a room in the basement below the old guard tower. They went up another flight of steps, and through an exterior door. They ran down an embankment to a small boat near the mouth of the river.

"We need to cross quickly. Illi won't stop the clock for us."

"Maybe we should seek high ground, on this side," said Barthon.

"We can't be seen here. We need to get lost in Libertaria."

"It beats a wet cell."

"The wind is with us. We can land anywhere, but we have to get away from the water fast."

Back on Central District Isle, Feli met her first patient. Tear came to the infirmary complaining of nausea. Feli asked if she had other symptoms. Tear told Feli that her period was late. Feli asked if Tear could be pregnant.

Tear said, "Yes."

"Dr. Sexapopis can give you a pregnancy test after she returns form Queen's Port. For now, I can give you tablets for the nausea," said Feli.

Tear accepted the tablets and said, "Zell says you and he are like brother and sister, is that how you see him?"

"Not at all. I see me and him as sister and brother, but he and I are like brother and sister. At one time we toyed with more. We even taught each other how to kiss, but we are too good as friends to mess ourselves up with the physical stuff."

"How would you feel about him and me being together?"

"If you are as sweet as your sister, Gretchin. I'm all for it."

"You think Retch is sweet?"

"Of course she is. She acts tough, but she would do anything for the people she loves. A woman like her could be just perfect for Zell."

"Why don't you try to fix them up?"

"Sweetheart would be perfect for Zell, but your sister
needs something else. Zell respects women as equals, and he
expects equality from them. Giving all of himself for a
fraction of a woman won't work for Zell. He is not stable
material."

"Men can be tamed," replied Tear.

"But women never can be," retorted Feli.

"You disapprove of our way of collecting men?"

"To the contrary, I admire it. I plan to start a
collection of my own."

An empty casket is no surprise at a Royal funeral. Embalming
is not practiced in any quarter of Epodlo. Bodies must be
interred quickly to avoid odor and the other indignities of
morbidity. Adults in the Kingdom know caskets are empty.
Young children may be allowed the illusion that the body of a
loved one is contained in a wooden box. Funerals are more
memorial services. There is generally a eulogy given by a
respected friend. Friends and relatives express emotional
support for the grieving. People say their silent farewells, and
life is adjusted in accordance with long-held traditions. The
tradition of having caskets must date back to a time when the
dead were actually buried in such things. No one alive could
imagine why anyone would want to slow the decomposition of
a corpse by encasing it.

For Theites death is a different matter. In the
Theocracy, death is but a transitional process. The faithful fall
asleep in God's grace. They awaken in the glory of God's
imminence. They are judged by God, and pardoned of their
sins, if in life, they accepted God's grace. The Kingdom of
Heaven is to be theirs as kings and queens in the eternal
service of God. There is a memorial service on the sixth day

after death and another abbreviated remembrance ritual on the thirty-sixth day.

For Humanists in the Republic there was yet another tradition. Northerners favor cremation over burial, not because of any Humanistic ideology, but because the cold frozen ground of the North often makes burial impractical. For Humanists there is no afterlife. Death is the end for an individual organism. A species and its culture may continue, but the dead are done. Dust is destiny. This fact is not good or bad; it is simply empirical reality. The reality of death does have utility however. Death reminds the Humanist that there is a very real and unavoidable limit on the opportunity for action. What a person accomplishes is done in this life, not in some future life to come. The Humanist cannot wait, cannot settle for complacency, cannot repent and expect a reward. Life's brevity makes it both sweeter and more urgent. The loss of life, especially an unaccomplished one, is a source of grief. A Humanist funeral normally incorporates a eulogy in which the service of the decedent to humankind is emphasized.

In Libertaria the dead are simply buried. There is no eulogy and no monument, other than the famous one in Battle Tree. The living are free; the dead are not. A tree is often planted over the body to liberate the molecules, giving them life in a new form.

As Risky sat between Dean Smith and Xiny, her thoughts were not of death. She hoped that this funeral would allow Xiny to process her grief and return to happiness. Xiny could again find happiness, if she could just let go of the past. The past was a place Risky shunned. There was pain in her past. She had known grief. Her mind was now in the future, a future with her lover. They were together in this place, but they could not be open about their love. They had to conceal how they felt. Risky longed for the day she could share her love openly, a time when traditions, conventions, and erroneous beliefs could be disregarded. She believed that time

would come. Deep within her heart, she believed that she
would be one with her lover.

Xiny felt numb. Sitting between Risky and Gretchin,
she also felt safe, and she felt loved. However, her feelings
were somehow distant, as if not a part of herself. The pain, the
fear, and the sorrow, had all been so great; she had to turn off
her feelings. Lissy was gone. She accepted that cruel fact. She
had wanted to die herself, to somehow trade her life for
Lissy's; but the universe would not accept that deal. One does
not negotiate with the laws of nature, the will of God, or
whatever. There would be other people in her life. There were
already. Risky, Antwanesta, and Gretchin had all offered their
lives to save her. Feli would have done the same, if she had
been faster. She had four dear friends who loved her, and she
vowed to herself that she would never take her own life, so
long as any of these four lived. She owed them everything.
She owed them each a duty to live and to be happy. As a
Royal, duty was her essence. Until Lissy's death she was
bound by duty and love to her. Now these four friends held her
allegiance, and she would serve them in any way possible. Her
love, without question, belonged to them.

Gretchin did not like funerals. She was here for one
purpose, to support her dear friend. She truly loved Xiny. She
wanted to take her pain away, but all she knew to do was to sit
next to her, and hope that Xiny would understand how loved
she was. Gretchin hardly noticed that Zell was two chairs to
her left. All amorous aspirations were on hold.

Antwanesta, was in a state of silent prayer. To her
Lissy was alive. Her soul was eternal. She could reside forever
in God's memory, or be excluded from God's presence. Lissy
had been the sweetest, kindest, and most generous person she
had ever met. However, Antwanesta had been taught that *all
fall short of the glory of God,* and that salvation can only come
through *Him.* Antwanesta knew that Lissy did not accept God.
Antwanesta began to weep. She wanted to be strong for Xiny,

177

but she felt she had failed her dear friend. Antwanesta thought, that if only she had been a better witness for God, she could have saved Lissy, perhaps not her corporeal life, but her eternal one. The more she thought of her own failure, the more sorrow she felt.

Gretchin held Antwanesta's hand, and then took Xiny's too.

"Greetings!" The voice was amplified and coming from all sides. Speakers energized with medipower were not unknown. They were used by monarchs, pontiffs, and on the floor of the General Assembly of Thirteen. God bless those Royal plumbers and their black boxes. "I am Alfide Stewart, Chief Councilor to the Monarch. I bid you welcome, countrymen and friends." Alfide was now also *Prince*, given that he was now the Monarch's second, but it would be a breach of etiquette to refer to himself as such, especially in these circumstances. "This is a grievous occasion. Speaking to you now is a heavy burden. That burden is lightened however, by knowledge that our sweet Queen has been succeeded by a new monarch in whom I have seen wisdom, courage, and benevolence befitting his status. I present to you, his Royal Highness, the Majestic King Gregorious Regalis!"

All stood and applauded as Gregor replaced Alfide at the podium behind the flagged casket. As the applause died down the King spoke.

"Thank you, kind people of the Southern Kingdom. Thank you, friends. The burdens are lightest when borne by the most. We of the Royal Kingdom know how to work together in unity, with curtesy, duty, and discretion, to achieve great things, and to endure even great sorrow. You have lost a queen, I have lost a cousin and the dearest of friends. Lissy was a model of virtue, who guided us to be better, kinder, and more loving than we realized we could be. We have lost her in life, but she lives on. She lives in our memories and our hearts. She will continue to be a model and an inspiration to all

people of goodwill. We stand here in the town of Queen's
Port. It has long been a tradition for this place to change its
name from Queen's Port to King's Port, and back as monarchs
rise and pass. By my authority, this tradition will end. We now
stand in a place which shall now and forever be Queen's
Port!"

Applause roared from the crowd.

"We are a people of tradition. However, as I have just
demonstrated, traditions can change. As your monarch I will
be demanding many changes in the months and years to come.
Some will resist change. Some may even believe I dishonor
Lissy's memory by changing polices she allowed to stand.
What I will do I will do for the good of the Kingdom. It has
long been a habit of public servants to say that it is an honor
and a privilege to serve. I will not say this. Being your
monarch is no honor. It is *not* a privilege. This office does not
have my gratification as its purpose. I am here because I
accept my duty to serve my Kingdom. This duty calls me. It
defines me. The duty mandates that I do hard and painful
things. I say goodbye to Lissy, because I must. I thank you all
for your commitment to this duty."

The King stepped away from the microphone to more
roaring applause. Alfide again stepped up to speak.

"Next we will hear the gracious words of a dear
friend and trusted advisor to our late Queen, his Eminence,
Bishop Korack"

Polite applause followed.

"Thank you, Chief Councilor Stewart. As I look out
and see the white and gold before me I am reminded that you,
the people of the Royal Kingdom are very blessed, as am I.
One of the greatest blessings we have enjoyed is knowing
Lissy Regalis. I mean no disrespect in calling your Queen by
her nickname. That is what she asked me to call her. She was

modest in that way. Lissy was the exemplification of many virtues. I remembered when I accompanied Lissy on her first trip to the Western Theocracy. After a long meeting, the Pontiff confided in me that he thought Lissy was a better Theist than most people who were baptized as such. By saying this it was clear that he saw what we all saw. Lissy was special. The energies of God flowed through Lissy and blessed us all. Thanks in no small part to your lovely Queen, the people of the Theocracy have a courteous and peaceful neighbor. The people in the Republic have a gracious and forgiving creditor. The people of Libertaria have enjoyed peace for two centuries. All people of Epodlo have been blessed by the benevolent policies of the Kingdom, as perpetuated by your beloved Queen. When a great blessing is lost to us, especially when it occurs suddenly, it is natural to ask why God would will such a thing, or even allow it. God did not will Lissy's death, but God's will shall be accomplished despite this great tragic loss. God will even find a way to turn this tragedy to serve His good purpose. We may not see this purpose, or comprehend the complex chains of causation which bring the purpose to its fulfilment, but God's will shall be done."

At that moment a violent shift in ground, tossed Bishop Korack hard to his left. All the chairs and people shifted south and fell. Risky fell on Dean Smith. Gretchin fell on Xiny. Zell fell on Antwanesta. Before they could stand, water flooded out from the lake, onto the field, while inundating the town of Queen's Port.

Parents grabbed their children. Soaked people stood The Earth shook no more, but there was a thunderous sound which rumbled from all directions.

Antwanesta prayed for God's mercy, and then turned to look into Zell's eyes.

Maidens of Epodlo, Book 1 — Antwanesta Agape and the Mystery of the Red-dot Moon

Azunia and Picius had been enjoying each other on the deck of the sail boat when the Earth moved. As they reached the peak of their mutual orgasmic pleasure, they began to feel the boat move down as if sinking. The boat was floating on the surface of the lake, but the water level was falling rapidly. Azunia and Picius tried to stand on the slippery deck of the sail boat. The keel bottomed and the boat listed hard port. The naked Azunia and Picius were thrown into the now shallow water.

On Central District Isle the sudden seismic shift was also felt. Feli was toppled off of the chair in Risky's office. She got off the floor and looked out the window in time to see water flooding the campus from the north. It was four balls high at the shore but quickly dissipated across the campus lawn. The first floor of both the sophomore and junior dorms flooded. Water barely reached the tower. Just a little water seeped into the north corner of the auditorium. The gym and infirmary building stayed dry, but the jolt caused Hardy Weaver to drop the barbell he was bench pressing. Thanks to Histina Bowright, who was spotting for him, the weight did not impact Hardy's chest with its full force. Hardy did have two cracked ribs and became Feli's second patient.

The sea water moved with greater ferocity than the water in the lake. North Point was first to flood. Every house was under freezing water in seconds. Buildings collapsed in Democratica City and Newton. The houses along the beach in Newton and North Tower were swept away.

Lord's Landing and Merchant Town were not, at first, subjected to flooding from the rising lake water. The northern part of the lake was sinking, at first. However, the Northwest River and Northeast River ran backwards. As seawater rushed into the lake from the rivers, Azunia scrambled back onto the sail boat. She then pulled Picius aboard. The two scurried into the boat's cabin as the vessel was buffeted by the churning lake water.

"Feli!" said Azunia.

"She will be ok," said Picius. "She is on the second floor in the infirmary. The water won't get that high."

The water was deeper, but less rapid as it flooded God City on the west coast and East Bend on the east.

As sea water rushed into the lake the water level rose again, and this time it totally washed over the campus on central District Isle, but only at a shallow depth. The Tower building atrium was flooded, as were the dining halls, the administrative wing, and the auditorium.

In Merchant Town the Fisher family boat might have been set adrift had not Zell's cousin, Duggy been handy to drag it further on shore and tie it to a tree, before the now brackish water rose above the lake bank.

Chapter 14

Xiny's Secret

As Zell lay on top of the soaked Antwanesta, he said, "Don't
worry I won't let you drown."

Antwanesta replied, "I know I won't drown. Lissy
taught me how to swim."

Chief Councilor, Alfide Stewart made his way to the
microphone, with the poise of an actor in a well-rehearsed
role. The speakers still worked because they were elevated
above the risen water. "Stay calm. Move in an orderly but
rapid manner to the south, away from the lake. Give priority to
children and their caregivers." While Alfide spoke he
motioned cryptically to Xiny with his arm.

Xiny nodded and ran to the stage. Gretchin and Risky
followed her.

Alfide stepped away from the microphone and spoke
to Xiny. "You are in charge of the evacuation of foreigners.
Your contingency pack is backstage. Grab the pack, and get to
the south before the second lake surge. After the surges
slacken, set up the evacuation staging area over there." He
pointed toward the lakeshore.

"Yes, Father," replied Xiny. She turned to Risky and
Gretchin. "I'll take you south. Then I'll get you back to the
college."

Risky and Gretchin looked at each other. Gretchin
said, "*She* will get *us* back?" They followed Xiny to the south.

Thomas David Valentine

They and the rest of crowd moved south of the field in an orderly and rapid manner as instructed.

South Tower, Free Beach, West Tower, East Tower, and West Port were flooded next, However, since the southbound wave had to wrap around the east and west bends in the Epodlo shoreline much of the waves energy was lost.

Barthon and his companion were already ashore in Libertaria. They had run into the woods avoiding notice. There they removed their tunics and buried them. Their blond hair still made them look very Royal. Royals hiking on Libertarian trails were uncommon, but not so rare as to attract attention, especially with earthquakes and floods.

The water at Royal Beach rose and flooded over Beach Trail, but then rapidly receded. No one was in Royal Beach to see it. A great swell of ocean rolled south growing ever higher. The mighty wave then became the horizon.

The ocean-fed surge of water entering Unity Lake from the rivers reached Queens Port. It took down the stage and the speakers, and moved the portable toilets forty balls south. The crowd had already moved to higher ground south of the field. The casualty count at Queen's Port was zero.

On Central District Isle, the glass paneled roofs of the baths withstood the shock of the quake. They had been engineered to do so. The first surge of lake water had not been heavy enough to break them. The second surge, fed by the sea water rushing up the Northwest and Northeast Rivers, was too much for the junior bath roof. It broke and crashed on the bathers below. The wounded were brought to the infirmary. Five students had wounds that were bad enough to worry about loss of blood. Feli stopped the bleeding of all five with the help of Histina, who had put on a white coat to become Feli's assistant, after having helped Hardy up the stairs.

Hardy helped as he could by cheering his fellow
patients with his indomitable optimism. "It's your lucky day
he said to a bloody junior man. We have the most beautiful
medics in all of Epodlo. I hear they can sow well too. They
will fix you right up."

Harolod Agape did not appreciate Hardy's comment
to the extent that another patient might. Harolod prayerfully
thanked God of his deliverance. He had faith that whatever
angels God saw fit to send him would be adequate the task of
caring for him. He was calm, but hoped that the blood would
be sponged off of him before Jillissa found him.

The ground shook no more. The water receded. The
rivers flowed in their proper directions. The water kept
receding. The island of Epodlo was larger than it had ever
been as water continued to rush south. There was an eerie
calm as people checked on neighbors. The Theists who had, at
the Pontiff's direction, gathered in fields far from shore and
buildings, praised God in great earnest, giving thanks for their
deliverance from harm. Rescue efforts began in Democratica
City and Newton, where several structures had collapsed.

Luckily the building that housed the medical
convention in Democratica City did not collapse. The venue
had been changed just one week before, from its usual location
at the Hypocrites Medical College. The usual building, which
had housed the convention for decades before, was now
rubble. It was an apparent miracle that the urgently needed
physicians were in Democratica City for the convention, but
were all uninjured. The Humanists dismissed the improbable
event as a coincidence, but were thankful all the same.

About half an hour after the calm had begun, there
was a thunderous roar greater than any which had yet been
heard. A massive tsunami 450 balls high rolled across Royal
Beach, lifting even native granite blocks. Every building in
Royal Beach was utterly destroyed. Every palm and bush was
uprooted and shreaded. What was left was scattered rubble,

eighty percent buried by sand. Royal Beach was now nothing but sand with rectangular blocks, and torn bits of palms and shrubs scattered about.

Now water rushed up the Southeast and Southwest Rivers. The southeastern towns of East Tower and Free Beach were deeply flooded and largely destroyed. The southwestern towns of West Port, West Tower and South Tower met the same fate. The dungeon, which had held Barthon two hours before, was now submerged in water and sand. Smithtown was badly flooded. The water rose in Queen's Port and the other lake towns. Central District Isle was inundated from the south this time. The chapels both flooded and the arboretum dock was washed away. It was now Merchant Town's turn again. The water rose and fell ruining the inventory of almost every business in town.

God City was also flooded, but the worst damage there was from the quake. A full third of the buildings had collapsed. Casualties were low thanks to the holy retreat to the countryside. God had indeed answered the Theites prayers for mercy. At least so it appeared.

As the lake calmed, Xiny lead the foreigners to her staging area. She opened the backpack which she had claimed from behind the stage. The stage was now wrecked south of its original position. From the backpack Xiny withdrew two telescoping metal poles. She extended them and mounted a banner on them. The banner was made of cotton with well-cut contrasting cotton letters sown in place. The letters spelled words which read, "Foreigner Evacuation Here."

Antwanesta was puzzled. She said to Xiny, "How could you Royals be ready for such a thing?"

"I planned it," said Xiny"

"You Planned it?" The words came from Antwanesta and Zell in unison.

"Not the flood, just the contingency response. I drew up the plans three years ago. My father delegated the disaster planning project to me."

"Three years ago you were fifteen," said Antwanesta.

"Yes, Father said I did a good job. Logistics is fun. I like to plan."

The foreigners, including Bishop Korack, assembled at the banner. Upon the Bishop's approach Antwanesta asked his blessing. He smiled, and granted the blessing according to ritual. Risky and Dean Smith each greeted the bishop politely, but with no reverence.

Dean Smith, Risky, Bishop Korack, Antwanesta, Gretchin, Zell, Xiny, Professor Solider, her husband, Jandarian and their two children, boarded the small sail boat, manned by the same two Royal soldiers from the trip to Queen's Port. The lake was calm now. They sailed North toward Central District Isle.

Jandarian spoke with the Dean about the damage he expected to find at the college. He knew the buildings were all well-fortified against earthquakes. Even the otherwise vulnerable bath rooves were built on skid plates to protect against lateral movement. Jandarian was concerned about flooding. The first floors of all buildings would have been infiltrated by water. There were no sump pumps or drains.

Risky was worried. She had left the infirmary in the hands of a college freshman with no formal medical experience. With the quake and flood surely students were injured. She had to get back as fast as possible.

Bishop Korack spoke to calm Risky. He said that change is just a manifestation of God's will. "The status quo can never be stable. God is the only constant."

Risky was not comforted by his words. She had always been free to do as she willed. The laws of nature and the needs of others were starting constrain Risky too much. Seeing he could not comfort Risky, Bishop Korack turned toward Antwanesta who was standing near the boat's starboard side near the stern.

It was no surprise to Antwanesta that the bishop would seek her out. She was the only other Theist on the boat. As he approached, Antwanesta, in her muddied Royal tunic, suddenly realized that her Holy Hexagon pendant was framed by her cleavage. She felt immodest. As Antwanesta looked toward the Bishop, her eyes grew wide. Shock came over her face. She said, "The moon."

Past Bishop Korack's shoulder the waning moon was rising over the eastern horizon. It was bright white. The red dot was *gone*. The red dot which had always been there, luminescent regardless of the moon's phase, was no longer there.

The passengers and crew all marveled at the amazing sight. The dot had been there all their lives, all their parents' lives, all the lives of 984 years of ancestors. The dot had come with a quake and left with a quake.

Antwanesta and Bishop Korack both made the sign of the hexagon across their chests. The bishop then turned and made a similar gesture toward his shipmates. All silently looked up.

"That was no lava field," Antwanesta said after a few minutes. "There are impact craters where the dot was. Lava would have melted them away."

Several more minutes passed. It was Antwanesta again who spoke. "Your Eminence, do you have an explanation for this?"

"No Sister. I do not. God does not share His mysteries until we are ready to understand." That answer was no better than what Professor Medic had told her. *Even worse,* Antwanesta thought.

The dock was gone. The boat's keel would not allow it to reach the beach. The vessel stopped short of the destination. The water at the bow was chest deep.

Risky looked the bishop in the eyes, and jumped in the water immediately.

"Shall I give you your robe, Dean?" asked Gretchin.

"No, Miss Quadrapopis, I shall relax the dress code for the evening."

"Thank you, Dean." Gretchin hopped in the water holding her backpack over her head. She kept her already wet and muddy tunic on, not out of modesty of course. The bishop was just another man to her. It just wasn't worth the effort to remove it, until she reached the shore.

When Risky reached the shore, she ran toward the infirmary. Her robe was in Gretchin's backpack. In her Royal tunic she ran with speed deer and rabbits would respect.

The bishop observed, "God has blessed us. He let the chapel stand."

Then Antwanesta said. "God blessed the Humanists with the preservation of their chapel as well. It's good to know He loves us all." Antwanesta hopped in the water holding her backpack over her head like Gretchin had.

Xiny did the same. The Dean and the Solider Family also hopped in. Zell tried to toss his backpack to shore. He missed. It landed with a splash five balls from the beach. Gretchin picked it up and waited for Zell.

When Zell reached the shore, Gretchin said with a smirk, "Walk with us on the trail. A man without a woman's guidance is just a man."

Zell walked with his female friends. It was a longer route for him given that the sophomore dorm was directly across campus. However, the company was hard to forsake, especially with Gretchin clinging to him for warmth, in the cold evening air.

Risky reached the infirmary, which was dimly lit with oil lamps. She called for Feli.

"Here, Doctor." Feli stood up from between two patient beds. Histina entered the room wearing a white coat and carrying a bed pan.

Risky asked urgently, "What is the status?"

Feli replied. "We have six resident patients, five with severe lacerations, one with two fractured ribs. Fifty-eight others were treated for minor injuries and released. We did not lose anyone.

Risky slumped with relief. "Thank you, Feli."

"Histina helped me. A second set of hands is priceless."

"I know that." Risky hugged Feli, long and hard. She released her and then said, Thank you, Miss Bowright. May I call on you again when I am short-handed?"

"Yes, Dr. Sexapopis, I am happy to serve," said Histina.

Risky examined the patients. "The sutures are excellent. Who? How?"

Feli replied, "My family does not have much money, so I have sewn up a lot of holes in my clothes. I have also sewn prototype clothing designs. Skin and blood vessels aren't much different.

"You did vascular repair with no medical training?"

"It had to be done. You gave me responsibility for the patients. I did not want to let them, or you, down."

"You girls go to the dorm and get some sleep. Check in with me in the morning. Gym class is canceled."

Histina kissed the sleeping Hardy on the forehead. Feli and Histina took off their lab coats, and walked back to their dorm room through the gym tunnel. There were two centiballs of water in the tunnel. That was well below Feli's blue standard Republican dress and cotton thigh warmers, not to mention Histina's purple hair ribbon.

Zell left his female companions at the freshman dorm, and walked alone along what was the running trail (sand now washed away). In the dorm he was warmly greeted by Tear. She took off his wet tunic, and refused to let him out of her arms.

Antwanesta, Xiny, and Gretchin, were happy to see their beds. Xiny did not need her warm life-sized teddy bunnies anymore. She had her duty for which to live. They all fell fast asleep. On the second floor Feli and Histina did the same, unaware of the curious event in the sky.

Jandarian put his family to bed in his apartment in the family dorm. He would have a busy night. Students with first floor rooms were being reassigned to upper levels. His team of plumbers had already conducted an initial damage assessment, which confirmed what Jandarian expected. They would begin the clean-up in earnest in the morning. God bless the Royal Plumbers.

Risky released all but the two most badly injured patients in the morning. She told Hardy to take a two-week break from exercise. That was like the Pontiff telling people to eat meat and attend orgies. She also told him to cut his calorie intake in proportion to his decrease in activity. She said, "If you don't, your belly will pouch out, and you will discover which of your girlfriends really love you." That made Hardy laugh painfully.

Classes were cancelled for another week. The first floor of the tower building was closed for clean-up. Food was served outside on a take-out basis. Xiny negotiated the use of the remaining vacant dorm space for Royal refugees (the families of the students).

The junior bath was closed indefinitely. Juniors were authorized to use either the senior or the sophomore bath. Every junior man chose to be in the senior bath to continue bathing with women. Even gay men made this choice generally, preferring the company of women outside of a sexual context. Every junior woman chose to bathe in the sophomore bath to be without men. This did not affect the freshmen. Their segregated bath continued with its usual population. It was still more crowded than usual because with classes cancelled many students chose to swim and soak two or three times per day, Gretchin, Antwanesta, and Feli included. Xiny was in the bath half as much due to her logistical duties.

As they soaked in their usual pool Antwanesta's favorite topic of conversation was the moon. She seemed obsessed with finding out what the red dot was and why it was now gone.

This did not interest Gretchin. She wanted to man her stable. So concerned was she about this subject, that she was even willing to give Feli an ear, albeit with frequent reminders that Feli was a "total bunny-brain." Feli enjoyed speaking with Antwanesta and Gretchin both. She seemed to have more in common with each, than Antwanesta and Gretchin had with each other.

Maidens of Epodlo, Book 1 — Antwanesta Agape and the Mystery of the Red-dot Moon

There was a particular commonality Gretchin and Feli shared which was totally outside the galaxy from Antwanesta's perspective. Both favored the idea of forming a collection of men. They disagreed only in that Gretchin wanted a passionate loving relationship with each of her men, while Feli, from her psycho-theoretical perspective, thought it better to use a collection of men for dispassionate sexual stimulation, and to not get emotionally involved. Antwanesta observed Feli and Gretchin were both like children confidently devising strategies for a sport they had never played. Antwanesta did not want to play. She further opined that polygamy was not a proper game to be played by anyone.

Assessment and recovery was conducted all over Epodlo. Fortuitous circumstances had mitigated loss of life in each quadrant. There was the rural retreat in the Theocracy, the Queen's funeral in the Kingdom, the medical convention in the Republic, and in Libertaria the tall brothels had been recently reinforced, and Frontaris Mason had organized a consumer trade fair outside Freetown, with free admission and very generous prizes few could resist. These were no doubt coincidences, like those Professor Medic had mentioned in his Nature class. Bishop Korack would call them blessings. There did indeed appear to be an intelligent hand at work, something or someone quietly manipulating events for some unknown end.

Jandarian Solider prioritized the clean-up of the tower building. Merchandise was salvaged from the atrium stores, and sold on clearance. Feli bought a fur coat, Gretchin said could be cleaned. Feli had enough cotton leg warmers, but Antwanesta and Gretchin bought more of them for the Winter.

Xiny assumed her special project with Dean Smith would be canceled. Surely the records Xiny was to review were destroyed in the tsunami with the rest of Royal Beach. On Thursday Xiny asked Dean Smith about it. The Dean

193

responded, "You would be surprised how much of Lissy's legacy remains. The project is still on. You will dive in on Monday.

By Monday, Antwanesta had several examples of phenomena in nature that seemed too orderly to be natural. Why is the weather so uniform year by year? Why is Epodlo almost bilaterally symmetrical on a north-south axis? Why is the climate so dramatically different over the 4400 kiloball distance from North Point to Royal Beach? Why are natural blocks cubes? Why are metals found in spheres of uniform mass? Why is an Earth-year evenly divisible by its rotations?

Xiny went to Dean Smith's office for her special project. As she entered the dean smiled. "Good to see you Miss Stewart. You are a Royal. You understand confidentiality. What you are about to see you must share with no one."

"Of course, Dean."

"This way."

Dean Smith opened the door behind her desk which appeared to be a closet or a toilet. Xiny looked in the door. It was a toilet.

"Follow me," said the dean.

Xiny did not understand. *Why would Illi want me in a toilet?* She stepped in tentatively.

"Close the door please."

Xiny complied, but said, "This is very unusual Illi. I don't know what you are up to, but…"

Illi pressed a button hidden under the front edge of the toilet stone. The toilet moved. It sank at a forty-five-degree angle down and away revealing a painted steel staircase. Illi

194

descended. Xiny followed in silence. After three flights and two landings they reached a textured metal platform.

The platform ended in a vertical ledge. Just passed the ledge was a silver cylindrical object twenty balls in diameter. It was tapered to a point at one end. The silver cylinder had an opening at the top just behind the tapered area. In the opening there were two seats, side-by-side.

Illi directed Xiny into the seat with her hand. Xiny sat. Illi sat beside her.

Illi said, "Close."

With a sharp short hiss, the cylinder sealed itself with Illi and Xiny inside. Illi pressed a white button. There was a pulsating whooshing sound and a feeling of acceleration. In less than one minute, there was a feeling of deceleration and the sound stopped. The hatch opened without command.

"Here we are."

"Where?"

"Under Royal Beach. This way."

Royal Beach? thought Xiny, *That's not possible. It's way too far.* Xiny did not give voice to her incredulity. She wanted to see what Illi had in mind.

Illi lead Xiny through a number of hallways and doors which opened without knobs or handles. Behind the final door she saw what could not be. Standing in front of her wearing a light purple jumpsuit was *Lissy*.

Chapter 15

Newton Day Break

Xiny was shocked to see Lissy. However, the shock on her face quickly changed to anger. "How could you do this to me!"

"I did what I had to do to save the Kingdom," replied Lissy calmly.

"I'll be back in forty minutes," interrupted Illi. "You two have a lot to talk about."

Without taking her eyes off Xiny, Lissy tossed Salbird Keysmith's keys to the dean. Illi caught them with casual ease and left through the door.

"You faked your death for the Kingdom, but keeping *me* in the dark served no purpose, but to hurt me. If Gretchin, Antwanesta, and Risky had not all risked their lives to save me, I would be dead from grief. I almost died, because *you* don't trust me. *You don't love me!*"

"That's not true Xiny. I *do* love you. I have always trusted and loved you. It was Illi. She insisted you be kept in the dark. She wanted your grief to appear authentic, and she wanted to contain the secret."

"Illi and her secret! You were Queen! You didn't have to submit to Illi. You could have stood up to her! When she comes back I sure will."

"Xiny, please. This is bigger than us, bigger than the Kingdom. All of Epodlo is at stake."

"That still doesn't explain why I wasn't told that you were alive."

"Illi was afraid that if you knew, Antwanesta, Gretchin, and Feli would find out. They are very smart and very perceptive. If you knew I was alive, they would read it in your face. Feli can almost read minds. Antwanesta will dig down to bed-metal to solve a mystery. An army can't stop Gretchin. We had to distract them by framing Zell and scapegoating Barthon."

"Barthon! You killed my brother!"

"No, Xiny, Barthon is alive. He was in on it. We escaped through the Libertarian forest together."

"Barthon too. Who can I trust?"

"I'm sorry Xiny. The secret is too important to risk disclosure. You have to understand that."

"How can I? I don't even know the secret."

"I don't know it either, but Illi does. She says that when the secret knowledge was broadly disclosed last time; it lead to war, not Gretchin knocking down toy soldiers, or men fighting over venison in the woods, but *real war*."

"The war before the quake, 984 years ago?"

"Yes. That's what truth can do. That's why we must hide it now."

"Xiny paused as Lissy's words soaked in. Why did you have to appear to die to evacuate Royal Beach? You were Queen. You could have just ordered people to leave."

"How could I have explained it? How could I have known a tsunami was coming? If I said that scientists predicted it, there would be too many questions leading to too many answers."

197

"How *did* you know a tsunami was coming?"

"Alfide and Illi told me what would happen. They did not share the basis of their knowledge."

"Father knew too? He lied!"

"Deceiving you pained him greatly, but he did his duty to save the Kingdom. Dr. Grocer and the soldiers also lied on my orders."

Xiny looked at Lissy and then said, "I don't know who to trust anymore. You are no longer a queen. Things are different between us. I expect to be treated as an equal."

Lissy replied, "We can never be equals, Xiny. *I* will always be *your* servant." Tears came to Lissy's eyes.

Xiny looked into the watering eyes of the woman she loved. She had Lissy back, or did she? "I still love you Lissy. I just don't understand what we have anymore. I lost you. I replaced you with Gretchin, Risky, Feli, and Antwanesta."

"Antwanesta?"

"I don't mean sexually; I mean emotionally. You know how Feli is about diversifying emotional assets. It's like Professor Solider said; we are too dependent upon each other."

"Are you going to leave me?"

"No. I will be *mad* at you for a while, and I'll never fully trust you again, but we are still partners."

When Illi returned she found Lissy and Xiny soaking in a hot bath. This hidden underground zone was protected from both the quake and tsunamis. Lissy's subterranean apartment had all the comforts of a Royal home, albeit a small one. Handing Xiny a towel, Illi said, "I see you two are getting along again."

"If I weren't a Royal, I'd drown you in this tub, Illi," said Xiny.

"I thought Lissy would explain my motives," defended the dean.

"She did, but as you are both a Libertarian and a Humanist, I expect you to respect my liberty to feel angry at you."

Illi made an evil looking grimace, and said, "Barthon sends his regards and apologies."

"Barthon?"

"Yes, I have him on another mission. He is doing quite well."

"What other mission?"

"You know better than that," Illi said with a smile."

Xiny responded, "I'm sick of your secrecy Illi. Why can't you be straight with me?"

"I put Miss Agape and Gretchin in your room so you could acculturate them. I see it backfired. You have become far too curious and impertinent for a Royal."

"Don't evade my question. I want to know why you think you are morally justified in turning my life upside down, and how you knew a tsunami was coming."

"The end justifies the means, Xiny. I knew when the tsunami would hit *because I caused it*. Now stop asking questions, or I will adjust my appraisal of your utility!"

Back at the college, Antwanesta, had an interesting Nature class. Professor Medic was not surprised by Antwanesta's list of odd *natural* phenomena. Antwanesta was surprised when the professor did not dismiss them all as coincidences.

"Yes, Miss Agape, some things aren't right. A lot of us scientists know it. Too many things are just unnatural. However, I don't posit *supernatural* explanations for *unnatural* events. Humans were around much longer than the time captured in our records. Our ancestors were as smart as us. They had advanced technology we don't understand. Look at medipower, a useful artifact from a bygone age. We don't know how it works. Perhaps our ancestors made the metal spheres and cubic stone blocks. Maybe they even altered the climate beyond repair. Perhaps the island of Epodlo itself was created by people from our past. That would explain why it appears on no globe. Epodlo is isolated from the rest of the world. Our ignorance is profound. However, empirical reality is, *in principle*, knowable. We will figure things out. That's what humans do."

Professor Medic is right, Antwanesta thought. *I was foolish to look for evidence of divine influence. Faith is a mystical experience, not a way to explain the universe. Science with its self-correcting empirical methodology is the way to explain God's creation. Only a pitiful god, unworthy of the name, would create a universe which required incessant tinkering and repair through miraculous intervention. The mystical experience of God transcends empirical reality. God, in His ineffability, is superior to empirical reality.* Antwanesta smiled at this insight, and she felt a sense of awe.

After a brief and wordless subway ride back to Central District Isle, Xiny and Illi assumed their roles as Miss Stewart and Dean Smith.

Xiny went to the freshman bath for her final class of the day. After her anger and frustration over Lissy and Illi's deception, Xiny swam hard in Physical Training. Risky was pleased to see her intensity. Xiny's energy had reignited. Gretchin was also pleased to have her perky, energetic friend returned to her. Xiny appeared almost back to normal. There was still some sullenness, but Xiny was obviously trying to be

her old self. How does one conceal the knowledge that Illisima
Smith (Dean of the Central College of Epodlo, Governor of
the Central District, a person fondly known from childhood)
admitted to causing the tsunami which destroyed Royal
Beach? Only a Royal could keep such a secret. That's why Illi
trusted Royals, and used them for her unknown ends. They
were worthy of trust, *to a fault.*

After Physical Training class ended, Gretchin
proposed a soak in their favorite hot pool. Xiny had been in a
hot pool just two hours before, but she had to conceal her
reunion with Lissy, so she cheerfully accepted. She would not
be "read" by her clever friends.

"I owe you an apology for exploiting you the way I
did," Xiny said to Gretchin. "You risked your life to save mine
after I made you spoon-feed me in the dining hall."

"I did what I did because I love you, Xiny. Ant,
Risky, and bunny-brained Feli love you too."

"I know that. Thank you."

"If you really want to thank me, you will give me
something."

"I will do literally anything for you, Gretchin. What
do you want from me?"

"Your life."

"You mean you want to become what Lissy was to
me? Do you want me to be your partner in life?"

"No, I just want you to promise me that you will
never try to kill yourself again."

"You have my promise. I will give you something
more if you like."

"What I would like is a stable of strong healthy *men*."

"Sorry, I don't have that to give. I have only myself, and even that is bound by my duty."

"Why do you Royals bind yourself with duty? Just be free. I know you don't want to marry a man that some deer dung tradition assigns to you. Just give it up. Be with whom you want."

"Should I want you?"

"Not unless you want to share me with a collection of men. I don't think you want to be a stable carl. I can't be like Lissy was for you, but someone else can be."

"Only for a time. My duty is my destiny."

"You now owe me the *duty* to live. Life without freedom is not *living*."

"You are right, Gretchin. Destinies can change."

Gregor was dealing with his changed destiny. On behalf of the Southern Kingdom he had politely refused all of the generous assistance offered by the Western Theocracy, the Northern Republic, and the people of Libertaria. However, King Gregorious expressed the Kingdom's gratitude to the other nations, for their kind offers of aid. The King offered generous trade to the Theocracy and to businesses in Libertaria. To the Republic and its citizens, King Gregorious granted five years of interest relief on all debts, public and private. For his own people, he oversaw the most ambitious building project ever imagined on Epodlo. Royal Beach would be rebuilt, better and stronger than it ever was, and on an ambitious schedule only Royals would impose upon themselves.

At the college the routine of classes, meals, exercise, and baths was restored. On campus, leaves and lawns were covered by light snow. Runners wore more fur, sweat clothes, or Smith & Mason extremity garb. Life seemed normal again. It was now

Maidens of Epodlo, Book 1 — Antwanesta Agape and the Mystery of the Red-dot Moon

December, and the students anticipated the coming of Newton Day break. The break was reduced to just one week this year to make up for some of the time lost to Lissy's death and the flooding. In the prior month, Hypatia's Day break had also been cut to just one day.

Antwanesta still could not risk a return to the Theocracy for what, to her, was Saint Isaac's Day. She needed to go elsewhere. Royal beach would have been great under other circumstances. Before events changed her plans, she intended to go there with Lissy and Xiny. What was left of Royal Beach was closed to people other than Royals. The whole Kingdom was closed to outsiders with only one exception. Bishop Korack was allowed back in to minister to the spiritual needs of the displaced Royals living in temporary housing around Center Town, midway between Queen's Port and Royal Beach. The Kingdom was out of the picture as a holiday destination for Antwanesta. Libertaria was also unavailable, because Gretchin had too much, "family business" to which to attend. Gretchin promised to take Antwanesta to Libertaria for the Summer. Feli invited Antwanesta to Newton for Newton Day Break.

"How perfect," Feli said, "Newton at peak season, you will love it. I'll show you the museum. It will be so wonderful." Feli hugged Antwanesta with excitement, forgetting, *or ignoring*, that Antwanesta was uncomfortable with physical displays of affection in public or private.

Xiny went south for Newton Day Break. She would see her father, her hidden brother, and her beloved Lissy. Her father, Alfide was in on Lissy's conspiracy, though Gregor was still not privy to the scheme. Xiny would also see the progress being made to resurrect Royal Beach. Royals are amazingly industrious and efficient, especially when no one is looking.

Gretchin's "family business," was not serving as a bone-breaking thug for her mom's disreputable enterprises.

Thomas David Valentine

Gretchin's mother kept Gretchin out of her wide-ranging business activities. In her mother's eyes, Gretchin was not *Royal* enough to be trusted. Gretchin needed to lay the ground work for Antwanesta to visit during the Summer. Her pops had to be prepped. They had to understand that Mom wanted her relationship to Gretchin and Risky to be unknown to her friends at school. Pops One and Three would do whatever Mom asked of them. Pop Four would be no problem. Gretchin and he were estranged, ever since the humiliation he had caused many years before. Everyone in Libertaria knew of his infamy. Only Risky blamed Gretchin for not speaking to him. Pop Two would be the challenge. He said lots of things he should not. He saw conspiracies everywhere. He spoke about the Knowers, the Masons, the Royal Plumbers, and extraterrestrials copulating to build an army for invasion. In short, Pop Two was really *out there*. He would be hard to manage.

Zell's younger cousins Wago and Naragadug (Duggy) came to the isle to pick up Zell, Feli, and Antwanesta in the good old aluminum rowboat. The trip to Newton was with the current to and down the Northwest River. That made rowing relatively easy. The boat would get to Newton rowed or not. The dead volcano beneath Central District Isle had long ago become a great spring from which water flowed at a constant rate and even temperature.

Antwanesta wore a thick cotton jacket. Feli had the fur she had bought on clearance with Gretchin's guidance. Both wore their standard Republican dresses, and their Smith & Mason leg and arm warmers. Zell had thicker-than-usual beige pants, two shirts, a sweater, and a neatly tailored deerskin coat lined with cotton. All his cloths were clean, unwrinkled, and well-matched. This was Zell (always the smart dresser).

Tear had gone to Libertaria with Gretchin. Her pregnancy was now public knowledge. Paternity was a matter of speculation, at least among people who were not Royals. Zell knew who the biological father was (a very dutiful young man), but in Tear's culture a mother decides who the fathers are. Zell would not tell anyone. He respected Tear, and would honor her wishes.

Antwanesta looked at Zell's cousins. She then looked Zell in the eye. "I guess this is it," she said.

Zell smiled at Antwanesta's apparent interest.

Antwanesta still smiling asked, "I'm going to find out now, aren't I?"

Zell thought maybe Feli had told her about their kissing lessons. *Did Antwanesta want tutoring?* "Find out what? Zell asked."

"What happens with Republicans in rowboats?"

The whole boat erupted into laughter.

Antwanesta still did not have her answer, but she was the life of the party. She was not about to admit that she did not know the punchline. She laughed too, but in a forced uncomfortable way.

As the boat passed Lord's Landing, Antwanesta saw the home she had left. The bushes, where she had hidden her raft, had been washed away. Many buildings she knew from childhood had been toppled. The sight prompted Antwanesta to pray silently. "Lord God of the Holy Hexagon, have mercy on me a sinner." She said this six times in her mind, and made the sign of the hexagon.

When Antwanesta finished, Feli, who was sitting next to her, asked, "Have you heard from your mom?"

Antwanesta replied, "Not since the Quake, but Brother Ir... I mean Professor Agape, the Red said that God had spared Saint Hypatia's Convent. It was reinforced like the buildings on campus. No one has been getting mail. Very few people in the Theocracy were hurt in the quake, I'm sure she's fine."

"Of course she is," said Feli. Feli kissed the left shoulder of Antwanesta's cotton coat.

The river would pass just three-hundred kiloballs from the convent before reaching Newton at its mouth. At Saint Hypatia's, Antwanesta's Mother, Dothina was lying on her back, naked after being shaved and bathed in preparation for her coming blessing. She was both very relaxed and very happy, just the way she was supposed to feel. The drug she had been administered was intended to have that effect.

As Zell's cousins rowed the boat near to Newton, past the fallen trees now buried in snow, the festive decorations could be seen. Red, green, and white were traditional Newton Day colors, but purple was also used for many decorations in the Republic. Garlands were strung on buildings. Newton Day trees sported red painted wooden apples and purple triangles speckled in silver and gold. Each tree had a star at the top to symbolize humanity's inseparable connection with nature, humans being composed of atoms created by stars. The famous Newton Museum even had colored medipower lights strung upon it. What a great wonder it was to behold.

Back in the reconstructed portion of the Stewart family home in Royal Beach, siblings were reunited.

"What are you up to these days Barthon?"

"Where is my sister? Xiny would never asked such a thing. You must be Antwanesta with bleached hair."

Xiny and Barthon laughed.

"You shouldn't be up here Barthon. What if you're seen?"

"I am very elusive, and if a Royal sees me, I can expect discretion."

"The secret passage to below is intended for Father and me to go down to see Lissy and you, not for you to come up here?"

"You're right Xiny. I just wanted to see the sunlight, such as it is."

In Freetown, Libertaria, Risky examined Tear. "You are doing just fine. You should deliver in June. Are you excited?"

"Yes," replied Tear with a smile.

"Are the perspective fathers excited too?" It would have been impolite for Risky to have said, *father* in the singular. That would have implied that there was only one, which would be insulting to a free woman.

"I'd rather not talk about it."

Given that Tear's roommates included the King of "Monogamy Land" and the disgraced murderer, Barthon; it was clear to Risky why she would not talk. She made light of the situation to ease Tear's anxiety, "You are free not to talk, and I'm free to bug you. Where's Retch? She should bug you too. She's your sister. I'm just your doctor-in-law, or something like that."

"She's at the beach house training Quinis to be *Royal* about your Mom."

"*Good luck* to her with that. Last time I saw Quinis he asked me if red-haired people were spawned from a different species of extraterrestrial than the God-kissed people."

"What deer dung; he has more rabbits in his head than the Pontiff himself. Poor Gretchin has both Quinis and Pargog as fathers; it's not fair." Then after a moment to realize

207

what she had said, "I'm sorry Risky. I forgot Pargog is one of your pops too."

"It's ok, Tear. Maybe Dussy can help. She's good with Quinis. Stable carls can be more persuasive than daughters in some ways."

Chapter 16

Newton Museum

In Newton, Feli, Antwanesta, and Zell walked to Feli's parents' house. Feli's mom, Azunia, hugged Feli, and greeted Antwanesta and Zell warmly. Azunia remembered Antwanesta from the time she was at the college representing Zell. Zell excused himself, and went to his father's house next door.

Azunia asked Feli if things were ok with Gretchin.

"Gretchin is fine, Antwanesta is another very dear friend."

Azunia did not want to judge her daughter's social life, but thought she would benefit with more stability in her relationships. This was the second person her daughter brought home from college. The first was a polygamist. This one was likely an asexual. She wished Feli would bring home a normal boy or girl for a change. Inwardly Azunia chastised herself. She knew that she should be tolerant of the sexual choices made by adults, but she lived monogamously with her devoted husband Picius. Azunia truly believed that pair-bonding was the best approach to interpersonal relationships, but she could only teach by example.

"Zell's grown up to be a nice young man," said Feli's mom to provoke an intrusive personal discussion.

"Yes, Mom. He is a good friend. Antwanesta, Gretchin, and Xiny are also good friends. I try to diversify my emotional portfolio to avoid becoming too psychologically vulnerable."

"Your dad and I enjoy our *vulnerability* just fine," Azunia replied.

"Speak of the devil…" It was Feli's father, Picius. "Not that I believe in devils or demons."

Feli hugged her father.

"This is my friend, Antwanesta."

"Hello, Antwanesta."

"Pleased to meet you, Mr. Smith."

After light conversation Picius said, "Excuse me, I'll get dinner on the table."

Antwanesta felt at home in Feli's house. It was much like her house in Lord's Landing. The earthquake had shifted some of the stone blocks, but it was still structurally sound.

As night came Antwanesta asked Feli, "is this the *infamous* bed, Gretchin complained about?"

"What did she say?" responded Feli.

"She said you make a warm blanket for a bunny-brain."

"Feli smiled, and said, "That's my Sweetheart. I hope you will not be uncomfortable sharing the bed with me. I assume your hexagon does not regard me as a threat to your virtue."

"I did the calculation," replied Antwanesta. "Taking into account that you care deeply about me, that you regard me as valuable friend, that you are devoutly committed to Humanistic compassion, that you show great restraint in using your formidable power to manipulate people, and that you have a near pathological fear of combining emotional intimacy with physical intimacy; the probability of you allowing your prurient impulses to motivate you to exploit my proximity is approximately… zero."

"You know me too well," said Feli. "Doesn't lying close to a woman as overwhelmingly gorgeous as me, create the risk that *you* may have feelings that won't fit into your hexagon?"

"Given the number of baths, physical training classes, and runs on the trail we have shared, I think I have been well-inoculated against your charms. The risk is very low."

"Suppose you were next door lying with Zell. Would the calculation be the same?"

"No, it would be a more complicated calculation. Cylindrical geometry makes proximity problematic, and I don't want to talk about it. Now please let my pray."

"By all means do." Feli felt a twinge of guilt thinking her statement, intended to show tolerance and respect, might constitute an act of enabling a religion addict.

Antwanesta recited the prayer of the Holy Hexagon thirty-six times, while kneeling on the bed. Feli sat quietly next to her, patiently waiting for her to finish, and make the sign of a hexagon across her chest.

Feli then spoke:

Our reason, which has evolved, existing in our brains, give us this day the means to produce bread, and help us to apply compassion, to ourselves, as we apply compassion to others. Lead us not into tedium, and deliver us from inhumanity. Ours is the kingdom, and the glory until extinction. Human.

"You said a prayer," said Antwanesta. "It was a grossly blasphemous prayer, but it was a prayer. Why did I never here you say that when you slept in our room to comfort Xiny?"

"I don't say it often anymore. It is not a prayer; it's a meditation. It is taught to Humanist children to teach them our values."

"It sounded like a prayer to me."

"The difference is," Feli instructed, "you pray to *nothing* thinking it is *something*, I meditate to *nothing*, with the correct understanding that it is *nothing*."

"How do you know there is nothing?"

"I know, because your god is not necessary to explain my universe."

"You understand the universe? Do tell."

"No. I don't have a comprehensive understanding of the universe, but positing supernatural beings in no way helps to explain it. It just adds complexity."

"Oh yes, the self-existing universe is *so* much simpler," said Antwanesta borrowing Feli's characteristic sarcasm."

"It *is* simpler. A god is a big fat unexplained concept plopped on to a theoretical system. It's not parsimonious."

"Looking past your characterization of the Ineffable as fat, what is so essential about parsimony?"

"It is a matter of probability. You understand probability better than anyone I know. You know what happens to a predictive model when you add unknown variables. The more undefined terms you add, the less likely it is that your theoretical model will predict or describe reality."

Antwanesta could not extemporaneously refute the argument of her Humanist friend. She made a strategic retreat to safe intellectual terrain. "Maybe that is where faith comes in."

"Not a chance," said Feli. "Faith does not tell you
what to believe, it only hardens your resolve to believe in a
proposition that you have otherwise selected."

"You have given me a lot to think about, Feli. I think
that is why I love you so much."

"You make me think too, Antwanesta. It is fortuitous
that both Humanism and Theism share love as a central value.
Good night. Try to sleep. You will want to be well-rested for
the museum tomorrow."

Tomorrow came, and after breakfast Feli and
Antwanesta joined Zell for the walk to the Newton Museum.
Feli held Zell's right arm. Antwanesta held *Feli's* right arm.

"Did you sleep well here in the cold North,
Antwanesta?" Zell's breath was visible in the cold as he
spoke.

"It wasn't easy at first. I was excited about going to
the museum, and I was processing the philosophy symposium,
Feli gave me."

"Say no more. I know when Feli starts talking about
metaphysics it's a blood sport," said Zell.

"Oh, I'm not that bad," defended Feli.

"You are with Histina."

"That's different. Histina fights back, and with her I
get to play god's advocate."

"God's advocate?" Antwanesta was both surprised
and curious.

"That's when I advocate the opposing side of an
argument, said Feli. I have gotten so much better at it having
you around to train me."

"I'm pleased to be of service, said Antwanesta."

Both Feli and Zell laughed at Antwanesta's use of the common Humanist idiom.

The Newton Museum looked much larger up close. The architectural structure created the illusion of a smaller building because of the massive scale of its doors, windows, and archways. The building was crowded because this was peak season. Many people made the long hike west to the museum from Democratica City as a pilgrimage each year. That made for a long cold walk in Winter, but for devote Humanists the trek was a ritual that strengthened their confidence–*Faith* is an offensive word for Humanists–in humanity. The crowd was smaller than in years before due to the distraction with reconstruction projects at the capitol.

As they entered the museum from the south, the first exhibit which caught Antwanesta's eye, was the official ball. It was housed in a glass case and centered at the front of the great hall of the museum. It was the standard unit of measure for all of Epodlo. Presumably the rest of the world used an identical ball as the official standard, given Epodlo's geographic isolation. It was solid gold and weighed one <u>ball</u>. It also had a volume of one (ball) and a diameter of one ball. It had been extracted centuries ago from a pristine part of a Royal mine, and was selected because of its amazing perfection even when examined under great magnification.

On each of the four walls of the great hall hung one of the four flags of Epodlo.

Directly across the hall from the entrances was the flag of the Northern Republic, a vast purple field with nothing in it. The Assembly of Thirteen had never been able to agree on anything but the color. The agreement on color had only been achieved because the two formerly existing political parties had been symbolized by red and blue. In a rare display of bipartisanship, the red and blue were blended to make purple. The two political parties were subsequently dissolved into the one which they *de facto* always had been. Purple was

214

coincidentally the color often used to represent Humanism. Despite a strict principle of separation between religion and government, the purple's long association with Humanism was tolerated. The tolerance was facilitated by the fact that, under the dominant conception, Humanism was *not* a religion, but the rational rejection of religion. Exceptions would of course be made, if a Humanist were subjected to discrimination based on antireligious beliefs. Laws protecting the free exercise of religion were interpreted to include freedom from religion. Reason could allow no other conclusion.

To the left was the flag of the Western Theocracy. It was a vast black field with a great white image of the Holy Hexagon. Antwanesta made the sign of the hexagon across her chest at the sight of it. The white of the Holy Hexagon was God's light shining in the darkness leading flawed, frail sinners to virtue and salvation. The Theocracy did not struggle with an ethic regarding the separation of religion and politics. It's very existence was the rejection such a principle. For most Theists the separation of religion from government was nothing to be sought. Such a concept was seen as a product human ego and perversion. Could there possibly be greater hubris than to willfully exclude God from governance?

On the right wall was another empty flag. This one was forest green. Libertaria had no government. There was no way to adopt an official flag. However, the lumber, paper, and navy stores industries had long represented themselves with the forest green color. Although the economic prominence of forest products had been eclipsed by manufacturing, and more recently medical services; the forest green color was, by default, the symbol of the wild ungoverned anarchy to the east.

On the wall above the entrances, unnoticed by most passing beneath, was the Royal flag. It had a white field with a red stylized capital letter, "R" centered with very little space above and below. The "R" stood for "Royal" or "Regalis."

215

Either term represented the monarchy and fidelity thereto. The rationale for the Royal preference for white is lost to history, though purity (of both blood and character) was generally taken as its meaning in modern the time period. Perhaps, in clothing at least, it is as simple and practical as the desire to reflect more sunlight to stay cool in the southern heat. The red of the "R," undisputedly represents blood, both the blood shed by heroes in wars to defend the Kingdom, and familial bloodlines guarded by generations of Royals protecting their pure genetic heritage from the adulteration of outsiders.

Zell lead Feli and Antwanesta under the Libertarian flag and into the Hall of Armor. This was Zell's favorite exhibit. On the walls were maces, swords, and polearms of various sorts. In front of the weapons stood suits of armor.

Before the Republic and the Theocracy came to power, and the minor kingdoms in the eastern quadrant fell into ruin; all of Epodlo was under monarchical rule. Not one monarchy; sometimes there were four, each occupying one quadrant of Epodlo geographically separated by the wide rivers. At other times quadrants were subdivided into multiple kingdoms. Once the East had sixteen politically independent subdivisions. The artifacts in the Hall of Armor were from a small fraction of the more recent kingdoms to fall. The Southern Kingdom was the last to remain, in no small part due to both the beneficence of the Regalis family, and the deep metal mines which blessed the Kingdom with the means to express that beneficence in tangible ways.

Zell had no love of monarchy, though even he respected the current Regalis family. Until recently Gregor, now King, was his roommate. Zell and Gregor continued to regard each other as good friends, despite the recent unfounded allegations against Zell. Zell's interest in the Hall of Armor was its sense of history. Zell loved history. He wanted to be a part of it. He knew he would never be a solider in armor. His place in a war would be safely behind real warriors, like Gretchin and Tear. His first semester of weapons

216

class had brought him only marginally ahead of the average
pacifist Theite in martial proficiency. Nonetheless, Zell
envisioned himself as an agent for change, a liberator who
would one day help bring Humanistic democracy to the entire
human family.

Without his allies, Gregor and Barthon to protect
him, Zell's defenses had fallen to the compelling feminine
allure of Tear. Zell had no place to run, and no will to resist.
He had fallen to *her* will.

Zell sought victory elsewhere. His ambition was to
take direct, albeit nonviolent, action to affect moral change.
He had bent Gregor's ear on the virtues of democracy.
However, his vocal criticism of the ineptitude and
ineffectiveness of his own country's democracy undermined
his rhetoric. He had also aided a young Theite women's
escape from the oppression of the Theocracy. Here she was;
with him, beautiful and happy, now free to live, learn, and
dress as she pleased.

Zell was following the example set by his father,
Comaz Fisher. A decade before Comaz had been on the
Assembly of Thirteen. He had advocated an aggressive foreign
policy to liberate women deprived of sexual autonomy in the
Theocracy. He failed, and was voted out of office. Zell had no
patience for a political solution. He dreamed of taking his boat
across the river to rescue women from Saint Hypatia's
Convent. The women he saved could speak publicly, and
expose the depraved, oppressive practices which must be
occurring under the vail of pious modesty.

After the Hall of Armor, the three went to the Hall of
Sacred Art, passing the oldest known representation of their
island's name on the way. The name was on a steel plate. It
was engraved in the old style, with a hyphen after the "E," and
a space after the "d." Both the first and last letters were
capitalized, as was presumed to be the convention centuries
before. In the Hall of Sacred Art were several paintings and

drawings of the Holy Hexagon, and one depicting a mysterious woman holding a baby. The woman was thought to be some unknown saint, because the style of the work was the same as that of the icons now in churches. It could not be the famed Hypatia, because she died a virgin, and thus could not have borne a child.

The hexagon paintings were in many styles, all of the same holy artifact. The administrators of the museum had long given up on acquiring the *real* thing. The Theocracy would never let it go. The Holy Hexagon was displayed respectfully on public view in God City. The Newton Museum just had paintings and drawings. Antwanesta made the sign of the hexagon several times as she passed among the holy images.

In the next room were more hexagon paintings. These were of the black hexagon in the sky. Antwanesta had seen the real thing, eight years ago, on a fieldtrip to Saint Isaac's College. She noted that the fuzzy looking sketch was the best representation of what she had seen through the Saint Isaac's telescope. The representation was *fuzzy* in that the sides of the hexagon were not smooth. The sides had ridges. The Newton Museum had a telescope too, but it was closed on this day because of cloud cover. The Newton Museum telescope offered less magnification than the one at Saint Isaac's. On a clear day the telescope would reveal just a tiny black dot in the sky. No features were discernable.

Another exhibit was very interesting to Antwanesta. Above the familiar globe of the Earth, appeared the words, "Where is Epodlo?" There was a wide shaded line covering a range of latitudes in each of the northern and southern hemispheres. These were the proposed zones for the presence of Epodlo based on its median temperature. The southern temperature zone was based on the theory that there was confusion between north and south due to a conjectured polarity shift. The fact that no almond-shaped island, between the sizes Sicily and Ireland, existed in either of the zones was explained by several theories of apocalyptic geologic change.

218

Such change was to have occurred subsequent to the creation of the ancient stone globe upon which the globe in the exhibit was based.

Antwanesta was disappointed that none of the theories explained or even acknowledged the basic problem she had discovered. The distance between North Point and Royal Beach had a climatic difference which represented and arch of latitude far greater than that which could be attributed to the length of the island.

Another exhibit was "Hypatia vs. Hypatia" The exhibit presented two side-by-side narratives of the legend of Hypatia. There was the Theist version and the Humanist version.

In the Theist version, St. Hypatia was a scholarly virgin who turned to God at age fourteen. She was martyred at age eighteen by a godless mob after using her prodigious reason and eloquence to convert hundreds of people to Theism including fifty learned philosophers an evil king had sent to persuade her that she was wrong.

In the Humanist version Hypatia was murdered by Theists in a church. The Theists also burned a great library which represented the greatest collection of knowledge the world had known, most of it irreplaceable.

Antwanesta thought of how she had failed to live up to Hypatia's standard. She had maintained her virginity, but had converted no one to Theism. To the contrary, others she met made *her* faith waver, especially her beloved Humanist friend, Feli.

In another exhibit hall, there were examples of animal life. The deer, rabbits, and turtles, though fine in the artistry of their taxidermy, did not have the beauty and wonder of the extinct animals represented. There were fish. Oh, what wondrous fish. There were mounted examples of red drum, flounder, speckled trout, black sea bass, striped bass,

219

mackerel, sheepshead, jacks, snappers, pinfish, and mullet. The ferocious blue fish seemed compelling and fearsome with its sharp teeth. Even now long after its extinction, the thought of blue fish schooling just offshore could leave bathers fearing for the safety of their genitalia.

As Antwanesta looked at the extinct creatures, she was struck by the fragility of living existence. Before her eyes were but shadows of vibrant creatures which had inhabited the very web of life she too occupied. Would the last homo sapiens also be displayed in a museum, or would our kind exist only in the memory of God? Antwanesta felt so finite, so small, so vulnerable.

After several other exhibits Feli, Zell, and Antwanesta, came to the Newton Museum's most famous artifact, the mysterious Golden Arm. It's origin and age were unknown, but the artistry and workmanship were nothing short of amazing. It was nearly twice the size of the average adult man's arm. It was made of an unknown golden alloy. From the articulations in the elbow, wrist and fingers, it appeared to have been able to move. The prevailing theory was that it was part of an animated statue. However, it looked much more functional than representational. There were many static sculptures with more realistic contours and textures. Under a minority theory, it was part of a mechanical man which could walk. This theory was dismissed by most because of the mathematical complexity of approximating human locomotion. How could any device make calculations fast enough to accomplish the complexity of bipedal ambulation? Evolution took millions of years to achieve such a wondrous feat.

Antwanesta agreed with the assessment that the mechanical man theory was impossible. She was also reminded of her Mom's habit of blaming sinful behavior on *golden demons*. Perhaps there was some connection deep in history.

Feli walked over to the arm's guard. "Hi, I'm Feli
Smith, I worked this station last Summer, I don't think we've
met."

Feli's initiation of conversation with the museum
staffer drew Antwanesta's attention. Suddenly, Antwanesta
had a sense of recognition. That guard, *she was... No. How?*

"Zillestra?"

Antwanesta could not believe her eyes.

"Antwanesta. Wow, it's you," said Zillestra.

In the discussion which ensued, Zillestra explained
her story.

Zillestra didn't drown. She did wash down the
Northwest River. She came ashore exhausted in the Northern
Republic southeast of Newton. Naked young women seldom
wash up on the river bank, but the given that respect for
women is a strong pillar of Humanist culture, Zillestra came to
no misfortune. I kind man found her, and let her in his house
for a shower and a warm place to sleep. From there, Zillestra
reported to the nearest police station. She was referred to
immigration authorities, who assisted her in an application for
asylum. A confidentiality law kept Zillestra's transition a
secret. She converted to Humanism, and changed her name to
Zillestra Human. She enrolled in Newton Junior College, with
plans to go to Central College as a sophomore next year.

Feli invited Zillestra to join Antwanesta and her in
the public bath the next day. This made Antwanesta vaguely
nervous, but she did not protest. Zillestra accepted
enthusiastically, eager to learn all she could about Central
College. Feli quietly asked Zell not to join them at the bath so
as to protect Antwanesta from embarrassment.

Being at the crowded public bath was at first
uncomfortable to Antwanesta. These were not her friends and
classmates whose nudity she had come to accept as the

221

unnoticed backdrop of her normal existence. These were strangers. Many were mature adults, others just children. Eyes were drawn to Antwanesta's red hair and Holy Hexagon pendant. She felt naked again and stayed between Feli and Zillestra for moral support.

In one hour Antwanesta was closer to Zillestra than she had become in twelve years of Theite classrooms. Zillestra had the zeal of one new to an adopted religion or philosophy. She lacked the depth and nuance of understanding which was so clear and alluring in Feli's devotion. Zillestra's conception of Humanism was oddly stark, and ironically dualistic, with right-wrong, and us-them. She was devout but shallow, more like Histina than Feli. Because of the similar experiences the two had in common, Antwanesta now truly liked Zillestra; but she loved Feli. Antwanesta had been taught to love everyone, but she couldn't help but feel that her bond with Feli, Gretchin, and Xiny was something special. The relationship she had with them seemed to be an awesome blessing from God. Antwanesta thanked Him ardently for it every day.

Antwanesta did not love Feli in a sexual way. When she lay close with Feli each night she did not connect with Feli's body, except in the literal sense, shoulder-to-shoulder or knee to thigh. Their bodies touched, but Antwanesta *cuddled* with Feli's soul. She connected spiritually to this woman who claimed to have no spirit.

Of course from Feli's perspective souls or spirits did not exist. In Humanism, parsimony excludes the existence of supernatural substances. At best, for Feli, she and Antwanesta shared thoughts and feelings which brought them together in mutual compassion as friends.

Feli was neither bound by the limitations of strict heterosexuality, nor constrained by moral standards, imposed by some in the past, to prohibit same-sex intimacy. However, the connection she shared with Antwanesta was not sexual

from her perspective either. She too felt a strong bond with her
friend. Physical proximity to Antwanesta felt warm and safe.

Safety was not a feeling Feli associated with
perspective lovers. Feli feared sexual intimacy in general. It
was not a fear of sex *per ce*, but a fear of sex being joined with
passion. Passion, for Feli, was reason's enemy. Passion could
steal her self-control. Self-control was what Feli desired above
all things.

It was Feli's conscious and subconscious fear of
losing self-control which drove her selection of friends. Feli
had an extremely broad social network. She knew almost
everyone, at least at a superficial level; but her truly close
friends were few. They included a celibate Theist, a duty-
bound woman resolute in her commitment to marry a random
Royal man she did not love, a polygamist with as single-
minded commitment to phallic adoration, and a charming male
friend she conveniently categorized as a brother. Feli could
love these friends deeply and freely without fear of losing
control. Sex could be found in some emotionally sterile way.
Feli was safe. Feli was brilliant. Feli was just as bunny-
brained as Gretchin had always said.

Chapter 17

Feli the Matchmaker

Feli and Antwanesta agreed not to exchange gifts for Newton Day (Saint Isaac's Day). They shared a true deep friendship. Neither could want more from the other.

Wago and Duggy had taken the Fisher family boat back to Merchant Town after dropping Zell, Feli, and Antwanesta off in Newton nearly a week ago. The rowboat had to be towed by a sail boat up river to Merchant Town because, despite the proximity to the ocean, there was never any incoming tide. The returning students would also need to sail up river. Picius used his aquatic research vessel to ferry Feli, Antwanesta, and Zell back to Central District Isle.

When Feli got back to her dorm room, on the second floor of the freshman dorm, Celina was there. Petina and Histina were at the cafeteria and bath respectively.

"May I ask you something, Feli?"

"Yes, Celina, What?"

"I don't think you would approve, given your unique way of seeing things, but you know psychology, and I thought you could help me. You are so good helping Petina with math, and Histina with diplomacy, I thought maybe you could advise me on something."

"Maybe. How can I help?"

"I think I'm falling in love."

"Who is the lucky person?"

"Eltwando."

"Of course, you fall in love with the only celibate man in our class. Are you asking me to help you stop loving him, or do you want him to love you?"

"Him to love me."

"That is challenging, but not impossible."

"You'll do it?"

"I will at least teach you some psychological principles you should learn anyway, for your own good. Whether Eltwando will benefit is too hard to predict."

"Oh Thank you, Feli."

"Does he know you love him?"

"No, I have been afraid to tell him."

"Good. Let's keep it that way for now. The first thing you need to learn is how to recognize the flow of emotional energy."

Feli explained to Celina that all people were either net donors or net sinks of emotional energy. The same person could be a donor or a sink depending on the circumstances. Feli gave examples for clarity.

She said that generally Xiny was a powerful donor. Xiny was full of energy. She made people feel good by her mere presence. With a word, gesture, or small act, she could drive people to action. Even if the people did not understand why they should comply with Xiny's direction. Xiny's uniquely compelling charisma made her nearly impossible to refuse. However, when Xiny lost Lissy, and her brother,

225

Thomas David Valentine

Barthon confessed his betrayal; Xiny broke. She became a
sink for emotional energy. At that time Xiny was such an
emotional drain on her friends, it took all the energy
Antwanesta, Gretchin, and Feli could produce just to support
her. For reasons Feli did not understand, Xiny returned to her
normal state as a powerful donor. Her emotional energy
overflowed once again.

Antwanesta was another example of a powerful
donor of emotional energy. Antwanesta had great inner
confidence, and a deep reservoir of moral resolve. Antwanesta
would say she had faith and was blessed to have the guidance
of God's spirit within. Regardless of the source, Antwanesta
was, in a way which differed from Xiny, a powerful source of
emotional energy.

Gretchin was another interesting case. She was both a
sink for some and a donor for others. Specifically, Gretchin
was an emotional sink for men and an emotional donor for
women. Despite her undeniable physical appeal, Gretchin was
quickly seen by men as needy and demanding, even
exploitive. She wanted to collect men like some kind of pets.
Men rejected and resisted Gretchin because they did not want
to be captured and caged in her zoo. Gretchin did not want to
collect women. Women saw her as strong and brave. They
could respect her, admire her, and feel safe with her. For
women, Gretchin was like a secure, supportive man, without
the emotional and sexual complications.

Feli did not disclose to Celina that she herself used
Gretchin as a major source of energy. Feli knew it was not in
her interest to reveal her own vulnerabilities. Feli did not draw
upon Gretchin's energy in a parasitic way. She reciprocated by
returning the energy in a complicated way which even she did
not fully understand.

Celina was awed by the insights Feli was giving her.
She was eager to learn more, but Feli said, "That is enough for
now. I want you to observe other people and yourself, and

226

watch the flow of energy from person to person. Don't tell
anyone about this. If you discuss this with people who are
themselves energy sinks, they will sap your enthusiasm, and
derail your progress. The weak-minded will tear you down
just to delude themselves into believing you are as sick and
hopeless as they are. That ends our lesson for today."

As Feli said the last few words, Histina walked in.
"Lesson? Are you teaching Celina how to pleasure men?"

"In a manner of speaking," Feli replied. Would you
like a lesson?"

"No, I do my training with Hardy."

"Hardy is reputed to be quite talented. He tutors lots
of girls." Feli could not resist the jibe, which she knew Histina
would have given her, if positions were reversed.

With her first semester behind her, Antwanesta felt more
relaxed. The culture shock which had so characterized her
initiation to college, was now largely behind her. Without the
constant bombardment of surprises in her environment, she
could begin to examine herself. She could review her
thoughts, her ideas, her beliefs. She could really just be herself
and feel the way… This was a problem. Feelings. She was
having feelings which were just not right. She understood
feelings in a theoretical way. She understood intellectually,
but this was *her*. She didn't want to feel. She did not want to
have feelings, feelings about men, feelings about a man,
feelings about *Zell*!?!

Faced with her inconvenient emotions, Antwanesta
did as she had always done. She prayed. She prayed to God to
give her the virtue she needed to face the challenges and
temptations which had been set before her. She admitted that
there were times when she really wanted physical intimacy.
There were times when her soul and body seemed
disconnected. Her soul ardently wanted God, but parts of her

body acted on their own. It was like a mutiny. Parts of herself would act against her will, with firmness here or moistness there. She knew God would not challenge her beyond her capacity for virtue. Father Alfonzo had told her so. She could control herself; no, not *herself, God.* She would give herself to God. God would relive her of this burden. God would do it. Yes, God. Antwanesta gave herself over to God, and God comforted her.

In Celina's next psychological training session, Feli addressed Celina's anxiety, which Celina herself had, upon introspection, discovered to be an impediment to the development Feli was mentoring her through.

"Each day exists in isolation from all other days. Spend no more than twenty minutes in a day planning the future, and spend *no* time in rumination about the past," said Feli like a spiritual teacher from a mountain in a distant land.

Celina trusted her guru. She endeavored to comply with Feli's prescriptions. Celina's anxiety did diminish.

Feli soon had another patient.

"I think I'm turning into Gretchin," said Antwanesta.

"Really, said Feli. Where's the fur?"

"I'm serious. I'm having thoughts about, about, Zell."

Feli, smiled. "Zell? You *are* Gretchin. No, it's ok. You're normal. Welcome to the human species."

"I'm not supposed to be normal. I'm supposed to resist temptation. I'm—I don't know what I am. I try to give myself only to God, and that works. It really works, for a time, but the feelings keep coming back. I have *desires*."

Feli hugged Antwanesta. "You are a sexual being. How can you be eighteen and not know that?"

"I do. I mean physiologically everything works. I know, but I feel I'm less in control now. I want it more and more, and I want to be with another person."

"I'm with you, Antwanesta. Passion is a scary thing. I use a lot of energy avoiding it, said Feli."

"How?"

"That's the problem. I don't know. I have theories and plans, but they are all very experimental. They are not for you; *trust me*."

"What should *I* do?"

"For now, let's just stick together, and keep each other out of trouble."

"You mean Tear's kind of trouble?"

"Tear's not in trouble. She wants to be pregnant. She is very happy. Better her than me, the pregnant part I mean; I don't mind being happy. Pregnancy can be a wonderful thing for people like Tear, who are ready to take on the responsibility of parenthood." said Feli.

"Do you think Zell is the father?"

"I'm going to take a page from Xiny's book on that. Let's not gossip, especially about the people we love."

So much for Antwanesta as a donor of energy. Feli felt stressed and drained. However, talking with Antwanesta about her intimate desires, and having Antwanesta's trust, did give Feli a deeper sense of closeness with this friend who she found at once both naive and wise. Feli really had no advice. She was struggling with the same problem. She did not hold to the idea that virginity was a virtue, but nonetheless *reason* was like a god to Feli. Reason and passion were always in a state of tension. The solution which Feli had chosen for herself, but would not impose on others, was to separate sex from love. If sex could be somehow quarantined, so that it did not invade her emotionally intimate relationships, she could grow closer to her dear friends, without the instability of passion. The tricky part was that the people with whom she wanted to have sex were the people with whom she had emotional intimacy. There was one person in particular she desired more than others. She had a crush on a friend. This was an unstable situation. She could not even discuss this with Antwanesta. No, she had to handle this one alone. *Reason rules*, Feli thought comfortingly.

Feli had more success with Celina. She gave Celina another tool. She called it the *Mighty As If.* She told Celina to act *as if* she were confident; *as if* she were desirable; *as if* she could not fail in achieving her goal, assuming she followed all the rational steps prerequisite to the goal's attainment. This tool had an amazing effect on Celina. By Darwin Day, what was left of the chronic anxiety, which had so long been an obstacle to her, was simply gone. Men who had so easily dismissed Celina as too high-maintenance, now saw her as a very interesting young woman. She even caught the eye of the young man next door, named Eltwando Agape.

Next session with Celina, Feli gave advice specific to Eltwando. "Eltwando is a Theite who values modesty. He does not want to be set apart as better than others. He resents being called *God-kissed.* Other women praise his skin, hair, and unusual facial features. He does not want to be objectified in that way. Ignore those superficial futures. Show him *what you really love*. Appreciate his intangible characteristics."

"I'm not sure I want Eltwando anymore," said Celina. "What attracted me to him was his calmness. He never seemed to have anxiety like me. Now I *am* that person that I loved. I'm calm and self-assured. I don't need him."

"It is only now that you do not *need* him," Feli said, "that you are really capable to fully *love* him."

Celina, began to cry. "Oh, thank you Feli." Celina hugged Feli.

Feli took both of Celina's hands into her own. She looked into Celina's eyes, and said "Your welcome." As she said the words, Feli gently squeezed Celina's hands.

Xiny did not talk about her personal life with Feli, Gretchin, Antwanesta or *anyone*, so far as Feli knew. Feli could only imagine how hard it would be for Xiny to move on, and open her heart again. Xiny politely rebuffed all efforts by Feli to get her to open and share her feelings. This made it seem all the more peculiar when Xiny seemed to make a sudden and remarkable recovery. Feli could see Xiny was not pretending to be ok. She wasn't even using the power of the *Mighty As If.* No one could hide emotions from Feli. If she looked into a person's eyes, she could see inside, not thoughts, but emotions. She could see that Xiny was once again filled with love. Her love was over-flowing and contagious. *Xiny had someone in her life.* Feli could sense it. There was no other explanation. The ever-discrete Xiny would never talk of course, and Feli knew better than to ask. She would just bask in the warmth of Xiny's radiant emotional energy.

Gretchin of course did not talk to the "bunny-brained psycho-nut" about her social life or her feelings. Gretchin had her worries, concerns, and flawed expectations, but "If it is broken, don't break it more." Feli had grown on Gretchin a little (like a fungus). Gretchin steered well clear of Feli's theories and schemes, but in the spirit, of Professor Irigon Agape's determinism Gretchin's fate was sealed.

In Professor Agape's Religion class Salbird Keysmith asked a question. "Professor Agape, who are the Knowers?"

"The most candid answer I can give you, Mr. Keysmith, is that I don't know. In history there have long been legends of elite members of larger groups, who were said to know secrets concealed from the rank-and-file members of

231

organizations, both religious and secular. They went by various names, 'Gnostics, illuminati, enlightened ones,' and others. I have never heard of the present variant of *Knowers* as being a religious group. They do have an odd shrine in North Point. I've seen it, at least from the outside. It looks like dirt. I expect it washed away in the flooding." As Professor Agape spoke, he thought to himself that perhaps the flooding had exposed some Knower secrets, secrets waiting for some clever mind to decipher. Irigon now had the genesis of a plan.

The classes of the second semester were continuations of those in the prior semester.

Physical training was more advanced. In addition to running, swimming, and weight training; yoga, and wrestling were added. Dr. Sexapopis assigned lots of homework. Antwanesta's muscles were sore, but in a good way. She found rigorous exercise was a good outlet for her sexual tension. She could sublimate her lust, to run faster, lift more, and swim harder. Her desire for sex became so connected with her desire for exercise that her motivation for exercise was even stronger than her passion for math. On the running trail she would target a sexually appealing runner, a little faster than herself, and give chase, telling her subconscious that her reward was in front of her. As her body leaned and her muscles grew, she became stronger and more confident. Neither Feli, nor even Celina could pin her in wrestling. Antwanesta refused to wrestle with men because that was just too intimate. Gretchin was not in her class, but Antwanesta practiced hard with her. Gretchin always won. However, in time wrestling with Antwanesta proved to represent a good workout for Gretchin, simplify because Antwanesta would never surrender.

In Nature, Professor Medic taught as much the history of science as he did physics, chemistry, biology, geology, and astronomy. It was clear in every discipline that the people of the past knew more, and had better methods of measurement than existed in the present day. Epodlo's isolation and violent history had apparently taken a toll on the preservation of scientific knowledge and the technology through which it had been obtained. Antwanesta, learned that medipower was *electricity,* electrons traveling through a conductor. There were means by which electricity could be generated, but generation was oddly unnecessary, as the plumbers had found "hot" lines underground. The lines could be tapped, and the power distributed just like hot and cold water. Scientists and plumbers were developing many new gadgets to run on the power source, however economics seemed to be the biggest impediment to actualization of the potential being promised. The innovative Northerners lacked the capital. Wealthy Royals lacked the incentive. Libertarians made only limited progress due to a lack of internal cooperation. The Theites gave priority to spiritual matters, and were wary of the potential abuse of electrical power in the hands of innately sinful humans. There was promise for battery power. If electricity could be stored and ported, perhaps small-scale entrepreneurial ventures could bring useful devices to market.

One Nature class was devoted to zoology. Though the microscopic world seemed to remain rich in diversity, the macroscopic portion of the animal kingdom was ominously small. There were two species of mollusks, commonly known as the large snail and the small snail. There were only four species of arthropod, all crustaceans, (the wharf crab, the blue crab, the hermit crab, and a tiny creature discovered by Feli's father, Picius when he was researching the food supply for the minnows in Unity Lake). The lake minnows were the last of the fish. There were no amphibians, and just one reptile, the musk turtle. Domesticated chickens were the only birds. Mammalian diversity was reduced to three species, deer, rabbit, and human. The deer and rabbits were no less dependent on humans than the hermit crabs on the large snails. Without their only predator, the deer and rabbits would eat

233

many of the island's plant species into extinction before starving to death themselves.

In History, Professor Soldier taught about past civilizations, the Greco-Roman Empire, the British Empire, the Sino-American Empire, the Neo-Russian Empire; each in turn destroyed from within by political mismanagement.

Professor Solider also had an interesting lecture about historic sea exploration attempts. None could remember when Epodlo was last in contact with the rest of the world. In the centuries past, expeditions of sailing ships had been launched north, south, east, and west. However, none returned with news of contact with other lands. The voyagers sailing south were forced to turn back by extreme heat which left the crewmembers dead or dying. Frostbite and hypothermia took those who sailed north. To the east and west were dead seas, where the air and sea did not move. If a vessel was rowed past this still and windless zone, strong currents forced the ship north or south toward death by heat or cold. Many vessels did not return, but enough did to make it clear that it was unlikely that the missing encountered a happy fate.

Xiny's *Special Studies* were conducted with great efficiency. Xiny forgave Lissy for her deception. She still held a grudge against Illi, and made sure that Dean/Governor Smith knew that she would not tolerate being treated in such away in the future. Even threat of war would not contain her, if Illi crossed her. Xiny and Illi reached a state of mutual respect and accommodation. Illi knew Xiny could expose some her delicate operations, and secret instrumentalities. Xiny knew that Illi was right to be canny about unwarranted disclosure of secrets, and that Illi also controlled the subway she needed to connect with Lissy. This cooperation won Xiny five precious hours per week with her beloved. This was *their* time, and so they made it quality time. They shared their love without interruption or inhibition. Lissy and Xiny were again one committed unit in a state of deep unconditional love.

In Math, the subject had reached the point where Antwanesta could be more student than teacher. She loved the advanced calculus. *Math is so pure, so beautiful*, thought Antwanesta. Feli and Antwanesta did their math homework together. When they reached the correct answer in unison, Antwanesta felt the same way she did when Gretchin pined her in wrestling. The struggle was over, and the thrill of its completion was not hers alone. She had a partner participating the same emotion, a release of tension, a victory sheared.

As the air warmed, off came the clothes on the running trail, and in Freedom Park. Physical Training was again outdoors. Zell's arrows still missed the mark. Tear's runs had been replaced with very slow walks with Zell and Gretchin. Antwanesta joined them sometimes as well.

Under a red maple Celina and Eltwando shared a kiss, nothing sisterly about it.

Chapter 18
Freetown

The school year ended as the Summer heat replaced the pleasant coolness of Spring. Antwanesta, Xiny, Gretchin, and Feli all had excellent grades. There was never any question about that. All were in good spirits, but for Gretchin's complaint that Xiny and Antwanesta had mutually procrastinated her out of selecting a roommate for next year to replace Lissy. There had been and ongoing disagreement on the subject. Gretchin wanted a *man* for a roommate. Xiny and Antwanesta both wanted Feli. Feli resolved the dilemma too late to recruit another candidate. She had made arrangements to room with no less than three men next year. Gretchin felt she had been out maneuvered by her nemesis once again.

At the dock Xiny was about to board a sailboat to the Southern Kingdom. She hugged and kissed Gretchin and Feli. She knew hugging and kissing were behaviors with which Antwanesta was not comfortable. Xiny had previously pushed Antwanesta too far by asking her to sleep next to her when she was grieving the loss of Lissy. There was certainly nothing sexual about lying with her, given her emotional state at the time, but Xiny felt she had asked too much of her dear Theist friend. She wanted to tread lightly now with Antwanesta on the issue of physical contact. In compromise, Xiny took both of Antwanesta's hands, clasped them together between her own, and held them to her sternum bringing her nose to nose with Antwanesta. "After you are done frolicking in the woods with Gretchin, you will come to me in Royal Beach. I will see you two at noon July 25th at East Tower Dock. When I get you

home, I will pamper you in every way I can, and you will love
me enough to *enjoy* being the very special woman you are."
Xiny then smiled and released Antwanesta's hands. She
boarded the boat and sailed off.

Gretchin and Antwanesta were next to leave. Feli
hugged and kissed Gretchin without reciprocity. She then
hugged Antwanesta, who did reciprocate with the tentative
beginning of what could fairly be characterized as some
gesture resembling a hug. Feli did not press her luck with a
kiss. No sooner did Gretchin step on the boat than she shed her
student robe revealing her natural lean form. "Free at last," she
said. Antwanesta removed her robe too, but beneath it was her
black standard Republican dress with her bronze Holy
Hexagon pendant hanging over the front of it.

Feli had a tear in her eye as she saw them leave. She
would go to Newton with Zell in his father's rowboat. They
would drop off, Zell's cousins in Merchant Town on the way.
Wago and Duggy had brought the boat the day before, and
stayed with Zell and Tear in the sophomore dorm. Tear had
taken the earlier boat to Freetown to avoid the sun, in her
condition. Zell would have his father's boat for the Summer,
as usual.

After dropping Wago and Duggy in Merchant Town, Zell and
Feli were alone in a rowboat.

"Is it safe for a gorgeous raven-haired beauty like me
to be alone on the water with such a compelling hunk as you?
asked Feli."

"Of course not. All men are your slaves, and most
women no doubt, responded Zell with equal sarcasm."

"If Mom is to be believed, she and Dad can't stay off
each other, alone in the water like this."

"I really don't need to hear about your parent's sex
life."

"Sorry, I forgot you have a crush on Mom."

"When I was ten."

"I saw you at the trial. You were very uncomfortable when Mom hugged you. You even blushed. You're not over it."

"There is no *it* to be over."

"How about us? Are the doors to romance between us forever closed?"

"What are you up to Feli? You know we have no chemistry. We're buddies, not lovers. Where are you going with this?"

"Is Tear your 'buddy' too?"

"You could have jumped over the teasing, and just asked?"

"I thought I might hit a *Royal* wall."

"Then you know?"

"Yes, I know." Feli slid closer to Zell and placed her hand on his knee. "What are you going to do?"

"What do you think I should do?"

"It's not for me to say, Zell. Fatherhood is a major life decision. It is a big responsibility, and a big commitment for a revolutionary who wants to save the world."

"It's up to Tear."

Feli removed her hand from Zell's knee. "Zell, look at me."

Zell looked into Feli's eyes.

With her pupils fixed on Zell's, Feli said, "Tear will not deny you. Barthon and Gregor are not waiting for Tear in Freetown. *You* could be the father if you *choose* to be."

"But I'm not. We never had sex before she was pregnant."

"No one cares about biology, especially in Libertaria. Tear wants you. You know it."

"Yes, but she doesn't want *just* me."

"So, does anyone want just *one* person?"

"I don't know. I think *you* would be happy with a certain someone."

"Don't change the subject. My love life is another level of complexity."

"It's not that different. What if Gretchin were pregnant, and she wanted you as a partner, and parent to her child?"

"You know the answer."

"Do I? Is that easy?"

"What about your cherished emotional and financial control? You would give all that up to give yourself to a lover who would force you to share her with whoever she chose?"

"That's the problem with passion. Reason gets pushed out the window. What *I* would do in a state of passion does not govern *your* choice now. I will not make the choice for you. I just won't let you delude yourself into believing you don't have a choice. Agape the Red may not believe in freedom, but I do, at least until passion steals it away."

Elsewhere, as the sailboat approached Freetown, Antwanesta felt ambivalent. She grew up being told that the land to the east was populated by savages who engaged in acts of

239

violence and unspeakable perversion in the open light of day, and in unimaginably worse behaviors at night. Her friendship with Gretchin had largely dispelled the propaganda fed to her in childhood, but to some extent, had also confirmed it. Gretchin was undeniably a loving person who would do anything for her friends. However, by Theite standards (Antwanesta's standards) Gretchin was sexually perverse. It was not just stripping off her clothes whenever permitted—Antwanesta had gotten used to that—it was Gretchin's open and enthusiastic advocacy of polygamy and fornication. Antwanesta loved Gretchin, but how does one reconcile such open and unrepentant sin? Despite this, Antwanesta felt oddly safe with Gretchin. Antwanesta had great faith that Gretchin could and would protect her when no one else could or would dare. Gretchin was an enigma, but in some strange way Gretchin was *hers*.

Antwanesta had heard that the people of the East were violent. Gretchin had confirmed this by her own actions. She had seen Gretchin with her own eyes as she beat Barthon bloody. Antwanesta heard, but had not seen, that Gretchin, had in cold blood and with an even taunting attitude, defeated three trained, armed soldiers with her bare hands. The Holy Hexagon stood for, among other things, peace. How could virtue be found in one such as Gretchin? How could such a sinful woman be redeemed? Why did Antwanesta feel Gretchin was *not* so bad?

The sailboat pulled up to the dock. Gretchin and Antwanesta hopped off the boat with their overstuffed rucksacks. Men on the dock wore heavy deerskin aprons, obviously to protect themselves, from the splinters and ruff edges of the crates they loaded and unloaded. As Gretchin and Antwanesta moved along the dock Antwanesta saw that other people wore less.

"I feel naked," said Gretchin.

"You are naked, so is everyone but me," said Antwanesta.

"Look closer, said Gretchin"

Looking closer was exactly what Antwanesta was trying not to do. When she complied with Gretchin's suggestion she did notice something. Everyone except her and Gretchin was armed. They all wore belts or straps with knives, swords, or axes. *This is bad*, thought Antwanesta. *These people are very dangerous*. Even children as young a five carried real knives.

"Why is everyone armed?" Antwanesta felt uneasy.

"Freedom isn't free," said Gretchin. "These people are protecting their right to bear arms by exercising it."

"Why do they need to?"

"They take their responsibility seriously. There is peace and freedom in Libertaria because enough people take the responsibility to deter those who would take freedom away."

In addition to the ominous presence of the ubiquitous weaponry, Antwanesta felt uncomfortable because she stood out. She was in her black dress; while on paths, alleyways, doorways, benches, chairs, and everywhere she could see people; all were nude, but for the straps, belts, or chains to carry blades. Antwanesta did not want to stand out, but she even more did not want to conform. Back at school she had been nude with her peers, but with reason. It would be just silly to wear clothes in a bath. Exercise was another reasonable exception; clothes would get in the way, and get sweaty. In the dorm she did without cloths for comfort; she was at home. *Here is public*, she thought. *This is just gratuitous nudity*. There was no moral basis for it. At least in the public bath in Newton she was swimming, and indoors no less. Here people are just out there (*everywhere*). She stayed in her dress. It was a bit hot, but morality was at stake, and as clothing goes a standard Republican dress is as comfortable as it gets.

In front of the docks was downtown Freetown, a wide deep area of one, two, and a few three story shops and apartment buildings. A few were still in disrepair due to the quake. Behind these lower buildings were three strong but elegant towers of nine or ten stories. They looked like luxurious hotels. They had exterior structural reinforcement like the tower back on campus. Gretchin saw Antwanesta looking up at the architectural wonders.

"Those are the brothels, Ant," said Gretchin, with what sounded a little like pride.

From Antwanesta's education in the Theocracy, she associated brothels with sin, not just sin, but sin of the most disgusting sort. She felt nauseated as her imagination took she to places she did not want to be.

Antwanesta's reaction had the roots of its origin in historical fact. Brothels were places of prostitution. Prostitution was an ancient practice. Historically prostitution had been, at best, an economic opportunity for financially disadvantaged women, and, at worst, *and far more often,* slavery, by which vulnerable young women were exploited to pleasure customers, and enrich pimps and crime syndicates. That was the past. Now a brothel was a very different place. A brothel, in modern Epodlo, was an educational institution. It was a place to train men in the very important art of pleasing women. There was sex, no doubt of that; but there was much more. Men were trained by mature experts to serve women, physically *and emotionally*. It wasn't just about how to give women external and internal orgasms of varying length, number, and intensity. Men learned how to behave like MEN. They were even taught *common sense*. A man educated in a good brothel could be exactly what a woman wanted, even when she didn't know herself *what* she wanted.

Maidens of Epodlo, Book 1 — Antwanesta Agape and the Mystery of the Red-dot Moon

There were variations in quality. The three tall luxurious buildings served collectively as an iconic landmark for Freetown. They were much like, in the distant past, the Statue of Liberty or the Eifel Tower had been for their respective cities. All three were owned by one corporation. They were undeniably the best, the top tier brothels. They offered the best education, at a high tuition. The women, fortunate enough to have graduates of these institutions in their stables, would say, "You get what you pay for." The second tier was composed of the "want-to-be" brothels. They did not have the best of the best women to render instruction, but men still truly benefited from the education they received. The men got a basic education in the art of pleasing women. Graduates, and even men seeking refresher courses, were clearly far better equipped to serve their mistresses than untrained men. The third tier institutions were small-scale entrepreneurial ventures, often just one or a few women who could neither found a stable of their own, nor get a good position as a stable carl. They were generally the blind leading the blind. They were cheap, but instructionally, just going through the motions.

The word, *prostitute* was not used because of the dark association with the distant past. The women who instructed men in the brothels, were *women of the brothels*. They were some of the most highly respected and highly paid people in Libertaria.

Antwanesta was unaware of this reality. She averted her gaze. She turned to see the small shops. The shop right next to the southernmost brothel sold prosthetic limbs. In the window there were realistic wooden arms, legs, etcetera. Antwanesta concluded that her misgivings about the nude practice of swordplay were well-founded. Otherwise, such a store could never generate the revenue necessary to be self-sustaining in peacetime.

Thomas David Valentine

There were also small markets selling fruits and vegetables. Others sold live chickens. A butcher shop sold fresh venison and rabbit. There were jewelry shops, a fletcher with the most perfect of arrows, a knife emporium, black smith, and a shop for deerskin accessories. There were even clothing stores, with red circles on the doors, closed until Fall.

There were shoe stores open. Antwanesta found herself lusting for what she could never have. There were the finest deer leather shoes and boots in the most extravagant array of styles. "Oh my…" Antwanesta almost uttered her Lord's name in vain. She had to settle for frail cotton shoes. It would be a sin against peace to use animal products, but Antwanesta coveted the finely crafted creations, which only her eyes could consume for the vicarious pleasure of her feet. She tried to bury her desire with prayer, but she *wanted* those shoes so very much. Libertaria was indeed a place of sin. Oh, the temptation. *God save me. Have mercy on me as sinner. You would not show me this without granting me the power to resist.*

Then God spoke to her, not in words. It was more of a vision. She saw it. *Here? How? Who?* Antwanesta was surprised by the unmistakable sight of a *Theite church*. It had black doors with hexagons. It was wedged between two shops and in the shadow of the brothels, but it was here.

As she looked at it, a young man approached her unseen until he spoke. "Mother, bless," He said.

"I'm not a priestess," Antwanesta said, taken aback by the error. She quickly realized that to these nude wild-folk, her skimpy black dress with the Holy Hexagon pendant made her look like one who had been called by God to serve in the special capacity of performing sacred rituals, and bestowing God's blessing.

The young man scurried off to his shopping. Then
seconds later, a real priestess stepped out from the door of the
church. Antwanesta trotted up and said "Mother bless."

Gretchin who had been examining knives at the shop
next door, followed her. Gretchin generally trusted her people
to behave in a responsible manner, as free people must, but
she did not trust Antwanesta. It was not Antwanesta's
character which was in question. That was never a question
with her. Gretchin kept close watch over Ant, because she did
not trust her judgement. She was like a child in Freetown.
Antwanesta was not just ignorant. Gretchin had every
expectation that her dear friend would find some novel way to
do something stupid. It was bad enough that she went about
teasing men with that *oh-no-you-can't-see-it* dress.

The priestess made the sign of the hexagon, and gave
Antwanesta the ritual blessing. "It is so good to see you here
Sister." I am Mother Bethunia. Welcome to our Lord's house.
Please come in."

"I am Antwanesta. I'm not dressed to enter a church."

"If I only allowed people in long black robes to enter
the church here in Freetown, I would have an empty building,
and I would have to answer for that. You're fine. Please come
in."

"I want to go in and pray, but I am here with my
friend."

"You can go in and talk to the gods if you like, Ant.
I'll wait here for a few minutes," said Gretchin.

"You may join us if you wish. God loves you and
wants you here. So do I." said Mother Bethunia to Gretchin.

This shocked Antwanesta. Is was bad enough that she
was wearing a skimpy Republican dress, but Gretchin was her
fully nude self.

"Ok, but I'm not talking to any gods," replied Gretchin.

They entered the hexagonal stone structure. The interior was very similar to the church in Lord's Landing and the chapel back on campus. It differed primarily in its iconography. Instead of being dedicated to Saint Hypatia, or Saint Charles, this church was dedicated to Saint Albert. The icons to the to the left of the opening to the Holy Hexagon depicted Saint Albert. In the one farther left he was lying on a hill apparently daydreaming. The right one had his traditional formal pose with his hair all askew. His usual iconic position was occupied by Saint Hypatia. How ironic it was; Saint Hypatia wore clothes in the icon here, and in the church at Lord's Landing *she* was the nude one in the church. Antwanesta smiled at the thought that the iconic could be ironic.

Antwanesta, knelt at the front of the church. Gretchin sat gingerly on the front bench hoping to avoid splinters. Antwanesta silently recited her prayer thirty-six times. Gretchin looked at the golden emptiness of the icon to the right of the hexagon.

After her prayer and some light conversation with the priestess, Antwanesta said goodbye to Mother Bethunia, who said, "Please come again, both of you. God's house is always open, and God always loves you."

What do you see in that spooky deer feces, Ant? Gretchin said as Antwanesta made her parting sign at the door.

"It gives me comfort," said Antwanesta

It gives me the creeps," said Gretchin. Look who's over there."

Across from the church Antwanesta saw some familiar nude bodies. They were not fully nude, each had a silver chain above her hips to hold the scabbards of small

daggers. Relisha had three. Wondina had just one, but slightly
larger. Gretchin and Antwanesta knew the Metropopis girls
from the third floor of the dorm. They had lived at the other
end of the hall, near the stairs, with the two Royals, Oluga and
Mulucia.

"Look Relish, said Wondina."

"Gretchin, Antwanesta. Hey!" Relisha waved.

Gretchin and Antwanesta smiled.

Relisha said, "A bit over dressed aren't you,
Antwanesta?"

Before Antwanesta could answer, Wondina said,
"She's hot."

"In two ways," said Relisha. Relisha and Wondina
both giggled.

"Look Gretchin, is unarmed. Are you Antwanesta's
stable carl now sexy girl? If you're not I have a place for you,
said Wondina."

"No thanks," said Gretchin. "Don't think that I need
weapons to take you."

"I agree, in close quarters, you can lick us both, but
give me twenty balls, and I will lay you down," said Relisha.

"Twenty-five, and only if you see me coming," said
Gretchin playfully.

"I don't know if you are talking about violence or
sex, but either way count me out," said Antwanesta.

"We're just playing," said Wondina, "but seriously,
aren't you hot in that black dress?"

"Yes," said Antwanesta.

Thomas David Valentine

"Why wear it?"

"To be modest," said Antwanesta.

"Whatever, said Relisha. I wouldn't want to wash a dress every couple of days. I have a life."

Back when she was in the Theocracy, Antwanesta washed two robes every six days in Summer. She remembered as a girl wanting so much to be free of the robe in the heat. That was as a girl, before she understood the importance of modesty. However, the rationale she had used back in school was coming back to her mind. She had thought it may be immodest to stand out where nudity was the norm. That rationalization had worked in the moment, but it was never really satisfactory. What if the norm were to eat meat, have sex, or kill people? "Everybody is doing it," does not really seem like a truly rational justification for anything. *This dress is hot and I will need to wash it every three days so I don't stink.* That is a line of reasoning which is much more compelling. *Maybe I will just wear the dress outdoors, or just in town*, Antwanesta thought.

Relisha and Wondina went on their way. Gretchin and Antwanesta were headed to the house of Gretchin's "Pop One." However, they didn't get far before meeting another classmate. It was Petina, one of Feli's two Libertarian roommates.

"Gretchin, Hi. Antwanesta. Gretchin, I just want you to know I am ok with everything. Everything is fine right?"

"Yes, fine. There is nothing else to say," said Gretchin.

"I accept that Feli is yours,"

"Whatever; we're fine; don't worry about it."

248

"Thanks Gretchin, I have great respect for you and your mother."

"Yes, I get it."

Petina nodded and jogged off.

Antwanesta asked, "What was that about?"

"It's just Feli. She drives all her roommates insane. It's a hobby I think."

"What?"

"You know; Petina, is a babbling idiot, Histina is delusional, and Celina is afraid of her own shadow. What they all have in common is an overdose of the ultimate bunny-brain."

"How is Histina delusional?"

"She thinks she's funny."

"Celina does not look too frightened at the moment,"

"What do you mean? Oh. Your Brother Eltwando does not seem to have your clothing hang-up."

"Let's go say Hi."

"No, We've seen them all year. Let's get to the house. Pop One will worry, and I want to check on Tear."

Pop One? Antwanesta realized she did not know what to call Gretchin's Father. When Antwanesta was in Newton for Saint Isaac's Day break, she knew to call Feli's father, "Mr. Smith." In the Republic all married men take the last name of their wives. However, in Libertaria last names are not passed parent to child. The name reflects the number of fathers a child has. Gretchin's Pop One was probably not a Quadrapopis. His last name would reflect the number of sexual partners, his mother had. Antwanesta decided to ask

249

Gretchin. "What is the proper way for me to address your Pop One?"

"Call him Ottarian. That's his first name. It's ok."

"Ok. What is a stable carl?"

"If I try to explain it, you will misunderstand. You will meet my mom's stable carl when we go to the beach house. Dussy is a very good carl, she can explain what she does better than I can. She will give you the lecture *and the lab* if you want."

Gretchin walked along a path away from the center of town.

"Are there toilets areas in Libertaria?"

"Yes! Ant, we aren't savages urinating from tree limbs. We have Royal Plumbers just like you."

"Well I need one now,"

"You are in luck. We're home."

Chapter 19

The Key

Celina and Eltwando had not seen Antwanesta and Gretchin,
despite the visibility of Antwanesta's black dress. Celina was
taking Eltwando to her parent's house. Like Antwanesta,
Eltwando could not visit the Theocracy for the Summer
without the risk of being detained. Eltwando's mother wanted
him to take an apartment in Merchant Town for the Summer,
but he trusted his good friend Celina. He wanted to be with
her. When she invited him, he accepted without hesitation. He
accepted readily, not because he was overcome by lust; but
because he knew that God was looking after him. God would
protect him from harm, and lead him away from temptation.
He shed his cloths more readily than Antwanesta, not due to
lesser modesty; but because he knew that if he were clothed in
Libertaria, he would inspire curiosity. His rare features already
drew interest he did wish to receive. If he covered himself, the
people of Libertaria, might think he was even more *different*
than he really was. What onlookers could imagine might
inspire lust. He could quell their lust by showing to all that he
was just a man. He was a member of the human species, not
some alien. He was no more kissed by God than each and
every one of God's beloved children. Being named *Agape* did
not make him unique or even special. He was not different. He
knew where he came from. He had put the pieces together. It
was no coincidence that the lust reduction ritual in the
monastery and the Humanist sperm donation program were so
similar. He knew what the monks at the monastery were doing

with his seamen. There was no *immaculate conception*. He and the other young men of the Theocracy were being duped into providing the *seed of God*. The men of the Theocracy were being robbed. One of the most precious blessings God could grant men was being taken against their will. *The church leaders, had become corrupted*, Eltwando thought. They were stealing *fatherhood*.

Faculty members were also free for the Summer. Risky had ridden the boat with Tear, just in case she went into labor. Dean Illi Smith would go to her home in Libertaria, before going to North Point to visit her father. The other professors also went to their home lands, except one. Professor Irigon Agape (The Red) would do some field research in the Republic. This was a bit of a secret, clandestine research one might call it. He told Illi something vague about studying old books in the library atop the Newton Museum, and in the Republic Archives at Democratica City. He said nothing concrete, nothing specific, such as his subject of study. Illi might disapprove.

He sailed for Merchant Town. In his pocket was some property he told the dean he would return to its owner for her. The owner lived in Merchant Town. The owner's father had a shop on the main square. No one could miss it (the only locksmith shop in Epodlo). Irigon returned Salbird Keysmith's set of keys, and then, with permission, borrowed one back. Sal had no objection. Had he not inspired this little adventure?

Irigon assembled his provisions for the trek north. Travel was far easier in the Northern Republic in Summer than in Winter. The weather could still get cold. There was still snow on the ground north of Democratica City. However, there is a vast difference between being cold and, *"You will die unless you get in a geothermally heated house NOW!"* That is a general description of the state of the northern part of the Republic in Winter. The intrepid pilgrims, hiking west to Newton each December, dressed very well for the cold.

It is a 900 kiloball walk from Merchant Town to Democratica City. The path was straight, well maintained, and with fully plumbed toilet facilities at regular intervals. God bless those Royal Plumbers. He could make it in nine or ten days allowing for reasonable rest stops, and with the good weather, which was assured except for light rain on June 8th. He made the trek last year with a friend. Walking alone this time would give him time to think, pray, and introspect about who he was, and what destiny would make of him. Illi would be pleased if he would lose a little body fat. She could be as dogged as Risky about fitness. She was always pushing faculty members to run the trail on campus. Morgont Medic was a committed runner. Elonora Agape (the Black) never ran. Irigon (the Red) was in between. The long walk would be good for him.

Gretchin opened the door of her Pop One's house with no knock. "It's me!"

Out from the kitchen came Gretchin's Pop One, Ottarian Dipopis. He was wearing a cotton kitchen apron. He had apparently been cooking. He was a tall, strong, fit man in his mid-forties. He hugged Gretchin. Then he nodded to Antwanesta, and said "Greetings Antwanesta." Gretchin had trained him in the standard touchless greeting of Theites. He even knew not to call her "Sister," an error which outsiders often made. The sibling titles were intended for use only by other Theites themselves (Paternal siblings).

Antwanesta, said "Greetings Ottarian," and nodded back.

Risky came from another room holding the very round-bellied Tear by the arm. Tear shared a sisterly kiss with Gretchin. Risky did not. She was being *Royal* about the secret sisterhood in front of Antwanesta. She and Gretchin would substitute their kiss with hidden winks when Antwanesta was distracted by Tear's blossoming nude form.

"Hi girls," said a cheerful Risky.

"Hi Dr. Sexapopis," said Antwanesta.

Risky responded, "I put up with the dean's *curtesy and respect* deer dung on campus, but *here* I'm 'Risky,' Antwanesta."

Antwanesta, smiled. It felt good to feel a sense of friendship with this woman she admired and truly respected. "Ok, Risky."

Risky was not one of Ottarian's children. She was at the house to check on Tear as her physician. "If there are any problems or the water breaks, send Retch for me, I'm guessing three weeks, but labor could come at any time now. Make her take it easy." Risky left. She was staying nearby at the house of a pop who was not mutual with Gretchin, but Gretchin obviously knew where to find her.

Ottarian was kind, smart, and pleasant to speak with, even after his apron came off. Antwanesta was now used to that sort of thing. She felt over-dressed, but stayed in her black standard Republican dress through dinner.

"Gretchin tells me she loves you are like a sister. That's the highest praise Gretchin can give. Nothing comes between Gretchin and her sisters."

"Pop," Gretchin interjected with wide eyes. Antwanesta was only supposed to know of one sister.

Ottarian was quick on the uptake, and shifted the subject before Antwanesta could inquire about the plurality of his ill-chosen word. "I haven't met many Theites, but *you* are a charmer. How did you get to the school?

Antwanesta related her story. Ottarian listened with
interest. Tear too. She had only heard the tale secondhand or
from the perspective of the *valiant crusader* who comes in
near the end.

"What made you get on that raft?" Ottarian's
question lay in the air. All were eager to hear Antwanesta's
answer.

"I don't know."

That answer was a disappointment to Ottarian, Tear,
and even Gretchin, who did not expect to hear anything
profound or enlightening.

"I mean that's why. I don't know. I don't know a lot
of things. I wanted to learn. I thought I could learn more from
people with whom I disagreed, people who saw the world
differently. I didn't want to be taught by professors who were
*imbued with the spirit, rightly teaching from a God-center
perspective*. I had enough of that, *too much*. I wanted more. I
wanted to be challenged. Then the Church and my mother
cracked down, and tried to force me into a mold I did not
choose for myself. That was it. I had to leave. I had to be who
I am. I had to make myself who I am."

After a silent pause, "Amen Sister!" It was Ottarian.
"That was liberty talking. You wanted to be a free woman, and
you *took* your right by force of your own will. On behalf of
the fathers you should have had, let me say, *I'm proud of you*."

Antwanesta blushed, and in that moment she really
felt that Gretchin was her sister.

The house had three bedrooms. Ottarian had his. Tear
had her own. Antwanesta was with Gretchin. After sharing
beds with both Xiny, and Feli, proximity with Gretchin, naked
in a small bed did not even register. There was no sin in lying
with her friend. They weren't having sex, and even if they
were, so what? Antwanesta did not think this, at least not with

255

her conscious mind. She loved Gretchin, and if it was with her mind, body, or both she was ok with that. *Oh my, that second glass of wine was too much.*

Antwanesta shed her dress and said her prayers as usual. She felt at one with herself and with God. Was there a difference? Did it even matter?

She lay next to Gretchin and asked, "How do you think it is with Xiny?"

"I'm sure she is fine at home doing Royal stuff."

"No, I mean, how it is to be the way she is?"

"Ant, Xiny is a Royal. Royals do not talk about the personal lives of others. Let's honor the friend we love by not discussing her sex life."

"Your right, Gretchin."

"Now you did it."

"Did what?"

"Put Bunny-brain in my head!"

"Feli?"

"You said, 'You're right Gretchin.' I immediately thought of the sarcastic flirtatious remark Bunny-brain would make in response. She's in my head. She does that to people."

"You're getting paranoid."

"See! Even you can see it. She is a psycho-menace."

"I can't even say you're crazy without you thinking you're crazy. Just shut up and sleep, Antwanesta said with a smile."

The further north Irigon hiked the colder the nights in his tent became. He began to yearn for her. Yes, *her.* Irigon had

stepped away from the chastity corner of the Holy Hexagon
long ago. It was his destiny of course. He wanted to feel her
warmth, her touch, her love. Even as his body was yielding to
age, his passion was strong. He had forgiven her for
everything, for all of *them*. He had no control over the
deterministic universe which had brought him into orbit
around the star in his life. He was captured by her gravity, his
destiny.

However, destiny can be cruel. Irigon's love was not
his alone. She was a woman who willfully rejected fidelity (at
least as willfully, as the illusion of liberty may allow). He was
not her *only* man. He knew this. He opposed this. He even
hated it, but he loved her more. He would not (could not)
resist the deep passion which drew him to his beloved, and
compelled him to submit to her will.

From an objective intellectual perspective, Irigon
rejected the polygamous lifestyle which had become the norm
in the wild East. Women would never *share* a man. Why
should men be forced to *share* a woman? Where is the equity?
The Libertarians would say, "You are free to leave." However,
there is no truth in that. The chains of emotion are stronger
than any metal extracted from the Royal mines. He was not
free. No one is ever free, but he was somehow less free than
her.

Feli was in another part of the Republic. She was back home
in Newton. She was in the Newton Museum, the place Irigon
had led Illi to believe he would be doing research. Feli was not
guarding the Golden Arm, or cleaning delicate exhibits. Her
shift was over. She was on her own, just enjoying this place
she loved. She smiled as she remembered the shared joy she
had with Antwanesta in this place on Newton Day break. She
was saddened that she had no time to bring Sweetheart here
when they came to retrieve her mom to represent Zell at his
trial.

The telescope to see the hexagon in the sky was now open. It had been closed when Antwanesta was at the Museum in December because the sky had been overcast. The geosynchronous black hexagon looked like just a tiny shapeless dot at the magnification provided by the museum's telescope. Feli had never seen it through the more powerful telescope at Saint Isaac's College in the Theocracy. Antwanesta had seen it. She told Feli that she saw it on a fieldtrip when she was ten. The shape was visible at the higher magnification; even then it was only roughly hexagonal in shape. Humanist scientists had no good explanation for the black satellite. Perhaps it was some piece of ancient technology, for communication, or a platform to view the stars without the obstructing atmosphere. No one knew, except the Theists of course. "It was a message from God to live in virtue, and to serve Him now and in the age to come." So said the Pontiff and many Theists before him.

"Feli? Feli? Oh my Dear, I am so glad I found you. I need you, Dear. You're the best. There is no one I would rather have."

"Professor Boatman?"

"Yes Dear, I am so glad I caught you. You must say, Yes. Please tell me you will say, Yes. You have to. There is no one better. Say, Yes."

"Yes, to what?"

"I got the grant, and then I got permission. *Permission!* Do you know what that means?"

"Generically yes, but in this context, No, *because I don't know the context*. What is it? What are you talking about?"

"I got permission to measure it."

"It? It!" Feli now understood. "They will let you. You want me to help, to go *there*?"

"Yes, Dear."

"Is it safe?"

"The Bishop of God City signed off on it herself. Of course it's safe."

"YES!"

Professor Gerluke Boatman, archology professor from Newton Junior College, had received permission from the Bishop of God City to make detailed measurements and a magnified examination of *the* Holy Hexagon.

Professor Boatman was 62, but no man a third of his age had his energy and enthusiasm when it came to research. Feli knew this was *big*. She would have a very interesting Summer.

Xiny came home to Royal Beach. Her family house and the neighboring Royal Palace, had been largely rebuilt. The interior and trim work had yet to be done, but the main exterior structure was complete. Any person not of Royal blood, who compared the total destruction which existed after the tsunami with the amazing progress which existed now, would conclude that this was not humanly possible. That was exactly why foreigners were kept away. The Kingdom had proprietary secrets, and every Royal knew that no outsider was allowed to discover them. Royals could see the most amazingly improbable things, and *never say a word*.

Xiny was not surprised by the progress. She knew better than most how long projects should take. She had been trained in logistics management, and had in the past, overseen construction projects for her father. She saw that all projects were right on schedule, the optimally efficient schedule of course.

259

Thomas David Valentine

Like Antwanesta, Eltwando discovered the Theite church in
Freetown. He also had the same misgivings about entering
naked. Mother Bethunia gave him the same encouraging
words Antwanesta had heard. Celina, like Gretchin found the
church creepy. Eltwando prayed and spoke to the priestess.
Mother Bethunia was curious about his story. He gave her a
much abbreviated version, and then spoke to her about the
matter which interested him. He asked her about *marriage*.
Marriage had not been practiced in the Theocracy for a couple
of centuries. However, it used to be a sacrament. There was a
ritual whereby God's blessing was requested and granted. God
not only tolerated the union of two people; He sanctified it.
Marriage had generally been seen as a substitute for the purity
of chastity, a second best choice. It was thought better to have
a monogamous relationship blessed by God, than to fail in
chastity in a base unregulated way. Surly it was better to be
committed to one spouse, reflecting God's love, than to
bounce from person to person, copulating at random,
producing unknown children.

Mother Bethunia said that she had not performed
such a ritual, but she knew of someone who had. Bishop
Korack, with the approval of the Pontiff, had performed
several holy marriages between Royals who had come to the
Lord. Royals had a deep tradition of monogamy, to have
refused to sanctify their marriages would have brought
missionary activity in the Kingdom to a dead stop against an
immovable wall. A similar approach was considered in
Libertaria, but the Pontiff was not about to condone
sanctification of a polygamous relationship. The priestess said
she would make inquires. She thought that a marriage could be
sanctified if the couple were both Theists and committed to
monogamy, but she could make no commitments without
consulting with Bishop Salestina. Libertaria did not have its
own bishop. Its programs were administered out of God City.
Mother Bethunia would write to her bishop for guidance.

After leaving the church, Eltwando asked Celina, "What do you think?"

"About marriage?"

Eltwando nodded.

For the first time since Feli had trained her, Celina was nervous. "I don't know. I want you in my stable. I very much do, but this religious stuff. It's just so weird. You want me to give up other men?"

"I'd give up other women?"

"What other women?"

"Hypothetical other women, who I would not be with because I'm committed to you."

"It's bad enough that you refuse to have sex with me. Now you want to lock me in a box and say I can't have other men."

"I love you Celina. That's why I want to do this. It is not easy for me to relinquish celibacy."

"Not easy for you! How do you think that makes me feel! 'It's not easy to put my penis in your vagina. It is such a sacrifice to endure the horror.' You don't love me!"

"I do love you Celina. Love is more than sex. You know that."

"Shut up Eltwando! If I weren't responsible for you being here, I'd leave you here in the street to be *raped*! A pretty pacifist like you wouldn't make it to the dock, with your precious chastity." Celina knew full well that Eltwando would not be raped in the streets of Freetown. Libertarians had great respect for the bodily autonomy of others. Rapists were almost as rare as fathered rabbits. However, the people of the East, had long allowed outsiders to see them as violent and dangerous. Some outsiders did not respect freedom. For them fear served and a practical substitute for respect. "Now come with me, and don't say another word until you figure out how to calm me down." Celina fought back her tears, and dragged Eltwando to her family home.

At the Newton museum there was a similar altercation. Histina and Hardy were visiting the museum. Upon meeting Zillestra, Hardy expressed flirtatious interest in her, *with Histina on his arm.* With self-restraint only Feli's training had enabled, Histina held her tongue until Hardy and she were out of Zillestra's earshot.

"Are you with me or *not*!?" snapped Histina.

"This is a trick question, right?" Humor was the only defense Hardy knew.

"I'm serious. I am with you, but you want every girl you meet."

"Just the pretty ones."

"Why am *I* not enough?"

"I give to you. You give to me. We're square. What does it matter what I do with other women? You even get more than I do."

"Hardy! I'm trying to create a deep emotional connection with you, and your maintaining some kind of orgasm score sheet. This isn't working, Hardy!"

"Why not?"

Histina walked away, hurt and furious.

"God exists. I have proof." These were Feli's sarcastic words, coming from behind Hardy.

"Another one. What? Are you two taking turns trying turn me gynophobic?"

"No, my God." Feli bowed.

"I can think of better ways for you to worship me than that. What's the punch line, Feli?"

"God must exist. Only a Divine hand could combine your wit, charm, and anatomical perfection with such abysmal stupidity."

"Histina has earned the right to insult me. You never give me anything, Feli. At least tell me what's wrong with Histina. You know her better than anyone."

"Yes, I do. I lived with her nine months, and every time you gave her a yeast infection, she asked me for a pelvic exam."

"Yea, so what's wrong with her?"

"After diligent observation, intensive examination, and the application of several psychometric analytical tools, I found that Histina is…." Feli beckoned Hardy close. She whispered into his ear, "…*normal.*"

"You've had your fun, Feli. What do I do?"

Feli, put her arm around Hardy's back. Now with a tone of sincere compassion she said, "You need to decide what *you* want. Do you want the maximum number of superficial sexual experiences you can have, or do you want to have a deep personal connection with a person who loves you?" Feli then withdrew her arm.

"The second choice is really scary to me, Feli."

"I know. It scares me too. The question is not as easy to answer as it sounds."

"Histina's great. She does everything. Nothing grosses her out."

"It's not about that, Hardy. Histina loves you. You need to decide if you are going to accept the wonderful gift she is offering you, or if you want take a pass, and let her find someone else to give her the love she deserves to receive."

Hardy sighed. "Your right, Feli. Histina is special. She deserves someone special. I just don't know if I can be that person."

"Look inside yourself, Hardy. You are a human. You are the greatest wonder the unconscious forces of nature ever created. Greatness is within you. You can be the man Histina wants, or you can be something less. You decide." With a final caress of Hardy's shoulder, Feli walked away.

Chapter 20

The Birth

Irigon made it close to the southern outskirts of Democratica
City. He just wanted to find the first hotel, check in, and have
a nice warm bath. Professor Irigon Agape, found no room at
the inn. All hotels were booked and would remain booked for
the foreseeable future. That meant more camping, but not just
for Agape the Red. The area south of Democratica City had
become a city of tents. Earthquake refugees were everywhere.

Recovery in the North was going at a snail's pace,
not even the pace of the big snail, the pace of the small one.
Many buildings in the city had been destroyed or were too
dangerous to occupy. To repair the public buildings required
the governmental agency responsible for building maintenance
to undertake the legally prescribed competitive procurement
process. The agency (the name of which was changed every
few years) had to draw up detailed specifications for each
building repair. The agency also had to develop criteria for
selection of a building contractor which met the rationally
defensible needs of the Republic. A notice of intent to procure
services also had to be drafted. All these documents had to be
reviewed and approved by several layers of management, as
well as specialists to check for compliance with a myriad of
applicable laws. This took time, so government buildings lay
in ruin.

There was a similar problem with private buildings.
Competitive procurement was not compelled, but compliance

with a long list of legal prerequisites was. Building permits required plan review, which required the drafting of detailed plans to check for compliance with building codes. The backlog of plan reviews would take many years to process. Also many of the more obscure pieces of building hardware, required to comply with the building codes, were not available in near the quantities necessary. Many more building contractors, carpenters, masons, tilers, etc. had to be trained and licensed. All plumbing, at least, was handled by Royals. The Kingdom had negotiated a treaty with the Republic to exempt Royal Plumbers from licensure, regulation, codes, and plan approval. This was fortunate because if the Kingdom had not been given a free hand to address the plumbing needs of the Republic, both the drinking water and heating systems would have failed. For the next election most voters would have been dead, and given the very high standards of integrity in the Republic, dead people never voted.

God bless the Royal Plumbers, Irigon said aloud. Even in the tent city there were plenty of baths. They were not made of stone. They were portable modular structures made of shinny aluminum, and there were lots of them, open and free. Irigon indulged himself in the nearest. The water was hot and clean, and the women there were marvelous wonders of God's creation. Irigon had long ago learned to interpret modesty and chastity in ways which did not prohibit his appreciation of feminine beauty. Clean, warm, and with esthetically pleasing company, Irigon, reflected on the objective of his expedition.

Salbird Keysmith had asked about the Knowers. Irigon was troubled, even embarrassed, by his own ignorance. He had said that he did not know if the Knowers represented a religious tradition. He didn't know. To the best of his knowledge he had not met a Knower. Would he even know if he did? No. The Knowers were presumably a secret society. If a Knower could keep secrets half as well as Royals, Irigon would be blind to the presence of a Knower right in front of him.

However, Irigon did know something about the
Knowers. This was something which even had a religious
quality to it. He knew that the Knowers had a shrine. He had
even seen the shrine in North Point, a short walk from his
friend's house. Everything was a short walk within North
Point. It was so tiny that even the term, "village" seemed to
carry a connotation of something more grand in scale. Few
had reason to live in the coldest place on Epodlo. The shrine
was locked behind a simple mesh cage, with a common
padlock, if it didn't wash away in the flood. Thanks to Mr.
Keysmith, Irigon had a key. He might not even need it. The
shrine's protective cage may well have been destroyed. Mesh
cage or not, he would sneak in, probe around, and just maybe
find something to lift the ignorance which obscured his view
of the knowledge he did not possess. He planned to seek
forgiveness for trespassing, but only if he were to get caught.

Democratica City was hit harder than Newton,
because it had many more buildings with several stories. The
only tall building in Newton was the museum which was built
to withstand a massive quake. Also building code enforcement
was laxer away from the seat of government. In Newton if a
stone had to be levered into place, or a wooden beam needed
replacement, the homeowner just did it. This was much like in
Libertaria where people could do as they pleased, and it
pleased them to act in a responsible manner.

The Government in the Republic was dysfunctional
in many ways. The Assembly of Thirteen was always
polarized. Those who advocated low taxes and fiscal restraint
clashed with those who sought to optimize governmental
power for the rational management of human need. In
compromise, taxes were increased but called, "fees,
assessments, fines, cost-sharing, apportionments, penalties,"
anything but "taxes." Governmental agencies were delegated
responsibility, but not legal authority, to implement all manner
of public welfare programs. When authority was granted by a
law enacted by the Assembly, the authority had to be
exercised in compliance with a vague, cumbersome, and

267

internally inconsistent administrative procedure law. That law required that delegated legislative authority be limited to the standards contained within the laws implemented. If the implemented laws were vague the regulations thereunder were legally invalid. Additional administrative procedural requirements required regulations to be promulgated whenever a government agency implemented or interpreted law. The net effect was that agencies were compelled to make regulations which were invalid, or ignore legally mandated duties. This generated litigation as well as angst in both the population and in the Assembly.

The Assembly responded with more procedures, more legislative committee oversight of executive function, and more mandatory reporting which drew resources away from the actual implementation of Assembly mandates. Agency failures were punished with budget cuts without reduction in mandated functions. This increased the inefficiency, and lead to demands for more outsourcing of government services. The outsourcing only made the problem worse. The companies to which the governmental functions were outsourced were more efficient. They were efficient at making a profit that is, as was the duty of the corporate management ethically bound to the company's shareholders.

Monopolies, liability shifting, forced change orders, and unilateral contract amendment provisions ravaged the Republics coffer's. The Northern Republic's government amassed an unpayable debt, owed to Royal Bank, an enterprise owned by a powerful government based on antidemocratic principles. Many decried this hypocrisy, both in and out of the Assembly. Many became openly skeptical of democracy itself, long a pillar of Humanist tradition. Ironically the foundation upon which the Northern Republic rested was not its values or its institutions. It was supported by the character of one nineteen-year-old monarch, elected by no one, in a kingdom to the south, with grave problems of his own.

268

Back in the Southern Kingdom, King Gregorious was briefed on the state of affairs by Chief Councilor, Prince Alfide Stewart. The King had thought it would be necessary to remove Prince Alfide from the office of Chief Councilor. Even if Alfide had no knowledge of his son, Barthon's treachery. How could the new King keep the father of the Queen's murderer in such a position of trust and power? The appearance alone would undermine confidence in the monarchy. On the other hand, to fire the man who in fact ran the Kingdom, and ran it well for twenty years, was not a good choice either. The situation was further complicated by the fact that Alfide's status of *Prince* could not be removed, even by the King. It was determined by blood. Alfide was the oldest member of the second ranking family, and Gregor was, at present, the last of his bloodline. At least the rebuilding was on schedule, and humanitarian endeavors had not been interrupted.

However, Prince Alfide identified a problem bigger than his own fate as a public servant. The Kingdom was dying. Death was very literally coming to the Southern Kingdom. They might have ten generations left, probably less. The point of no return may already have been passed. Gregorious had alluded to this in his speech at Lissy's funeral, in a most indirect way. That part of the speech was written by Alfide. Gregorious did not even know what he was talking about. Now Alfide brought him the grim undeniable truth. Centuries of strict monogamy among the small number of shrinking families in the Southern Kingdom had resulted in inbreeding, yielding a loss of genetic diversity which was leading to a concentration of genetic anomalies, congenital disorders, sterility, and a birth rate lower than the death rate. Prince Alfide advocated the obvious. The long tradition of protecting the bloodline was now killing it. The long-standing system of arranged marriages had to end. Royals had to mate with outsiders.

How many times had Gregor spurned Tear's advances? How many times had Gregor cautioned Barthon about risks to the blood? Is that what drove Barthon to murder the King's beloved cousin? Had Barthon gambled with the Royal bloodline and lost? Did Lissy know? Did she somehow try to save the Kingdom? What a cruel irony it would now be for him to forsake the tradition Lissy died upholding, and to do so at the insistence of the traitor's father.

Gregor's duty was clear. It had fallen upon him to decide the fate of the Kingdom. He could allow the Kingdom to die by upholding the long-held tradition to his nation's doom, or he could stand boldly for the change which might still be the salvation of his people. His duty was clear. King Gregorious dismissed Prince Alfide from the position of Chief Councilor.

"Fate," thought Irigon, that's what it all came down to. He had been born in the Eastern Theocracy. He was a Theist and a Theite. It was his fate to study theology, his fate to see what others did not, his fate to be discredited for his vision, his fate to be taken in by Illi, and to become Professor of Religion at the Central College of Epodlo. In that role studied Humanism.

He looked at the philosophy which had been disparaged by clerics, teachers, and mentors all his life. He examined Humanism, not with an open mind, but a critical one. He now understood Humanism. It informed him with a new perspective from which to see reality. It helped him to see even his Theism in a new light. Whenever Irigon now said that he "believed in God," he meant that he aligned his will with the good; with the Logos (the order, beauty, and essence of reality). This was Irigon's God, and Irigon existed in the warmth of God's love, revealed only in the shadow of empirical reality, the only reality a human could know.

Humanism is a philosophy, based on the humble acknowledgement that all we know about ourselves is what is processed through our brains, brains in which perceptions are modulated by sensory input. Our perceptions, and the conceptions built upon them, inform us that we are animals

who evolved on planet Earth. We exist because our ancestors
had the characteristics which allowed them to survive, and
procreate in the environment in which they found themselves.
We invented culture and technology to enable us to adapt
faster than the mere selection of genes by a changing
environment.

The Northern Republic had a culture. Humanism was
a large part of that culture. Irigon knew better than to attribute
the intractable bureaucratic legalism of the Republic to
Humanism, or even to democracy. Humanism did not cause
the Republic's flaws any more than the innumerable sins of
Theites were the inevitable consequence of Theism. Elected
bodies make bad choices. Monarchs make bad choices.
Pontiffs make bad choices. Even individuals acting
unencumbered by government with the purest of motives
make bad choices. However, regardless who makes a choice,
or what causes the person to choose; the measure of the
goodness is *service to human need*. Most Theists would put
the *will of God* over human need, but in turn would assert that
God loves humanity, and therefore humans are called to love
one and other. Humanists just skip that step. *Perhaps
parsimony is another word for laziness*, thought Irigon with
sarcasm that Feli and Zell would relish.

There was no utopia on Epodlo. There was not even
one dystopia. There were four interdependent dystopias. All
four societies had strengths and weaknesses. All missed the
mark. *The archer who has a history of missing the target
should shoot lots of arrows.* Irigon thought. That seemed an
odd metaphor for a pacifist. Perhaps he had heard that one
from Largot Cook, the weapons instructor; or perhaps missing
the mark is something all sinners know well.

Lots of arrows, in deed; How could the learned
professor be so prescient, and yet not see the insight buried in
his own thoughts. Perhaps cultural diversity existed because of
its adaptive utility. A gene pool exists with many variations to
allow natural selection to select those traits a situation

271

demands. Perhaps the existing cultures on Epodlo coexist because each has elements which were adaptive at one time in the past. Irigon had just missed this intellectual plateau, but others were standing on it.

Irigon Agape, was pleased to move beyond the northern perimeter of Democratica City. He headed further north toward North Point. He was pleased it was Summer, and that he had dressed for the chill. He had to replace his cotton boots in Democratica City. New ones were hard to find. It took three days, but he needed the rest. The Humanists of the North had no qualms about wearing deer leather. Cotton boots just did not have the durability anyone would choose to fill a need for rugged footwear, except Theists, who would make any sacrifice for God. That is to say any sacrifice which could be plotted on a line in between weak point one and weak point two. All sin and fall short of the glory of God in some way. For Irigon wearing animal products was not the way he would fall. He was a gentle man, and the burdens of peace had, to date, been light on his shoulders.

The weather was cold, but with Irigon's warm clothing and steady walking pace, he was warm. Two extra layers of clothing hung from is backpack. He would need them on colder mornings.

On June 6th, Ottarian made a crumbly, eggless cake to celebrate Antwanesta's nineteenth birthday. The day after was Sunday, and Antwanesta went to the liturgy service at the church downtown with Eltwando and Celina. Antwanesta again wore her black standard Republican dress. Eltwando conformed to the Libertarian dressing norm, a fair compromise to get Celina to church. Celina was still not keen on conversion to the faith, but she was there. Antwanesta prayed for Tear, her baby, Gretchin, Feli, Xiny, her mom... oh yes, and for Lissy. Antwanesta never forgot to pray for Lissy's soul. She would not forsake her dear friend, even in death. She similarly remembered Father Alfonzo, but she felt he needed her prayers less. That was no reflection on Lissy's personal

virtue by any means. It was just that Father Alfonzo formally
qualified for God's grace, by repenting and believing. Lissy
was depending on her. If only Antwanesta prayed hard, long,
and often enough, surly she could buy God's grace for Lissy.
All fall short of the glory of God, but Lissy was a very kind,
loving soul. If anyone deserved postmortem salvation it was
her.

On July 11ᵗʰ Tear went into labor. Ottarian was
downtown. Gretchin ran for Risky. Antwanesta was alone
with Tear, holding her hand. When Tear had a contraction she
squeezed Antwanesta's hand. Antwanesta was in a small way
sharing Tear's pain, and she felt like a real sister. Antwanesta
recognized that in a biological sense she could be as much of a
sister to Tear as Gretchin. Gretchin had four pops. Tear had
three. Assuming each pop had an equal probability of being
the biological father of Gretchin or of Tear respectively, there
was only an 8.33% chance that Tear and Gretchin were
biological siblings (and then only half-sisters). The calculation
made Antwanesta to feel even closer to Tear, that is closer
than standing naked, holding the hand of a woman giving
birth.

*Shouldn't a prospective pop or pops be doing this, a
protopop or something*? thought Antwanesta. *What if there is
no pop? Will I be asked to be a popette, a popelle, a stable
carl? This is all just too weird.*

There was a knock at the door.

"Get that Antwanesta," said Tear.

Antwanesta did as she was asked. Swinging open a
door to a stranger while naked was now so normal, in an
everybody-else-is-doing-it sort of way. Antwanesta was
happily surprised. This was no stranger. This was a man who
had seen her naked a hundred times. She had even copulated
with him; if imagination counts, sinning with her heart or
whatever. It was Zell. Wearing only a rucksack.

273

Thomas David Valentine

"You're just in time," said Antwanesta. She stripped off his rucksack, grabbed Zell by the hand, and shuttled him into Tear's bedroom, like Xiny taking a terrified Theite girl to her first communal bath. Antwanesta held Zell's waist in her hands, as if a woman in labor wants to see her boyfriend dancing with her sister's naked roommate. Like Xiny, Antwanesta turned the surreal into the normal. Tear smiled. Zell hurried to her. They kissed until Zell made a hasty retreat with the next contraction. He barely escaped Tear's mouth with his tongue intact.

Gretchin returned with Risky. Risky smiled at Zell, and with her smile the tension in the room dropped. Tear was in good hands now.

Two hours later, as the baby began to crown, Tear said, "Get down! Get down there. Down there, Zell. See your child come into the world."

"Yes," said Risky. "You have earned this."

After several more minutes of pain and joy, Zellick Dipopis was born.

Zell expected the "Dipopis." He knew who the other pop was. He also knew what that meant. It meant that he would carry the burden of two fathers rather than just himself. From another perspective, he would be the only father, *the* father, just like fatherhood naturally was in the Republic where pair-bonding was the norm.

"Zellick?"

"He would have had a different name if you hadn't walked in that door," said Tear.

"Ick?"

"It means, *son of a.*

"Son of a?"

Maidens of Epodlo, Book 1 — Antwanesta Agape and the
Mystery of the Red-dot Moon

"Son of a Zell, Bunny-brain."

After a welcome cry the baby boy was happy and
hungry. He soon attached himself to Tear's nipple, eager to
taste the sweet flavor of Mom. Mother and child savored the
joy of their mammalian heritage.

Gretchin was happy too. She had seen a new life
come into the world. Zellick was her sweet wonderful nephew.
She was an aunt. Aunts were special in the land of the free.
Aunts of Gretchin's age were especially valued. They were
called *pacifiers*. There were no latex nipples with plastic rings
attached. That technology had been long forgotten. Now, in
Libertaria, when a baby had enough to eat, and had been
burped, but still needed to be distracted from the inclination to
cry; a mother would hand the baby over to a young bare-
chested aunt. For most pacifiers the service was a bit painful;
some enjoyed it. It was a role for which Gretchin was
obviously not well-equipped. The prudish *Ant* would be a
better pacifier than her. Gretchin was jealous. She was jealous
that Tear won Zell, jealous that Tear had Zellick, jealous that
Tear had full breasts with dark nipples dripping with the
sustenance of life. Gretchin was also angry at herself for
feeling this way. She turned and walked slowly out of the
bedroom and out of the house. She sat on the doorstep outside.

Zell was preoccupied by his new son, and the mother
of his child, but even he noticed the abrupt shift in Gretchin's
mood.

"Ok, let's get out and let the Momma sleep," said
Risky.

Zellick was on Zell's shoulder almost asleep. Zell
asked Antwanesta to hold the newborn, so he could talk to
Gretchin. Antwanesta took Zellick who fell promptly to sleep.
Risky went to the kitchen to wash her hands and talk with
Ottarian.

Zell went outside and sat on the step next to Gretchin. In Zell's culture women were respected as equals. Zell had absorbed this egalitarian ethic. He also grew up with Feli, so he couldn't help but pick up a few things about psychology.

"I have a problem," Zell said to Gretchin, while looking straight ahead so as to seem not to see the tears in Gretchin's eyes. "I had hoped to talk with you about it."

"What?" Gretchin was relieved he did not ask about what she was feeling. She did not want to share her jealousy and feelings of inadequacy, especially with him.

"Some people are not good at some things, and now that I am a father, I'm worried that I can't be all Zellick needs me to be. Men here in Libertaria and in the Kingdom, they know how to use swords and bows. Despite Professor Cook's efforts, I'm not good at those things. I never will be. I started too late. I want Zellick to learn to shoot, fight, and hunt from someone whose better, better than I am."

Gretchin turned her head to look in Zell's eyes. "You know I'll teach him. I'm an aunt. That's a special person you know." She began to cry, and hugged Zell.

Zell hugged her back. "Thanks, Gretchin, I really needed to know that you will be there for me."

They both got up and went in.

They found a distressed Antwanesta with Zellick on her nipple. Every time she tried to pull him away he started to cry. She did not want the exhausted Tear to wake up so she was stuck with a baby on her breast.

Risky came back from the kitchen with a smile. She gently took Zellick from the panicked and blushing Antwanesta. Zellick latched on to Risky's breast and fell immediately asleep.

Zell and Gretchin smiled.

Zell turned to Gretchin and said, "I guess you are sort of my sister-in-law; or is it *sister-out-law*, now?"

"We don't really have a word, but we are family," said Gretchin with a gentle smile.

"Well, if you are like a sister to me, and I am like a brother to Feli. That makes you and Feli sisters." He had been so sweet. Why did he have to spoil the moment? Gretchin had all the kinship with Bunny-brain she wanted.

Later Risky went back to the small two-bedroom house of her Pop Six, just five kiloballs away.

Her houseguest from the night before had left as expected. Her friend had come to make plans with her, secret plans to enter the Kingdom. The Kingdom was still closed to outsiders. *Those Royals and their secrets, enough already*, she thought hypocritically. Risky had a secret of her own. Maybe it wasn't hers; it was her lover's secret. No, it was *their* secret. They were in this together. *Together*, that's how they would be most of the Summer. Together, without rules, without criticism, without doubt, without pretending to ignore each other, but with the privacy to enjoy themselves *together*.

The next day Gretchin and Antwanesta were headed east. They were going to the beach house in East Bend, a tiny village on the coast where rich Libertarians go to relax, stare at the ocean, and coordinate their conspiracies. Gretchin's family had a house there, as did the Mason clan. The famous and infamous stone magnate, Frontaris Mason met his wife, Uvinia in East Bend. She was his neighbor's stable carl. Gretchin only vaguely remembered Uvinia. Dussy was more of a mother to her. Gretchin looked forward to seeing Dussy. Gretchin's three younger brothers were also at the beach house. They were always fun, except when they were being annoying, which from a big sister's perspective, was most of the time.

Chapter 21

To the Point

Antwanesta heard the spray of water. She turned.

"What are you doing?" Antwanesta had not finished the question before Gretchin stood.

"You are one dumb doe, if you can't figure that one out."

"I mean, there are no toilets on this trail?"

"No the Royal Plumbers wanted to install them, but the Pine Tree Union protested. It was messy. The trees threw needles and everything."

"No, seriously are there toilets?"

"No. Who needs toilets in the forest?"

"There were nice normal toilets in Freetown."

"Yes, Freetown is a town. It has houses and stores. This is a forest with trees and humus. No one needs a toilet."

"I do." Antwanesta squatted despite her words. "Don't look at me."

"We met in a toilet, Ant. We have been urinating together for months."

"When we met I had the decency not to look at you, and we had toilets and walls. It's not the same."

"Ok, I'll go look for fat wood."

Antwanesta released. She wanted to thank the Royal Plumbers, but she really was not very happy with them right at the moment, and they certainly had not earned her praise today.

Gretchin and Antwanesta continued east, along a trial which meandered around tree falls and native stones, and their fragments.

"It will rain tonight," said Gretchin. "The tent will keep us dry. It's sealed with wax from tree leaves. I normally stop at the third spring to camp, but today we will stop at the first spring, so we can make our stew before the rain puts out the fire. The site has a good pool. I normally stop there coming from the other direction."

Antwanesta trusted Gretchin to handle the travel details for the eight-day hike. Antwanesta's mind was elsewhere. She asked Gretchin, "How do you feel about Zell and Tear being together?"

"She won. I'm happy for her."

"I thought you wanted Zell."

"I did, but the game's over. He's in my sister's stable. Blood flows faster than seaman?"

"What?"

"It's an expression. It means family gets priority over sex partners. In principle people are free to fight, hold grudges, kill each other over jealousy; but people who choose to live *that way* have short lives, and so do their families. I am happy for Tear, for Zell, and for Zellick. My family continues strong and united. There are more men out there for my stable.

279

Also, with Tear distracted, she will be less competition for me."

"I know I should look at it that way too. All six virtues sing in harmony on that point. God took away a source of temptation. I should be glad."

"You wanted Zell? I thought you weren't supposed to want men."

"I'm still a woman. I still have desires. I'm celibate, not asexual. I have chosen my path, but it is by no means easy."

"There will be other men, said Gretchin in a reassuring tone."

"Other men that I'm not allowed to have. You may be free to copulate with whatever man you want, but I am called by God to serve *Him*. More men are more temptations, more obstacles in my path."

"You're free to think what you want to think, Antwanesta. If I had a belief system which forced me to deny my needs as a woman, I'd choose to believe something else."

"Until I find something better, I'm going to stick with what I have, and pray for God to deliver me from temptation."

"Whatever."

For Irigon, finally reaching North Point was like coming home. He had been there three times before, with Illi. Irigon knew Illi's father and was assured of a place to stay even though he had not written ahead.

Illi grew up in North Point, a lonely place for a child. Her father was her best friend and teacher. North Point itself was a quiet desolate place. Beneath the snow was a crust of ice. After the flood waters came in last October some of the water never left. It froze to the ground. There was a layer of

ice two deciballs thick in most places. Irigon had to walk
carefully not to have his feet slip out from under him.

There was one place, one patch of soil, one small
square, which had no ice; not even snow. That little patch of
black soil was under a rusted wire mesh cage, on a weathered
wooden frame. There was a door made of the same wire mesh.
The door had a latch. The latch was secured by a shiny new
lock.

*I wonder how much faith I will need for Keysmith's
key to fit that new lock*, thought Irigon.

"Irigon." A short elderly man limped over and
hugged him. The man was not ignorant. He knew that Theite
culture discouraged hugging outside of maternal relationships.
However, Irigon was like a son to the old man. "Illi, told me
you were coming."

"How did Illi know?" responded a surprised Irigon.

"You've known her long enough to know she is three
steps ahead of everyone."

"Come on in. Have some tea."

The door to Illi's father's house was in sight of the
shrine. As they walked slowly to the small stone house, Irigon
asked, "But how?"

"You told her you were going to the Republic to do
research. She gave you the locksmith's son's keys. She knows
you are too curious for your own good. She says all red-hairs
are like that. She knows that you know that both the shrine and
a warm bed are here in North Point. She knows you would
rationalize the long walk as getting the exercise she harps on
you about. The only mystery is why you would be dumb
enough to think she wouldn't know. Even I haven't figured
that one out." The old man laughed.

Irigon laughed too, "She's got me. You do too, I see."

"I taught her everything she knows."

"You look good for eighty-one, Jarn."

"I could be half decomposed and look good for eighty-one. There is no secret to a long life. Just eat a whole food vegetarian diet, exercise right, and stay out of the range of your enemies."

"Is that why you live up here, to stay out of range?"

"I fought my fights; lost most. My last term in the Assembly I advocated hardening infrastructure against earthquakes. I got run out of D.C. as a tax-and-spender. Some fights you don't win. Being right is no satisfaction at all."

"Didn't it flood up here? How did you survive?"

"We North-Pointers know what cold water can do. The first sign of it we hit the high ground. The first rise of the water was relatively low and slow. We were all in the hills before the violent water came."

"The houses are all still here. How?"

"The Assembly never listened to me about hardening infrastructure, but my neighbors did. Also, what we had here wasn't half as bad as what hit Royal Beach. No hardening would have saved that place."

"Praise God, the people had evacuated," said Irigon.

Jarn Smith smiled, and opened the door to his house.

"Some tea, Sweetheart?" It was Illi, handing Irigon a cup that she had just poured before he entered the door.

"Illi?"

Illi stood before Irigon looking fresh and rested in her purple standard Republican dress. She gave him a casual kiss and said, "Sit. Dad will tell you about the dirt garden."

"Dirt garden?"

"Our little shrine," said Jarn. "I've maintained it for decades. I just got it cleaned up again last week. It's dirt. We Humanists like dirt, as a symbol that is. Dirt to dirt, we come from it and return to it. Dirt reminds us who we are, what we are. It tells us that we must act in the present, because in the future, and in the past, we cannot act. You Theists may be able to put things off to a purported afterlife. We can't. When we are gone we're gone. All we leave are the effects of our actions during life."

"So you are a Knower?"

"It's meant to be ironic. What we Humanists *know* is that knowledge is relative. It's probabilistic. Nothing can be known in any absolute sense. There are propositions, theories, and hypotheses which we test against our perceptions, our models of empirical reality. We are, more or less right, to the extent our propositions match our perceptions."

"So Knowers are Humanists?"

"Yes and no. All humans do the same thing. We go through the same basic process of proposition and test. We do it every day, all the time, over and over again. You may call yourself a Theist, but you are always testing your propositions, no matter what you believe or how much faith you have."

"That's it, no conspiracy, no secret society, no rituals?"

"That stuff is Illi's department."

"You go take a shower and I will show you a ritual in a *secret place*," said Illi with a wink.

283

Irigon went and took a shower. He then dressed in some clean cloths. He had been had. *This was all a gag, a trick Illi laid, just to laugh at me. Here she is fifty-six, and acting like one of her students*, he thought. *Humility is the essence of modesty, and Illi is God's chosen angel teaching me a lesson. Now there is irony.* Irigon smiled.

"Ready?" It was Illi. Was there more? Illi stood in front of Irigon with a thin piece of black cloth in her hand. "It's a blind fold. I can't allow you to see the way to our place of secret rituals, can I?"

In another part of the Northern Republic another woman named Smith was holding a piece of black cloth. This one was much larger than a blindfold.

"I have to wear *this*?"

"Yes, My Dear. It's the only way. The Theocracy gave us access; we must play by their rules."

"They're sick people; you know that."

"I know who they are Feli, but right now they are our doorway to knowledge. Scientists must make sacrifices for knowledge."

"But it's like giving in to oppression, being complicit to the denial of freedom. It's acquiescing to sexual subjugation."

"Think of yourself as a spy. You're infiltrating enemy lines. Perhaps the information we acquire will help to set the oppressed free."

Professor Boatman and Zell are cut from the same cloth, thought Feli. However, this was a rare chance to be on the cutting edge of discovery. She could learn something new, and Feli's passion for learning, could even pierce her conscience. Hiding under a black robe was a small price to

284

pay for knowledge. "You win, Professor, I'll wear the Theite robe. Antwanesta did it most of her life. I can survive a few weeks." Feli rolled her eyes.

Illi blindfolded Irigon. "No peeking. Got it?"

"Yes, Oh great *Knower of nothing*." Irigon was getting in the spirit of the fun.

Illi opened the outside door.

"Outside!?! It's cold!" protested Irigon.

"We won't be out in it for long."

She walked him this way and that, rattled some metal, and said "You must bow in humility."

"I only bow to God."

"Lower your head or you will bump it. We have low clearance here."

Irigon complied.

"Watch your step. There is a stairway down." Unknown to Irigon, he was truly probing below the shrine's soil.

Illi held Irigon's arm and walked him down one flight then another. "You are going to sit. I will sit next to you." Illi sat Irigon on a soft seat, and put his hands together on her lap with her left hand on top of his. "See its warm here. You didn't need to worry about your *cloths*." Illi kissed Irigon's cheek. There was a pulsating whooshing sound and a feeling of acceleration. She kissed his lips. Her lips, her tongue, her sweet perfume—Oh blessing of blessings. In less than one minute there was a feeling of deceleration, and the sound stopped. Illi's lips pulled away from Irigon's.

"We are going to stand now." Illi took Irigon's arm.

285

"I don't understand. I feel strange. Maybe I should..." Irigon reached for the blind fold.

"No Sweetheart. Illi took his hand and kissed him again deeply mouth to mouth. Pulling away long enough just to say, "Its better this way." She kissed him again. "This way, up some stairs." She lead him up, up, up. There was a hum.

"What's that?"

"We Knowers have our secrets, Dear. You will keep our secrets won't you?"

"I don't know."

"You'll do it for me. I know you will."

A door opened and another. There was a little more walking. Illi turned Irigon, gave him one more peck on the lips and pushed him backward.

For an instant Irigon felt fear. His adrenaline spiked. There was relief when he landed on a bed. His heart was still racing as his shoulders relaxed and sank into the mattress. As he felt his pants sliding over his thighs, then down his calves and ankles, he said, "What are you doing?" The question was intended to be rhetorical, but he got an unexpectedly verbal answer.

"I'm buying your silence,"

This reply seemed odd to Irigon. He had always been discreet about his special relationship with Illi. No one on campus knew, except Morgont of course, but no one who would talk.

Then Irigon received the answer he expected and wanted.

After several minutes of erotic pleasure which Irigon savored, Illi slid herself up along his body. Sliding up his

286

abdomen, and then his torso, until she was face to face with the very satisfied man in the blindfold. Her breath was his breath. Then she said in a tone which seemed somehow more authentically Illisima Smith, "Next time will be all about *me*."

Irigon smiled and said, "Of course it will."

Illi stood and walked through a doorway.

Irigon, at last removed his blindfold.

He was in a familiar place. He had been here many times, but how could it be?

What? Had it been twenty, thirty, forty minutes? Not an hour. What difference did it make? It was just as impossible. It was 2300 kiloballs. He should know he just traveled it; for two weeks he had traveled. Now, in just minutes, he was back, back in Illi's bedroom, on the second floor of the tower, *back on campus*.

Irigon was in awe, in awe of the woman he loved. He knew he would keep her secret. He had no choice. He would do anything for her. She was a deterministic force he could never resist. Irigon would never be free.

Chapter 22

The Beach House

The campsite was a beautiful setting. Surrounded by maples, wax myrtles, willows, and hollies, was a clear spring-fed pond. No one else was at the site. There were three established fire pits with flat stone at their bases, to hold heat and block moisture. Gretchin set up the tent near the pond, well away from the place where the fire would be. Antwanesta sat on a rock facing to the west. She prayed as Gretchin gathered firewood and food.

Gretchin did not resent Antwanesta's absence from the chore of collecting firewood and edible mushrooms. Gretchin knew what she was looking for. She could operate more efficiently by herself than with a girl who had no knowledge about collecting what was needed. Without experience a green girl would pick-up rotting wood as fuel, or would mistake a poison mushroom for a good one. Gretchin cherished he her independence. Being in the woods with just her sandals and a knife, she felt at home. The air, was fragrant with life. The wind-pollinated flowers of her childhood were all about. A warm breeze caressed her skin like a gentle lover.

The knife Gretchin carried was longer than that worn by most Libertarian women. The blade was sharp on one side flat on the other. The daggers worn by Relisha and Wondina back in Freetown looked more like jewelry, like the one Gretchin had returned to Xiny at the end of the year, after both Gretchin and Risky were convinced Xiny was again in command of her faculties.

Some young men in Libertaria (and some aging ones too) chose long swords and big knives for a reason obvious to all who saw them. Gretchin did not choose this knife because of insecurity about her physiological shortcomings. This type of knife was versatile. It was the kind Gretchin trained with as a child. It was a weapon and tool with which she had great proficiency. This is not to say that Relisha, Wondina, or even Xiny wore mere decorations. Relisha was not making an idle boast when she had said she could lay a person down with her throwing daggers. Wondina could strike a third lethal cut before her target felt the first. Xiny could do no less. She had been armed because handmaidens have a duty to protect their ladies. Royals are always diligent about *duty*. Antwanesta's only defenses were Gretchin and her bronze hexagon amulet. The amulet was no magic talisman, but when a Libertarian man saw it, he knew the fishing would not be good.

Gretchin returned to find a cheerful and relaxed Antwanesta. Apparently prayer was, for her, a source of comfort and power. Gretchin cut a sap-heavy piece of pine stump into chips and shavings. With this pile of tinder ready, she pulled a small deerskin sleeve form her rucksack. From that scabbard-like sleeve she withdrew a metal rod no longer than her middle finger, and thinner than her pinky. Gretchin held the small rod over the pile of tinder. She struck the rod with the back of her knife. A bright white spark fell on the tender pile, and it ignited immediately. With some blowing, and the addition of progressively larger pieces of fuel, she had a useful fire.

"How did you do that?" Antwanesta was impressed with the survival skills of the friend she still saw as a kind of jungle girl.

"It's a ferrocerium rod, the same technology used throughout Epodlo. Your people probably light fires the same way to clear the fields for planting. What, did you think, I'd rub two sticks together?"

"I don't know, something like that."

"We Libertarians are not the savage primitives you think. So what if we wear fur in the Winter and nothing in the Summer. Is that less cultured, or less educated, than hiding your body under a black tent all day because if a man sees a woman's skin he might lose control? We value freedom. That's it. Our clothing style is not dictated to us. Nothing is, but we know that freedom has a cost. The cost is *responsibility*. We pay that cost every day, and we are glad we do it."

"I'm sorry Gretchin. You're right. I shouldn't subject you to a stereotype. I know you are a smart and loving person. I didn't mean to imply I thought otherwise."

"I didn't mean to lecture you, Ant. It's just with you, Sinny, and Bunny-brain, I feel like I'm seen as the dumb one. I'm not dumb. I'm in the weaker in math because free children often don't commit the time they should to homework. I'm paying for that now. I have to catch up to you Theite geometry worshipers, and the Northerners with their statistics fetish."

"I never see you as dumb, Gretchin. No one has taught me as much as you. I thank God for you every day, by name, over and over."

Gretchin made stew in a steel pot which had been lashed to her rucksack. Stew was made from mushrooms and vegetables from the market in Freetown. It tasted good, like all camping food does after a long hike. The light rain began to fall. The gentle storm brought its own clean fresh fragrance, but the raindrops felt cold on naked skin. The two crawled into Gretchin's small tent.

"What about tomorrow?"

"We hike along the trail to another campsite. It's seven more days to East Bend," replied Gretchin, to

Antwanesta's vague query. "I made it in two once, but *we* are taking it easy."

"No, I mean when I need to use a toilet."

"I thought we covered that."

"I can urinate on the ground, but in the morning I will want to do more."

"For a curious genius, it seems strange you would not notice the hand trowel hanging from my rucksack."

"I did. I thought it was for digging roots and mushrooms."

"In the morning you will use it to dig a little hole, to make a payment to the tall green guys outside, for the use of the shade and firewood."

"What about the blue button?"

"If I were a primitive, I would say use leaves to wipe yourself. The pond is your bidet appliance."

"You thought you looked like the dumb one," Antwanesta replied with sincere humility.

"I said you were a *dumb doe*, that's one step short of a bunny-brain."

The two fell asleep to the sound of the rain on the canvas of the waxed cotton tent, each knowing she had the love and respect of the dear friend lying next to her.

Two nights later at a campsite further east, Gretchin and Antwanesta met too classmates, Quistina Unipopis and Yarvan Quadrapopis.

Upon seeing Yarvan, Gretchin said, "I thought you would be in the Republic seducing snow does."

"I was up there a couple of weeks, but I came back to visit my parents."

"Looks like Quistina captured you," Gretchin said with a smile.

"No, we just enjoy each other. She knows I want a committed monogamous pair-bond, and I know she wants a stable. In the meantime, we are both available to pleasure each other. It's what the Royals do while they wait for their arranged marriages. Why not us?"

"It works well for the moment," said a grinning Quistina.

Later alone with Gretchin in the tent, Antwanesta said she did not think Yarvan and Quistina's arrangement for casual sex was wise, because one of them would fall in love, and the other would leave for a relationship with someone else, producing heartbreak.

"It could be worse," said Gretchin without sarcasm, "They could end up in a committed monogamous pair bond like Yarvan wants."

"Why is that worse?'

"In twenty-five years Quistina will reach her peak of sexual desire. Yarvan will be half-impotent. A woman needs to be able to add new stock to her stable. The utility of men expires early."

"That's twenty-five years away."

"You Theists think life is forever. Twenty-five years is a short time, and so are the years after that. I don't want to lock up my freedom with one limp man."

At the halfway point of the hike to East Bend, Gretchin and Antwanesta came to Middle Village. Middle Village had nothing but a tavern, an inn, a public bath, a two-room brothel, and some chicken farms. The bath and a bed were welcome. Antwanesta even indulged in two servings of wine at the tavern.

A man, who had even more to drink, decided to test the power of the Holy Hexagon. "Your necklace says, 'No, No, but the rest of you looks like a *big yes.*"

With courage enhanced by wine and the proximity of Gretchin, Antwanesta replied, "You obviously don't know body language."

The drunken man continued, "I never tasted your flavor before. You look sweet. Just one taste, come on."

"Antwanesta, looked nervously at Gretchin."

Gretchin interjected, "She tastes just like me, and she's taken for tonight. Despite your undeniable charm, I don't think you are up to pleasing both of us."

"I could try."

"I appreciate your sweet offer, but the two of us are *together*, and though many women surely want you, you're not *our* type."

"Oh, I see. Well, have a good night."

"You too."

"The man walked away passively."

Antwanesta said, "Didn't you just imply that we are lesbians?"

"Yes."

Antwanesta blushed, "Why? You could beat ten of him in a fight."

Thomas David Valentine

"Twenty, but getting in a fight, I could avoid, wouldn't sit to well with your hexagon, the people in this town, his family, my mom, excreta. I chose not to antagonize him, and I saved his pride by giving him a good face-saving reason why two young women would not be interested in him."

"I concede. You *are* the smart one," responded Antwanesta.

After passing millions of oak trees and pines, and greeting an occasional westward hiker, each with rucksack and blade, Gretchin and Antwanesta reached East Bend. The village consisted of seventeen houses and one store. All the houses were at the beach fount, and past the last house at each end was a massive pile of granite native stones, positioned at random orientation rather than stacked face-to-face. The native stones extended into the ocean to form two jetties. The houses ranged in size from one-room cottages to small mansions with over twenty rooms. With one exception, all were in the familiar style of pink granite blocks and heavy timbers. The larger of these were remarkable only in scale, and not the novelty of architecture. A few had three stories, and large wooden decks overlooking the sea to the east.

The one exceptional house was *very* strange. It stood on four angled metal pilings, not driven into the sand but resting on metal-plated native stones. Antwanesta had seen this plate-on-base arrangement on the buildings and bath rooves at the college, and at the base of the brothels in Freetown. In neither of those places were there pilings. The pilings she presumed were to allow storm surges to pass under the house. Some of the smaller houses were on pilings of wood driven in the sand, nothing nearly as strongly engineered as this structure. The plate-on-base arrangement, she now understood, was for seismic shock protection. In contrast to the rectangular structures neighboring it, this house had rounded edges. One could not call them walls; because, except

294

for a two-story window facing the sea, the roof tapered down, and the floor tapered up, until roof and floor almost met. The glass wall between was just four balls high on the part of the house facing inland. The glass expanded in height around both sides. Jandarian Soldier had to wait weeks for a single section of glass for the sophomore bath roof. This structure must have taken forever to build. There was one stairway into this clam-shaped house. It was from beneath, with metal steps facing west, away from the sea. Gretchin walked Antwanesta to the base of the steps resting in the sand.

"This is the house?"

"Yea, Mom had techno-kook taste when she designed it."

"Gretchin!" A very happy auburn-haired woman, in her early thirties, wearing nothing but a bright smile and a sword-shaped pendant, suspended between soft, ample breasts, came bouncing down the steps to greet them. Dussy hugged Gretchin, who returned the hug enthusiastically.

Dussy turned to Antwanesta. "You must be Antwanesta. Gretchin told us you are a very good friend of hers. I know you are a Theite so I will try to accommodate any special needs you have. Vegetarianism is no problem, Risky would be make *me* into a vegetable if I fed meat to the family. You will fit right in."

"This is Dussy," said Gretchin. "She is Mom's stable carl, sort of my second mother."

"I'm pleased to meet you Dussy," said Antwanesta. "I asked Gretchin what a *stable carl* was, and she said I just had to meet you to understand."

"There is nothing complicated about a stable carl," said Dussy, "I am the right hand of my mistress. I do for her what she can't, or does not want, to do. If a woman has more than three men to manage, she needs a helper sometimes."

295

The three walked up the stairs. As they entered there was motion near the wall of the kitchen. A boy peeked at them a moment, and ran out a glass door in the center of the ocean-side glass and onto a large wooden deck beyond.

"That was Mars. Don't mind him. He's eleven, that age when boys see girls as, intriguing but fearsome aliens."

"I have a dress," said a suddenly embarrassed Antwanesta. She had been naked so long, she forgot that it might not be appropriate to be nude in some places. "Shall I put it on?"

"Please don't," said Dussy. "I don't want the boys thinking you have something we don't. They are ill-mannered enough as it is."

"There are other boys?"

"They are in the pool with Quinis."

Dussy walked Antwanesta to the pool area out back, while Gretchin took the two rucksacks to the bedroom.

"This is Karis, Lander, and Quinis." She ignored Mars, who was grinning sheepishly from behind a small metal storage building at the corner of the pool area.

At that moment, Gretchin came up from behind Antwanesta and Dussy.

Lander yelled, "Retch, Retch, Retch!" He climbed out of the pool, Karis five steps behind him. Quinis, a well-muscled man of forty-five with thinning hair, made his way to the steps at the shallow end of the pool. Lander and Karis hugged Gretchin excitedly. Mars jumped into the pool vacated by the others.

"Gretchin." Quinis hugged his daughter then turned to her friend. "Antwanesta, I'm pleased to meet you. Call me

Quinis." He nodded his head as Gretchin had instructed him
when she visited for Newton Day break.

"I'm pleased to meet you, Quinis," replied
Antwanesta.

"You're a *Red*," said Quinis. I always wanted to
meet one. Dussy bring dinner out on the pool deck."

"When its ready, I will, another fifteen minutes, or
so." Dussy winked at Quinis.

"I'll help with dinner, you girls watch the boys," said
Quinis.

"Then it will take *forty* minutes," said Dussy with a
smile.

The girls played in the pool, with the boys. Karis
proudly demonstrated he could pick up a rock from the bottom
of the deep end. All three could swim very well. Antwanesta,
thought of how, as a child, she was not allowed to wade past
her knees. Here a five-year-old could swim with ease. She
decided that she liked freedom. Responsibility seemed a small
price to pay. Antwanesta thought Gretchin was lucky to have
so many siblings. Antwanesta had a whole country full of
brothers and sisters, but she couldn't help thinking that this
was in some way much better.

After forty-five minutes Quinis and Dussy returned
with dinner, baked bell peppers stuffed with tomatoes, onions,
and three whole grains. There were also steamed vegetables
and a fruit salad. The adults sat at a tall round table on the pool
deck. Antwanesta could see Dussy was no mere servant, or a
slave as she had feared. Dussy was a member of the family.
Apparently she had a status, at least equal to the men of the
stable. Much like Xiny, Dussy held a higher station, than her
title implied.

Thomas David Valentine

"Maybe we should eat on the beach," said Quinis, "Evy is always spying on me."

"*She is not*," said Dussy decisively.

"Every time I see her she's looking at me," Quinis insisted.

"That's not spying. It's *ogling*. She just thinks you're sexy,"

"No."

"We carls talk. I know she wants you. She said she'd like to trade places with me when you're here."

"She would?"

"Don't get excited. Two women are enough for you."

"I don't have two. I have two-fourths. That is just half a woman."

"If you do the math that way, it is less than half. Mistress has two exotics you didn't count."

"Two more in the denominator makes the fraction five-twelfths. That's 0.4167 women," interjected Antwanesta. She blushed when she realized what she was talking about.

No one was offended or laughed, but Quinis reacted. "Ha, it's those alien genes isn't it. That's how you can do math so fast."

"Pop," said Gretchin with the tone of a parent giving a child a first warning.

"I mean *alien* in the sense that Antwanesta is from a foreign country. Theites are good at math. That's what I mean," said Quinis defensively.

"Get the knife out of the pool, dry it, and give it back to him!" Dussy was yelling at Mars, who had thrown Lander's knife in the pool."

"I'll get it," volunteered Karis. He dove in.

"You boys get up here and eat your dinner," Dussy added. "You eat too Karis," she said as the youngest boy emerged victorious with the rescued knife.

"Sorry Antwanesta, I had hoped, with you here, they might calm down, and be civilized for a change."

"That's ok," said Antwanesta "I like seeing a real family." I was an only child, so I missed out on this.

"What's it like over there? Over in the Theocracy I mean," asked Quinis.

"Well, people wear long black clothes year-round. We pray, meditate, and grow food. That's about it."

"What do they tell you about where you come from?"

"My mom was annunciated at Saint Hypatia's convent. I was born there. We moved to Lord's Landing when I was one. The Humanists at school say women at Saint Hypatia's are raped by monks, but that can't be true. Mom speaks only of happiness when she remembers her time there."

"What do you know about your father?"

"What does anyone know? He's ineffable."

"So he might be from another planet?"

"Pop, we talked!" Gretchin was losing patience.

"I'm just making conversation. I don't know if *they* are tied in or not. I wouldn't put it past them. The Masons and Knowers are involved in everything big."

"Enough Pop!"

"It's ok," said Antwanesta, "I'd like to hear about the Mason's and Knowers."

Dussy kissed Gretchin's shoulder and hugged her. She knew Gretchin had no patience for conspiracy theories. "Let him get it off his chest, Dear," Dussy whispered to Gretchin.

"The Masons—that's their house right next door— they are into stuff, *big stuff*. I used to work in their stone quarry up north, at their compound by the Northeast River. I overheard some plumbers, not real Royals like you see above ground. These were the ones recruited locally. They were talking. Their words were clear as the dot on the…well clear anyway. One said to the other, 'We've got to keep the aliens copulating. The invasion is coming.' The other one laughed. Then they stopped talking when they thought I might overhear."

"Maybe it was a sarcastic remark. You said the guy laughed," said Antwanesta to the man clearly glad to have an attentive audience.

"Maybe, but there's more. What do you see over there down the beach?"

"Rocks, the jetty?"

"And the other way?"

"The same."

"What are they there for?"

"To protect from erosion?"

"Three major storms hit each year. Only the July 8th Storm comes from the east. It hits every year, messes up the beach a little, then the currents build the beach back in three weeks. Mason built those ugly rock piles, for no purpose, at least so as anyone could tell. Then the Tsunamis came, and oh, what a genius Frontaris Mason turned out to be. He *knew* the tsunamis were coming. He knew, and his friends knew. And who reinforced the brothels with steel bracing and slip plates? The cost of that project must have been three times the annual revenue generated by the brothels. Mason also organized and funded a big party away from the buildings which were not reinforced. How lucky that it was *the day of the earthquake*. Mason is a knower. He pulls all the strings. He even has his claws in *my* mistress."

Dussy interrupted. "They are business partners. Our mistress controls Frontaris as much as, or more than, he controls her."

"Frontaris took Uvinia from her," countered Quinis.

"Uvinia freely decided to marry the richest man on Epodlo. I'd walk too, if I could anchor a stable with one like that."

"You'd never do that to me," said Quinis.

"Sure I would. Mistress wouldn't let me take you with me."

"Why not. I'm a free man."

"Freedom is relative, Pretty Boy. In a state of freedom, women *always* rise to the top."

"Thanks for dinner, Dussy" said Gretchin. "I'm going to *freely* show Antwanesta the bedroom. It was a long hike for her."

Antwanesta added her thanks, and followed Gretchin to the bedroom. The room was large with a bed as big as a whole dorm room. There was a private bathroom. The toilet and tub were steel rather than the stone which was otherwise so uniformly used throughout Epodlo.

"You could have your own room, but we have been sleeping together so long I thought you'd rather share with me."

"Your right. In a bed that size I want Xiny and Feli too. I'll need a compass to find you."

Later, lying near the middle of the large bed, Antwanesta asked, "How can your mom share your pops with Dussy. Doesn't she get jealous?"

"They don't *share*. *Women* don't share. Mom delegates duties to Dussy. Dussy enjoys her work to be sure, but she serves at Mom's pleasure. They make a very good team. Mom has clear dominance, but Dussy has the freedom to leave at any time."

"Did I understand right that Frontaris Mason's wife used to be your mom's stable carl?"

"Yes, Uvinia married Mr. Mason. She has a carl of her own now."

"How many men does she have."

"Just Mr. Mason, I think."

"If she has only one man, why does she need a carl?"

"As you see with Dussy, a carl does more than have sex. Stable carls are very helpful."

"Will you have a carl someday?

"Let me find some men first."

Quinis would remain at the beach house five more days. Even Antwanesta grew weary of his wild conjectures. He claimed that the moon was the ideal staging area for an

invasion of Earth. Perhaps the red dot was a giant space vessel
which was parked on the moon. Maybe it had a mass so great
that its movements triggered seismic activity in this
geologically unstable region. Quinis took a collection of
seemingly unrelated facts to weave a tapestry of fantasy with
numerous large holes. Professor Medic or Histina Bowright
could easily tear apart his silly theories of an alien invasion,
with Knowers and Masons collaborating with an
extraterrestrial occupation force, ready to dominate Earth.

Antwanesta said to Quinis, "So where did the big red
spaceship go?"

"It may be on the far side of the moon for final
preparation of its weapons, or maybe it landed elsewhere on
Earth. Perhaps the invasion is underway, and Epodlo is too
isolated to have been reached by ravenous alien hoards."

Chapter 23

Feli's Revelation

After listening to the wild speculations of Quinis more than she wanted, Antwanesta practically leapt from the stainless steel living room tub, when Gretchin said, "Ant, lets walk on the beach." The two had walked and run on the beach several times since their arrival in East Bend. They had even climbed over both tall rock piles anchoring the jetties, to enjoy the beach on the other side to the north and the south. This time they walked between the rock piles in the light of the bright white moon. The moonlight seemed to mock Antwanesta. God had given her this puzzle. Surely He did not intend for her to fail in solving it.

Gretchin said, "Pop Two is a sweet man, but you have to ration him out in small amounts. There is just enough truth in what he says to drive a person turtles. Maybe I should bring Bunny-brain here next Summer. I could watch them melt each other down."

Antwanesta laughed. "Why do you give Feli such a hard time?"

"Me give Feli a hard time? Everything she does is to rearrange the universe to scramble my brains?"

"You don't believe that do you?"

"No, I don't. She and I play with each other, because we don't want to take each other seriously. I wish I knew what she was doing now."

The next day Quinis left the beach house to return to his small house in Hunt Town. There were three days at the beach house with no men, not counting the boys. Mars had gotten used to Antwanesta, and was now even talkative, after concluding she was safe, and that red hair was just as boring as any other color. Karis thought "Ant" was "Aunt." The women thought that was cute, and Karis would remain in the dark for three weeks, until Lander would finally correct the error. With Quinis gone, Dussy had more time for Gretchin and Antwanesta. Antwanesta liked Dussy. Being only thirty-two she seemed more like Gretchin's sister than a mom. Dussy was the biological mother of both Lander and Karis, but in Libertaria kinship was a bit of an ethereal concept. She said it was easier to handle the boys with no man or mistress to service. Dussy had more authority in the eyes of the boys without another parent around.

Another parent arrived. Daro Pentapopis was tall and thin, in his late forties with black curly hair. His weathered deerskin rucksack flew up the stairs before him. "Where's my Dussy!"

Dussy went to the top entrance way where the rucksack had landed. When Daro reached the top of the steps, she and Daro shared a deep kiss. "Say hi to the kids and Gretchin's friend, Antwanesta; then it's straight to the shower with you, and don't forget you have ears to wash."

Daro hugged Gretchin and the boys.

He extended his hand to Antwanesta, apparently thinking she was from the Republic, despite the prominent bronze hexagon between her breasts. Antwanesta shook his hand.

"I'm Daro, Gretchin's prettiest pop, please to meet you. Speaking of pretty, Gretchin you must have big stable by now. Those college boys must be ripe for the picking."

"Not exactly, Pop."

"Don't worry. That means you've got good taste, like your mom."

"Shower, *now!*" Dussy pointed her index finger toward the shower.

Daro went where directed.

"Men can be worse than children," said Dussy. "Daro is not as bad as he pretends. He knows all the best women of the brothels, and they did not leave him dumb. He just plays at being a stupid rooster."

Dussy was right. Daro was playing. After cleaning he was a gentleman. Dussy thanked Antwanesta for inspiring him to behave. Daro was charming, and he did learn it all in the brothels. A brothel owner gets first pick of the most talented men. Gretchin's mother picked Daro for her stable twenty-nine years ago, when she wanted to raise the passion level of her collection. Dussy considered him the best of the stable, not counting the two foreigners she did not yet have the pleasure of serving.

"Congratulations *Aunt* Gretchin. Risky told me about Zellick," said Daro.

Gretchin tried to signal with her eyes for Pop Three not to mention Risky, because Antwanesta was not supposed to know she was her sister.

"I don't play your Mom's games, Gretchin," said Daro.

Gretchin's face grew angry.

Daro softened his position. "Dr. Betriski Sexapopis is a very well-respected Libertarian. Everyone knows her, and holds her in high esteem. Her Pops must be very proud of her. I passed her headed to Free Beach. She was going to see one of her pops and meet a friend."

Antwanesta noticed the exchange between Gretchin and Daro, but she thought that if they wanted to hide a personal matter, it was their business. She imagined Xiny smiling in approval.

"What friend?" Gretchin was the curious one now.

"She didn't say. She said, 'her;' it must be a woman. That's all I know. How long are you girls staying?"

"To July 9ᵗʰ," said Gretchin. "I don't want to camp in the storm."

In the Kingdom, Xiny was in a hurry. It took more time than she allotted to brief the construction supervisor who was to cover her position while she was away. There were three malfunctioning D-units to be reprogramed, so she had to remap the project schedule to optimize the construction process with the unexpected resource downtime. She was afraid to miss the boat to Free Beach. She was uncharacteristically twenty minutes late. The boat pilot had waited. She was no longer the Queen's Handmaiden, or even daughter of the Chief Councilor, but she was still Xinonina Stewart, now Princess, being third from the throne. The boat pilot would have waited much more than twenty minutes for her. The sail to Free Beach was uneventful. Rooms had been reserved for both her and her boat pilot. The boat pilot did not mind a free night in a resort town. It was no Royal Beach, but then Royal Beach was no Free Beach. It had its own charms. Xiny was met by Risky's pop, Pargog, the owner of the Free Beach Inn. The inn was still far from fully repaired after massive Tsunami damage, but if *Risky* wanted two rooms, she got two rooms.

Risky soon arrived and hugged her pop and Xiny.

"Yes?" Risky asked Xiny.

"We're on," replied Xiny.

Risky gave Xiny a warm hard hug.

The two visited with Pargog for a couple of hours, and then retired to their room. The walls were crooked, and what was left of the roof leaked, but Pargog had put forth a truly heroic effort to meet his daughter's request for a place to stay. The next morning, Xiny and Risky sailed to the Kingdom.

In the West, Feli stepped off her father's boat at the God City dock. Her father helped her step down. The long black robe, she was required to wear, hindered her mobility considerably. She promised herself that she would be forever kind to Antwanesta. Surly Antwanesta had suffered enough in one life, walking around in a black tent, for seventeen years. She imagined Antwanesta and Gretchin swinging naked from vines in some Libertarian jungle. She would have envied them even more, if she knew they enjoyed the most extravagant beach house in Libertaria, and were waited upon by the most charming of servants. Professor Boatman had it relatively easy. He wore a long-sleeved black shirt, and black pants held by a black cotton belt. His clothing was hot for Summer, but his mobility was not impaired. Feli felt almost chained to the ground by the bulky Theite robe which women were expected to suffer under, in order to protect the world from lust.

Feli and the professor said their farewells to Picius. He would return for them in two weeks. He smiled at his daughter, taking joy in her suffering the way parents do when a child feels oppressed by a hardship, which the parents know will do the child more good than harm.

The professor and his assistant were met at the dock by a man with God-kissed features, and a tiny scar on his left cheek. With a nod of the head, Brother Ifarbis explained that he was to take them to drop off their things at the rooms they were being provided. He then was to escort them to meet Bishop Salestina.

308

After Father Alfonzo had fallen asleep in the Lord, Brother Ifarbis felt called to the priesthood. Seminarians were assigned to assist priests and bishops. Brother Ifarbis was clearly strong in the faith, and was blessed with the temporary assignment to assist the Bishop of God City.

God had apparently seen it fitting to bless the Theocracy with the preservation of the buildings which housed the offices of church/government administration. Surly it was God who spoke to the bishop to guide the Pontiff to have the buildings reinforced. Private businesses and apartment buildings were toppled, but the heart of the Theocracy was preserved, as were the lives of all who obeyed the Pontiff's directive for a holy retreat to the countryside on that fateful day of the quake.

Professor Boatman and Feli were quartered in different buildings. It would be improper for women and men to sleep under the same roof. Such a practice would create temptation to sin. Even Brother Ifarbis could not show Feli to her room. A personable sister was assigned that task. Feli was relieved to find that the apartment provided was, to her taste, very normal, almost identical in size and features to her bedroom and bath at Newton. The consistent style of the Royal Plumbers was obvious down to the blue and red buttons on the pink granite toilet slab. Feli was comforted to know that, at least at night, she could strip off her clothes and be a human.

The sister returned Feli to Brother Ifarbis and Professor Boatman. The three went to Bishop Salestina's Office, which was located on the second floor of the building which housed the Holy Hexagon itself. As they passed the great white relic, Brother Ifarbis casually made the sign of the hexagon across his chest. Feli and Professor Boatman paused. They each felt a sense of awe which seemed incongruous with their Humanist convictions. Ifarbis lead them up from the Hexagon Atrium to the office of Bishop Salestina. Brother

Ifarbis kissed the Bishop's hand. The bishop then extended her hand, not to be kissed, but to shake the hands of Professor Boatman and Feli in succession.

"Welcome to the Western Theocracy." Bishop Salestina was a God-kissed woman, buoyant, with gregarious charisma. She was warm and sparkling with good cheer. Feli's anxiety level dropped immediately, after having expected either a tedious bureaucrat or a zealous proselytizer of the Theist faith.

After introductions and casual ice-breaking conversation, it became clear that the bishop had a message which would not be welcome news to the investigative team. Professor Boatman had applied to both measure *and inspect* the Holy Hexagon under magnification. What had been granted was something less. The bishop said that the Theocracy consented to measurement, but not inspection under magnification. The professor protested gently but insistently.

When the professor asked for an explanation. Bishop Salestina said, "I will be candid. We are concerned that the magnified inspection would identify imperfections, scratches, or dents. You or other Humanist scholars would cite your data as proof that God is imperfect, or that the Holy Hexagon is not a message from God. The relic is an important source of inspiration to our people. We will not be accomplices with those who would discredit God's message. Measurement is another matter. We have measured it at 30.0000 balls across, side-to-side. It is expected that your more precise measuring tools, and your less-than sympathetic perspective, will lend credibility to our prior measurement. If our measurements are off, we have explanations which will satisfy the faithful."

Daro left the East Bend beach house after four days. He took the three boys with him for, hunting, camping, hiking, and a trip to see their new nephew in Freetown. They left in time to shelter at Middle Village for the storm. This left Dussy

310

without boys to watch or a man to entertain. She savored eight
days of relative tranquility, being with two self-sufficient
women.

Antwanesta grew close to Dussy, who taught her the
culture, philosophy, and practices of the free people of
Libertaria, with more patience and enthusiasm than Gretchin.
Antwanesta was an eager student, and she ate ravenously at
the banquet of knowledge and wisdom Dussy provided with
cheer. Dussy spoke candidly, but from her, even the most
physically intimate information did not seem prurient. Her
seemingly promiscuous lifestyle was not a source of shame.
For her, a stable carl's life was normal. Dussy did not see
Antwanesta's cultural heritage as a reason to edit her
instruction or personal disclosure. To the contrary, she pitied
Antwanesta in her deprivation, and spoke with all the more
detail, recognizing that Antwanesta might not know some very
obvious things a woman needs to understand. However, Dussy
did conceal the many secrets of her mistress. She always did
that.

July 4th was Gretchin's birthday. Antwanesta, Dussy,
and Gretchin enjoyed cake, sparkling sweet wine, and the hot
bubbling water of the stainless steel living-room tub. Dussy
used eggs in the cake. This did not comply with the rules of
either Theism or of Risky, but the eggs made the cake hold
together better. Antwanesta ate it anyway. Dussy could seduce
anyone into anything, but much like Feli, she used her power
judiciously, with compassionate consideration for those upon
whom she applied her charisma.

For her part, Antwanesta, though eager to learn from
Dussy about philosophy and even the biology of erotic
pleasure, was steadfast in her faith. While she thought Theites
had much to learn from Libertarians about freedom, she held
fast to her conviction that her purpose was to serve God, not to
bestow orgasms upon others. She thought such to be a gross
perversion of the ideal of loving one's neighbor.

311

The storm hit on July 8th, as it always did. Dussy and Gretchin knew the house was safe. However, with the roar of the waves, the thunder, and the wind driven branches and pine cones pounding on the metal roof, Antwanesta could not sleep. While silently praying, she held Gretchin like a teddy bunny. Gretchin and Dussy both slept soundly. The next morning, they visited the beach. The beach was well-packed with saturated sand and had some tree limbs washed up on it, but there was no meaningful damage. It was now safe to hike south. With goodbyes and sincere hugs to Dussy, Gretchin and Antwanesta trekked southwest toward Hunt Town.

The first night in the forest the two camped near another spring-fed pond. The sky was now clear. There was a native stone near the pond. Its top surface faced the still pool at a fifteen-degree angle. Like all native stones its face was thirty balls by thirty balls. The two young women lay side-by-side looking at the moon and stars.

"I do like the white moonlight better than the red," said Gretchin.

"I still want to know what it means," said Antwanesta.

"I don't buy Pop Two's flying disk deer dung. Do you?"

"No, it's not parsimonious enough," replied Antwanesta. "We have no evidence of extraterrestrials."

"So Humanistic of you to say. If you keep talking that way, Feli will declare *you* her "Sweetheart" too."

"I wouldn't mind. You call me 'Ant.'"

"You want me to stop?"

"Don't you dare. I'm 'Ant' to you, except when you introduce me to people. The pet name makes me feel special."

312

"I thought Theites weren't supposed to be special, too immodest. I guess that doesn't apply to women lying naked on a rock with legs spread for the whole galaxy to enjoy."

"I look at modesty differently now. It's not about hiding skin. It's about being humble. It's accepting that we just don't know a lot of things."

"So you are an Agnostic Theist now?"

"I guess I am. When you say you believe in freedom, you don't mean that freedom exists; you mean you align your will with freedom. Maybe God's the same way. I can't know anything about God's existence or nature. At best I can align my will with His energies."

"You're going into Feli's territory again. I wish I could find a man who could go as deep into me, as you two go into metaphysical rabbit holes."

"Why is everything about *men* for you?"

"Maybe because all my closest friends are women."

The second night Gretchin and Antwanesta set up camp at an established site two-hundred kiloballs north of Hunt Town. After pitching the tent and starting a fire, they were joined at the site by two handsome men in their mid-twenties.

"Hi, I'm Tolmov, may we join you for the night?"

"Please do," said Gretchin with a welcoming smile. "I'm Gretchin, this is Antwanesta."

This was the first time Antwanesta heard Gretchin use her real name. It was a bit jarring, after being 'Ant' so long; but she appreciated being introduced by her proper name to strangers. Standing naked in the woods in front of strange men with grins on their faces was inherently uncomfortable.

"I'm Bari. Are you from around here?"

"I'm from Free Town, but I get around, my friend is from the Theocracy."

"A Theo? I thought you were all into dark clothes and hiding your beauty, said Umbar." "Bari" was a nickname he had adopted after bringing such disrepute to his given name.

"*Theite* is the preferred term," said Antwanesta. "I have temporarily adopted local clothing customs for convenience and curtesy."

"You look both convenient and courteous to me," said Umbar.

Antwanesta was now acutely aware that these men were armed, and she was not. *Could Gretchin fight off two skilled men if necessary? Would she?* Antwanesta's heart began to race, and it was *definitely* not the result of any sexual arousal.

Gretchin appeared to see the situation much more favorably. "Have you boys' hearts been captured, or are you looking for a stable?"

"I could use some *stabilization* in my life," said Umbar.

"Gretchin," said Antwanesta, very uncomfortable with the proximity of Tolmov.

Gretchin began to kiss Umbar deeply mouth-to-mouth, tongues licking and penetrating. She was becoming excited. She enjoyed Umbar's warm body embracing her, as if in a slow close dance. She could feel his excitement firmly caressing, wanting to be united with her. Gretchin so wanted a man, a man to be hers, a man she could have, a man of passion, a man…

"Hey Tolmov, I want some red head. How about I take the top half, and you get the bottom half. Then we can finish with this local one for dessert."

Gretchin, saw the world in a blur. It then came back into focus, as if reality blinked. Blood which had rush *down*, now rushed *up* into Gretchin's head with heat, not heat of passion, but *heat of rage*. Reality was back, and Gretchin saw it all too clearly.

"*Dessert!*" Gretchin pushed Umbar hard on the shoulders. He fell backwards into the wet leaves and humus.

"Umbar! You Stupid…," Tolmov scolded. "Flat-and-Fluffy was hot for us man, and you go and talk about dividing up the frozen strawberry! What third-rate brothel did you flunk out of?"

GET OUT OF HERE NOW!!! Gretchin was livid.

"We'll go; we'll go," said Tolmov, nervous and embarrassed. Then as his traveling companion rose, Tolmov kicked Umbar's left buttock as hard as he could, sending him sprawling face down in the forest muck. Umbar again staggered to his feet. The two men slinked up the trail and away, too ashamed (or indifferent) to turn and see the emotional trauma they had wrought.

Gretchin's body went limp. Antwanesta caught her in her arms.

Gretchin began to cry. Among the tears, words began to form. "Why…Why ca-ca-can't I have…"

Antwanesta said, "They are gone Gretchin, and I am thanking God for that. Those beasts were not good enough for you." Antwanesta hugged Gretchin as the tears flowed.

"They liked you b-better than me," said Gretchin.

315

"I was called a 'frozen strawberry.' I'm not flattered by that."

"They w-w-wanted you more than me."

"They wanted to use both of us for their own selfish lust. They saw us as nothing but convenient holes. You don't want to be wanted *that way*. You want a man to *love* you, and a man *will* love you. I know because I love you, and I know God would not be so cruel as to make a world were all men would be too blind to see what I see in you."

Feli and the professor made measurements by various means. The Holy Hexagon was 30.00000 balls across between each pair of parallel sides, but only if one accounted for the curve. The hexagon was not flat. It bowed in like a piece of paper wrapped around a giant sphere. The geometry was simple. Feli did not need Antwanesta to help her comprehend its radial summitry. Measuring the curve was not hard, but it was tedious. The professor went for a much-needed nap while Feli worked on. The depth from a hypothetical plane at specific points had to be measured. The edges needed to be compared to the center. The point markers required precise placement for accurate measurement. While examination of the relic by magnification was prohibited, Feli felt that using a magnifier to place the point markers would comply with the limitation. When placing one of the point markers Feli noticed something at an edge of the hexagon. There seemed to be a tiny inscription somehow *inside* the edge. It could not be read because of the blurry translucence of the material at the relic's surface. The lack of transparency teased Feli's curiosity. The blurriness was due to tiny scratches caused during the time the hexagon had been washed about in the sand on the ocean floor.

It occurred to Feli that the application of a clear liquid might fill the scratches enough to see what was beneath the surface. She couldn't just go get water. That would be too indiscrete. Her next idea would be a desecration. No Theist

would tolerate it. Feli was torn between breaking a trust, or
adding, in some small way, to the body of human knowledge.
She made her choice. She brought her hand to her mouth, as if
pensively thinking about her measurements. She moistened
her right index finger with her tongue. Feli wasn't actually
spiting on the Holy Hexagon, just moistening it. Feli discreetly
applied her saliva to the edge of the venerated object.

Feli tried to read the inscription, C-e-i...

"Miss Smith."

Feli jumped.

"Forgive me Miss Smith," said Brother Ifarbis. "May
I ask you something?"

"Yes," said Feli with the anxiety of a guilty
conscience.

"You said that you go to school at the college on the
lake. Do you know Sister Antwanesta?"

"Yes." Instant relief poured over Feli. "She is a good
friend."

"Would you please tell her that I understand that my
injury with the stick was an accident. There is nothing for me
to forgive, because she did nothing wrong; but I want to be
sure she understands that."

"I will tell her," said Feli.

Ifarbis bid her farewell. He was returning to Saint
Isaac's College to continue training for the priesthood.

Feli was again alone with the Holy Hexagon, not
counting the anonymous passersby. She read the inscription.
She was shocked at what she read. She reread the words she
had put on the paper. She did not want to again chance being

caught looking through a magnifying lens. The words read, "Ceiling Tile E10-00000098725646657."

"Is your work progressing well, Miss Smith?" It was the voice of Bishop Salestina.

Chapter 24

Gretchin's Reconciliation

"Y-Yes, Bishop Salestina. The c-curvature is radially uniform. The formula is simple, and you will be p-pleased that your measurements were confirmed to another decimal place."

While looking toward the paper in Feli's hand the bishop asked, "Is that the formula of the curve? "

"No, No, this is just a measurement. It's just raw data. It would not be of interest to you?"

"That's strange, said Bishop Salestina. "Last time I read the inscription, I found it *very* interesting. Let's go to my office where we can speak in private."

Feli thought through her options. She could run. She could lie. She could face the bishop, and then reevaluate her situation. She followed the bishop up to her office.

"Shocking isn't it?"

"Yes," replied Feli.

"What do you plan to do?"

"I don't know. I need to think."

"Are you going to tell Professor Boatman?"

"I don't even know that."

"There is a lot at stake here Feli. Sometimes an explicit truth is even worse than a falsehood."

Feli did not know what to say. She did not want to debate ethics with a Theite bishop. She had just lied to the bishop about the content of the paper in her hand. Was she now going to defend the principle of honesty? She sat in silence.

The bishop continued, "Many civilizations arose and fell on Epodlo before we were born. Some kingdoms prospered for a time, before succumbing to human frailty. Some of our distant ancestors had a stadium or theater under a great roof. A ceiling tile survived under the protective sand of the sea bottom, until a storm released it, to be washed up on one kingdom's beach. That piece of debris was a source of inspiration which God used to draw thousands of people into His embrace, bringing God's peace to what became the Western Theocracy. That peace spread to the rest of Epodlo. I know you do not believe in God, but do not your *reason* and *compassion* compel you to tread lightly here?"

"You are right. I cannot act here without due care."

"Will you promise to keep our secret?"

"No, I can't," said Feli. "Normally humans are best served by the truth. There are many, myself included, who think the death of Theism would be a good thing. I, more than many, would like that death to be a gentle one. The sudden revelation that one's faith is based on fraud would not be gentle, and may lead to consequences I can't predict, so I don't know what to do."

"Then will you promise me that before you unleash this revelation on the world, you will at least talk to your cousin, Illi?"

"Dean Smith?"

"Yes. She is a wise woman. When my technicians discovered the inscription three years ago, they came to me. I went to your Dean Smith." Illi has no love for God, but God uses her as His tool. Go to her. Let her advise you before you tell Professor Boatman or others. "Will you promise me to do this, if not for God, *for humanity*?"

"Yes, I will talk with Dean Smith."

"You can talk with me right now." Dean Smith appeared from a doorway wearing her purple standard Republican dress.

"Dean Smith," said a shocked Feli.

"We aren't at school. Call me Illi here. We *are* cousins."

In the emotional intensity of the moment, Feli's mind grasped for the mundane, amid the momentous "How—How come you don't have to where a robe?"

"Theites are pacifists. I'm a head of state. They put me in one of those, and its war," said Illi with a smile.

Feli smiled too, thinking of Gretchin singlehandedly conquering the Theocracy.

"It's very important that you keep this ceiling tile information quiet. It is more dangerous than you know," said Illi.

"How is it dangerous?"

"We have four peaceful societies on Epodlo. You take Theism away from the Theites what will happen? Will they all turn into rational, compassionate Humanists overnight? Will they be responsible lovers of freedom like the Libertarians? Will they somehow join the Royal bloodline? No. there will be a cultural void, and in that void we don't know what will arise."

"We could educate them in Humanism. They could learn. We could teach them," suggested Feli.

321

"Why didn't I think of that?" responded Illi.

"Oh, I see," said Feli as she realized that such education was exactly what Central College was all about.

Illi continued, "It takes time. Eventually, with our help, the Theites will dispose of their supernatural rubbish, but telling them their religion is based on a discarded architectural feature will not serve the purpose of achieving a *peaceful* transition. They will find other excuses to believe in nonsense. Without empirical grounding, their next fallacy may be less benign than this one. In the past people used religion to justify torture, murder, and depravation of liberty. We don't want that to come back."

"Can't people be trusted to be rational, compassionate, and responsible?"

"I wish they could Feli. I really do. Someday maybe, but not yet. Do you understand?"

Feli reluctantly replied, "Yes."

"Then you need to keep quiet about the ceiling tile, ok?"

"It doesn't feel right. Professor Boatman, I'm his assistant. I have a duty to him."

"Your duty is to humanity, Feli. You're not alone in this. You have me. You have Salestina. We live with this. You can too."

"Ok, for now. I was worried about the news hurting Antwanesta anyway. Now I have a rational justification to deny her the truth."

"So you promise to tell no one about the ceiling tile inscription?"

"Yes, I promise I will tell no one about the inscription," said Feli.

"Thank you Feli, now go before the professor gets curious about your whereabouts. I'll see you back at school."

Feli got up form here chair and turned to leave. Before she reached the door she paused and turned back.

"Bishop, there is another problem which may involve some preparation on your part."

"What is it, Dear?"

"It's the arc of the ceiling tile. The curve extrapolates into a sphere with a radius which when measured in kiloballs is a big round number divisible by *thirteen*. You will need to come up with an explanation which will satisfy your people."

"Thanks for the warning Feli. Illi and I, will have an answer ready. God bless you, Dear."

Feli left.

"You sounded very convincing," said Bishop Salestina to Illi.

"She saw through it. That one is very smart." said Illi. "However, I think we have her plugged."

"It sounds like God has finally blessed you with the virtue of faith."

"No, it's not that. Feli is as rational as they come. The nice thing about rational people is that their behavior can be predicted. She's on our side now. The other leaky girl is more dangerous. You never can tell what stupid thing a religious person will do. I have my people on her."

Two days after her promise to the Illi and the Bishop of God City, the wind filled the sails of Feli's Father's sailboat. Feli lay on the foredeck at the bow, showing her

323

nakedness to the sky, and the sky showing its nakedness to her. The sky was blue, spotted with clouds here and there. The clouds seemed far away, but the smell of the salt air gave Feli a refreshing sense of reality. She looked to the northwest, she had never seen the black hexagon in the sky with her naked eyes. Why did she expect to see it now? It was too far away, too small. Thanks to the measurement's she and Professor Boatman made, she could calculate exactly how far that black hexagon in the sky was. She did not know the exact distance from the boat, but knowing the orientations of the telescopes in Newton and at Saint Isaac's College, she knew its height above the point on the water directly below it. She was not Antwanesta, but she could still do the math. *Below it? Was down still down? Yes, down is always relative to a gravitational reference point, a point (the center of gravity). Point? No line. A curved line in a great arc, an arc even greater than the arc of the sky?* Oh, how Feli wanted to talk this through this with Antwanesta, to use her fast brain, and to share the awe of her realization.

That was the problem. She could not tell Antwanesta. She could not even tell Professor Boatman, or her father, and they would love the awesome discovery. Boatman would die of joy.

Antwanesta would die of grief. Xiny lost her friend and lover, and tried to kill herself. It must be worse to lose a god. Histina and Zillestra would say otherwise. "She's an addict. Stop enabling her," they would both say. Feli agreed, agreed with her mind, agreed with her reason, agreed with her Humanistic values; that truth should be shared. Humans have the right to know, to have the best information to make decisions. If a person was hurt because a truth unsettled a cherished falsehood, surely it was the falsehood that was to blame, not the truth. It was Feli's heart that held her back more than that promise she had made. Feli knew it was her brain, not her literal heart. (Humanists can think in metaphors too.) Feli loved Antwanesta, she would not be the agent of this pain. She could not tell her friend that, in a tiny inscription on

the most holy relic of Antwanesta's faith, there was
undeniable proof that her religion was a lie. However, maybe
she could tell her something else.

The bishop had spoken of an ancient stadium or
theater. Did *she* know the truth? Did Dean Smith (her Cousin
Illi)? Feli was keeping secrets within secrets. *This is what it
must be like to be Xiny*, Feli thought.

After the short boat trip to East Tower, Xiny and Risky
walked west. They were now campers like Gretchin and
Antwanesta. However, Xiny and Risky wore white Royal
tunics except when sleeping or bathing. The Royal Plumbers
had installed baths and toilets along the trail from East Tower
to Center Town, just as Antwanesta had hoped to find on the
trek from Freetown to East Bend. The Kingdom was still off-
limits to most foreigners, but Xiny knew better than anyone
where the confidential technology was hidden. There were no
red tarps along the trail to Center Town. There was nothing to
hide here, except the secret Risky already knew.

Gretchin and Antwanesta stayed at the house of Quinis in
Hunt Town. It was much like Ottarian's house in Freetown,
less one bed room. The two went to bed early to cut off the
fantastic rambling speculations of Quinis. After three nights
back in the tiny tent, the guest bed seemed as big as the huge
one in East Bend, though it was as small as the one they
hardly fit into in Freetown.

"Why didn't I get to meet your mom?" Antwanesta
asked from her side of the pillow.

"She's very busy. I see more of her than my pops
anyway."

"Why don't you talk about her?"

Gretchin was ready for this one. "She is a bigshot
entrepreneur who owns the brothels. I know Theites don't

325

think highly of that business, so I don't talk about her. What else do you want to know?"

"Why am I not supposed to know that Risky is your sister?"

"Who told you?"

"I figured it out. Dussy said Risky would turn her into a vegetable if she fed meat to the family, then you nearly wanted to strangle Daro when he mentioned Risky, He said something about your mom's games."

"Mom wants us to keep a low profile. If one of us is connected with her, the other is still secure. Big people are targets, and so are their children. Look what happened to Lissy. Mom wants to protect us. I'd appreciate it, if you didn't let on about Risky and me."

"Of course. Does Xiny know?"

"Yes, she knows, and Feli knows Mom owns a big interest in the brothels. I don't know if she knows about Risky."

"Why haven't we seen your Pop Four?"

"Because he is not worth seeing."

"You shouldn't talk like that about your father."

"You wouldn't think kindly of him either, if you knew what he did."

"What?"

"You know Risky is my sister, so I guess I can tell you now. The Summer after Risky graduated from Central College, she brought home a boyfriend to meet her pops. My Pop Four, Pargog Metropopis is her Pop Two. None of her pops liked her boyfriend, and they told her so. However, one pop went far beyond what any responsible person would do. He severed her boyfriend's penis with a knife."

"How terrible," said Antwanesta with a true sense of revulsion and pity.

"Risky and the boyfriend broke up. He went back to his home county. She went to medical school in Democratica City.

Her boyfriend was from the Republic?

No, a Theite."

"A Theite?"

"Korack is now a Bishop. You met him. Our pop disgraced the family. Everyone knew. Everyone was appalled. I was thirteen. Just as I wanted the boys to like me, they all saw me as the girl from the lowest, most irresponsible family in Libertaria. I was hated and ridiculed. No boy ever liked me. I thought things would change at the college, but I'm still alone. No one loves me."

Antwanesta hugged Gretchin. "I love you Gretchin. You know I do. However, as one who truly loves you, I need to tell you *that you must forgive your pop*."

"Risky says the same thing, but why should I?"

"The Holy Hexagon…"

"Ant, I don't believe in your hexagon."

"You don't need a hexagon Gretchin. It's just a symbol. Virtues aren't virtues because they fit in some geometric shape. Forgiveness is good because people need it. Both the forgiven and the forgiver need it. You need it Gretchin."

Gretchin wept. Antwanesta held her close.

After three days the two left for Battle Tree, and then on to Smithtown. Battle Tree was another tiny village, like Middle Village, but with a larger brothel and no chicken farms. It only existed because of a small stone monument at the base of a sprawling live oak, which drew tourists in scant numbers. There were presumably enough visitors to support the tavern, the brothel, and the inn; but only just. The monument was to honor those who had sacrificed their lives in defense of liberty, fighting in the war of 783. The inscription at the monument's base read:

> *Here did fight the valiant three.*
>
> *For us they died. For them we live,*
>
> *For now, and forever free.*
>
> *Liberty's cost we each must give.*

Over wine in the tavern, Antwanesta again raised the issue of Gretchin forgiving her pop four. Antwanesta thought. *If I can persuade Gretchin to reconcile with her Earthly father, I will have the momentum to get her to reconcile with her Heavenly Father. Perhaps God has put me here for that very purpose. I can be the tool God uses to save Gretchin's soul.*

"No, Ant. Stop trying to fix me. *You* are the broken one. Irresponsibility earns its consequences. If forgiveness is given to those who have not earned it, society will fail. Freedom will be lost. I have been more than tolerant of your religious idiocy, don't try to push it on me."

The warmth which had grown between Antwanesta and Gretchin had chilled even as the climate grew hotter and the foliage more tropical. On the morning of July 19th they skipped breakfast and broke camp before dawn. Antwanesta wanted to leave early to get to the Theite church in Smithtown in time for the liturgy. Gretchin was happy to move fast and talk less, since the portable god-girl had decided to save her soul.

Maidens of Epodlo, Book 1 — Antwanesta Agape and the Mystery of the Red-dot Moon

In Smithtown Antwanesta would attend her first liturgy in several weeks. She extracted her black standard Republican dress from her rucksack, and dressed on the church steps. She tried to coax Gretchin into the church. With a cold stare of resentment, Gretchin refused, saying she would go to the knife and sword market. Smithtown was named, not for Illisima Smith or any of her relatives; it was named for the profession which crated it. Smithtown was the weapons manufacturing center of Libertaria, of all of Epodlo for that matter. Even Royal soldier's short swords were manufactured there, right across the Southeast River from the Southern Kingdom. The market was a bustling place, with crooked rows of makeshift stalls, and wood-framed kiosks. There were swords, knives, axes, maces, polearms, arrows, bows, bolts, crossbows, and various deerskin accessories. There were no red circles on any doors here. There were hardly even any doors.

Gretchin browsed among the weapons. She even bought two small daggers, more decorative than the one on her hip. There were more goods at the sprawling market, than just weapons and weapon accessories. Some stalls sold jewelry. There were finely crafted items of gold, silver, and platinum. Gretchin did not try on earrings, or sift through the racks of bracelets and bangles. She wanted a gold pendant with a matching chain. She quickly saw what she needed, and bought it. She did not wear her new acquisition, or even try it on. She buried it in her rucksack, in case she needed it next year.

At the church service Antwanesta was the only person dressed, except the priestess in her traditional vestments. Aside from the lack of attire, the service was very much the same as she had always known. The nine other members of the congregation were even weaponless, though Antwanesta had seen several daggers and swords in the narthex, close to the door, when she had entered. The other people in the sanctuary sat on the first three rows. Antwanesta sat on row six, so as not to be intrusive. At the end of the service, the parishioners lined up to greet the priestess. Based on her seat Antwanesta was last, behind the others. When the forth parishioner turned back after greeting the cleric, Antwanesta had a flash of recognition. This was the same bearded man who pulled her out of the lake eleven months ago.

He recognized her too. "I see you made it, Sister. You found your way to freedom."

"It's you. I never thanked you for saving me. I would probably have drowned without you."

"You're very welcome. I hope things worked out for you."

"They did, thanks to you. My name is Antwanesta."

"I'm Pargog."

"Pargog Metropopis?"

"Yes, *that* one. I'm infamous."

"Come with me!" Antwanesta grabbed his hand and dragged him from the church.

"Where are we going?"

"Just come. This way."

Antwanesta dragged Pargog into the weapons market around this corner and that. Pargog did not understand where he was being taken. The priestess had recently told him he should trust God's will. Even before he had subjected himself to the counsel of the Theist cleric, he would have regarded being dragged enthusiastically about by a beautiful young woman as a blessing. He had left his dagger in the narthex of the church. Its absence made him feel as naked as he was, here in such a public place. There was no risk that he would really need to defend himself here. There was surly no safer place in

the world than the Smithtown weapons market. Soon the tall
tan flatness of Antwanesta's beloved friend came to her eyes.
She jerked Pargog's arm and dragged him directly to Gretchin.

Gretchin saw him.

Pargog saw his daughter. "Gretchin?"

"Ant! I said no!"

"Gretchin wait," said Pargog. "I'm sorry."

Gretchin ignored his apology.

"Risky forgave me. Korack forgave me. God forgave
me. That just leave us, you and me. We are the only ones who
don't forgive me. The priestess said God washed away my
sins, but I need *your* forgiveness, before I can forgive myself."

Gretchin responded, "Why? How could you have
done such a thing?"

"It was love of my daughter," said Pargog. "Korack
had convinced Risky to go to the Theocracy and become a
Theist. She wanted to become celibate. He was leading her to
give up her sex life. I was frustrated and angry. My daughter
was going to surrender her reproductive freedom, for nothing.
In a spilt second of irrationality, I wanted to show Korack
what the loss of sexual liberty meant. I've hated myself every
day since. I can't forgive myself. I became a Theist myself six
months ago. I thought it was a small way to make amends."

Gretchin broke down and cried. She hugged her pop
four.

After the tearful reunion, Pargog invited Gretchin and
Antwanesta to his resort in Freedom Beach. They sailed down
river to the coast.

"I'll give you the same room Risky and Princess
Xiny had."

Antwanesta responded to Pargog's statement with, "Risky and Xiny were here?"

"A couple of weeks ago, just for one night. The Princess was taking Risky to the Kingdom for the Summer."

Antwanesta then asked, "Are they *involved* with each other?"

"I don't know. I'm the last person who has any right to pry into Risky's sex life."

"I don't think so," said, Gretchin. "Risky did say she had a lover that she wouldn't talk about. I assumed it was a man."

"Xiny is both a Royal and a student," interjected Antwanesta. "Those are two good reasons for Risky to be secretive. There is a school rule against physical fraternization between teacher and student. Risky could lose her job."

"I don't think they're together, but I guess we will find out in two weeks, when we go to Royal Beach," said Gretchin.

Back in the Kingdom, Xiny was busy. Her hiking trip with Risky had taken her away from time with Lissy. Her time with Lissy, conflicted with her construction supervision work. She wanted to wrap up as many projects as possible before Antwanesta and Gretchin came to visit under special permission from King Gregorious. At least the D-units were now working properly. D-units were golden human-shaped robots, twice Xiny's height, and very handy for excavation and construction.

Chapter 25

Royal Beach

Xiny stood at the bow of a sailing vessel in a white Royal
tunic. She could see Antwanesta and Gretchin, similarly
attired, standing on the dock at East Tower. Pargog had rowed
them across the mouth of the river earlier that morning to
make the rendezvous set for July 25th, today. As the boat
drew closer Xiny waved excitedly, as did Gretchin and
Antwanesta.

Xiny jumped off onto the dock and hugged Gretchin.
"I've missed you so much," she said with a broad smile before
releasing the embrace.

"We missed you too, Sinny."

Xiny kissed Gretchin on the right cheek, after hearing
the name which no other person would use to address the
respected Princess.

Xiny wanted to give Antwanesta a similar hug, but
remembered that Antwanesta did not approve of nonmaternal
hugs. Xiny also knew that a hug from *her* may seem all the
more sexual regardless of how platonic it may be.

Antwanesta resolved Xiny's ambivalence, by giving
Xiny a hug with all the warmth and excitement her discarded
inhibitions could no longer deny.

"It's so good to see you Xiny."

"You too Antwanesta, I see Gretchin has given you
freckles."

A crewman took the rucksacks aboard. The sailing vessel was 150 balls long, about the length of Feli's Father's boat.

"We'll depart in ten minutes, Princess," said the sailboat's pilot. Xiny was now called *Princess*. With Lissy gone her father was second to the throne, and *she* was third. Xiny and her father, Alfide were the only Royals above ground who knew Lissy was alive aside from Dr. Grocer, Captain Knight and a dozen Royal soldiers used in the operation to fake the Queen's death. Lissy did not resent Xiny's advancement. Lissy had chosen to step down as Queen, not just to save her people from the tsunami, but because she wanted freedom no queen could know. The arranged marriage process was no longer her fate, and now she with Xiny conspired further.

Xiny had to fight her feelings in order to conceal the truth of Lissy's situation from her dearest friends. Only a Royal could hold such a secret.

Xiny also had to protect the Kingdom's proprietary secrets. The ancient D-units had long been the secret of the Kingdom's mining success. The root of the Kingdom's power was monopolistic control of the gold supply. No one can extract gold as fast as a D-unit, much less 164 D-units. To the Theocracy the historic memory of the of the D-units was retained only in idioms about "golden demons." In the Republic, there was the mysterious golden arm. In Libertaria no one gave a thought about such things, except maybe Quinis.

The vessel set sail for Royal Beach.

"Pargog said you were with Risky in Free Beach," said Antwanesta.

"Pargog is not very discrete about the personal affairs of others. Risky said that he and Gretchin were estranged. I didn't expect you would be talking with him."

Antwanesta pressed further, "Are you with Risky?"

"If Risky and I were together, it would be none of your business."

"I just don't want you two to get in trouble at school," said Antwanesta.

"If, hypothetically, Risky and I were together as you suspect, I promise we would have the sense to save our intimacy for weekends in Freetown."

"You *are* with Risky?" Gretchin was only now thinking Antwanesta may be right.

"As I said, whatever there is between Risky and me is none of your business. Now let's talk about the fun we are going to have." Xiny successfully cut off the inquiry into a third area of secrecy.

Gretchin was pleased to think that her sister and good friend may be together, but Xiny was facing a future duty of arranged marriage with a Royal, and Risky had her own stable culture to consider. Gretchin did not dwell on it long. *Risky and Xiny are free women. They don't need to comply with anyone's rules or cultural traditions*, Gretchin thought. Whatever would make them happy was fine with her. A temporary lover was more than she herself had, having a celibate best friend was testament to that.

Antwanesta was comforted that Xiny and Risky would be discrete. She did not try to impose her values on others, at least not always. Celibacy was a hard path. Antwanesta herself had been wavering in her own resolve to stay on it. She knew her own feelings, her own weaknesses, the intermittently intense desires she felt. If an attractive someone with whom she felt emotional attachment had offered physical intimacy, could she say no? Antwanesta was modest enough to doubt it. If she did not have friends to protect her, unwittingly holding her accountable to the values they themselves did not hold, she would break. If she were not so overflowing with platonic love, she would fill her void with something else. She dropped the subject, and would say nothing more of Risky and Xiny being a couple.

As Royal Beach came into view, Antwanesta and Gretchin were surprised how many intact structures could be seen. There were places with scaffolding and broad red tarps, but most of the coastal city appeared intact.

"I thought Royal Beach was wiped out by the Tsunami," said Gretchin. "I thought you communists would take decades to rebuild."

"It was just sand and rubble," replied Xiny. "We have been busy. Royals work well if, left to our own devices."

"I don't see how it's possible. Even free people in a free market could not build so much so fast."

"You are right to call us Royals communists, Gretchin. We of the Kingdom are one community of people bound by a strong sense of nationalistic duty. Communist systems of the past did not fail because of any flaw fundamental to the idea of communal control of the means of production. The Royal bank, the Royal mines, the tropical fruit collective, these are all very efficient productive operations. Communism failed in the past due to a lack of resources."

"Deer dung, retorted Gretchin. Professor Solider said that the ancient Soviet Union had vast timberland, virtually unlimited fuel reserves, mineral wealth greater than 100 Royal mines, as well as a well-educated population. The Russians had plenty of resources. Communism robbed people of

336

incentive and killed the empire dead as any. The neo-Russian Empire occupied almost the same territory and lasted far longer thanks to capitalism."

"The Soviet Union was short on the most valuable resource any nation could have. The Russians are reputed to have been a very patriotic and self-sacrificing people. However, though they may have been the best of the best, there were enough among them who were corrupt of character to doom the system to failure. *Moral character* is the most precious resource any nation can have. Where character is deficient there is failure no matter how noble and wise a nation's founding principles."

The boat later pulled alongside the newly replaced Royal Beach Pier. A crewman took the rucksacks and handed them to a young woman, a servant in a standard Royal white tunic. The crewman then helped the women from the boat, not that they needed help. Royal curtesy required men to treat women so, given their special role in the perpetuation of the bloodline.

"This way." Xiny lead the two up the pier to Beach Trail, a long path of sand leading off into the distance as far as could be seen. To the left, the beach side of the trail, all the people were nude, but for an occasional sunhat. To the right everyone wore white tunics. On the wide path people were either dressed, undressed, or, as was often the case, dressing or undressing. As people disrobed they put their tunics into cotton canvas bags, which they carried on the beach. "I guess our dress code it pretty obvious," said Xiny.

Antwanesta was not shocked. After two months of nudity in Libertaria, the people on the left seemed more normal than those on the right. They were distinctive only in the characteristic blondness of the Royals.

Most of the buildings looked, not new, but in good condition. Scavenged blocks had been reused in recent construction. Some buildings where cloaked in red tarps, with the whine of machinery purring from behind their crimson concealment.

Antwanesta asked, "What is that noise?"

"Construction equipment." said Xiny, "Up ahead is the Regalis Palace, just beyond is our estate."

The palace was four stories of stone. The stonework was austere for a palace. The ornamental façade had not yet been restored. Likewise, the garden was devoid of the plants which had previously created a regal atmosphere. Still to erect such a structure from ground up in nine months was incredible.

"We are invited to lunch with King Gregorious tomorrow," said Xiny as they passed.

Antwanesta and Gretchin both looked forward to seeing Gregor. Last time they saw him was at Lissy's funeral. That was just looking up at him on stage. They had not spoken with him since before Zell's trial. So much had happened since then.

"Here we are. Don't look at the garden. It's a fright. We want to finish construction before we start landscaping. It would be most uncourteous for us to plant flowers while we still have citizens displaced from their homes. All homes will be restored soon," said Xiny confidently.

The servant carrying the rucksacks was well ahead, and already entering the Stewart House, while Xiny, Gretchin, and Antwanesta were still on Beach Trail.

When the three young women reached the house they were greeted by a familiar smiling face with a narrow blond goatee. "Greetings! Gretchin, Antwanesta, welcome to our home," said Xiny's father, Prince Alfide Stewart. "This is *your* home. You will want for nothing while here. If you have

any need, we shall endeavor to meet it. Dinner will be served
in two hours. Xiny will show you to your rooms to freshen up.

Antwanesta and Gretchin were each provided with a
large luxurious bedroom and a private bath. In front of the
rooms was a breezeway overlooking a rectangular swimming
pool. At one end of the swimming pool was a round hot pool
almost identical to their favorite pool in the freshman bath. At
the other end of the pool was an exercise area with an
assortment of gold-plated free weights and two benches, one
flat, the other inclined. There were also two massage tables
identical to those at school, except that these were clearly new.

Gretchin said, "I see being the second family of the
Southern Kingdom has its perks."

"Not really," said Xiny. Look out from your balcony,
and you will see that all Royals live in similar comfort. This
house is larger only because the reception and dining areas are
expanded to accommodate some functions of my father's
position. Even the palace is large only because it houses
administrative offices, and spaces to entertain visiting
dignitaries."

"What about the servants?" asked Antwanesta.

"In normal times servants are mostly foreigners
paying off debts to Royal Bank. Since the tsunami many
temporarily displaced Royal citizens have elected to serve in
domestic capacities. You cannot overestimate the will of
Royals to serve one and other. Our collective commitment to
duty is our strength. Whenever I tell the two of you, 'I am
your servant,' I mean it most sincerely."

At dinner the meal was whole vegetarian food, all
prepared with skill and style. Otherwise familiar dishes were
accented with pieces of banana, pineapple, papaya, and
tangerine. The salad had at least fifteen different ingredients.
For Antwanesta, it was the sliced avocado, its silky decadence

caressing her tongue, which made the salad so irresistible. The servants would not permit a wine glass to stand empty. Antwanesta's one glass of wine became four.

Gretchin noticed Antwanesta's unintentional intemperance and said, "If you keep drinking that you are going to have a *ménage-á-trois* for dessert."

"Does it have chocolate on it?" responded Antwanesta.

Despite the relaxing effect of the wine, and the regal comfort of her grand bed chamber, it was hard for Antwanesta to sleep the first night. Aside from the occasional nap in the dorm, she had not slept in a room alone in almost a year. For the past two months she had slept in the tent or a bed close to Gretchin. Antwanesta had not recognized how much Gretchin had come to mean to her. She thought of going to Gretchin's room, but then thought that maybe she was getting too emotionally dependent on Gretchin, like Xiny with Lissy. No, she would go to Xiny, talk a little, just the two of them. Antwanesta walked down the hall, still unsteady from the wine; or was it the cherry liquor she had with dessert? She knocked on Xiny's door. There was no answer. She tried the door knob. Xiny wouldn't mind. They walked in on each other all the time in the dorm. There was no Xiny. Where could she be? Down stairs perhaps, maybe the kitchen. Antwanesta went back to bed. In time Antwanesta relaxed. She knew she would be with Gretchin and Xiny the next day. If only Feli were with them, then she would feel the fullness of support from the three central friendships which sustained her.

The next morning, after a yoga, a run on the beach, a shower, a massage, breakfast, and a bath, it was time to visit the King for lunch.

Gregor was a gracious host.

"Don't even think of bowing to me. If you bow to me Gretchin, Tear will come down and sever my bloodline. How is she by-the-way?"

"Mom and baby are fine."

"Remind the happy family that I want to see them down here as my guests."

Gregor hugged Gretchin.

"Antwanesta, you're getting a tan, sort of. The freckles are cute. We'll make a Royal of you yet. I'd hug you, but Bishop Korack say's Theites are not comfortable with hugs."

"I've adapted," replied Antwanesta. She hugged Gregor.

Gretchin asked, "Are we supposed to call you "King" now?"

"To you, Lissy was Lissy, and I'm still Gregor, until I appoint you to an official post."

Gregor asked about mutual friends, not for gossip. He sincerely wanted to know of their welfare. Antwanesta asked how he was faring in his new demanding role.

He responded that the duty was a heavy burden, but he would wish it on no one. "Anyone who would want this job is less fit than I. I don't want this crown, but I can't trust the weight of the Kingdom to anyone. I need friends inside and outside the Kingdom. This is a critical time for us. Big changes are coming, and the Kingdom will need its allies."

"What changes?" asked Antwanesta.

Gregor looked Antwanesta in the eyes, "The Kingdom has a desperate need, a need which you would refuse to fulfill. However, with the good guidance of Xiny and

341

Alfide, the Kingdom will endure. I will say nothing more on the subject, until the formal announcement in a few months." He also did not mention that Alfide was no longer his Chief Councilor, at least not in title. Xiny had also become invaluable as an advisor. Xiny had her own perspective on the future of the Kingdom. She would mold it to meet *her* needs as well as her nation's.

When she went to bed the second night in the Stewart manor, Antwanesta left the door ajar to see when Xiny went to bed, so she could come to talk. The pillow-talk with Gretchin had been so sustaining to her. She longed to have similar moments with her dear Royal friend as well. She noticed Xiny pass quickly. By the time Antwanesta got to the door and stuck her head out, Xiny was gone, but a panel at the end of the hall was moving. It was closing like a door, perhaps it was a special passage for servants. Antwanesta went to Xiny's room. Like the night before she was not there. Antwanesta went to the end of the hall, and found the mechanism to open the hidden door. Inside was a ladder, a long series of metal rungs extending down into the darkness. "Xiny?" she yelled down. There was no answer, just a *clank* sound. Antwanesta could now see a small circle of light below. "Xiny?" Antwanesta climbed down the ladder through a cylindrical metal tube. Some 500 balls down, she found footing on a textured metal floor which felt warm beneath her bare feet. She only now noticed her own nudity, having become so accustomed to the state. This was a room, well-lit, but from what source? She saw no lamp. She turned.

Antwanesta's arm was grabbed quickly and with power which could not be resisted. *It was a golden demon,* Antwanesta thought at first. The robot was thirty balls tall, human in shape, but gold all over. Its face had two eyes, but no nose or mouth. It held her left arm in its right hand. It pressed her forearm against the upper left portion of its own chest, on what would have been the inner portion of a pectoral muscle on a real man. A golden band popped from the chest of

342

the robot. The band strapped Antwanesta's wrist to the chest of the golden brute. In another second her right arm was similarly secured to the other side of the robot's chest. The robot walked its suspended prisoner forward.

Antwanesta hung painfully from the manacle bands which secured her hopelessly. She pushed with her feet to no avail. This only hurt her wrists. She wrapped her legs around the golden beast's abdomen. She tried to crush it between her thighs. The machine between her legs was cold and ridged. The metal skin did not give under her pressure. Antwanesta lightened the grip of her thighs, and held to the golden man with her legs, like a child clinging to a parent.

Antwanesta was ready for this moment. She had trained all her life for a time like this. She knew how to defend herself. She had a weapon, a defense so powerful that no demon could ever prevail against it. Antwanesta drew her weapon. She drew upon the power of prayer.

Lord, God, I trust You with all my heart. There is no challenge too great for the power of Your love. If it is Your will that I should join You now, I will obey, and submit myself to Your mercy; but I ask dear Lord, please send an angel to deliver me from this. Allow me to serve You longer in this world. I know I can do more to serve You. I am but Your unworthy tool. Bless me with the power to serve You longer.

A metal wall panel opened. Xiny stepped out from behind it, nude and dripping wet. "Release Captive!" Xiny said with authority.

The metal bands on the robot's chest popped open, and the D-unit released Antwanesta. Then Antwanesta placed her hands on the giant's golden waist, unwrapped her legs, and dropped her bare feet to the floor.

"What, what is…?!" She backed toward Xiny.

"I'm sorry Antwanesta. The D-unit was on security patrol. Let's go back up the ladder and I'll explain."

Xiny followed Antwanesta up the ladder, and then lead Antwanesta into the bedroom where Antwanesta had twice found her absent. Xiny grabbed a towel from her bathroom and explained while drying herself. "You were not supposed to see that. That was a D-unit, proprietary Royal technology. You must promise me not to tell anyone."

"Why not?"

"Outsiders don't know we have mechanical men. If they knew we had them, people would be afraid. The D-units are not weapons. They are for digging and building mostly. They are just strong fast machines. They have allowed us to quickly rebuild Royal Beach."

"What about God City and Democratica City?"

"We can't let the Theites or the Republicans see what we can do. They would want the technology for their own use. Neither a theocracy nor a democracy can be trusted with such power. They are too unstable."

"What about Libertaria? The people there are responsible."

"They are free with their tongues, and some of them might see a preemptive strike as the best defense, against a perceived enemy with superior technology."

"Can I tell Gretchin?"

"No, not even Gretchin. Peace is one of the values of your Holy Hexagon. For *peace* you must be *Royal* on this." Xiny looked into Antwanesta's eyes. "You have to be *with me* on this. We have been through so much together. I need you Antwanesta. I need you to keep this quiet."

"Ok, for peace, and for you. I'll be *Royal*."

344

"You want to stay here with me tonight?" asked Xiny, wanting to mitigate against further snooping on Antwanesta's part."

"Your friend is waiting. I'm sorry I intruded on you."

"You saw her?"

"No, but you were wet, if you wanted to bathe alone you would do it up here. If you wanted to swim you would do it in the first floor pool. You must have a secret friend if you choose to bathe in the basement guarded by a D-unit."

"Why did you follow me?"

"I just wanted to be closer to you. I got so close with Gretchin in Libertaria. I wanted to be like that with you too."

"I love you Antwanesta, but I don't want you following me through secret passages. I can see my friend again tomorrow, she will understand."

"Then you do have a lover in the basement?"

"That is none of your business, Antwanesta. You know how we Royals are about personal matters."

"I don't mean to pry. I'm just happy you found someone. We were all so worried after you lost Lissy. We knew it would be hard for you to love again."

"I understand. You, Gretchin, and Feli were there to support me when I needed you most. I will never forget that, and I will always love you."

"When do we get to see her?"

"You don't. In the Kingdom premarital sexual relationships are not allowed to exist. So you can't meet my friend. Sorry."

"We were all discrete about you and Lissy."

345

"That was Lissy's call. This is mine. I will not surrender my friend's privacy to your voyeuristic curiosity."

"I'm not voyeuristic! I just care about you, that's all."

"I know, I'm sorry." Xiny kissed Antwanesta's forehead as a passive aggressive outlet for suppressed anger. "You slept cheek-to-cheek with Gretchin for two months without a single sexual thought, I know you're not voyeuristic." *I'm as sarcastic as Feli,* Xiny thought. *I need to tone it down. I'm not mad at Antwanesta. I'm mad at Illi for making me do this, and I am mad at the system I'm fighting to overturn.*

Antwanesta kept *Royal* about the D-units, the secret passage, and Xiny's hidden romantic partner. She enjoyed the infinite comfort and hospitality of the Kingdom. She did not even feel guilty about the immodesty of enjoying her comfort and pleasure.

However, deep within Antwanesta was a troubled spirit. She still lived in a world which made no sense. There was predictable weather, and a climate which was inconsistent with the latitude of any island, or any place, on Earth. The geology was absurd, and there was a moon which had stopped blushing, robots of unimaginable technology... Nothing was rational.

"Hey Girls, look at this treasure," said Xiny holding a folded piece of paper. "It's a letter from *Feli.*"

Antwanesta could not have been more pleased with a diamond necklace. This was word from her other dear friend, the only person missing from the otherwise perfect setting and company.

Gretchin too was pleased, but she only expressed her satisfaction, by not speaking disparagingly of the bunny-brain who had clawed into her heart.

Maidens of Epodlo, Book 1 — Antwanesta Agape and the Mystery of the Red-dot Moon

The letter read:

Dear Xiny:

I hope this letter finds you well and happy, and in the company of the two girls we both love so much. If you are not well and happy, just muddle through until you return to school and can get centered. I will gladly take on any handmaiden duties too challenging for our furbearing sweetheart. Please kiss her for me.

Dear Sweetheart:

Much as I love science, and have enjoyed my research with Professor Boatman, I admit I envy Antwanesta, the Summer she has shared with you. I'm sure she is quite the tanned Libertarian now. I promise you I will be free next Summer, so if you want to drag me through your jungle, I am all yours.

Dear Antwanesta:

I spent two weeks in the Theocracy in a Theite robe. I found the people there to be very nice and warm in their way. However, I can't dress like that. If I ever fail to show you the respect and tolerance you deserve, just remind me that you wore a Theite robe for seventeen years, and I will bow to you and kiss your feet. If kissing is still a problem for you, I will instead give you all the foot massages that you desire.

Here is a math problem to get warmed-up for school:

A plane intersects with a sphere creating a circle of intersection. The radius of the sphere is 13,000 kiloballs, but the plane does not intersect the sphere in the middle. You know three points on the plane, N, C, and S. Point C is at the center of the circle, and is 596 kiloballs east from Point S. Point N is 1403 kiloballs from Point S. The one known point on the sphere is 13.3 degrees up from S, and 14.1 degrees up from N. S and N are both close enough to sea level to ignore their respective altitudes, which vary by an inconsequential amount. Points N, S, and a point X (on the plane directly below the known point on the sphere) form triangle NXS, with angles 69.2 degrees at S and 83.3 degrees at N. What is the arc of the plane? Either do the math, or hug Sweetheart. For bonus points, find the diameter of the plane and the height at the peak of the dome.

My closeness with the three of you makes it comforting to know that it's a small world.

Stay Royal.

Your loving friend,

Feli

"Bunny-brained as ever," said Gretchin. "Why did she have to insult me? Hugging me is not some disgusting punishment for getting a math problem wrong."

Antwanesta laughed, hugged Gretchin, and saved the math for later. She already got the message.

Xiny, kissed the back of Gretchin's neck and also gave her a hug from behind, Including Antwanesta in the embrace. "Feli is a trusting soul isn't she?" Xiny said.

"Bunny-brain has no soul," replied Gretchin. "She gave us a bunch of useless numbers, followed by a trick question. Even I know that a plane has no arc. I get it. I'm the butt of the joke."

As the days of August passed the three could feel that they would soon head back to the campus on Central District Isle. They were on the beach again enjoying the sun, the salt air, and the wind-driven waves. As they soaked in the last joy of Summer, a taste of school met them earlier than expected. Before them stood an attractively curved older woman, wearing nothing but a white wide-brimmed sunhat.

"Hi girls. Ready for school?"

Standing before them was Dean Illisima Smith.

Chapter 26

Illi's Secrets Uncovered

In Royal Beach a steady wind blew from the south. The relentless sound of the warm, unobstructed air moving across the ears of beachgoers made it necessary for the women to stand close to each other to be heard. People just fifteen balls away could not make out a word of their conversation.

"So what do you think you know, Miss Agape?" Dean Smith spoke with cold confidence from under the wide white hat which she held to her head with he left hand.

"I know a lot," said Antwanesta. She sounded proud, but she really just wanted to give birth to the mass of half-formed ideas in her head. "I know this isn't real, the sky, the sun, the moon, the stars. It's artificial, some sort of projection. *People* made this world, not nature, not God. The weather is too predictable. The climate differential North Point to Royal Beach is inconsistent with the known diameter of the Earth. Geology is a joke with spheres and cubes, and an almost bilaterally symmetrical island centered on a dead volcano spewing water at a constant rate and temperature. The human species could not have evolved here. We struggle relentlessly just keeping most of the other plant and animal species alive in this place."

"Is that what you think?" Illi tried to look skeptical, but anxiety leaked out in subtle ways. Her eyes could not hide the fact that she saw Antwanesta as a threat. She was impressed both with Antwanesta's insights and her eloquence. However, this one was even worse than her clever cousin. Feli was easy to understand. Feli was a devout Humanist, programmed by reason to serve the good of humankind.

Maidens of Epodlo, Book 1 — Antwanesta Agape and the Mystery of the Red-dot Moon

Antwanesta was a Theist. What a volatile mass of random concepts and impulses. Illi could pluck Feli's *good-of-humanity* string, and the sweet music of her silence would follow the melody of logic. This one was unpredictable, an instrument Illi did not know how to play.

Antwanesta continued. "I did the math. Our world has a diameter of no more than 11,624 kiloballs, and it's *flat*. The sky stops about 1372 kiloballs above the school. It's lower here. A dome keeps our artificial atmosphere from leaking into space, or whatever is out there."

After a pause Antwanesta added, "I also know what the fake moon's red dot meant. On every closed store there is a red circle on the door to indicate business has stopped. We were—this place—this space vessel, was stopped, or at least whatever propels it was. The red dot was a warning, some message to those who would understand, that the ship was not moving toward the destination. We are going again. The earthquake was the jolt from the sudden acceleration of forward movement. Inertia held back the water of our make-believe ocean. As this great vessel moved forward the water accumulated against the stern bulkhead. Piled against that resistance it was forced back, causing the tsunami and destroying this city which is now being rebuilt. I'm guessing that the centrifugal force needed to simulate gravity is generated with a spinning motion which continued even when our forward momentum had stopped."

"That's bunny-brained Ant," said Gretchin. "No one could make something that big."

"Gretchin, I want to hear what Miss Agape has to say. Is there more?" asked Illi.

"Yes," Antwanesta continued, "People in high positions knew about the restart. Lissy's funeral, the Theist retreat, Frontaris Mason's trade show, the medical convention in Democratica City; these were all planned to protect people

351

from harm. Some people knew what was going to happen. Some people *caused* it to happen, and *you* were one of those people."

"Xiny!?!" Dean Smith turned to Xiny.

"I didn't say anything, Illi. Antwanesta figured it out on her own."

"Xiny? You knew about this?" Antwanesta was shocked to hear that her dear friend had hidden such important information. Xiny was a Royal, yes, secret robots, ok; *but this*?"

"I just knew about the intentional tsunami, not about the artificial vessel restart part."

"I've had enough of this, Mom!" said a clearly irritated Gretchin to Illi. "I played your mind game all year, but now you've stepped over the edge. You've gone way past Pop Two. If you don't come back to reality, I will get Risky to declare you a nut case."

Antwanesta looked at Xiny to see if the dean being Gretchin's mother came as a surprise to her. Xiny showed no sign of surprise. *This Royal secrecy has a real downside,* Antwanesta thought.

Illi ignored Gretchin, and said, "Now that you see reality from a new prospective, what do you intend to do, Antwanesta?" This was the first time Dean Smith ever called her, "Antwanesta."

"I don't know."

"Well then if you don't mind," Illi said, "let me tell you what happened the last time that what you now know became common knowledge. It was the year 1, B.Q. The Knowers of the time were all Humanists. They had confidence in humanity. They believed in the power of reason,

compassion, and creativity. They believed that if their fellow
humans only had enough information they would act wisely.
Those Knowers were *very* wrong. They told the population
that they, and countless generations of ancestors, were on a
spaceship travelling from a dying home-world to a distant
planet, with liquid water, and mass close to that of Earth. The
population panicked. Some wanted to press on to the new
planet. Others wanted to stop, and live as they always had.
Advocates of each prospective argued and negotiated. That
failed. Then they fought. Most of the population was killed in
the war. The pro-stopping forces found a way underground,
into a place only advanced Royal Plumbers know today. They
learned enough about the ship's locomotion mechanics to stop
it, or at least reverse, and then disable the thrust engines. They
did. That was the Great Quake of Year 0. It killed most who
had survived the war. It took nearly a thousand years to fix the
engines. We are going again, because we Knowers learned not
to ask for consensus. The end justifies the means, because
nothing but an end can justify means. The end we seek is
nothing less than the *survival* of the human species."

Illi paused. Even Gretchin was speechless.

Illi continued. "I need you girls to be *Royal* about
this. If the knowledge is not contained, we all die. I don't like
having to trust people, but given that I must, I could do worse
than you three." The dean then hugged her daughter, Gretchin,
and said to the three young women, "Tell no one. Humanity is
at stake."

Illi then looked into Antwanesta's eyes. Illi's cold
serious stare seemed to penetrate Antwanesta's soul. "I'm
testing your god, Antwanesta. I'm testing his love of
humankind. I hear you are a good teacher. I hope you teach
your god well. Don't let him flunk."

Then to all three young women collectively Illi said,
"The success of humanity rests upon the character of each of
you."

Illi then walked away toward the newly-restored Beach Trail.

Antwanesta, Xiny, and Gretchin all stood stunned.

Gretchin spoke first. "You two fell for that deer dung! Listen; I know Mom. She has more rabbits in her head than anyone. This is just one of her games to drive me crazy. It is what she does. She lives to mess up my head."

"Can you at least be *Royal* with us, Gretchin?" asked Antwanesta, looking not at Gretchin, but to the flat horizon across the water.

"Yes, Ant, I can. If you stay *Royal* about my familial connection with Dean Demented, I won't tell people you think we live in a metal can flying through the galaxy."

After a pause, Gretchin's eyes widened, "No!" Gretchin cursed. "I forgot to ask her about our new roommate. Now she will give us the most intolerable female weirdo she can find, just like last year."

Antwanesta and Xiny looked at each other with raised eyebrows.

Gretchin looked in the direction of Beach Trail searching the beach crowd for her mom's white hat.

"Look it's Risky," said Gretchin. "She's with Bishop Korack. Of course Korack! Risky's back with him. *He's* her secret lover. Leave it to my sister to form a stable composed of the one man in Epodlo with no penis."

Antwanesta, looked at Xiny.

Xiny said, "I liked your theory about me being an irresistible seductress, who could inspire such passion that a respected professor would risk her career to have sex with me. The reality of being Risky's messenger and travel coordinator, is just *so* ordinary."

"Maybe Risky can talk Mom into putting a man in our room," said Gretchin.

Gretchin ran.

Antwanesta yelled, "Gretchin!" Gretchin was running toward Risky before Antwanesta could again make her case for a female roommate.

Antwanesta's speculation's seemed more real now, having said aloud the truth she found too fantastic to believe. Dean/Governor Illisima Smith had confirmed her theory. Her world was forever changed, and yet she still cared who her next roommate would be. Was there some defense mechanism in the brain which forced it to concentrate on the mundane, when the awesomeness of reality became too overwhelming to handle? She would have to ask Feli that. *Can I discuss this with Feli? Yes, Feli knew*, Antwanesta thought. *Feli gave me the data for the calculation of the height of the dome. Does she know to be Royal? Yes. She must. She told us to "be Royal" in her letter.*

"You're going to think yourself silly," said Xiny.

"I have to think a lot. *You* won't tell me anything," responded Antwanesta.

"You get to play the secret game too, now," said Xiny with a mischievous grin.

"Will you give me lessons?"

"On being secretive?"

"No, on being seductive." The sarcasm made Antwanesta feel closer to Feli."

Risky had already dressed and crossed Beach Trail. She and Korack were rounding the corner into an ally when Gretchin reached the north edge of the path. Gretchin skidded

Thomas David Valentine

to a halt. She turned, and then returned crest-fallen to Xiny and Antwanesta.

"Too slow are you?" chided Antwanesta.

"I couldn't cross Beach Trail because I left my tunic back here."

Antwanesta and Xiny laughed. Antwanesta hugged Xiny. "You *are* a seductress," Antwanesta said.

"You've come a long way Antwanesta," said Xiny.

"Only because God has blessed me, by giving me his most wonderful angels to be my friends."

In a star system in some backwater neighborhood, near the edge of the Milky Way Galaxy, there rotates a wheel slightly smaller in diameter than Earth's moon. Attached along the perimeter of the spinning wheel there are eighty-seven almond-shaped expeditionary pods and a number of gaps which some would attribute to bad luck. Through the axis of the wheel, extending fore and aft is a cylindrical body, tapered at the front and silently expelling energy out the back. The fusion reactor within the cylinder continues as it has for thousands of years, but now the forward thrusters are again engaged on a course for the target planet.

On the hull of one of the pods an inscription reads, "E-pod 10."

Coming soon:

Maidens of Epodlo Book 2

Feli Smith, Adventures of a Stable Carl

maidensofepodlo.com

www.ingramcontent.com/pod-product-compliance
Lightning Source LLC
Chambersburg PA
CBHW061311170626
46817CB00001B/142